# SNAKE
## DREAMS

ALSO BY JAMES D. DOSS

# SNAKE DREAMS

## DREAMS

JAMES D. DOSS

ST. MARTIN'S MINOTAUR
NEW YORK

www.minotaurbooks.com

Library of Congress Cataloging-in-Publication Data

Doss, James D.
   Snake dreams / James D. Doss. — 1st ed.
      p. cm.
   ISBN-13: 978-0-312-36460-1
   ISBN-10: 0-312-36460-1
   1. Moon, Charlie (Fictitious character : Doss)—Fiction.  2. Police—Colorado—Fiction.  3. Ute Indians—Fiction.  4. Colorado—Fiction.  I. Title.
PS3554.O75S63 2008
813'.54—dc22
                                                     2008025099

First Edition: November 2008

10 9 8 7 6 5 4 3 2 1

For

Gerald Plain
La Grange, Kentucky

What—you have already crossed that beckoning boundary, are even
now entering into the dismal regions?
Then it is too late.
You have purchased your share of the nightmare.
Be advised that all such transactions are final.
There are no refunds.
*And no returns.*

# PROLOGUE

## NIGHTMARE

YOURS? NOT TONIGHT.

This particular horror is reserved for two souls already deep in sleep—and a third who burns with a perverse appetite.

You have nothing to fear from this nasty business.

Unless . . .

Unless you should assume too intimate an interest, allow yourself to become unduly absorbed—*irretrievably entangled.*

Not a chance?

Very well.

But there are invariably some who do. A few. Perhaps one or two.

For those reckless souls, the following cautions are hereby provided. First, a suggestion: Refrain from focusing too closely on the stark desert dreamscape—such intense concentration is likely to unduly excite the fertile imagination, which will conjure up all manner of poisonous viper, rabid rodent, and other vile nocturnal characters that slither and scuttle about in the darkness.

Second, a recommendation: Do not incline your ear to the unwary pair's sighs and groans and snores and moans, and firmly refuse to hear the lurid murmurings of the third wretched creature, who—in frantic anticipation of the atrocity—*giggles.*

Last, this warning: Remain where you are. Resist any temptation to drift off into the shadowlands, and beware any glib stranger who might invite you to witness the unsavory event. Yielding to such an enticement could prove dangerous.

◆ ◆ ◆

WHILE NO guarantee of absolute safety is made or implied, paying close heed to the aforementioned counsel should keep you reasonably—

# SNAKE DREAMS

# CHAPTER ONE

## WHEN AND WHERE

ALL THESE BIG BROUHAHAS HAVE TO GET STARTED SOMETIME AND someplace and this one commenced two summers back, about midway between Pecos and El Paso.

It was a few owl-hoots past sundown when a brand-new moon floated up to shine a fine, silvery sheen on the favored side of the mountains. Very nice. And it should've stopped right then and there, but no—like some folks you know, that two-faced satellite has a dark side, and just as it was brightening up the eastern slopes, it flooded that big dusty trough between the Delaware peaks and the Sierra Diablos with shadows, and we're not talking about a widow's veil of night shade that wouldn't keep you from seeing what o'clock it was on your granddaddy's dollar pocket watch. Nosiree, this was sure-enough mucky stuff, black as Texas Tea, too thick to churn and firm enough to slice with Mr. Bowie's knife.

If we were to wait around until that pockmarked face gets about four hours high, the murky lake would start to drain and dry and any poor soul who happened to happen by and got blinded and drowned in it would be able to see and breathe again. But this is right now and that'll be then and it's not night-meandering pilgrims we're interested in, so let's mosey on over to where the trouble's about to begin.

Watch your step, now. Don't put your foot on them prickly pears. Or that feisty little sidewinder.

See that tattered old tent over yonder? Aim your eyeball a tad more to the left.

They're camped right beside the rusted-out pickup that's hitched to the horse trailer that's empty just this morning the rider swapped his piebald pony for a shiny Mexican trumpet and three bottles of Patrón Reposado tequila. The feller still has the brass horn, but he's too high to toot on it and too far under to have the least notion of the serious Bad News that's about to bite him in the neck.

◆ ◆ ◆

THE FORTY-FOUR-YEAR-OLD woman (married, mother of one) is entwined in the arms of a broken-down old rodeo cowboy who never asked her name. Oblivious to his indifferent embrace, Chiquita Yazzi has drifted away into a twilight place. While she watches a splendid black swan glide upon a mirrored pond, a bright-eyed little girl runs along the grassy bank to hug Momma's neck. How do mother and daughter while away these blissful hours? They laugh at fluttering but-terflies, sing happy songs, pick pretty flowers. In even this feeble fac-simile of paradise, only the sublime should be called to mind—ugly memories should not be permitted entry. Sadly, it is not to be. The bright vision takes a dark turn into a vermin-infested alley. The mother—as only mothers can—senses danger close at hand. She instinctively reaches out to pull her child close. The little girl, a moment ago so warm—is cold to Momma's embrace.

An unhappy turn of events. But it is merely a dream, which will quickly fade from memory. What we desire is a change of scenery, so let us return to the world of flesh and blood and see what is afoot there.

For the most part, ordinary events common to the nighttime desert. In a shallow arroyo, a scaly something glides silently by.

A melancholy breeze heaves a wistful sigh.

Inside the tent?

Already stinking of beer and sweat, the has-been bull rider adds urine to the pungent brew. Thus relieved, he sinks ever deeper in his drunken stupor.

And the woman is . . . But what is this?

No. Don't look.

A tarantula strides oh-so-deliberately along the lady's forehead. Be-fore moving on to explore other parts of her anatomy, the fascinated arachnid pauses—extends a bristly foreleg . . . strokes her dark eyebrow.

Altogether too dreadful? Then let us depart from the canvas shelter.

On the way out, we shall encounter the third member of this ill-fated trio.

## SNAKE DREAMS

BUT DO they, really?

This is a highly controversial subject, hotly debated among distinguished zoologists and eminent herpetologists—which shall be settled here and now. The answer is:

Yes.

They most certainly do.

The more fascinating, and not quite settled, issue is—*what* do slithery-slimy serpents dream *about?*

We are about to find out.

## THE SERPENT'S NIGHTMARE

UNDERNEATH *a shadowy sea, unseen by the rusty red moon-face hanging high in the dusty West Texas sky, the night crawler watches. Waits. Is this entity a human being? By the most generous definition—yes. A he or a she? Moonlight has not yet illuminated the subject sufficiently. We must wait and see. What do we know with certainty?*

*That the assassin is cold sober, wide awake, recently bathed—and near enough to hear the woman's raspy breaths, the boyfriend's intermittent snores.*

*The time has come to settle scores.*

*Inching along on its belly, the sinister pseudoviper wriggles into the tent, rises above the intended victims. A crooked grin splits the hate-twisted face—a silvery straight razor glistens in a pale hand.*

*Flickity-flash!*

*Snickety-slash!*

5

# CHAPTER TWO

## CENTRAL COLORADO

WHEN THE HIGH PRAIRIE STRETCHED BETWEEN THE MISERY AND Buckhorn Ranges transforms from snowy white to bright green, and wildflowers start sprouting up like this was a sweet little girl's happy dream, you know for sure it's Springtime in the Rockies.

But is it time to start picking a bouquet of posies for the favorite lady, perhaps making plans for an alpine picnic? Let's put it this way: Don't put your long underwear in the cedar chest just yet. The weather at these altitudes doesn't care a whit about hardware-store calendars or showy spring blossoms. And genuine, gold-plated summer (if it doesn't pass by altogether) might tarry for a week or two.

At this very minute, huge, rumbling thunderheads are boiling up over the blue granite peaks and you can hear that icy wind come a-roaring down the mountain like ten thousand runaway freight trains. It's been huffing and puffing all night, whipping spruce and cottonwoods left and right.

Pete Bushman, a crusty old stockman who's been with the outfit since way back then when men were men and women were mighty glad of it, has seen all kinds of weather, so when he chomps down on a big chaw of Red Man and spits and declares, "That wasn't nothin' but a cool little breeze," not one of the hired hands will argue with him. Not to his face. That might be partly because the old-timer's the foreman of the Columbine Ranch.

As might be expected, your regular cowboy who rides the wide-open spaces and mends fences tends to experience Pete's "little breezes" from a different perspective. Here's a f'r instance: "When that there wind came awhistlin' over Pine Knob, it had a edge like a brand-new butcher knife and it was whacking off stalks of buffalo grass and when it took a slice at the bunkhouse, it shaved the frost right off the winda glass!"

6

Now that's what Six-Toes claims, and ol' Six never tells a bare-faced lie unless he has his mouth open. And even if he is touching the weather report up just a mite, that norther did rip a few shingles off the bunkhouse roof and almost shook the door off its hinges. The cold winds also kept most of the day-shift cowboys hunkered down in their bunks with the blankets pulled up to their bloodshot eyeballs.

Shameful behavior for fellows who pack six-guns, strut around like bowlegged peacocks, and generally act like they're just itching to strap a saddle on the worst Texas tornado you ever saw, and spur Mr. Twister all the way from here to Laredo.

Pete Bushman has something to say on any subject and will be glad to inform you that "today's cowhands ain't what they used to be." To hear the foreman tell it, there's only two sure-enough cowboys in this outfit—himself (naturally) and that Ute Indian by the name of Charlie Moon, who happens to be the owner of the Columbine Ranch, which makes him the big chief hereabouts.

Fact is, there are at least a dozen top hands on the Columbine who can perform any chore from shoeing a fractious quarter horse to overhauling a sixty-year-old Farmall tractor. But there is a reason for the foreman's confidence in the boss: Charlie Moon can outwork and outfight the best of his employees. And there is also this: The hardy fellow is not bothered by any kind of weather. He likes mornings that're brisk, don't you know—and *brisk* for Mr. Moon is ten below.

Which is most likely why the Ute came out onto the ranch-headquarters porch while the wind was still whipping up a fuss, sat down on a redwood bench with an old banjo, and began to pluck all five strings. Is he good? Honest reporting compels one to admit that Charlie Moon is no Earl Scruggs, but he has been working at it for months, and if practice does not always make one perfect, it generally leads to marked improvement. And as Grandpa Jones or Stringbean (bless their souls) might have observed: *That long tall drink a water sure does make that banjer ring!*

Moon could also sing. Loudly.

Which did not please everyone.

The porch where he picks taut banjo strings and croons lively blue-grass ballads is only about two stone throws from the bunkhouse down by the river, which is where a bunkhouse should be, because water rolling over rocks has a fine way of lullabying a tired man off to sleep. On the contrary, Moon's instrumental and vocal efforts have a way of waking that same fellow up. Him and all his bunkhouse buddies did not appreciate it.

Didn't matter. The sun was about to explode over the Buckhorns and it was by-gosh time to be up and at 'em.

Among those residents who did not share the Indian cowboy's brand of sunrise enthusiasm, the twanging and singing particularly annoyed Sidewinder, who, in case you two have not been properly introduced, is the official Columbine hound. At the beginning of the impromptu recital, the long-eared, sad-eyed canine was stretched out under the porch, dreaming about a mighty fine lady hound who was following him around, licking at his face. Now the dog was awake, and mightily ticked off. The Ute's booming baritone also startled a skittish little mare, who kicked a board loose in her stall.

Even way out here in the wide-open spaces, there is no shortage of critics.

The performer accepted it all in good humor. Mr. Moon was feeling *good.*

You want to know why?

We will tell you.

This final frigid blast of winter, which drifts down from the Never Summer Mountains every year about this time, is potent stuff for a fellow who enjoys invigorating weather—especially on top of a breakfast of three fried eggs, a slab of Virginia ham thick as a boot sole, a heap of crispy home-fried potatoes and a quart of steaming black coffee fortified with a generous helping of Tule Creek honey. The potent combination is sufficient to persuade a pessimist that good times are just around the corner and convince a man like Charlie Moon that he is alive on one of those golden days when life is fine and dandy and that he can accomplish anything. *Anything.*

Such as persuade Lila Mae McTeague (aka Sweet Thing) to accept a diamond engagement ring.

And why not? Here on the high plains stretched between two snow-capped mountain ranges, where a rolling river rollicks and chuckles its uproarious way to the western sea, anything is possible.

Almost anything.

One hates to be heard saying a discouraging word at Moon's home on the range, but despite a hardworking fellow's best efforts, his plans will occasionally go awry. Putting it another way, the Ute has plenty of the *right stuff* but sometimes his best effort is not quite *up to snuff*.

The full-time rancher and part-time tribal investigator knows how to handle hardcase cowboys, high-spirited horses, cranky internal-combustion engines, leaky plumbing, and—when absolutely necessary—deadly weapons. Sadly, Moon's expertise does not extend to an understanding of the daughters of Eve.

Case in point—the diamond engagement ring. It is not brand new. On the other hand, the ornament has never encircled a lady's finger and so cannot be categorized as used merchandise.

It happened like this. Quite some time ago, and at considerable expense for a man of his means, Charlie Moon purchased the ornament for another charming lady. It is a melancholy story that he would just as soon forget. He particularly prefers to disremember the stunning finale, where (after refusing the ring) the potential fiancée roared away in a shiny Mercedes-Benz—spraying dust and grit in his face.

Why bring up such a disagreeable event? Surely, Charlie Moon does well to forget the bitter disappointment and move on. But, unless we are badly mistaken, the residue of that unhappy romance will come back to haunt him.

And we are not.

# CHAPTER THREE

## CHARLIE MOON'S AUNT

FOR AS MANY HARD WINTERS AS SHE CAN REMEMBER, DAISY PERIKA has lived in the eastern wilderness of the Southern Ute reservation where long, brown mesa fingers stretch out from the San Juan Mountains to grasp at the arid prairie. Her home, situated near the mouth of Spirit Canyon, is miles from her nearest neighbors—an arrangement best for all concerned. Unlike so many little old ladies whom we hear about, Daisy is not burdened by a sweet disposition. As we shall shortly see, neither is patience to be counted among the tribal elder's virtues, which list (so her detractors say) could be inscribed upon the nail of Daisy's little toe. With space left over for the Preamble to the Constitution and St. Paul's Epistle to Philemon. This is an uncharitable and wholly unwarranted exaggeration. There might be room for either the Preamble or the Epistle, but certainly not both.

## REGARDING THOSE MECHANICAL CONTRAPTIONS THAT AGGRAVATE US

DAISY PERIKA had things to do. As she stood watching the school bus that Sarah Frank had just boarded, the tribal elder fidgeted and fumed. Her steely gaze was not directed at the driver, who was vainly attempting to restart the engine. She knew her thick-skinned third cousin to be unresponsive to helpful advice, angry threats, and scorpion stings. The shaman used her left thumb to draw an invisible spiral in the air, spat twice in the yellow dust, and muttered a guttural instruction to the recalcitrant motor vehicle: "Start up!"

The flooded engine coughed. Sputtered. Coughed again.

Daisy rolled her eyes at a pale turquoise sky. *I might as well be talk-*

*ing to a brick.* But this caster of spells knew another trick. Switching to the Ute tongue, she whispered a thirteen-word incantation that almost never failed, the gist of which was that a subject that did not respond to her subsequent order would immediately be infested with lice, cockroaches, and various other vermin. She followed this awful threat with: *Now start running and get a move on, you rusty old bucket of bolts!*

Instantaneously, cylinders sparked to life, gears meshed, clutch connected engine to transmission, and big rubber tires began to rotate. Thus empowered, the small yellow bus jerked and jolted away to transport Sarah Frank to Ignacio for the final day of school before summer vacation commenced.

Gratified by this victory, Daisy returned a cheerful wave to the Ute-Papago girl who shared her home.

## THE SHAMAN'S SECRET MISSION

THE MOMENT the boxy vehicle was out of sight, Daisy slung a hemp bag over her shoulder, got her sturdy oak walking stick firmly in hand, and set her leathery face toward the mouth of Cañón del Espíritu. It was a short, easy walk past Cougar Tail Ridge and she made good time for one of her years. About a hundred yards into the canyon, she paused to gaze at her lofty objective on the cliff wall, which loomed almost two hundred feet above the canyon floor—just short of the crest of Three Sisters Mesa. As she made her way slowly up the steep path, taking care not to stumble and tumble down the crumbling talus slope, her ascent came at a painful price. She gasped for every breath.

Just as Daisy thought she could not go another step, she arrived at the end of the trail, where a brownish red sandstone shelf jutted from the sandstone wall to hang over the abyss. Leaning on her walking stick and wheezing like an overworked mule, she surveyed the floor of Cañón del Espíritu, where tall ponderosas and spruces looked small enough to slip into her apron pocket. The tribal elder had not made this climb for the view. Daisy expected to find the object of her tiring trek concealed in a small cavern, which was behind her. She was not yet ready to peer into that darkness. Indeed, she would have preferred to be at home, in her comfortable parlor. But last night, when a sliver of silver moon sailed through the starry sky, the shaman had heard his raspy voice.

Not with her ears.

She had perceived the urgent summons as she slept. But do not tell Daisy that this was merely a dream. Oh, no—the little man was definitely *calling* her. And there was nothing the least bit vague about the message; she was instructed to bring specific items to him, and right away—his need was urgent! Moreover (and this was peculiar), the dwarf had informed the shaman that he was not in the long-abandoned badger hole that served as his residence on the canyon floor. He was high on the side of Three Sisters Mesa, in the tiny cave she had often visited as a girl.

Before setting out, Daisy had given the matter careful thought. The *pitukupf,* who rarely left his underground home, was a slippery little fellow. The sensible decision would be to ignore the summons. But, as is so often the case in such matters, there was an "on the other hand." By some mysterious means, her eccentric little neighbor seemed to know about everything that went on in the vicinity, and on occasion he would exchange useful information for bits of food and inexpensive trinkets. Also, Daisy was curious. *I wonder what that little wart's up to now.*

Father Raes Delfino, former pastor of St. Ignatius Catholic Church, had sternly warned Daisy Perika to stay away from the *pitukupf.* But the wise old Jesuit was no longer present to advise this perpetually backsliding member of his flock.

*I might as well get this over with.* Daisy set her jaw and turned to peer at the opening in the cliff wall.

Mimicking a gouged-out eye socket, the dark portal stared blindly back at her.

Nothing stirred in the inner blackness.

Daisy cocked her ear to listen.

A fat black cricket ratcheted a clickety-clatchet.

A sage-scented breeze whispered over the mesa.

From a branch on a lightning-killed ponderosa, a jovial raven croaked a crowish joke.

In no mood for fowl humor, the footsore woman called out, "Well, here I am—are you in there?"

He was.

Now, if Daisy had brought along a companion, would that person have seen the dwarf? The unambiguous answer is: It depends.

Charlie Moon certainly would not have; he did not believe in the Little Folk.

Sarah Frank *probably* would not; the Ute-Papago girl had not quite made up her mind on the matter.

Daisy's cousin Gorman Sweetwater, who was a traditional Ute? Quite possibly.

The aged shaman saw him quite clearly, and what met Daisy's eyes almost unhinged her jaw. Unconsciously, she took a step backward, then another, until her left heel was at the very edge of the precipitous shelf. One more step and— Thankfully, she did not take it. But what exactly did she see?

The little man—usually well dressed for one of his ilk—was naked except for a tattered rawhide robe clutched around his emaciated frame. The *pitukupf* reeled this way and that on knobby, wobbly little legs. His yellowish eyes were crisscrossed with bloodshot vessels that throbbed with each beat of his heart. Moreover, spittle dribbled from his lower lip.

Daisy Perika got a grip on herself and the walking stick. *The ugly little booger is sick.* This called for a diagnosis. *I bet he ate some spoiled jackrabbit.* Or was he drugged to the gills? *Maybe he's been smoking some jimson weed.* Dr. Daisy assumed her best bedside manner. "You'd have to get lots better just to look like death warmed over."

In a version of the Ute tongue so archaic that the tribal elder strained to understand, the smallish person explained the reason for his pitiful appearance.

*Oh, my!* Daisy swallowed hard, croaked, "You're *dying*?"

The decrepit little fellow (who understood English perfectly well) nodded.

*I thought I'd be gone long before he would.* After taking a moment to absorb this grim news, she managed to speak. "Is there anything I can bring for you—like some medicine?"

The *pitukupf* shook his shaggy head, thanked the Ute elder for coming to visit. Her presence would make his final hours easier to bear. And he wanted his neighbor to know that despite her occasional harsh words—such as that instance just a few weeks ago when she'd said he was a nasty lying old trickster who'd cheat his own mother out of her last copper penny just for the fun of it—he had forgiven all. Daisy had always been his best pal, and now as he was about to draw his last breath, she was his *only* friend. As if by an afterthought, the prospective corpse inquired whether she had brought along those modest necessities he had requested.

Removing the hemp bag from her shoulder, Daisy placed the offering before him. Seeing a faint glow of joy brighten his gloomy countenance, the old woman felt her eyes well up with tears.

A sad little story. Very near to being poignant.

And one that is not finished.

Daisy watched the dwarf lick his bluish lips as he found a chunk of walnut fudge in the bag. The famished creature stuffed the whole thing into his mouth, and while still chewing he helped himself to a handful of vanilla wafers, a matched pair of peppermint sticks shaped like miniature shepherds' staffs, and a string of purple glass beads. Each of these gifts seemed to bring with it a small measure of healing. Indeed, as on those occasions when an unexpected beam of sunshine flashes though a momentary gap in the thunderclouds, there seemed reason to hope that the *pitukupf* might not be quite ready to find a bucket to kick, buy the proverbial farm, or—to put it more plainly—cash in his chips.

Daisy was astonished at the remarkable effect of such modest gifts on the diminutive invalid, who appeared to be regaining his health with every heartbeat. The *pitukupf*'s benefactor watched with fascination as his pallid funeral-parlor pallor was replaced by a leathery glistening such as one might observe on a healthy iguana's skin, and the dwarf's rheumy eyes were regaining a measure of their glinty sparkle. These were merely the preliminaries, and we shall skip the in-between phenomena—which included such displays as blowing disgusting spit bubbles, flexing barely discernible arm muscles, and grinning like a halfwit who's just heard an off-color joke—and get right to the good part, where the elfin clown popped two cookies into his mouth, hung a peppermint stick over each hairy-tufted ear, and began to yip-yip like a frisky juvenile coyote.

A most remarkable recovery.

Indeed, he had already gone about a yip too far. But even now, had he proceeded with just a smidgen of caution, the *pitukupf* might have gotten away with it. It was not to be. When your happy prankster savors that first heady taste of triumph, he tends to lose all sense of proportion and prudence. So what did he do for an encore?

You will not believe it.

The impudent little imp put his knuckles on his hips and performed an energetic jitterbug that was much like a Mexican hat dance, but without the impressive headgear. Oh, and how he did leap and prance! To his credit, the lively little acrobat stopped short of backward somersaults and triple cartwheels, which self-control a more charitable soul than Daisy might have attributed to innate admirable character traits such as discretion and modesty.

What was the icing on the cake?

While displaying the lively footwork, the brash fellow laughed. Loudly. And right in the Ute elder's ashen face. Why did he press his luck? Hard to say. Perhaps because a virile, clever creature such as himself had insufficient respect for a feeble old woman who was so easily made to look the fool. Also, the pint-size Fred Astaire was staying just beyond arm's reach.

Daisy's arms might be stubby, but he had not taken her sturdy walking stick into account. That multipurpose tool was a good two yards long.

As one of Charlie Moon's rustic ranch hands might've described what happened next: *That sassy little feller never seed it comin'.*

The oak staff caught him about belly-button high. The unexpected blow loosened the molars from his jawbone and the cookies from his hand, sent the peppermint sticks aflying, and laid the startled offender flat on his back. While the stricken dwarf was gasping to get his wind back, he felt the Ute woman's foot resting heavily on his chest. When he saw her dark face looking down at him, there was no mirth in Daisy's grin; rather, the keen foretaste of retribution.

Seeing as how they were best friends, and also as a professional courtesy, the shaman explained precisely what she was going to do to her diminutive counterpart, and how much she was going to enjoy it. The lurid details of what she said to the hapless practical joker shall not be repeated here. Even the mildest of her threats (about how she would reach down the small person's throat all the way to the other orifice, jerk out his entrails, and strangle him with them) is somewhat beyond the bounds of good taste.

Suffice it to say that her words had a marvelous effect on the *pitukupf,* who began (as well as one can with his lungs almost deflated) to apologize. The general tone of this expression of contrition was that he was mightily sorry if he had (however unintentionally) offended the kind old lady, but that she would surely understand why one such as himself could not be held accountable for having a sense of humor, which was deeply ingrained in his dwarfish nature, which he had inherited from his daddy's side of the family.

It was Daisy's turn to laugh in someone's face, and she did not allow the opportunity to pass. But, admiring his effort, she graciously offered to yank out only the *lower* half of his entrails. That long, ropy section was all she would need to choke him to death.

The potential victim gulped, made a desperate counteroffer. In exchange for mercy, he would tell the heavy-footed woman something important that she needed to know.

Daisy's derisive "Hah!" rattled him somewhat, but the cunning little customer knew he had her hooked when this hearty expletive was followed by: "What does a nasty varmint like you know that I'd care to hear about?"

It had to do with an unexpected visitor who would have important business to discuss with the Ute elder.

Daisy's derisive grin melted away to make room for a suspicious frown. *This sounds like another trick.* But two factors worked in his favor. First, she did not actually relish the thought of yanking out his lower digestive tract and wrapping it around his scrawny rooster neck. Second, curiosity once again got the better of her. "Who's coming to see me?"

He suggested that it would not be reasonable to expect him to reveal what he knew before she removed her foot.

The tribal elder's response was too vulgar to reproduce. Truly excessive. And to add weight to the harsh reply, she leaned heavily on the offending foot.

Thus pressed, the little man was obliged to cough up his secret.

After considering the involuntary testimony, Daisy's frown deepened. *We wasn't friends when Chiquita Yazzi lived in Ignacio—why would she want to come see me? He could make up a lot better lie than that.* But that very fact imbued the dwarf's report with an aura of truth. She removed the foot to give him a cheerful kick in the ribs—and followed the comradely gesture with this warning: "Don't you ever mess with me again!" Before departing for hearth and home, the victor ground the vanilla wafers under her heel and stomped the peppermint sticks to red-and-white flinders.

Cruel acts? Not from her perspective.

At an early age, Miss Daisy had been forcibly enrolled in that famous School of Hard Knocks, whose flinty-faced graduates live by such proverbs as "don't leave a job half done" and "he had it coming."

In fairness, it shall be noted that she left one gift intact—possibly because her victim had fallen on the necklace of purple beads and she did not notice it. But we shall give Daisy the benefit of whatever doubt there might be, and interpret her oversight as a deliberate act of charity.

# CHAPTER FOUR

## EVENING

IN THIS TUMULTUOUS, UNPREDICTABLE WORLD, IT IS A COMFORT TO know that some things can be depended upon. Daisy Perika's satisfaction at day's end could be attributed to a tribal bureaucracy that provided reliable transport for young scholars, an exquisitely tuned solar system, and a well-provided pantry.

Right on schedule, the little yellow bus brought Sarah Frank home from school. As twilight mists began to swirl in the canyon, our rotating planet produced the grand illusion of a sun sinking below the westerly horizon. As the bloodred sphere was performing the vanishing act, Daisy Perika and her youthful friend sat down to a hearty supper of flour tortillas and lamb stew.

Life was good. And about to get better.

Sarah volunteered to wash *and* dry the dishes.

After retiring to the parlor rocking chair, Daisy was warming her knees by a piñon fire that crackled happily upon the hearth. Her eyes appeared to be closed.

Did the tired woman doze?

Or was she mulling over this morning's confrontation with the *pitukupf*?

Perhaps the aged soul mused about bygone days repainted in rainbow hues by that sly artist Nostalgia, whose name sounds suspiciously like a dysfunction of the frontal lobe.

None of the above. Our subject neither dozed nor mulled, nor mused. She fretted.

Out of the corner of her shifty left eye, Daisy watched a spotted cat that seemed to be deep in sleep—and wished she could figure out some way of getting Mr. Zig-Zag's tail under the rocker. A mean-spirited old woman? We hesitate to judge the senior citizen, but let us take a poll of three persons who know her.

Charlie Moon, who is a generous soul, prefers to think of his aunt as *feisty*.

Sarah Frank, who was not in the parlor at this moment, would be horrified to know of Daisy's dark obsession to rock on the tails of innocent cats. But she is devoted to the grumpy old woman, and Love is blind to minor faults.

Mr. Zig-Zag, who watched his nemesis from the corner of his ever-vigilant right eye, views Daisy as a worthy opponent. Also an indispensable benefactor who, twice a day, pours cold milk into his saucer.

And so there it is. The vote is inconclusive.

But this modest exercise in democracy does serve to introduce us to Sarah Frank, the young lady who holds legal title to that small piece of livestock known as Mr. Zig-Zag. For quite some time now, the orphaned girl has been Daisy's companion and helper. Though Sarah is grateful for every blessing, including food, clothing, a roof over her head, and a bed to sleep and dream in, it is tough being a teenager.

## HER YOUTHFUL ANGST

SARAH GAZED at her image in the bathroom mirror. As was her daily habit, she appraised the oval, big-eyed face, black hair that stubbornly refused to curl, a skinny frame that seemed to be all elbows and knees. A pearly bead of salty water appeared in the corner of each eye. *I'm so plain.*

Do not be sorry for the little lady. She is far from plain; indeed, she loiters on the very threshold of pretty. And whatever the difficulty, Sarah is no quitter. She is *determined* to be attractive for a certain Someone. Well, of course the adolescent girl is in love. *Passionately.* With whom?

Charlie Moon, that's whom—a man old enough to be her father. Add to this drawback the well-known fact that the lean, seven-foot-tall

Ute already has a grown-up, drop-dead-gorgeous sweetheart whom he intends to wed.

But never underestimate a member of the so-called gentler sex, particularly when she is about to blossom into young womanhood and knows what (who) she wants, has set her mind to have it (him), and will fight tooth and claw with whoever (and whatever) might stand in her way. And Sarah will *never give up.* Never-never-never!

## NIGHT

ALL THREE residents of the snug dwelling near the canyon's wide mouth slept peacefully. Those envious insomniacs among us may ask what their secret was. The reasons for their sweet repose were as varied as the characters themselves.

Sleep comes easily to a cat with a full belly.

As Sarah Frank said her Now I Lay Me Down to Sleep, she had *cast her cares upon Him who cares for her.*

Daisy Perika was capable of fretting for hours on end about the current vexation, and the old backslider had not offered up even a perfunctory prayer. So why did she drift off to enjoy pleasant dreams? Put it down to not being concerned about the dwarf's prediction of a visit from Chiquita Yazzi, who was a quite ordinary person. Had the tribal elder had the least inkling of what she would encounter tomorrow in Cañón del Espíritu, she would not have gotten any sleep. Not a wink.

# CHAPTER FIVE

## THE TIME HAS COME (TO SPEAK OF MANY THINGS)

*SUCH A PICTURE OF CONTRASTS THEY MAKE.*

*The aged woman in the dark blue dress and black woolen shawl, hobbling along ever so slowly, pausing now and then to lean against her oak staff and squint at a noonday sun that seems to have stalled over Three Sisters Mesa.*

*The slender, full-to-the-brim-with-energy teenager in faded jeans and a red blouse, darting this way and that off the deer path to ooh! and ahh! at a pale pink butterfly fluttering by or admire yellow-and-purple wildflower bouquets that a kindly Someone has strewn across the broad, sandy floor of Cañón del Espíritu.*

◆ ◆ ◆

AFTER A painful eternity for Daisy Perika and in practically no time at all for Sarah Frank, they approached the particular (and most *peculiar*) destination the tribal elder had in mind when she had planned this trek into the cool, quiet depths of Spirit Canyon. The shaman stopped near a ponderosa that had been toppled by March winds ripping down the chasm between Three Sisters and Dog Leg Mesa. This venerable tree, like the scruffy raven perched a few paces away on a branch jutting from its surviving sister, was one of her old friends—and she viewed its untimely death as a dark omen. The weary woman addressed the fallen comrade: "Before very long, I'll be here in the canyon with you. We'll sleep together, you and me."

As the girl turned to see whom her elderly companion was talking to, the raven voiced a raucous squawk. Daisy tapped her walking stick on the horizontal trunk and spoke to the Ute-Papago orphan. "I'll sit there for a while."

This was easier said than done, but with the girl's assistance Daisy managed to make herself moderately comfortable on a pink-barked spot between a pair of jutting branches.

Sarah seated herself on a sandstone outcropping in front of the woman she called Aunt Daisy. The girl was aware that the *pitukupf*'s home was only a few yards behind her, and noticed that the Ute elder was staring intently at the badger hole.

Daisy was deliberating. *There's no smoke coming out. And I don't smell the little stinker.* Maybe the aggravating neighbor was not home today. *I bet it'll be a long time before he'll try to pull another fast one on me.* She allowed her gaze to drift up the talus slope, focused on a spot high on the mesa wall where the sandstone shelf protruded like an impudent tongue. *Someday, I guess he will pass away.* It occurred to her that someone should bury the little man. *But it won't be me. I'll be gone a long time before he bites the dust, and there'll be nobody left to do the job. Unless* . . . She eyed the Ute-Papago girl, stated the obvious: "I'm getting old."

Sarah put on a solemn expression, nodded.

"I probably won't live through another winter." Seeing a protest rise in the girl's throat, Daisy raised a finger to shush her. "And after I'm gone there'll be things around here to look after. So I need to pass on some of what I know."

Hardly daring to breathe, the girl waited.

The vexed woman commenced to explain her dilemma. "Some years ago, I figured Charlie Moon would have himself a nice Ute wife and some children by now, and that I'd have a sweet little niece I could teach." She scowled. "But Charlie hasn't got the job done and hardly any of the young people in the tribe are interested in the old ways." *And the few who are would rather talk to a sun-dance chief or a story-keeper than the likes of me.* She glared at the orphan. "You're only half Ute." A wistful shake of the gray head. "But you're all I got, so I guess you'll have to do."

At the same instant, Sarah felt a little hurt-feelings lump in her throat and a tickle in her funny bone—poor thing didn't know whether to burst into tears or snicker. Very sensibly, she cleared her throat of the impediment and attempted to suppress the giggle by imagining *a bloodred centipede creeping into my bed tonight, slithering along my neck, up my chin, across my mouth, and into my nose.* Not scary enough. Sarah could *see* the invader, and it was a cute cartoon centipede—wearing a black derby and fifty pairs of tiny yellow shoes. She could feel the smile pulling at her lips. *It'll bite me and the poison will make my nose swell up big as a yellow squash and I'll have to breathe through my mouth for the rest of my life and little children will be afraid of me and I'll have to go around with a pillowcase over my head.* That did it. Thus composed, she said, "Thank you, Aunt Daisy."

The old woman's indifferent nod communicated the fact that this undeserving recipient of her kindness was welcome. Sort of. With no further ado, the tribal elder pulled in a deep breath, got right to Lesson Number One, which had to do with how to put together your very own home pharmacy from resources that sprouted from the earth. During the next few hours, the old woman expounded upon such subjects as:

How to prepare a tincture of a plant that she identified as yellow smoke, which (taken in *very* small doses!) was useful in treating nervousness, twitching, and facial tics. It was not to be used by a woman who was pregnant or taking any of those expensive *matukach* prescription medications for a nervous/twitching/facial-tic condition.

She also described various ways to use the bark of the coffeeberry shrub. Depending on details of the preparation, you could (so Daisy claimed) end up with an effective laxative or a medication for reducing pain in swollen joints. Or maybe it was for treating diarrhea and reducing swelling in painful joints. Either way, it was good stuff and patients would pay twenty dollars an ounce for the medication.

She told the youth how to prepare Mormon tea for treating urinary-tract problems and how to use larkspur for killing body lice; she even revealed her secret recipe for using Indian mint and "gray fuzzy-leaf" to make a dandy stomach tonic. In every instance, the self-made pharmacist provided warnings about the potential dangers of these homemade medications. In the hands of amateurs, such preparations could be dangerous—even lethal. A medicine dispenser had to know exactly what she was doing, otherwise her patients might not live long enough to pay the fee.

Sarah listened in rapt silence, wondering how much of this lore she would remember next week. But the little scholar knew what to do. *Soon as we get home, I'll write this stuff all down, then I'll get Aunt Daisy to check it and make sure I've got it right.*

When a cool late-afternoon breeze drifted down the canyon, the educator announced that today's lesson was over. But on the way home, as the shadows began to grow longer and the thin little girl grew hungrier, the old woman paused occasionally to point her walking stick at a plant that Sarah should harvest. From one, a few leaves would suffice, while from another the blossom and roots were required. At a spot near the stream where the ground was soggy, Daisy directed the youth to dig a marsh marigold up by the roots.

Sarah stared at the pretty little plant in the black mud. Her jeans were clean and the flower appeared to be perfectly satisfied where it was. "Dig it up with what?"

Daisy shook her head, snapped, "With a stick!" *Does she think I've got a shovel in my pocket?*

The teenager followed the elder's order without any further hint of protest, but learning the pharmacy trade was hard, dirty work.

As Sarah dug in the mud, Daisy seemed to be keeping a sharp eye on her pupil, but she was paying scant attention to the girl's labors. The Ute elder was distracted. Ever since they had left the vicinity of the badger hole, their footsteps had been dogged by someone that Sarah had not noticed. No, not the dwarf—but rather that person whose visit the peculiar little prognosticator had predicted. Though Daisy had caught only a glimpse of the individual who stalked them, she had no doubt that it was Chiquita Yazzi—and that she was *dead.* Daisy had not been fond of the pesky woman when she was alive, and doubted that death had done much to improve her.

Ever since the tag-along game had begun, the shaman had pretended to be unaware of the spirit's presence. From long experience with displaced souls, she suspected that Chiquita would be one of those persistent ones that cling like cockleburs on your stocking. *Trouble, trouble—that's what dead folks are—nothing but aggravation!* Daisy ground the few molars she had left. *I hope Chiquita don't follow us home. I'd as soon have a family of rabid pack rats set up camp under my house.*

It is gratifying to report that during the approaching night, Daisy Perika would be plagued neither by pesky haunts nor by hydrophobic rodents. But who knows what trouble the morrow will bring? Or the day after that.

# CHAPTER SIX

## MR. MOON DREAMS

ACCORDING TO THOSE ERUDITES WHO HOLD PH.DS IN SLEEPOLOGY, some 92 percent of our dreams occur within the span of only a few seconds—this despite the fact that from the dreamer's point of view, the night-vision drags on for ever so long. As the Indian cowboy rode his particular nightmare through the dark labyrinth of his subconscious, he lurched and grunted and scowled and groaned—and aged about fifty years. But, happily, only within the confines of his hallucination.

While fascinating, the details of his dream shall be omitted. The gist of the experience was that Mr. Moon was viewing his *future self*, who was passing his twilight years on the Columbine. With every Moon of Dead Leaves Falling, the skin on his face hung more loosely, the eye sockets became more hollow, the wrinkles deeper, the jet-black hair faded to gray, then finally to snowy white. All the while, the energetic gait slowed, and all too soon, Scott Parris gave him a walking cane for Christmas. Oh, unhappy holiday! Then came those twilight days when Moon scuffed around the headquarters leaning on a shiny titanium walker with greenish tennis balls on the bottoms of the aluminum shafts.

It gets worse.

With each winter, Charlie Moon was *losing his appetite*. An inflamed gall bladder had made it necessary to remove fatty foods and zingy spices from his menu. What did this leave? Don't ask. Oh, very well—but it is depressing. Instead of three square meals a day and snacks in between, he was spooning mashed-up yellowish goop past his lips. It looked suspiciously like boiled summer squash with not a hint of salt. Tasted like it, too.

And having no teeth to speak of, he *gummed* the stuff.

It gets even worser.

There was no spouse in the house. Charlie Moon was *alone*.

No wonder the young man awakened in a cold sweat, sat straight up in bed, the first thought in his head: *I've got to have me a wife. And the sooner the better.*

But not just any wife would do.

Moon was a top hand, and even your run-of-the-mill cowboy knows that hitching up with the right companion for life is every bit as important as selecting a suitable quarter horse or pickup truck. Whether it be hoofed mount or wheeled vehicle or long-lashed mate, a man needs one that will stay with him over the long haul.

*Whom* to wed was not the issue for our hopeful bridegroom—he'd had his eye on the top-grade lady for quite some time now. For so long, as a matter of fact, that Lila Mae McTeague had begun to wonder whether the only man in her life was all that interested in matrimony.

### HE MAKES UP HIS MIND

BUT NOT before two cups of black coffee. A sensible man does not make a firm, life-changing decision immediately after getting up from a bad night's sleep, especially one that has ended with an unsettling dream. What he needs is a double dose of caffeine to get the brain circuits properly electrified, the cerebellum engine hitting on all eight cylinders. But the mind cannot run without glucose fuel, which energy he acquired by stirring heaping tablespoons of honey into his coffee. Not long after downing the last sweet sip of the hot, syrupy brew, he knew what he had to do—and did it. Which required picking up the kitchen phone, placing a call to a snug little bungalow in Thousand Oaks, California. *I'm gonna make this short and to the point.*

When a man like this gets his steam up, a lady is likely to get bowled over, swept right off her feet, or whatever metaphor that will get the job done. Look out, Lila Mae McTeague!

Sweet Thing answered on the fifth ring with a long, languorous yawn, to which she appended a "Hello, Charlie."

He helloed her right back. But it was time to hammer those shiny little brass tacks. Moon banged his fist on the kitchen table. "Lila Mae . . ."

The man who had stared Death in the face a dozen times . . . *choked.* Literally. Like a diner with a fish bone in his throat.

"Charlie—is something wrong? Are you okay?"

"Um . . . yeah."

This made her head ache. "Something's wrong—or you're okay?" Like so many of her colleagues, the FBI employee was one of those analytical types.

The source of her headache nodded. "Right."

The lady rolled her pretty eyes. Pretty *violet* eyes. No wonder the man was smitten. "It is rather early to be calling."

*Early?* That put some wind back in his sails. "It's an hour later here on the Columbine."

"I am aware of the differential between Pacific and Mountain time."

"Look, Lila Mae, we've got to talk . . . uh . . . what I mean to say is—the thing is . . ." His face seemed to be on fire. "You know what I mean."

And the lady did. She leaned back on her pillow, blinked the big violets. "You woke me up at dawn to discuss our future?"

"Well . . . yeah." He jutted the chin. "Yes, I did."

"That is very sweet of you."

*Look. See Charlie Moon grin.* "It is?"

"Certainly. But the subject is too important to discuss on the telephone."

"No problem." He glanced at the clock on the wall. "I'll make a dash over to the Springs, catch a flight, be in Los Angeles by noon."

"That would be delightful, except that I will not be here to meet you. In about three hours I'm off to Washington for a meeting this evening in the Hoover Building with the Homeland Security Liaison Team. I won't return until next week at the earliest, and—"

"I'll meet you in D.C." He recalled a nifty scene from a vintage Clint Eastwood flick about a couple of Secret Service agents who were of opposite genders. "How about the Lincoln Memorial?"

A long, wistful sigh. *He is so cute.* "How about I stop off in Colorado on my way back to L.A.?"

"Name the day, Lila Mae."

"My return schedule is problematic, but I'll let you know."

"I'll be at the airport to pick you up." Moon's heart was banging against his ribs. "And I'll have something for you."

Well, she could guess what *that* would be. What the lady didn't know was, *would she accept it?* Lila Mae adored Charlie Moon. She was also very attached to her FBI career. For the past two years, she had been trying to figure out how she could have both. So far, it seemed to boil down to one of those either-or situations. Tough call. Time to say, "Goodbye, Charlie." To this, she added a kissing sound!

Did this make an impression on Mr. Moon?

Here he comes, out of the kitchen, deep voice booming "I Walk the Line" with so much heart and soul that the most diehard fans of the Man in Black would sit up and expect to see Mr. Cash appear around some dark corner. But can our man sing and dance at the same time? *You know he can.* Hot-footing it along that well known Line, Moon is doing the best takeoff of your classic buck-and-wing that could be expected of a big, lanky fellow wearing heavy cowboy boots who has never had any formal training in classic ballet. Look at him go! He bops all the way across the dining room—and the performance does not end there. Charlie Moon's hard heels and sharp toes echo across the hollowness of the parlor, where juniper flames snap and crackle in the stone fireplace. Has our hoofer shot his wad? Not a chance. Up the stairs he boogies, to the second floor, down the long hallway and through his bedroom door—No. Hold on. Something seems to be amiss.

The dancer has not entered that sanctum where he suffered through the "I'm so old I creak" dream. Nor has he gone into his office. Or into any of the other rooms on the upper level of the ranch headquarters. This is most peculiar. So much so as to boggle the mind. It's like this—only about fifty percent of Charlie Moon is still in the hallway, his upper half is gradually vanishing and *his boots are not touching the floor.*

Neither Mr. Harry Houdini nor Professor Isaac Newton need be alarmed. Though Charlie Moon's mood is so extravagantly exuberant as to be deemed light-hearted, he has not gone so far as to defy the law of gravity.

The happy man has opened a spring-loaded overhead door, climbed a pull-down pine ladder hand-over-hand into the vast headquarters attic.

Now in that dusty space, he approaches an antique Mohler safe that has resided there since the 1920s, when a previous Columbine owner used the vault to store his hoard of gold coins, a substantial share of stock in the Fairview Golden Boulder Mining Company, and a single bottle of Napoleon brandy. The Ute cycles the dial clockwise and counterclockwise, opens a heavy door that is exquisitely balanced on oiled hinges. Sadly for the AA member, of the original treasures only the alcoholic beverage remains. But some time back, the potential groom placed another valuable item in the safe. He removes a paper bag from Pippin's Fine Jewelry. Inside is a bill marked PAID and a small box with black velvet skin. He opens the latter to gaze therein.

It glitters, it sparkles, this diamond ring nestled in its pink satin nest.

*Oh, she's gonna like this!*

# CHAPTER SEVEN

## DRIVING MISS DAISY TO TOWN

TRANSPORTATION WAS A CONTINUAL PROBLEM FOR THE ELDERLY woman who lived in the wilderness of the arid canyon country, which was why Daisy Perika had summoned cousin Gorman Sweetwater to take her and "the girl" to the supermarket.

Gorman's spiffy pickup was at the dealership for the thirty-thousand-mile checkup, so he was hauling Daisy and Sarah Frank to town in the backup motor vehicle. His trusty old Pontiac sedan rolled serenely along, rubber tires humming warmly on the sun-baked asphalt. Presently, it passed the Durango City Limits sign. Despite all the fascinating sights and sounds that might have distracted Sarah's attention—the rush of midday traffic, a flock of blackbirds peppering a cloudless blue sky, 1940s big-band music on the radio—the teenage lass was unable to keep her mind off of You Know Who. Charlie Moon was (in Sarah's opinion) good-looking, kindhearted, patient as a saint, very smart, brave as any man alive, reliable, and— But the list is too long, and no man is perfect.

Consider the "reliable" attribute. Why was the object of her girlish affections not present to act as chauffeur? It is a fair question. Charlie normally visits his aunt about once a week and drives the elderly lady and Sarah wherever they hanker to go, but, given one thing and another that has kept him busy (valuable purebred cattle dying from mysterious ailments, drunken ranch hands thrown in jail, vital equipment breaking down left and right)—Sarah's heartthrob had not shown up for several weeks. But he had called last night to assure Daisy that he would arrive on the following morning to take them to the Columbine for a visit. That news alone would have been sufficient to make tomorrow a *very special day*.

Sarah sighed. *Charlie is handsomer every time I see him.* Another sigh. *And he's so sweet.* A stomach churn as she considered a complication: *He already has a sweetheart.* The girl frowned at the sandblasted windshield. *But Lila Mae's in California and I'm here.* She also comforted herself with this thought: *That FBI lady is practically an old woman—probably at least thirty-five.* And wasn't it a well-known fact that men preferred women who were younger than themselves? Of course it was.

In her mostly unhappy life, the occasional lapse into wishful thinking, even outright self-deception, had often provided just enough hope to prevent her from falling into deep despair. But such remedies should be used sparingly. In large doses, they can prove deadly.

## MEANWHILE, BACK AT THE COLUMBINE

BLISSFULLY UNAWARE that he was the object of this adolescent adoration, Charlie Moon was also thinking about "that FBI lady." And admiring the contents of the black velvet box.

## MEANWHILE, BACK IN THE PONTIAC SEDAN

IT MIGHT have been purely coincidence, but as Mr. Moon gazed at the golden circle, Sarah was seized with a sudden flash of alarm: *If Charlie was to give that woman a ring, I'd just die!*

Gorman Sweetwater slowed, pulled the venerable automobile into the supermarket parking lot, smiled at the image of his grumpy cousin in the rearview mirror. In a voice just loud enough for Daisy to hear, he said to the girl in the passenger seat, "While I go get me a haircut, keep a sharp eye on that fussy old woman. Last time she was in this grocery store, she threatened a little boy with her walking stick."

The accused piped up from the backseat, "I may have one foot in the grave and the other on a banana peel, but I ain't dead yet and I sure ain't deaf." Daisy Perika got a firm grip on her oak staff. "And I should've done more than threaten—I oughta whacked him cross-eyed!" *That freckle-faced white boy put my hot roasted chicken in the same plastic bag with a half gallon of butter pecan ice cream.* The memory made her blood boil. *Dumb* matukach *kid must have a brain the size of a pinto bean.* The scowl darkened. *Which means by now he's probably the store manager.*

After escorting the ladies into the supermarket, Gorman Sweetwater departed in search of a beer. Or maybe two. If there was some time left over, he might visit the barber.

◆ ◆ ◆

AS THEY meandered through the bakery section, Daisy paused to inspect a transparent plastic bag of dinner rolls, pressed a deep impression into each of the half dozen with her thumb. *I bet these are a week old.*

Sarah edged over to a display of multicolored pastries. "They have some *really* big cakes."

As she fumbled through her purse, Daisy mumbled, "I wonder where I put those coupons. There was one for nineteen cents off on a loaf of Wonder Bread."

"The cakes don't cost all that much." No response from Miss Daisy. "And the sign says they'll make any kind you want."

The mumbling fumbler found what she was looking for. "Here they are—I forgot I'd put 'em in my coat pocket."

Having eliminated several perfectly presentable candidates, the youthful judge was attempting to decide between two stunning, high-calorie finalists. Would the winner be the Strawberry Dream with inch-thick pink icing—or the three-layer fudge-and-ice-cream creation? Sarah could not make up her mind. Not that it really mattered. *I'll never have a cake like those.* Her long, wistful sigh was spiced with a hint of self-pity.

Daisy snapped at her sweet-toothed companion, "C'mon—let's go load up on some groceries."

And so they did.

## DAISY MAKES A THREAT

A HALF hour later, after sending Sarah to get some bananas, Daisy Perika was gripping her oak staff with one hand, had the other fastened to the supermarket cart, which she had filled with such necessities as three gallons of pasteurized cow's milk, two dozen brown-shelled chicken eggs, four pounds of Snow-White Pure Lard, a dozen 100-percent pork hot dogs, and a package of grape Popsicles. As it happened, the tribal elder was blocking aisle 14, which (according to the overhead sign) was where the shopper could find canned and dry soups. Casting doubtful glances at several products, Daisy searched the shelves for the tried-and-true Campbell's Chicken Noodle. One of the more blatant imposters featured the entire alphabet, a second one little *O*s, while still another offered a swarm of tiny fishes. *Why would anybody in her right mind want to see little letters or circles or baby carp floating in their soup bowl?* The old woman shook her head at the craziness of it all. *Some of these aren't even made by Campbell's.* She glared at the perplexing display. *Just as soon as I get used to something, I can't find it in the store anymore.* A painful grunt. *And some of these shelves are so low I have to bend my back like a bobby pin just to read the labels on the cans.*

These musings were interrupted by a finger tap-tapping on her back.

Daisy turned her head to identify the tap-tapper. What she saw was a short, plump woman in a too-tight yellow satin party dress, yellow high heels, a yellow ribbon in her black hair, and a black ribbon around her neck. The tips of the high heels were soiled with mud that had dried, and the dark ribbon had been tied to suggest a rose.

Too much detail—move right along to the *good stuff*? Very well.

The woman's throat had been deeply slashed, literally ear to ear. The blood that flowed from the hideous wound was soaking into the pretty dress.

It was too late for Daisy to pretend that she had not felt the finger tap or seen the awful apparition. "Oh," she said. "It's you."

The ghostly remains verified that it was.

"What brings you here?" The shaman grinned. "Big sale on Band-Aids?"

Apparently not offended, the bleeding woman replied in the negative. The reason for her appearance was that she was worried *to death* about something. And she needed some help.

*That's what I was afraid of.* "Well, I'd just as soon not hear about it—I've got troubles enough to last me till doomsday." The curious old soul picked up a can of beef-and-barley soup, pretended to read the list of ingredients while (from the left corner of her mouth) she said, "But if you're in the mood to chat about this and that, why don't you tell me where your body is."

Apparently encouraged by this interest, the whatsit replied that she was buried in a sandy, rocky place where water flowed after a heavy rain.

The shopper arched a brow. "In a ditch?"

No. In a dry wash. Not far from some mountains.

Daisy asked for a more specific location.

Somewhere east of El Paso.

"Well, that narrows it down some."

Apparently oblivious to this sarcasm, the haunt began to describe the injury responsible for her untimely death, and how she couldn't get her breath and gagged and choked and coughed up a gallon of blood and—

"Excuse me, Chiquita—but *how* you died is plain enough to see." What Daisy craved was a dose of high-octane inside information. She returned the red-and-white can to the shelf. "You want to tell me who did it?"

The bleeding presence shook her head, which (and Daisy was thankful for this) managed to stay more or less in place.

"Why don't you want to tell me who murdered you?"

The spirit did not respond.

Daisy knew that playing coy was a favorite ploy of those who are barely containing a delicious secret. Confident that the dead woman was just *dying* to tell her, she offered a teasing speculation: "I bet it was some nasty man you took up with."

Chiquita informed the old know-it-all that she had it figured wrong.

"Then set me straight."

Ms. Yazzi refused the bait. Stood pat. And that was that.

Accepting a defeat that she believed was temporary, the aged Ute woman put on her most amiable expression, which suggested a Tasmanian devil suffering from severe gastritis. "So what did you come to bend my ear about?"

The haunt was worried about her daughter. Poor Nancy was in trouble. And the situation was about to get worse. Much worse.

Daisy was not surprised. *Nancy Yazzi's probably smoking dope and shoplifting dime-store jewelry and no telling what else and Chiquita wants me to give her a good talking-to. For all the good that would do.* For a moment, the old sinner considered playing the good Samaritan. The moment passed quickly. *No, I'd rather chew my foot off at the ankle.* In contrast to this internal reference to self-mutilation, Daisy's reply was flavored with sympathy and common sense. "I'm sorry to hear it, but whatever her problems are, Nancy'll just have to grow out of 'em." She set her face like stone. "There's nothing I can do to help you."

Ah, but there was. The wispy apparition smiled, and asked a favor. Just a *little* favor. Which she expanded upon.

"No." Daisy shook her head. "I won't ask Sarah to do no such thing."

The favor seeker began to wheedle and whine and plead and—

"Chiquita, listen to what I'm saying!" Daisy stamped her foot. "The *pitukupf* told me you was coming, and when me and Sarah went for a walk in Spirit Canyon, you followed us around like some sneak thief. And now, when I'm trying to find some chicken noodle soup, you come and aggravate me." The shaman shook her knobby walking stick at the offender. "If you don't vamoose right now, I'll put a spell on you—one that'll turn you into a horned lizard that eats nothin' but fire ants and burps up red-hot cinders!"

Clasping a trembling hand over her oozing wound, the apparition asserted that Daisy had no such powers. But even if she was capable of doing such a cruel thing, she surely would not.

"I can and I will." The spell caster assumed the narrow-eyed, flared-nostril, bared-teeth expression that terrifies little children. She used her stick to draw a triangle on the floor. Spat in it!

Truth was, Daisy couldn't and wouldn't. But the old woman knew how to throw a world-class bluff.

The ghost was gone before the spit hit the floor.

But if the presence seen only by the shaman was not merely a hallucination—and this is not an entirely academic question—*where* did it go? Those of us with inquiring minds want to know.

# CHAPTER EIGHT

## SARAH AND THE SINISTER VEGETABLE

DAISY'S HELPER WAS TRYING TO DECIDE WHICH CLUSTER OF GREEN bananas looked just right when she was distracted by a more interesting display—a tangle of gingerroots. After a careful inspection, Sarah selected a curious little sample for closer examination. Unlike its more ordinary fellows, this one had a face. Well, sort of. The imaginative girl turned it this way and that. Concluded that the countenance most resembled a certain genus of amphibian. She looked over her shoulder to make sure that no one was near enough to hear, addressed it in a whisper: "Poor little thing—you look like a frog. If I kissed you, would you turn into a handsome prince?" She could have sworn that the frog's mouth curled, as if it was about to speak, then—

*Help me, Sarah!*

"Aaaaiieee!" The terrified girl flung the unfortunate root far across the produce section, where the lumpy little missile impacted a yard-high pyramid of Vidalia onions, which commenced to tumble to the floor with a thunderous rumble.

At that inopportune moment, Daisy Perika rounded the corner with the shopping cart and found herself stumbling over the sweet Georgia onions. She was not amused. When the startled produce manager appeared to find out what the matter was, the elderly woman gave this victim of opportunity a condescending lecture on how to stack onions and got yes-ma'amed several times, which annoyed her no end. After leaving the ruffled supermarket employee to clean up the mess, Daisy gave Sarah the gimlet eye and posed what she supposed was a reasonable question: "Why'd you throw that carrot at the onions?"

The girl was a stickler for accuracy. "It wasn't a carrot."

"Well, I don't care what it was. What I want to know is why you threw—"

"It was a gingerroot—with an ugly little frog face!"

Daisy snorted at such foolishness. "I've never seen a gingerroot that was much to look at. And it being ugly is no reason for you to squeal like a stuck pig and pitch it halfway across the store."

Sarah leaned close, whispered, "It *spoke* to me!"

The shaman's face went blank.

"The gingerroot said, 'Help me.'" The teenager recalled an important detail. "And it called me by name. It said, 'Help me, *Sarah!*'"

The old woman hesitated. "This face you say you saw on the ginger root—did it have big, pop eyes and a silly little grin like this?" Daisy bulged both eyes, did her best imitation of a silly little grin.

"Yes!"

The shaman groaned.

Sarah wrung her hands. "What?"

Daisy shrugged. "Oh, nothing."

"Then how did you know what that face looked like?"

"Frog faces are pretty much alike. You see one, you've seen 'em all."

"Oh." (There was more than a hint of suspicion embedded in the girl's "Oh.")

Daisy pondered what to do. *It was Chiquita, all right. And if we don't help her she won't let Sarah alone. She'll come creeping around the house at night, scaring the poor little thing out of her wits, and I won't get a wink of sleep.* The surly shopper glanced in the direction whence she had come. "I happened to run into a certain person over by the soups."

The needle on Sarah's suspicion meter edged into the red zone. "Who?"

A sly smile cracked Daisy's leathery face. "I'll tell you if you'll promise to keep it to yourself."

Discretion was Sarah's long suit. "Okay."

"Cross your heart?"

The secret keeper's finger made an X on her chest.

Daisy whispered, "It was Chiquita Yazzi."

"Nancy's mother's come back?"

"Yes she has." *In her own special way.* "And she asked for a little favor. It'd make her real happy if you'd talk to her daughter."

"What about?"

Daisy avoided the girl's stare. "Chiquita said Nancy was about to get herself into some serious trouble—I guess she figures you could talk some sense into her head."

"Why doesn't she talk to Nancy herself?"

"Oh, after running out on her second husband and her daughter, I expect Chiquita has her reasons for staying out of sight." *Like a neck that oozes buckets of blood.*

Knowing this peculiar old woman only too well, Sarah addressed the issue that was still making her skin crawl: "Does this have something to do with a ginger root talking to me?"

Daisy reached into her bag of deceitful tricks, found her Appalled mask, put it on. "Well, that's a silly question!"

Having seen this phony face before, Sarah was not impressed. She assumed her I'm Waiting for an Answer expression.

For the longest time, the old woman and the youth stood toe to toe. Eye to eye.

It was Daisy who blinked. Appalled was reluctantly exchanged for Guilty as Charged.

*Aha—I knew it!* "Tell me."

The shaman sighed, shook her head. "Chiquita can't talk to her daughter because . . . because . . . well . . . she's *dead.*"

"Oh." The girl felt her fingertips begin to tingle. "How did Mrs. Yazzi die?"

The morbid old woman drew a finger across her neck.

"Oh my!" Sarah tried to swallow. Could not. "Who did it?"

Daisy headed for the banana display. "Chiquita won't say, but I figure it was one of her lowlife boyfriends." Another possibility occurred to the tribal elder. "Or maybe it was her husband. That Hermann Wetzel's a dangerous man—and jealous. He might've tracked Chiquita down and slit her throat."

In an attempt to dismiss this grisly scene from her mind, Sarah tried to remember happier times when she and Nancy Yazzi had been close friends. After her mother had abandoned her, Nancy was very angry and said she hoped she'd "never see that bitch again!" But when a long-haul trucker from Bayfield claimed that he'd spotted Chiquita in a Las Cruces honky-tonk, Nancy had dropped out of school for a few weeks and there were rumors that she'd borrowed her boyfriend's car and gone looking for the errant mother. Other tale tellers claimed that Nancy had simply shacked up with the boyfriend while Hermann Wetzel had gone searching for his wife. Whatever the truth of the matter, after Nancy returned to school, she never said a word about her mother. It was as if Chiquita Yazzi no longer existed. Sarah wondered aloud, "What are the police doing?"

Daisy treated herself to another snort. "Not a thing." But there were extenuating circumstances. "Besides me and the murderer, I guess nobody knows for sure Chiquita is dead—her body's never been found." She selected a cluster of medium-green bananas, put them into her shopping cart. "And that poor soul don't even know where she's buried." Which was no big surprise. *Chiquita couldn't find her head if it wasn't fastened on her shoulders. Which, come to think of it . . .* But that didn't bear thinking about. She pointed a crooked finger. "Go over there and get us a half-dozen Winesaps. And watch out for wormholes."

Sarah objected to this unjust insinuation. "Grocery-store apples don't have worms."

"Oh, that's what they want you to think." Daisy cast a sideways glance at the patient man who was restoring fallen onions to the stack. "Those *matukach* slickers stuff the holes with candle wax and paint 'em over with fingernail polish!" The crafty old woman cocked her head at the youth. "D'you know what's ten times worse than biting into a nice, shiny apple and finding a worm?" Gratified by the girl's apprehensive Please Don't Tell Me expression, she snapped, "Finding *half* a worm!" Almost overcome by mirth, Daisy banged her walking stick on the floor, cackled up a long string of "heh-heh-hehs."

◆ ◆ ◆

AS SARAH pushed the cart toward the apples, trying ever so hard *not* to imagine how half a worm would taste (the ick factor was very high), a wonderfully refreshed Daisy Perika approached the restored onion pyramid.

The produce manager was frowning at something he did not understand: This interloper did not belong among the Vidalia clan.

The Ute elder snatched it out of his hand.

His eyes popped at this outrage. "Hey!"

Daisy cocked her head at the man. "Hay is what Tennessee rednecks make while the sun shines. Come sundown, they run off a gallon or two of moonshine."

These jarring non sequiturs momentarily discombobulated the uncomplicated fellow. "Uh—excuse me, ma'am, but that item's been on the floor."

Ma'am stuffed the ginger root into her pocket. "So do I get a discount?"

"No. I mean . . ." He felt his facial tic kick in. "It's not for sale."

"Well, thank you."

Her victim blinked. "For what?"

"A free sample." Tapping away with her walking stick, Daisy tossed a parting remark over her shoulder: "I'll feed it to my three-legged billy goat."

He watched her go, shook his head. *Probably another old crank that slipped out of the nursing home.*

# CHAPTER NINE

## THE INVITATION

*PICTURE THE THREE OF THEM IN DAISY PERIKA'S COZY PARLOR.*

*Sarah Frank's black-and-white spotted cat is sprawled on an oval rug by the hearth. Mr. Zig-Zag's eyes are shut, but he does not slumber.*

*Daisy Perika has a white woolen shawl pulled around her hunched shoulders. The aged woman sits in a rocking chair, but she does not rock.*

*Sarah sits cross-legged on the couch. The Ute-Papago girl has a job to do, but she does not know how to begin.*

◆  ◆  ◆

THE AGED feline, who does little nowadays but eat and doze, was digesting tasty leftovers from supper. In preparation for a long night's sleep and exhausting dreams, Mr. Zig-Zag was resting.

As she mused about her stressful day, the wrinkled old husk of a woman had her knees close to the fire. *That trip to town in Gorman's car and not being able to find any real chicken noodle soup and having Chiquita Yazzi—bloody as a slaughtered hog!—sneak up on me and start yammering about her dopy daughter—the whole business has me all wore out. If the roof was about to cave in, I don't think I could lift a finger to help myself. No, I'd just sit here and let it fall on me and then all my troubles would be over.*

Sarah Frank was staring at the cordless telephone in her hands as if she had not the least notion what it was, much less what to do with it.

Though she seemed to be focused on the flames that curled lovingly around a pile of split piñon logs, Daisy's favorite way of looking at things was from the corner of her eye. Her *left* eye. Which was aimed at the girl. *Why doesn't she just do it?*

Sarah responded to the unspoken question: "I don't know what to say."

Daisy groaned. *These silly young people, it's a wonder they know how to breathe in and breathe out.* "Just say, 'Hello, Nancy—it's me, Sarah. What've you been up to lately?'"

"I mean after that."

The weary woman gathered just enough strength to roll her eyes.

Sarah squeezed the telephone. *I can't say anything about Aunt Daisy talking to her mother in the supermarket. Nancy would say, "Oh, that's wonderful—how is my momma doing?" I can't very well tell her, "Well, except for having her throat cut and being dead, I guess she was all right."*

Having rolled her eyes upward, Daisy was about to reverse the process when she happened to notice a tiny spider hotfooting it across the beamed ceiling, down the paneled wall toward the four-inch-thick oak mantelpiece. *I hate spiders. Especially when the nasty little buggers come into my house. If it wasn't so much trouble, I'd get out of this chair and roll up a newspaper and swat you flat as a pancake.* Not so many years ago, the traditional Ute woman would not have thought of killing an arachnid—not if it was tap-dancing across her nose. Such a crime could bring on all sorts of bad luck, like the well going dry and the cows and goats and sheep dying off. Not that Daisy owned any livestock. But she did have a fine well. The thing that was really scary was revenge by the dead spider's angry relatives, who would sneak into the house at night, crawl up the legs of your bedstead and under the covers and bite you all over, and you would swell up like a big tick on a dog's ear and die in horrible pain. But the tribal elder no longer feared any of these things. Last year, both Daisy and Sarah had demonstrated such incredible courage in facing down formidable eight-legged creatures that the Spider Clan would not dare attack *them.* Which reminded Daisy that there was nothing to keep Sarah from giving this tiny creature a good whack. She was about to suggest that her youthful companion perform this service, when—

Sarah took a deep breath, punched in the Granite Creek telephone number, and waited.

The frugal homeowner snapped, "It's long distance, so don't talk all night."

Sarah heard a highly gruff "Whoozis?" in her ear, mumbled, "It's me. Sarah Frank."

"You've dialed a wrong number, sis. Hang up, and next time watch where you're puttin' your fingers—"

"I'm sure this is the right number." She steeled herself to say his name. "Is this Mr. Wetzel?"

"Yeah." The voice softened to medium gruff. "Do I know you?"

"Uh—I don't think so." *I hope not.* "I just want to—"

"You one a them people who call up to sell me something I don't want?"

"—talk to Nancy."

"Well, why didn't you *say* so?" A rafter-rattling bellow: "Hey— Nance—it's one a your little dingbat girlfriends on the phone." A bang as Hermann Wetzel dropped the instrument on a table. "Keep it short. Three minutes flat and I pull the cord."

The caller waited, counted her thumping heartbeats.

"Hello."

"Nancy—this is Sarah."

"Sarah Frank?"

"Uh-huh." *Now what do I say?* "I just wanted to call you up, see how you're doing."

"That's real sweet of you."

"So—how're you doing?"

"Oh, okay I guess. How're *you* doing?"

"Okay."

"Things going okay at your new house?"

"Oh, you know."

"Yeah."

This fascinating exchange would likely have continued along this line had not Daisy Perika and Hermann Wetzel been eyeing the respective teenagers.

Sarah had no trouble reading her friend's mind. "Is your stepfather listening to you?"

"Mmm-hmm." A pause. "No, wait. He's going down to the basement."

"What's he do down there?"

"Oh, that's where he reads his hunting and fishing magazines and plays around with his guns and stuff."

"Guns?"

"He's got dozens of 'em. Rifles. Shotguns. Pistols."

Sarah had a sudden inspiration. "Tomorrow morning, Charlie Moon is coming to get me and Aunt Daisy. We'll be spending a week or two at his ranch." She took a deep breath. "What I wondered was—would you like to go to the Columbine with us? I'm sure Charlie wouldn't mind. He's got a great big house with lots of bedrooms and there's horses we can ride and a big lake where we can catch fish and—"

"I'm sorry, Sarah—I can't."

"Why not?"

A hesitation. "I've already got something planned for tomorrow night."

"Oh. With one of your boyfriends, I bet."

"Maybe."

That meant yes. "Does your stepfather know?"

"You've gotta be *kidding*."

"So Mr. Wetzel still doesn't let you go places—like on dates?" Nancy was almost eighteen.

"No. He likes for me to stay home." *Especially at night.*

"Does he still . . . you know . . ."

"Mmm-hmm. Sometimes."

"Nancy, you ought to *tell* someone!"

"Like who?"

"Your high-school nurse. Or the police."

"I can't prove anything, Sarah. Nobody would believe me."

"You could tell Charlie Moon—he'd believe you." *And he'd fix Mr. Wetzel so he couldn't ever do anything like that again. Not as long as he lived!*

"Let's not talk about it."

"Okay. But I don't know how you can live in the same house with him."

Nancy Yazzi almost said it out loud: *I won't have to for much longer.*

Six heartbeats.

Sarah broke the brittle silence. "So how're you getting out of the house tomorrow night?"

"Hermann thinks I'm going to help our landlady do some shopping." Nancy's laugh tinkled in Sarah's ear. "The old lady rents us this really nice house for like *half price,* so he's glad to do her any little favor he can—especially if I'm the one who has to do the work."

As if the evil stepfather might hear her query, Sarah whispered, "Where are you *really* going?"

The older girl hesitated, then revealed a portion of the plot: "Miss Muntz—that's our landlady—she's gonna drop me off at a dance."

It was Sarah's turn to sigh. "I'd like to go to a dance." *But only if Charlie Moon took me.*

Nancy giggled. "You ought to come to this one."

Sarah felt the intensity of Daisy's sideways stare. "Tell you what—in a day or two I'll call you from Charlie's ranch."

"Okay." Nancy suppressed a second giggle. "If you want to." *But I'll be long gone by then.*

"Goodbye, Nancy."

"G'bye, Sarah."

Daisy Perika had been straining her ears, also the corner of her eye. "So Hermann Wetzel still keeps a tight leash on his stepdaughter."

"I guess so." Sarah Frank was imagining Charlie Moon punching Mr. Wetzel in the face over and over. Then breaking both his arms and—

"Well, you talked to Nancy and even invited her to come to the Columbine with us." Daisy was glaring at a pint-size, pinch-faced version of Chiquita Yazzi. The dead woman was perched on the mantel-piece, between a pair of pale yellow candlesticks in pewter holders. "Nobody could say you didn't try your level best to help her." She glared at the unwelcome guest and whispered, "Nobody who didn't want to be a horned lizard that eats red fire ants and burps up hot cinders!"

At this, the apparition vanished.

Never to return again, the shaman hoped. Daisy also hoped for joints that did not ache, sufficient rain to help her parched little garden grow plump Better Girl tomatoes and crisp radishes, a hundred nights in a row when the wind didn't blow sand against her bedroom window, and sleep without dreams. She blinked at the girl. "It's past your bedtime and we've got a big day tomorrow." And indeed they did.

Not being a typical teenager, Sarah neither groaned nor whined. She got up, kissed the old woman good night, and headed for her bedroom.

Watching the girl go (from the corner of her eye), the tribal elder called out, "When you get up in the morning, don't forget to put on that pretty blue dress I made for you."

"I won't forget." Sarah smiled. Charlie Moon was coming and she intended to look her very best.

"And your new black shoes."

◆ ◆ ◆

AFTER THE girl had snuggled into her bed, Daisy Perika picked up the cordless telephone and began to rock back and forth. *Creakity-squeak* went the chair. *Poppity-snap* went the piñon logs in the fireplace. *Tickity-tock* went the old wind-up alarm clock.

How she does it is a mystery. But from time to time, the old woman *knows* the phone is going to ring. If you asked her, Daisy would tell you who was on the other end of the line and she'd be right eight times out of nine.

*Brrrriiing.* She slipped the instrument under a wisp of gray hair. "Hello, Charlie."

The voice in her ear echoed the greeting, asked how she was getting along.

"If you don't want to hear an hour-long organ recital, don't ask." She waited until his laughter had subsided. "So let's talk about our plans for tomorrow."

"A-hmm." (That was Charlie Moon clearing his throat.)

Daisy: *I don't like the sound of that.*

"Uh . . . something's come up. I got a call from Lila Mae a few minutes ago."

*I should've known.* "Oh you did, did you."

"She'll arrive at the Colorado Springs airport tomorrow."

"And she expects you to come pick her up."

"She said not to bother, she'd rent a car, but—"

"But you said, 'Don't you rent a car, sweetie pie—I'll be there when you show up.'"

"More or less."

"Well, that sure messes things up." *Of all the big gourd heads in the whole world, Charlie Moon takes the cake.*

"Everything will work out fine." Moon smiled at his mental image of the irascible auntie. "Jerome Kydmann will come to get you and Sarah."

In Daisy's opinion, of all the slack-jawed cowhands on the Columbine, the Wyoming Kyd was the best of a sorry lot. The tribal elder secretly liked the intelligent young man. But never one to pass up an opportunity to punish her nephew, Dr. Daisy searched her dusty pharmacy, found a black little bottle labeled EXTRACT OF GUILT, expertly injected a stiff dose via the telephone connection. "For weeks now—that sweet little girl's been looking forward to seeing *you.*"

Having developed a tolerable immunity to this toxin, Moon responded in the amiable tone that annoyed his relative, "That's nice to know. I'm looking forward to seeing the kid."

Daisy managed to detect something vaguely like a put-down in the reply. *He's looking forward to seeing Sarah, but not me.*

"So, are you two all packed to come spend some prime time at the Columbine?"

"Sure." *And now he'll ask me a whole bunch of questions, just to make sure I haven't forgot anything. And he'll remind me to turn off the well pump and the propane valve and all that other stuff.*

Moon asked his aunt a whole bunch of questions. Just to make sure that she had not forgotten anything. He also reminded her to turn off the well pump and the propane valve. And all that other stuff.

As the conversation gradually wound down, Daisy was playing with the notion of mentioning Chiquita Yazzi and suggesting that her nephew convince the Texas State Police to go looking for the missing woman's corpse. Charlie, who used to work for the Southern Ute Police Department, had cop buddies all over the Southwest. Not only that, the big-shot tribal investigator's best friend was Scott Parris, who was chief of police in Granite Creek, which town (about forty miles or so this side of the Columbine Ranch) was where Nancy lived with her mean-to-the-bone stepfather. By the time Daisy had mulled this over for about two seconds, Charlie Moon—who assumed that his elderly relative was getting sleepy—said "Good night, Aunt Daisy."

◆  ◆  ◆

THAT NIGHT, one member of Daisy's household slept in perfect peace. Mr. Zig-Zag.

Tired to the bone, Daisy Perika slept like a stone. But not a *peaceful* stone.

Sarah Frank? The girl would enjoy a few minutes of heavenly slumbers, in which the bright star of her dreams was invariably the same tall, lean, dark man, who was deeply in love with his new bride—who (in these nighttime fantasies) was much prettier than that aged "FBI woman." Sad to say, soul-chilling nightmares would shoulder their way in between these blissful interludes. In the worst of the lot, a huge, hairy-armed Hermann Wetzel would slit his wife's throat with a razor—or beat his screaming stepdaughter with his fists. Inevitably, the sweet dreams were abbreviated, then faded altogether, and the terrible ones dominated the girl's fitful sleep. To flee from bloody murders and brutal assaults, Sarah opened her eyes long before daylight, determined to wait out the dark night. Over and over, she whispered this consoling mantra:

"Charlie Moon will be here today—and take me to the Columbine." Then, everything would be fine.

Sarah dared not close her eyes, lest the horrible night-visions begin all over again. But you know what she did. Sarah yawned, drifted off into dreamland for more of the same. Except that Mr. Wetzel had traded the straight razor for a butcher knife.

# CHAPTER TEN

## SARAH'S EXTRAORDINARY ADVENTURE

*NOT AN EXAGGERATION.*

*Before this day was over, her bizarre encounter with the "talking gingerroot" would seem like a commonplace event—a big yawn. Which, by coincidence, was how the sleepy girl would greet the dawn. While nothing would seem particularly wrong, neither would things feel quite right. This was to be one of those peculiar awakenings where it is difficult to tell where dreaming ends and reality begins.*

*Sarah Frank's very special day bloomed from the prickly stem of night with a gray, sickly facsimile of light that scuttered under the curtains, and like a shroud searching for something dead that needed wrapping, went creeping across the bed where she was half napping. A chill, funereal breeze moaned dreadfully in the eaves, rattled dry cottonwood leaves, set a woody finger to tap-tapping upon the windowpane.*

*Otherwise, things started off just fine.*

◆  ◆  ◆

WEARIED BY her lurid dreams and wary of what awakening might bring, the frail little girl shivered and shuddered under the covers, pulled the hand-stitched quilt to her chin, kept her eyes closed tightly. *If I keep very still and think nice thoughts, I'll get cozy and warm.* The nicest thought of all: *Before long, Charlie Moon will show up in his big car to take me and Daisy and Mr. Zig-Zag to the Columbine.* A distant second: *A hot breakfast of eggs and biscuits.* Fleshing it out, Sarah imagined crispy bacon sizzling alongside plump sausage patties in Daisy Perika's black iron skillet. A big stack of pancakes soaked in syrup thick enough to snare a bumblebee. A steaming mug of black coffee, very sweet—just the way Charlie liked it. Her first sigh of the day. *Charlie Moon.* Having come full circle to the object of her affections, the youthful optimist managed a wan smile. *If I keep really still and think nice—*

*Bang-bang* on her bedroom door. "Up and at 'em!" Daisy yelled. "Wa-hoo!" As an afterthought, she added, "Tippecanoe and Tyler Too!" *Whatever that means.*

Sarah bounded out of bed, slipped into her pretty blue dress, pulled on a pair of socks and the brand-new black shoes, and admired herself in the mirror. Almost shrieked at the sight of the wild-girl image that stared back at her, hurriedly ran a comb through her long, black hair.

Breakfast was lumpy oatmeal, warmed-over biscuits, and a glass of outdated milk that left a slightly sour taste on her tongue.

There was no indication that Aunt Daisy realized what an important day this was, but Sarah was neither surprised nor dismayed. An elderly woman who sometimes had trouble remembering what *month* it was, and didn't give a hoot about Labor Day or Halloween or when Daylight Saving Time kicked in or kicked out, could hardly be expected to pick up on the teenager's pent-up excitement. And it really didn't matter. Before long, Charlie Moon would pull up in his Expedition with the blue-and-white Columbine logo on the door.

Daisy Perika—who did realize how important this day was to her youthful companion—decided that the bad news could wait.

After breakfast, Sarah leaned on the front windowsill and watched for his arrival. *He'll be here any minute now.* Minutes passed like snails going uphill. Old, feeble snails carrying big suitcases filled with rocks.

*Poor little thing.* Daisy was just about to open her mouth and tell Poor Little Thing that Charlie would be sending Mr. Kydmann. *But if I do, then she'll ask me, "But why isn't Charlie coming?" And then I'll have to tell her: "Because the big gourd head's going to the airport to pick up Miss Pretty Two-Shoes and then Sarah'll get all teary-eyed and go off to her bedroom and cry and cry like she didn't have a friend in the whole world and would just as soon die here and now and I'll have to go knock on her door and say, "Don't worry so much about Charlie Moon. He's not all that special. . . ."*

But he was, of course. Daisy knew that her nephew was one in a million or whatever big number anyone cared to mention. The old woman set her jaw firmly enough to crack a walnut between the molars. Exercised the gray matter. Looked at things this way and that. Came up with a solution to the current difficulty. Passing the buck, of course. *I'll just let Kydmann answer Sarah's questions about why Charlie didn't come.* Which reminded her that when it came to talking to girls—especially girls with tears in their eyes—she had never seen a cowboy in her life who could put three words together without getting all tongue-tied. Daisy grinned. *That should be fun to watch.*

The teenage girl was puzzled when Charlie Moon did not show up shortly after breakfast. Or shortly before lunch, which for Sarah was the dry, butt end of the Velveeta block sandwiched between two pieces of stale white bread, smeared with mayonnaise from the bottom of the jar. Another glass of almost-soured milk.

After the midday meal, the girl pulled a white cotton sweater over her pretty blue dress, went outside in her shiny-new black shoes, listened for the sound of the big automobile. What she heard was a raven, perched on the top of an electric utility pole. As members of the rude Crow tribe are wont to do, the black bird caw-cawed a rude haw-haw at We Know Who.

◆　◆　◆

UTTERLY DESPONDENT when her hero did not appear during the midafternoon, Sarah ascended the rocky ridge behind the house, brushed pine needles and dust off a sandstone boulder, and sat down to watch the long dirt road that meandered miles from Daisy's remote home to the graveled road, which crossed the Rio Piedras bridge to terminate at the paved highway whose name was Route 151, from which junction the rutted road came all the way back again. When a puffed-up cloud thundered overhead, insolently began to spit and sprinkle on her head, she returned to the house and, quiet as a mouse, tried to hold the tears inside.

◆　◆　◆

AT ABOUT half past three o'clock, Daisy's telephone rang. Sarah Frank jumped up to answer it, but the old woman got there first. It was Mrs. Bushman, the ranch foreman's kindly wife. Dolly B. said she had tried to telephone Daisy earlier, but the electric power had been knocked off all the way from Montrose to Salida by a big thunderstorm—even the cell-phone towers had been out of commission. Dolly was very sorry, but not to worry—Jerome Kydmann had left quite some time ago.

After listening to this report and hanging up, Daisy told the expectant teenager, "We'll be picked up in a little while."

Having some dignity to preserve, Sarah refrained from leaping and dancing. But she did pick up her cat and give him an enthusiastic hug.

◆  ◆  ◆

PER DAISY'S promise, not too many minutes had passed before a shiny red F-250 pickup pulled into the grove of piñon and juniper that dotted her front yard. Sarah ran outside, a smile splitting her little brown face. *Charlie's got a new truck!* When she saw Jerome Kydmann, aka the Wyoming Kyd (a genuine native of Wyoming, Rhode Island), getting out of the vehicle, her smile drooped at the edges.

He tipped his white cowboy hat. "Sorry I'm so danged late. I would've shown up bright 'n' early this morning, but just as I was about to leave I found out the starter wasn't working. Took me a while to get it up and running again."

Sarah had no interest in matters mechanical. "Where's Charlie?"

Charlie Moon's good-looking employee flashed the boyish grin. "Ah . . . some important business came up the boss had to attend to, so he asked me to bring you ladies up to the Columbine."

Sarah was struck dumb. *Important* business? The teenager hung her head, but she did not weep. The tough little lady balled her hands into knotty little fists, clenched her teeth. Growing up is hard work.

It got harder when the Wyoming Kyd, who realized that the girl was upset, figured that she might feel a notch or two better if he explained just *how* important the boss's business was. He cranked the engaging grin up to about three hundred watts and said, "Charlie had to make a run over to the airport and pick up a VIP."

Sarah asked who the Very Important Person was.

The Kyd told her. He might as well have plunged a dagger into her tender heart.

The girl turned her back on Mr. Tact, ran into the house. She passed Daisy coming out.

The handsome young cowboy's grin long gone, he looked to the old woman for help. "What's wrong—was it somethin' I said?"

"Oh, no, Knot Head." Daisy snorted. "You're a sure-enough silver tongue." He had, in fact, met her expectations. Nay, exceeded them. And revived her faith in the hairy-legged sex's innate ability to make asses of themselves at every opportunity. And though Daisy felt sorry for Sarah, to be proven right was quite gratifying.

The perplexed fellow stared at the peculiar old Indian woman. "I don't get it." Truer words had never been spoken.

Daisy took this member of the clueless gender by the arm and, in her hobbling gait, led him to a shady grape arbor, where a horde of small black wasps whined about in search of something to sting. "Charlie's change of plans has complicated things, and there's a few things we need to get straight."

The boyish grin appeared again. "Oh, right."

Daisy pointed to a hand-hewn pine bench. "Let's you and me sit down and have a little talk about what's what and what's not."

And so they did.

Fine. But what about Sarah's Extraordinary Adventure?"

*Shhhh. Ever so stealthily, it is creeping up on her!*

# CHAPTER ELEVEN

## SMALL TALK

AFTER THE MIND-NUMBING FLIGHTS FROM DULLES INTERNATIONAL Airport to St. Louis to Colorado Springs, the pleasing prospect of deplaning and seeing the Ute's smiling face for the first time in months had FBI Special Agent Lila Mae McTeague fairly tingling with anticipation. Charlie Moon was so full of life . . . so—so spontaneous! But he had sounded ever so slightly tense during last evening's telephone conversation. *Like perhaps I might be arriving at an inopportune time. I hope he's still the same old Charlie.*

The tall rancher—looking mighty fine in his tailor-made gray suit, gray John B. Stetson hat, and hand-tooled gray cowboy boots—enveloped the pretty lady in an embrace that left her—for a dizzying moment—breathless. And not entirely because he had squeezed Lila Mae's first good whiff of Colorado air right out of her. The moment was all too brief.

While Moon manhandled her luggage off the segmented track and out to the Columbine Expedition, it was all chitchat about how nice the weather was but it would sure be great to get some rain, and after all that time at thirty-six thousand feet, wasn't it great to get her feet on the ground again.

For the first time ever, they were not entirely comfortable together. It was like a first date.

Not that Charlie Moon didn't try. For reasons he could not entirely understand, the man could not bring himself to broach the delicate subject. Every time he made an attempt to mention what was on his mind, the words stuck in his throat. There was a deep concern that—*If I don't say it just right, she's liable to say, "No way, bub." Or, "Let's take some time to think about it, Charlie—this is a very important decision for both of us."* Which was just a polite way of saying, "No way, bub." The engagement ring in his jacket pocket was a fine prop and would be a considerable help when he got around to popping the question. As he drove along the mountain road, chasing the afternoon sun, the prospective groom rehearsed several brief speeches. But as he turned them over in his mind one by one, the cowboy under the fine gray hat rejected them all.

## AN OPPORTUNITY

ABOUT AN hour west of Colorado Springs, Charlie Moon pulled into a rural mom-and-pop grocery store and café that featured a couple of old-fashioned gas pumps that had no slots for credit cards. It was a friendly place, where Mom and Pop trusted their clientele. A handwritten sign on each pump advised customers to Get Your Gas Then Pay Inside. Moon shed his jacket, filled the tank, entered the store to pay for the fuel.

Lila Mae, who had no great interest in rustic roadside businesses, was staring straight into the future, musing about what it would be like to be Charlie's wedded wife. *Mrs. Lila Mae Moon*. The moniker did have a nice ring to it. As the muser happened to glance at the driver's seat, where Mr. Moon had left his jacket, she noticed something. A small, white plastic bag that was about to fall from one of the pockets. Now, the federal cop was not overly nosy. If the lady had suspected what was in the smallish sack, she would not have touched it with the pointy tip of an immaculately lacquered fingernail. But she was one of those very orderly souls who cannot abide the prospect of something escaping from its proper place, and so had no option but to correct the situation. Which was when she noticed the label on the bag:

**PIPPIN'S FINE JEWELRY**
**GRANITE CREEK, COLORADO**

Lila Mae reacted instinctively, withdrawing her hand as if it had encountered a hyperactive mouse in her pocket.

*Goodness—that's none of my business!* This was her conscience, bolstered by a formidable sense of integrity.

The let's-not-be-too-picky portion of her brain begged to disagree: *But it* is *your business—you're thinking about marrying the guy, aren't you?*

In support of this point of view, the sneaky lobe (which was prone to nauseating baby-talk) tossed in its two cents: *It won't hurt to take a teensy-weensy little peeky-weeky.*

Let's Not Be Too Picky was quick to agree: *Charlie's still inside, paying for the gas. What he don't know won't hurt him. Et cetera.*

So she did. Opened the bag, found the black velvet box. Opened it.

*Oh my!*

Well, what could she do? Just look? Not on your life. After glancing at the open door to the grocery store and seeing no sign of her practically betrothed, Lila Mae slipped the gold band onto her finger. It was a wee bit tight. As she held her hand up to admire the ornament, white light that had departed the nearest star eight minutes and twenty-two seconds earlier refracted along the diamond's multitudinous facets, lit up the lady's eyes with a dazzle of rainbow hues. *It is so lovely!*

Lila Mae is, in a word—*entranced.*

She is, in three more words—*not paying attention.*

But the lady is not so distracted that she does not hear the characteristic sound of boot heels crunching on gravel. That's right. Here comes Charlie Moon, big smile on his face, big Styrofoam cup of coffee in each hand.

"Eeeek—eeeek!"

No, really. This is exactly what she said, word for word—whilst pulling the ring off her finger, jamming it into the little black box, deftly slipping said box into the white plastic bag, the bag into the gray suitcoat pocket—and Charlie Moon, who is making yard-long strides—is now so close that she can see the whites of his eyes!

*Oh, I just barely made it—*

But wait. What is this small rectangle of paper that has fallen from the bag, fluttered down to the floorboard to rest near the pointy tip of her stylish shoe? A sales slip, no doubt. But there is no time to restore the receipt to its rightful place, so the FBI special agent—who has been trained to make lightning-quick decisions in the most harrowing circumstances imaginable—snatched it up, stuffed it into her purse, snapped it shut. And—like the arrival of the U.S. Cavalry with sabers raised when the war-painted Indians are about to make the final, bloody attack—*just in the nick of time!*

Whew!

◆ ◆ ◆

WHEN MR. MOON and his favorite companion were within a few minutes of Granite Creek, he mentioned—in an offhand way—his plans for the evening.

After listening intently, Lila Mae McTeague nodded. Yes, that would be fine with her. *But why didn't he tell me about this last night?* She thought she knew: *Probably because he thought that I might decide to put the Colorado trip off until next month. Or the month after that, or . . .*

But later on, as the lady and the Man in Her Life joined a group of Moon's rowdy friends, it wasn't long before Lila Mae was clapping her hands. Applause? Yes. Also her way of getting with the rhythm. The Ute musician was perched on a three-legged stool, plucking at all five strings on his red-hot banjo. Miss McTeague was delighted to be with her bluegrass beau and Mr. Moon was right happy to be with his special agent sweetie, also mighty glad to be picking his way up Cripple Creek and just as pleased to make his way back down again. And so it went, the lady's hands a-clapping, the man's long fingers pluckity-plucking taut banjo strings. *Twangity-twang-twang!* Foggy Mountain Breakdown.

◆ ◆ ◆

SOME MIGHT wonder whether Charlie Moon should have been giving some thought to that little slip of a Ute-Papago girl who adored the barnyard muck he made oozy boot prints in. It is a point worth considering. But one woman at a time was about all he could deal with.

Speaking of women, let us visit a kindly little old lady who loves to help her neighbors, and manages to do at least one good deed every day. A brief preview of essential facts will prove helpful. Her name is Millicent Muntz. The senior citizen resides in the western outskirts of Granite Creek, just across the street from the home she recently occupied, and now rents to Mr. Hermann Wetzel, who is Nancy Yazzi's stepfather.

And if Daisy Perika's suspicions are correct, Hermann is the cold-blooded rogue who slit Nancy's mother's throat. A enigmatic threesome, Mr. Wetzel and his pair of Yazzis. One wonders what will become of them.

But for the moment, it is Miss Muntz who interests us.

# CHAPTER TWELVE

## THE LANDLADY

MORE OFTEN THAN NOT, AN ADVENTURE BEGINS WITH A PERFECTLY ordinary act. Turning on the radio to catch the weather report. Turning off the radio to avoid the news. Waking up. Going to sleep. Never waking up again. Having lunch with a friend. Or—doing a favor for a neighbor. In this instance, the spine-tingling escapade had been launched when Millicent Muntz acquiesced to a request from the girl across the street.

The potential benefactor viewed herself in a full-length mirror that was affixed to the hall closet door. The image of a thin, five-foot-two, bespectacled lady with silvery hair in a black silk dress looked back at her. Aside from the bright blue eyes, there was no color. As if ready to claim their kin, gray shadows seemed eager to envelop her.

Miss Muntz raised a white-gloved hand to place a perky little black hat *just so* and was pleased with what she saw. *I may be pushing eighty-six, but I don't look a day older than seventy.* The woman, whose saintly Quaker mother had taught her to value Truth above all else, pursed her lips. *Well, perhaps seventy-five.* As was her habit, Miss M (she had never had a husband) addressed her plump Persian cat: "Well, Mr. Moriarty—the game, as they say, is afoot. The time has come to launch the charade." A nervous little smile. "I shall go fetch Nancy Yazzi."

Curled up in a snug wicker basket by the gas fireplace, Mr. M gave not a meow about the woman's plans for the evening. The cat (as was his habit) kept mum. No matter. She knew what Mr. M would have said, had he had a mind and mouth to. "Not quite the upright thing to do, you say?" *It is so like Moriarty to raise an ethical objection—the fuzzy little nitpicker.* She made a final adjustment to the hat, considered the straitlaced feline's point of view. "Very well. Your point is well taken. And I do admit to some misgivings about involving myself in a deliberate deceit. But after having given the matter considerable thought, I have concluded that this is one of those circumstances where there is no clear-cut right path. I am confronted by the need to make a choice between the lesser of evils." She adjusted an antique ivory broach at her throat, cocked her head. *There. That looks rather nice.* "Every now and then, Nancy deserves a chance to get out and kick her heels up a bit." She pulled on a black, knee-length raincoat and fastened four black horn buttons, then responded to Mr. M's pithy comeback: "You suggest that Mr. Wetzel is merely trying to protect his daughter?" She sniffed. "I know things that you do not, and assure you that his motives in keeping the girl *close at hand* are not so innocent as that." Miss Muntz turned to wag her finger at the cat. "And even if that were not so, it is not right to keep the poor girl cooped up at home all the time." She waited for Mr. M to make some catty remark to the effect that how her tenant dealt with his teenage stepdaughter was *none of her business.* But it seemed that her feline companion had lost interest in the debate.

Satisfied with this modest victory, she picked up a black leather purse off the telephone table, hung it in the crook of her left arm, and shot a mock-stern glance at the cat. "I'll be back in a jiffy—so don't get into any mischief while I'm gone. I would be shocked—*shocked,* I say—to return and find you with a paw in the guppy bowl." She winked. "Or chasing about the house after a wee mousie. Ha-ha!"

This was one of their little family jokes. Mice (and all others of the rodent persuasion) were strictly prohibited from the Muntz premises, and as for the aforementioned bowl of guppies, they were not in the least danger of being Mr. Moriarty's lunch, because— But that is of little importance. In due time, we shall address that fishy issue. Unless we forget to.

# 750 BEECHWOOD ROAD THE HERMANN WETZEL RESIDENCE (UPSTAIRS)

FOR ALMOST an hour, Nancy Yazzi had been in her darkened bedroom, perched on her bed, peering between red velvet curtains at the land-lady's house. Over and over, the questions cycled through her youthful brain: *What's keeping Miss Muntz? When is she going to come out of her front door and cross the road and knock on our door and tell Hermann that she needs me to come over and help her run some errands? I hope she hasn't forgotten all about our plans for tonight.*

Fortunately, after several dozen such loops, the desired outcome occurred. Across the way, the door of 751 Beechwood Road opened.

"Yes!" Nancy clapped her hands.

## (GROUND LEVEL, FRONT PORCH)

DESPITE A slight fluttering of her heart, Miss Muntz made a fist and rapped lightly on the oak panel. *It seems so odd, knocking on the door of the home I lived in for so long.*

## (BASEMENT RECREATION ROOM)

HERMANN WETZEL scowled at the can of Bud in his hairy mitt. *What was that?* Not Nancy, who was upstairs in her room. *She's just like her sneaky mother: never makes any noise.* Another possibility occurred to him: *Maybe it's a prowler.* His hand found the butt of the 9-mm automatic holstered on his cowhide belt twenty-four/seven. There it was again. *It's just some goofball knocking on the door.* Which was unusual, what with ten-acre lots and no close neighbors except the ditzy landlady across the road. *Must be old Muntzy. What'll it be this time?* He grunted his way up from the La-Z-Boy recliner. *Probably some excuse about how she thought she'd bring us another tuna casserole or a pan of brownies but what she really wants is to snoop around and make sure I'm taking good care of her precious house and furniture.* Up the basement stairs, through his office, into the kitchen. Heading down the hallway, he belched up a taste of his supper of canned spaghetti and meatballs. The gourmand savored the recycled flavor, smacked his lips. *Those brownies the old biddy makes with walnuts are first-rate. But I'd rather eat roadkill than the best tuna casserole that ever came down the pike.* Passing through the parlor, he checked to make sure that his shirt-tail (which was out) concealed the holster. Hermann figured that being a fussy old woman, Muntzy wouldn't like her tenant packing a gun. *But it's my legal right. I'm a part-time night guard at the lumberyard, and I got me a permit, so she ain't got no call to give me any static.* He jerked the door open. "Hey—my favorite little old gray-haired lady." He forced himself to smile at "Muntzy," but his lips lost the upward curl when he realized that she did not come bearing brownies, walnut enhanced or otherwise. Not even the dreaded casserole.

As she gazed at the barefooted misanthrope whose belly button was showing through his unbuttoned shirt, Miss Muntz smiled. "Good evening, Mr. Wetzel. I hope I am not interrupting your quiet time." She added, with a twinkle of the blue eyes, "For all I know, you might have been reading an editorial in *The Wall Street Journal* about financial instability in China—or perhaps perusing a slim little volume of Mr. Shakespeare's sonnets."

"Uh—naw, I was lookin' at a magazine."

"Ah, let me guess. The periodical was this month's *Scientific American,* the article entitled, 'Exploring the Deepening Mystery of Dark Energy.'"

*Old broad must have a screw loose.* "I was lookin' at an old copy of *Field & Stream,* where they was tellin' about this guy who caught a ninety-two-pound catfish in the Rio Grande."

"That must have been quite stimulating."

"It was better'n a sharp stick in the eye." Hermann Wetzel stood aside. "C'mon inside and tell me what's on your mind."

"Thank you." She closed the door behind her, followed him down the hallway. "If Nancy is not too busy, I am hoping that she might be available to help me for a few hours this evening."

"Doin' what?"

"I have a few errands to run, and would very much appreciate it if she could lend me a hand. I will pay her, of course—by the hour. The usual rate."

◆ ◆ ◆

NANCY YAZZI peeked through a crack in her bedroom door, her teenage heart pounding like it might burst. *Oh, if Hermann won't let me go with her I'll just die!* And she might well have. Fortunately, death was not in the cards. Not Nancy's, that is. She heard her stepfather's booming voice.

"Hey, Nance—c'mon downstairs. Miz Muntz needs you to help her do a thing or two."

*Goody—he's going for it!* The girl emerged from her bedroom, effected an indolent shrug as she appeared at the top of the stairs. "I don't know—I'm feeling kind of tired."

"Tired my ass!" He turned to mutter an apology for his language to the prim landlady, then yelled again at the lazy girl. "You get your sorry butt down here right now and go with this nice old lady."

◆ ◆ ◆

HERMANN WETZEL was not as stupid as his stepdaughter thought he was; the fellow had a keen instinct for chicanery—especially where a pair of conniving females was involved. As he watched the spry old woman and the slim girl cross the street and walk up the long, paved driveway to Miss Muntz's house and her garaged Buick (the landlady insisted that Hermann keep his black Hummer in the garage), he had a worrisome suspicion that something was wrong with this picture.

Couldn't figure out what it was, though.

And thinking about it made his frontal lobe ache.

As soon as they were in the landlady's automobile and backing out of the driveway, Hermann Wetzel gave up the painful mental effort, left the front window, padded along the carpeted hallway into the kitchen, turned into his office, and descended the stairway to the basement rec room, where he plopped into his comfy armchair and opened the *Field & Stream* to gaze admiringly at the photo of the gigantic catfish. *Maybe I oughta take a drive down to New Mexico, see what I can hook on some beef liver. Or maybe a big gob of cheddar cheese.*

# CHAPTER THIRTEEN

## THE RENDEZVOUS

THE COCONSPIRATORS WERE BARELY OUT OF SIGHT WHEN NANCY Yazzi hugged her elderly companion. "Oh, thank you thank you thank you—this will be the happiest night of my life!"

Disengaging herself from the startling embrace, Miss Muntz recentered her automobile in the right lane. Her dignity restored, she said, "Your assumption of a satisfactory outcome to this evening's business is premature. I suggest that you reserve your expressions of gratitude until our little intrigue is successfully completed."

"Oh, everything'll work out fine." Nancy clapped her hands and laughed. "You'll see."

"I certainly hope so." Miss Muntz tried vainly to remember what it was like to be young and full of hope—and utterly silly. *I suppose I have always been a rather sensible sort—even as a girl.* "After I make a brief stop at Sunburst Pizza, I shall take you directly to the dance."

Nancy fumbled in her purse until she found a compact. As she pretended to examine her hair, she used the mirror to view the rear window. There was a vehicle about a block behind them. *I hope that's Jake.*

"I shall be there to pick you up at nine forty-five P.M. If you should wish to return home earlier, you may call me on your cellular telephone."

Nancy smiled. "Right."

"And another thing."

The teenager rolled her big, brown eyes. With old fussbudgets there was always *another thing.*

"While you are at the festivities, I imagine you will encounter your young man." She wagged a finger at the girl. "I expect you to conduct yourself like a proper young lady. You must solemnly promise to be on your *very best* behavior."

"I promise." And she would be. But Nancy's notions of acceptable behavior would have shocked the prim elderly lady, who had been kissed only once, in November 1943 by a slim wisp of a farm boy about to board a troop-transport ship for Britain. Some seven months later, on D-Day plus nine, her paratrooper sweetheart died beside a Normandy hedgerow when a Wehrmacht sergeant tossed a "potato masher" grenade into the muddy ditch where he was sleeping. For all these years since, Miss Muntz had kept his photograph on her bedside table. Every night before drifting off to sleep, she talked to her absent lover as if he had departed only yesterday.

As she parked at the Sunburst Pizza Restaurant, Miss Muntz assured her passenger that she would be back in a jiffy. Upon entering the busy eatery, she made a beeline to the takeout-orders counter, where a pale, thirtyish fellow whose plastic name tag identified him as Al Burkowitz was attempting to remove a small obstacle from his left nostril.

"Hello, Alvin."

The Sunburst employee regarded her with a blank, glassy-eyed expression.

She forced herself to smile at the unpleasant face. "Are you making deliveries this evening?"

"Who else?" His grin exposed yellow teeth that resembled kernels of corn. "I'm the onliest delivery guy the joint's got." A strained frown. "I remember you—you're the calzone lady. You always get a carry-out and take it home yourself."

She nodded. "That is correct. But, as I have some other matters to attend to this evening, I prefer to have the order delivered."

"Not a problem." He pulled a Bic ballpoint from behind his ear. "D'you want the usual?"

She did. Carefully enunciating each syllable, Miss Muntz placed her order for a medium calzone with Italian sausage. No bell peppers, please.

"Where d'you want me to bring it?"

Miss Muntz recited the address, watched him pencil the information on a delivery pad. "It is rather unlikely that I will be there when you make the delivery, but I have left the front door unlocked. Go directly through the parlor, down the hallway, and into the kitchen, and put the calzone into the electric range oven."

"Not a problem," Pizza Man said.

Alerted by a flash of light, Miss Muntz turned her face to a filthy plate-glass window. *Someone has pulled up beside my Buick.* Very close beside it. *I hope they don't scratch my lovely car.* Her concentration on the arriving motorist was interrupted by Al's nasal voice: "With tax, that'll be nine dollars and fifty-six cents."

She wrote him a check. "You may pick up your gratuity when you make the delivery."

"My *what*?"

"Your tip, which it is my custom to pay in cash." Miss M watched his expression brighten with a glint of avarice. "But I do not leave money lying about the house in plain view." She told him where to find it.

◆ ◆ ◆

AS THE muddy Jeep pulled alongside Miss Muntz's immaculate sedan, Nancy Yazzi lowered the window. "Jakey—I thought that was you back there."

"You thought right, Peachy Pie." Jake Harper grinned. "Everything set?"

"Sure."

"What about your daddy?"

Nancy spat the words at him: "Hermann Wetzel is my *stepfather*."

"Whatever." The heavyset, bearded man unrolled a pack of Volcano Mexican cigarettes from the arm of his black T-shirt. "He buy your story about doing some chores for the landlady?"

"Of course." With a dismissive toss of the head, she added, "He's a moron."

He eyed her purse. "You got Hermann's bankroll in there?"

"No way—he's been watching me like a hawk." The girl unconsciously glanced over her shoulder, as if her stepfather might be in the backseat.

Harper tapped an unfiltered cigarette on the back of his hand, popped it between his thick lips. "Does he still have it stashed in his office?"

Nancy nodded. "It's in a black leather pouch, down in that little thingy where the hot air comes out—the heat duck." *I wonder why they call it that.*

"That *little thingy* is a heat register." He grinned. "It lets warm air outta the furnace ductwork."

"Whatever." *Big know-it-all smart aleck.*

The big know-it-all smart aleck jerked a kitchen match across his jeans, touched the sulfurous flame to the tip of the cancer stick, inhaled. "How much d'you figure the old miser's got squirreled away in that leather bag?"

"Enough to choke a horse." Nancy felt her heart pound. "There were five or six stacks of bills in rubber bands. Big *thick* stacks."

He clamped his teeth on the cigarette. "We could sure use that cash."

She held her breath before posing the critical question. "You want to go get it while I'm at the dance?"

"Damn right." He tapped his toe to rev the Jeep's engine. "You got your house keys with you?"

She did. But Nancy had also brought a spare set, which she fished out of her purse. "The big brass one works on the front or back door; the silvery key's for the garage."

Harper stuffed them into his pocket.

The girl reached across the open space to rub his hairy forearm. "Be careful, honey—just grab the money and get outta there."

"You worry too much, Peachy Pie." He jutted the lower lip, puffed a cloud of gray smoke up to his nostrils—apparently for recycling. "I expect ol' Hermann will be in the basement, swigging beers and reading his fishing magazines."

"That's where he spends all of his time."

Jake Harper sucked in a lungful of carcinogenic smoke. *After I get my hands on Hermann's cash, maybe I ought to stop his clock.*

◆ ◆ ◆

AS MISS Muntz exited Sunburst Pizza, various terms of endearment were being exchanged between the Buick and the Jeep.

Nancy squeaked, "Oh, here she comes."

"I'm outta here." Jake Harper released the girl's hand, departed with a squeal of tires.

Miss Muntz slipped into the Buick, smiled at the young woman. "One of your young friends?"

Nancy exercised the bored-teenager shrug. "Oh, just some guy I know."

*I'd bet a greenback dollar to a Georgia peanut, that was your mysterious sweetheart.* The elderly romantic inserted the ignition key, started the engine, consulted the dashboard clock. "We'll make the dance in approximately seven minutes."

"Great." The anxious teenager glanced at her wristwatch.

Six minutes and ten seconds later, Nancy sat up straight as a poker. "Let me off here—by the drugstore."

"But, dear, it's still another three blocks to—"

"That's okay. I need to pick up a few things."

Frowning at a little red motor scooter that was using up an entire parking space, Miss M double-parked. "Have a nice time, dear."

"I will." *You can count on it.*

The inevitable reminder: "I'll return at nine forty-five sharp to pick you up."

Nancy Yazzi slammed the car door, jammed her hands into the tight pockets of her Miss Texas jeans, and sauntered off toward the Corner Drugstore.

Mrs. Muntz sighed. *Young people nowadays, they all seem so unhappy. Like they were riddled through with angst.*

During the entire course of her long life, Miss M had never experienced the least bit of angst. Not the most minuscule molecule. And this was no happy accident that could be credited to top-flight DNA or fortuitous circumstance; it was a direct result of Millicent's Domestic Policy. The lady of the house was always telling her cat that what a body had to do to keep from worrying herself to death about problems was to spend her time *solving* them. Every Day, Make Something Right. This slogan, which was crocheted on white cotton and mounted in a frame, hung over her 1933 Singer treadle sewing machine. Such prudent proverbs could be seen on virtually every wall in her cozy dwelling, including the pantry and bathrooms. One of her favorites hung over the parlor couch:

Curse Not the Darkness
Light a Small Candle

In this evening's gathering darkness, had Millicent Muntz touched the flame to a candle wick . . . or a fuse?

# CHAPTER FOURTEEN

## WHAT IS IT ABOUT MEN AND THEIR PICKUP TRUCKS?

AS HAS BEEN REVEALED, MR. JEROME KYDMANN ORIGINALLY HAILS from Wyoming, Rhode Island, which is no teeming metropolis. And the Wyoming Kyd, despite his shy little-boy smile and gentle way of beguiling the ladies, was—like every mother's son of a gun on Mr. Moon's ranch—*macho to the core*. Why, give any of those roughneck cowboys a set of socket wrenches, a big ball-peen hammer, and a pair of rusty old *war plars* and he will roll up his shirtsleeves and fix any ailing machine on the Columbine, be it a GMC flatbed, John Deere tractor, or Allis-Chalmers combine. Which is what Charlie Moon did. Provided the Kyd with the necessary tool kit, that is—and turned him loose on a beat-up 1992 F-150 pickup. According to the cowboy mechanic, the worn-out engine soaked up thirty-weight oil like a sponge and would not go anywhere in reverse, and the brakes was so worthless that the driver tossed out a ninety-pound boat anchor to stop the contraption. A bit of an exaggeration, but there are no flies on the Kyd—he'd gotten his orders to turn this heap of nuts and bolts into a dandy truck barely two weeks ago, and just look at it now—all the rust is wire-brushed off, every single ding hammered out and smoothed over with Acme's Finest Auto-Body Putty, and there's a thick layer of rust-proof undercoat plus two coats of red paint so shiny that old geezers can see their nose hairs on any fender they want to gaze at.

All the way from the Southern Ute reservation to the southern outskirts of Granite Creek, Jerome Kydmann did not stop talking about how he'd fixed up this pickup so it was *better* than new. New pickups did not come with genuine chrome hood ornaments, and the one he'd bolted on was a fine facsimile of a cougar—about to pounce.

Sarah, who was sitting between the poster-boy cowboy and Aunt

Daisy, did little more than murmur and nod. Not that she didn't appreciate fine pickups and good-looking young men who took a bath twice a week, shaved every other day, and slapped on lots of Old Spice (the Kyd smelled right nice), but she was saddled with a big load of the blues. Sarah didn't want to talk to *nobody* about *nothing*.

The Kyd was not thin-skinned. Far from it. But the girl's obvious lack of interest in the admirable results of his mechanical labors tended to be a drag on the one-sided conversation. Which is probably why, from time to time, Daisy Perika would say something nice about the truck, like, "Except for the bird doo-doo that just fell on it, that new paint on the hood sure is shiny." Or, "That motor sounds good."

Even with this encouragement from the Indian woman who rarely had a kindly word to say, the Kyd finally gave up. Just as they crossed over the dashed line on the map and entered the Granite Creek city limits, he shut his mouth.

Combined with the light rain, this sudden silence enhanced the escalating sense of gloom.

As the tires whispered along the wet streets, Sarah began to feel sorry for the pleasant young man, and ashamed of her self-centered behavior. By way of apology, she made this observation: "It's a very pretty pickup, Mr. Kydmann. And it runs really smooth." She appended this addendum: "You did a very nice job on it."

"Why thank you, Sarah." The driver's smile went off like a flashbulb in a coal mine.

To show her approval, Daisy patted Sarah on the knee.

The teenager resorted to stern self-examination: *I'm not a kid anymore. It's time I started acting like a grown-up.* With this resolution, Miss Melancholy began to feel measurably better. She assured herself that by and by, things were going to be just fine.

# JOHN LAW

MORE PRECISELY, GCPD Officers Eddie "Rocks" Knox and E. C. "Piggy" Slocum. On this rainy evening in Granite Creek, they constituted one half of the on-duty law-enforcement staff. When the newly painted red pickup passed, both cops took a hard look at the license plate. As Piggy jotted the number down on his duty pad, Knox said, "Is that who we think it is?"

"Uh-huh. And he's got a couple a passengers."

"Well would you look at that." Knox shook his head. "That reckless cowpuncher just run a red light."

"Looked yaller to me."

"Pig—if I say that light was red, it was *red*."

"Okay, Rocks." Piggy had aimed a portable radar transponder at the pickup. "Mr. Radar says he's doin' thirty-nine in a thirty-five zone."

"The man is a danger to innocent pedestrians and law-abiding motorists."

Officer Slocum jutted his double chin. "Then let's go get 'im."

Knox turned the headlights on, eased unit 240 out of the alley, hung back about a block behind the pickup.

# CHAPTER FIFTEEN

## BIG RHUBARB

JEROME KYDMANN, WHO COULD SEE A COYOTE A MILE AWAY ON A twilight prairie, had spotted the police car as he passed the dark alley and was eyeing it in the rearview mirror. As he eased the pickup into Granite Creek's downtown business district, the black-and-white suddenly picked up speed, closed on him. When the red and blue lights began to flash, he didn't even blink. And he didn't slow down. When the siren made a gut-wrenching yelp-yelp that caused Sarah to practically jump off the seat, the driver's heart did not miss a beat. A thin, ready-for-action smile creased his youthful face.

Cool customer, the Kyd.

Neither was Daisy Perika alarmed.

Sarah Frank, who had been intermittently hugging her cat all the way from Daisy's remote home at the mouth of Cañon del Espíritu, squeezed Mr. Zig-Zag so hard that the poor animal let out a yowl. "What was that?"

Daisy snorted. "Your dumb cat."

"No, I mean behind us."

"Nothin' to worry about." The Kyd sneered. "Just some cops."

When they were about even with the Silver Mountain Hotel, the siren yelped again.

Kydmann pulled the truck to the curb.

Sarah turned to squint at the flashing lights. "What's wrong?"

"Who knows?" As the black-and-white pulled in behind him, Kydmann cut the ignition. "Maybe I got a taillight out." In the mirror mounted on the driver's door, he watched Eddie Knox and E. C. "Piggy" Slocum emerge from their unit, approach the pickup from both sides. He lowered his window and advised Daisy to do the same, which she did.

Knox's broad, muscular frame blocked Kydmann's open window.

Piggy used a five-cell flashlight to illuminate the inside of the cab.

Daisy swatted at it. "Don't you shine that thing in my eyes!"

The chubby cop withdrew the flashlight.

Knox addressed Kydmann as if the well-known Columbine cowboy were a stranger. "Sir, could I please see your driver's license and registration?"

The driver produced the requested items, gave them to the cop.

Knox shone a penlight on the documents, returned them. "Sir, you was violating the posted speed limit. And you ran a red light."

"I didn't know I was speeding, Eddie. But if you say I was, I won't argue. But I'm *danged* sure I didn't run no traffic light."

"I saw you do it." Knox stuck his face halfway into the cab. "You callin' me a liar?"

"Naw, Eddie—I wouldn't do that. Let's just say you made a mistake."

"And just what's *that* supposed to mean?"

From the expression on his face, it looked like the Kyd was getting steamed. "Maybe you're a little bit color-blind."

"Now I don't like the sound of that remark!"

"Okay—then try this on for size: You're incompetent."

Knox's reply was barely above a whisper. "What did you say?"

"You're an incompetent *boob*—and you don't hear so good. Maybe it's time you retired, Eddie."

"That does it, big-mouth—haul your butt outta the truck!"

The cops on both sides opened the doors.

The Kyd came out swinging. His right hook barely missed Knox's head but came close enough to knock the copper's hat off.

Energized by this example, Daisy let out a wild-eyed war whoop and took a healthy whack with her wooden staff, which landed on Piggy's shoulder.

Sarah screamed, hugged her cat so hard that his eyes popped.

◆ ◆ ◆

MUCH MORE *could be said about the Kyd and Knox struggling and scuffling in the wet street, Daisy getting bear-hugged by Piggy whilst aiming vicious kicks that just missed landing on the copper's shins, about Sarah's frightful wails—but to avoid dwelling on gratuitously violent details, we shall skip approximately thirty-eight seconds of the scandalous encounter and fast-forward to the point where the hardy law-enforcement officers have prevailed.*

◆　◆　◆

AS KNOX frog-marched the Wyoming Kyd into the lobby of the Silver Mountain Hotel, the cowboy's hands were pinned behind his back, his wrists restrained with plastic "handcuffs."

Officer Slocum was close behind, helping Daisy up the curb. For this favor, she whacked him one on the leg with her walking stick. Piggy snatched the club away, deftly restrained the old woman with plastic strips on her wrists.

Sarah Frank, who had snatched her cat from the pickup (which was to be impounded by GCPD!) was yowling, weeping copiously.

As soon as the arrestees were in the hotel lobby, where a few well-dressed guests and gape-mouthed employees viewed the vulgar scene with no little alarm, Knox stood Daisy and the Kyd back-to-back, used another plastic strip to fasten their wrists firmly together, and bellowed, "That oughta hold you!"

Sarah warned the police officers that if either one of them so much as laid another finger on Aunt Daisy she would scratch his eyes out. They knew she meant it and she dang well did—*literally*. We are talking two pairs of cop eyeballs dangling on optic nerves—gouged-out eye sockets oozing blood! Sarah had not been so flat-out furious since a sly-eyed old coyote had attempted to kill and eat her cat. Matter of fact, she was even angrier than that.

Officer Knox put in a radio call to GCPD dispatch, requested a female officer to assist with the arrest of a "hostile offender" of the same gender. (Watch his happy face droop into a petulant scowl as he is informed by the dispatcher—loud enough for bystanders to hear—that no officers are available.) Worse still, he was advised that he and Officer Slocum were to respond *immediately* to a silent alarm at the Cattleman's Bank and Trust. The policeman shouted at the dispatcher, "What'll I do with these prisoners we just arrested?" Secure them as best as you can, he was advised, and (though not precisely in these words) to make haste to the Cattleman's Bank and Trust.

◆  ◆  ◆

BEFORE HE and Slocum left to put the kibosh a possible bank robbery in progress, Knox used still more plastic strips to fasten the glowering Indian and her red-faced cowboy partner to a sturdy iron gate that deterred thieves' access to a small room where guests' luggage was temporarily stored. After the policemen had departed, the hotel lobby was so quiet that a local used-car salesman insisted that he had *actually heard* a bit of cigar ash fall onto the two-inch-thick red carpet: "Cross my heart and hope to die—it made a kinda little *puff*."

Daisy broke the silence with this command: "Sarah, reach into my purse and get my keys."

Though puzzled about how keys might be of any use in the present situation, the girl complied. On the brass ring, in addition to a quarter pound of mostly useless old brass keys, was a Swiss Army knife with black handles. Aha! Sarah opened the scissors and attempted to cut the plastic handcuffs. No dice.

Daisy explained that while the little scissors were fine for small jobs, such as trimming a cat's whiskers, they were not up to this task. Sarah opened the blade. No problemo. In about three and a half jiffies, the deed was done and the alleged felons were free as the prairie breeze singing in the piñon trees.

Seeing as how Officer Knox had relieved him of the ignition keys, the Kyd revealed his intention to "go hot-wire the pickup." The escapee advised his female conspirators to lie low until he honked the horn, then to hit the street at a dead run, pile into the F-150, and hang on for dear life. He aimed to aim the mountain lion hood ornament toward the Columbine and "not stop for flash floods, earthquakes, or tornadoes!"

Daisy shook her head, said that she had not lived so many years just to get killed dead by a reckless cowboy who was more likely to wrap that red truck around a telephone pole than get them safely to Charlie Moon's ranch. She and Sarah would get away the best they could. If they hitchhiked back to her home on the res, the Ute police would protect them from such bone heads as Knox and Slocum, which paleface *matukach* cops didn't have no whatchamacallit (jurisdiction) on the res.

After the Kyd wished the spunky womenfolk luck and showed them his back, Sarah Frank voiced her opinion that the ladies' room was a good place to lie low while they figured out what to do next. Daisy, who had urgent need of the facility, agreed, and as soon as her bladder was relieved, she announced that she was awfully hungry and determined to find some eats that would stick to her ribs. Maybe a bean burrito with lots of cheese.

Absolutely desperate to be elsewhere, and quickly, Sarah suggested that they could find something nutritious at a convenience store in Durango or Ignacio.

Daisy's appetite could not wait. Accompanied by Sarah (who was protesting that they should be a long way from the hotel when the police returned) and the male cat (who was purring contentedly), the Ute elder marched out of the ladies' room, straight across the hotel lobby, and right up to the entrance to the Gold Nugget Ballroom, where a tastefully lettered sign advised potential customers that the dining-dancing area was currently reserved for members of the Rocky Mountain Birdwatchers' Society. Daisy addressed a tall, well muscled, immaculately dressed man whose apparent assignment was to discourage hungry diners from entering. "Hi ya, spud. Take us to a nice table."

Pierre Brigance raised his clefted chin an extra notch. "Excuse me, madam, but I am obliged to inquire—are you a bona fide bird-watcher?"

"You bet your boots. Why, I've watched more birds in my time than you can shake a stick at." Daisy shook her walking stick at him. "But just between you and me, I'd rather chow down on the handsomest chicken or duck you ever laid eyes on than *watch* it strut around." She aimed the stick at her youthful companion. "Me 'n' this skinny little girl are hungry enough to eat last week's roadkill."

Pierre looked down his nose at the pair. Being a gentleman who kept himself well informed about such matters as alleged felons who got marched into the Silver Mountain Hotel by the local constabulary, the maître d' was aware that these folk were not genuine birdwatchers. But they were genuine Native Americans, and their presence presented an unprecedented opportunity. With utmost gravity, he inquired, "Do you ladies have reservations?"

"Sure we do." Daisy cackled a merry laugh. "But we're way too hungry to be picky, so we'll eat here anyway."

The joke was so old that it had varicose veins, calculated planetary orbits with a slide rule, and voted for Grover Cleveland.

If Pierre was offended by Daisy Perika's response, he had far too much class to show it. The elegant fellow bowed gallantly, gestured. "Ladies, please walk this way."

No. Neither the maître d' nor Daisy did any such thing. (Walk *that* way.) Certain standards must be maintained.

For the distraught little girl, this entire day had been just *too* bizarre. Charlie Moon, the most reliable man on earth, had utterly failed her. In his place, Moon had sent a normally sensible employee who could do nothing but talk about a stupid pickup truck. Then, when they're stopped by a couple of crazy cops, both Jerome Kydmann and Aunt Daisy put up a fight and they get arrested and— *It's got to be a bad dream. I'm still in bed in Daisy's house.* Sarah knew how to find out: She used her free hand to pinch herself on the left arm. *I could barely feel that—this must be an awful nightmare!*

But everything seemed so crisply real.

*Maybe my arm has gone to sleep from carrying Mr. Zig-Zag.* Another, more dreadful possibility occurred to her: *Maybe my arm is paralyzed because I've been bitten by a prairie-dog flea and I've got a rare disease that'll spread all over my body and I'll die right here in this fancy restaurant and Charlie Moon will haul my corpse away in the back of that red pickup truck and wrap it up in an old blanket bury it on Pine Knob where the wind blows day and night.*

As if he sensed her growing panic, Mr. Zig-Zag provided what would have been (in a run-of-the-mill crisis) just the prescription. He licked Sarah's chin with a sandpaper-surfaced tongue. It did not help.

Sarah trailed along behind Daisy, who was following the maître d' through a clutter of tables. Things were getting scarier by the second. In the dancing shadows cast by flickering candlelight, the girl caught brief glimpses of hard faces, big calloused hands, worn work boots; heard an underlying mumble of guttural mutters, the use of phrases like *I reckon he'll be here drekly*; *must've got bushwhacked*; *drunk as a skunk*; *cold as a whore's heart*; and worse. These patrons were definitely not birdwatchers.

Pierre paused at a long, vacant, linen-covered table where sixteen tallow tapers in crystal candleholders were aligned along the center. He seated Sarah at one end, Daisy at the other.

Wishing that she could become invisible, Sarah sat very still. *I wonder what'll happen next.*

Right on cue, a soft glow of blue light revealed a bandstand. An ensemble of elegant ladies in white gowns and tuxedoed men began to pull bows across violins and cellos. Vienna Woods, that's what it was, and for an audience that might start tossing beer bottles at the musicians. But this was merely the beginning. Things were about to become stranger still.

Sarah watched with horror as uniformed Officers Knox and Slocum appeared in the gloom, marching to the long table like determined men on a serious mission. They stopped on both sides of Daisy Perika's chair. The tribal elder realized that the cops were there. Obviously didn't care. Not a whit, iota, speck, or smidgen.

Knox reached out, tapped Daisy on the shoulder.

The aged woman leaned her head, listened to something he said, then nodded and *smiled.*

Sarah watched in utter disbelief as Eddie Knox helped Daisy to her feet and escorted her to the dance floor, which was suddenly illuminated by an almost blinding array of overhead lights. At the precise center of the forty-by-sixty-foot rectangle of inlaid oak and maple, the Granite Creek cop put his arm around the Ute elder . . . and they began to waltz.

From the now-quite-visible audience came a thunderous roar of applause.

Sarah watched the Wyoming Kyd—a big six-gun strapped to his hip—appear as if out of nowhere, approach Officer Slocum. She wondered what would happen. Would Mr. Kydmann shoot the chubby cop right on the spot? You might think so, but no.

Why, the Kyd bowed and asked if he could have this dance! Slocum tipped his cop hat and grinned, which the Kyd took as a consent. The high-tone ensemble shifted quickly from Strauss to "Turkey in the Straw." Do-si-do, and off they go, stomping across the hardwood floor.

This unseemly display brought on loud hoo-ha's, shrill whistles, and rude catcalls.

Oh so slowly, the lights begin to dim.

As the scene faded to black, the small orchestra fell silent.

Poor Sarah. The spotted cat clutched to her bosom, she sat numbly at the long, linen-enshrouded table. Once again, only flickering candle-light illuminated the night. And aside from the rapid beat of her heart and the purring of her cat, not a sound. The girl was miles beyond bewitched, bothered, and bewildered. She felt her skin going all prickly-cold, hugged the cat closer to her chest. Something was very wrong. *This has to be the weirdest dream I ever had.* Any second now the lights would come on again, the cops would turn into shaggy were-wolves, and Piggy Slocum would snatch Mr. Zig-Zag from her grasp and eat him whole!

Then, there was the other, far more alarming possibility: *If I'm not asleep, I'm going crazy.*

# CHAPTER SIXTEEN

## HEART STOPPER

THE TRUTH BEGAN TO DAWN ON SARAH FRANK WHEN—OUT OF THE darkness—a throaty chorus of some two hundred voices began to sing (quite a few off-tune and out of synchronization) a piece that had been composed and rehearsed especially for the auspicious occasion. The men boomed out the odd lines, the womenfolk trilled the evens, both genders joined in to repeat the entire song:

> *Dear Sarah,*
> *Dear Sarah,*
> *We wish you a happy birthday,*
> *We wish you a happy birthday,*
> *And all of God's blessings,*
> *And all of God's blessings,*
> *Dear Sarah, for you!*

Yes. The dreaded *surprise party.*

For a few heartbeats, the birthday girl's mind was as numb as her limbs. She was startled to full consciousness by a man's voice that roared from speakers mounted on the ballroom ceiling: "Ladies and gentlemen and cowboys—let's give a great big wa-hoo for the little lady who's just turned sixteen!"

Which they did, and that wa-hoo! just about blew the roof off.

Which is when Sarah realized that Daisy, huffing and puffing from her recent exertions, was back in her seat at the far end of the table and that they had been joined by such notable citizens as Granite Creek Chief of Police Scott Parris, Southern Ute Tribal Chairman Oscar Sweetwater and his shy wife, Vera, Oscar's brother Gorman, who was Daisy's cousin, Daisy's friend Louise-Marie LaForte, Columbine foreman Pete Bushman and his wife, Dolly, the Wyoming Kyd, and those glittering stars of the police farce—Officers Eddie "Rocks" Knox and E. C. "Piggy" Slocum. The women (even Daisy) were smiling and chattering a mile a minute, and all the men were laughing and whooping it up.

What a party!

But there were a few empty seats in the hotel ballroom.

The unseen announcer's voice boomed out again: "And now, let's give a great big welcome to the Columbine Grass!"

A roar of applause, a hollering of raucous catcalls, a thunder of boot stomping.

Mr. Zig-Zag, who may have interpreted this outburst as that final, flesh-mangling clash of sword-swinging troops at Armageddon, let out a terrified yowl and slipped from Sarah's grip to take refuge under the table, whence the climactic battle could be viewed by one who had no stake in the outcome.

The lights flashed on over the bandstand platform, which was little more than spitting distance from where our birthday girl was seated.

Right away, Sarah noticed two things. First, that a couple of the seats at her table had been vacated. Second, that the chamber orchestra had been replaced by four hairy-chested men and a tenor. No. The tenor was a blonde of the other gender, whose shapely form (starting at the top) was outfitted in a red sequined cowgirl hat and a frilly silk blouse with lace at the neck and cuffs. Her black jeans (cinched with a Mexican silver concho belt) were tight enough to read the date on an 1886 Indian Head penny in her pocket. All this was bottomed off by shiny black cowgirl boots.

The men were dressed to match the eye-stopping lady. Except that their white shirts weren't quite so frilly and their belts were plain black leather, with tasteful brass or pewter buckles advertising the likes of Coors beer, Ford pickups, Winchester rifles, and Buck knives. Picture the brawny maître d' on bass (Pierre Brigance was the Columbine blacksmith), the bearded foreman Pete Bushman with his granddaddy's

Arkansas Traveler fiddle pressed firmly against his chin, the Wyoming Kyd with the pearl-inlaid mandolin, and the long, lean Ute, ready to let go on his five-string banjo!

Sarah's mouth was . . . well, there is no other word. Wide open. *Oh—all this for me!* After teetering right on the brink between nightmare and insanity, this was just *too* wonderful.

While the pretty tenor, a local librarian whose name was not Marian, danced and pranced in place, the cowboys kicked it off with "Choctaw Hayride"—and oh, what a ride that was. After the applause died down, Charlie Moon introduced the girl singer—one Patsy Poynter—and laughed at the whistles and wolf howls from appreciative hairy-legs amongst the crowd.

Patsy, as it turned out, was not only pretty and a fair-to-middling dancer—the shapely librarian was a spellbinding crooner, her voice velvet smooth and sweet as honey in the comb. Backed up by the Ute and his cowboy friends, she took the microphone and electrified the audience with "I Don't Believe You've Met My Baby"—all the while giving Charlie Moon the big-eye.

Talk about your red-hot class act.

The rudest fellows in the ballroom were silenced. And the tears? It is no surprise that they fairly poured from quite a few ladies' heavily mascaraed eyes, but the measure of Patsy's effect was this: Here and there a pearly bead of salt water coursed down a leathery cheek that hadn't been wet since Daddy's funeral. We're talking about the sort of fellow who would laugh out loud if his best friend got bucked from his saddle into a bristling bunch of prickly pears, then kicked in the head by the horse that'd throwed him. Even Daisy Perika dabbed her eyes with a linen napkin.

What about Sarah Frank? As Miss Sweet Sixteen watched the good-looking librarian make goo-goo eyes at Charlie Moon, it took all her willpower to maintain a passable poker face. But behind her lips, her teeth were clenched. Not quite hard enough to bite a ten-penny nail in two, but your unwary yellow number-two lead pencil would definitely have been cleaved in half. Under the table, her little hands were balled into fists. Now some might say that Kid Frank, who weighed in at about ninety-six pounds, was not up to slugging it out with a world-class heavy-weight blondie who had years of experience, not to mention other—ah—attributes. No matter, Sarah was a scrappy fighter. But she did not realize that the really serious opponent was sitting two tables behind her.

What about Lila Mae McTeague? Moon's sweetheart was not en-tirely pleased with the onstage flirting, but she assured herself that it was all part of the act. After all, Charlie wasn't flirting back. Was he?

But this reference to Moon's almost fiancée raises another question: Why was she not seated at the table of honor? Because Lila Mae had told Charlie that she preferred a smaller table, in the shadows. This preference for fading into the background might have been merely force of professional habit for one employed by the Federal Bureau of Investigation. Or perhaps, being endowed with the grace of humility, she was one of those Christians who takes the command about "taking the lowest seat" quite literally. Perhaps.

Backed up by his friends, Charlie Moon began to sing his version of "Goin' Back to Harlan"—to his *little* lady. His motives were pure as morning dew on wild mountain roses, but had he gone a song too far?

It was enough to cool an already icy Special Agent McTeague an-other degree or two.

On the plus side, Moon crooning made a giddy sixteen-year-old forget all about the pretty blond canary from the local library. Sarah was about to faint or swoon or whatever it is young ladies do when life doles out altogether too much unadulterated pleasure. Could things possibly get more interesting? Yes they could. And would.

But not immediately.

So before Charlie Moon gets himself into serious trouble, let us leave the Silver Mountain Hotel ballroom behind. We shall pay a brief call on Granite Creek's shadowy suburbs.

◆ ◆ ◆

NANCY YAZZI'S boyfriend switched off the Jeep's headlights, turned off Beechwood Road and onto a dirt lane that circled behind the GC

Propane Company's nine-foot chain-link fence. He parked the four-wheel-drive vehicle in a cluster of junipers, eased his 238-pound frame to the ground, hitched up his thick leather belt, and took the first step in a short walk to the Hermann Wetzel residence.

The young man was not afraid, but neither was he a fool. Jake Harper felt just edgy enough to sharpen his senses—and his instincts. But would it be enough to see him through the next few minutes? That remains to be seen.

But let us leave the fellow to his dark business, and return to the festivities.

# CHAPTER SEVENTEEN

## A DELICATE SITUATION ARISES

AS SOON AS CHARLIE MOON HAD CROONED THE FINAL VERSE OF "Shady Grove," plucked the last *twang* on the banjo strings, the object of Sarah Frank's affection set aside his instrument, bounded off the stage to take several long-legged strides (the spotlight tagged along) in the general direction of Lila Mae's table, where he planned to ask the lady to dance, after which he would—if he could get up the nerve—offer her the engagement ring.

The fact that the potential fiancée was seated in the shadows beyond Sarah turns out to be a detail that is of some significance. As Moon was approaching the birthday girl's table, he realized to his horror that *both* ladies were smiling; *both* were about to get up from their chairs and accept his gracious invitation. Uh-oh.

Just about everyone else had realized this, too, which led to one of those *expectant hushes* we hear so much about.

The audience watched, wondering how Charlie Moon would deal with this terrible dilemma.

Might he pretend to stumble over some imaginary object and simulate a sprained ankle, which rendered him incapable of dancing? Not a chance. Such a cowardly subterfuge would be beneath the man's dignity. Besides, he did not think of such a clever ruse.

Should he yell "Fire!" and clear the ballroom? This had worked like a charm for Paul Newman when Alfred Hitchcock placed him in that Eastern bloc opera house where the snake-eyed ballerina recognized him as a spy and summoned the dreaded Secret Police. The Hitchcock/Newman ploy might well have solved Charlie Moon's immediate problem, but it did not occur to the banjo picker to create a riot where dozens of innocents might be trampled to death. (Do not be overly critical; keep in mind that he had only a fraction of a second to come up with a plan.)

So what did he do?

Nothing.

Moon's deliverance appeared in the form of an attractive lady with golden hair that flowed over her shoulders like spun honey.

No, not the girl singer. Patsy Poynter was onstage with the other players.

The attractive lady was Beatrice Spencer, who had taken an interest in Charlie Moon when their paths had crossed about a year ago. Bea had been eyeing the Ute ever since she had arrived (uninvited) at Sarah's birthday party. As if conjured up to rescue him, the shapely apparition appeared between Moon and an uncertain fate, stretched out her arms, and murmured with a seductive smile, "Dance with me, Charlie."

Does this woman have brass? Indeed she does—tons of it. Also gold and silver and bank accounts and blue-chip stocks and gilt-edged bonds and deeds to the Yellow Pines Ranch and Spencer Mountain.

What happened next? Just what you'd expect.

The bass player picked up Moon's left-behind banjo, the Columbine Grass Minus One hit a few hot licks of "Pike County Breakdown," and Charlie Moon danced Bea away like his feet were on fire.

How did the two abandoned ladies respond? Imagine gaped mouths. Gasps exhaled from those gaped mouths. Moreover, *little daggers* came zinging from their eyes. Sarah's delicate stilettos and Lila Mae's over-sized butcher knives were focused on Charlie Moon. Sounds fanciful? Maybe so. But he felt them sting the back of his neck.

Almost everyone in the ballroom had witnessed what had happened. Most had sense enough to keep quiet, and did so by holding their breaths. The other 49 percent (the men) were either snickering or haw-hawing like jackasses.

Still unaware of the presence of Charlie Moon's sweetheart, Sarah Frank was humiliated to the core or the marrow, whichever is deeper. She wanted to crawl under the table with Mr. Zig-Zag, hug him and have a good cry, and die. Or fall into a faint and expire of a broken heart. Whichever was faster.

The FBI lady was (unconsciously) reaching for that place where she normally carried her Glock automatic. It was merely a subconscious reflex. Lila Mae would not actually have *shot* her sweetheart with a 9-mm slug. Not in front of so many witnesses.

It did not help that Charlie Moon, who thought he'd carried things off pretty well, was obviously having a fine old time. Kicking up his boot heels with vim and vigor, grinning ear-to-ear at the delightful armful.

And it also didn't help that Bea Spencer, who had never danced with a man of this caliber, was quite swept away in his arms. Or that she snuggled just a little closer to Charlie than was absolutely necessary.

Things were about to go from bad to badder when, out of nowhere, the Wyoming Kyd appeared, snatched Sarah up, and danced her to the middle of the ballroom floor. It is not for nothing that Mr. Kydmann is known as Charlie Moon's right-hand man. Within a heartbeat, a tall, handsome gent outfitted in hand-tooled ostrich-hide boots, a three-thousand-dollar suit, and a white Stetson asked Lila Mae McTeague would you like to dance, ma'am. Ma'am allowed as how she would and away they whipped across the floor like a couple of West Texas whirlwinds.

It seemed that the pair of lady bombs had been defused.

The women in the room exhaled the breaths they had been collectively holding.

From their dates: loud shouts of "Wa-hoo!" "Whoopee!" "Let 'er rip!"

As if on cue, a grizzled, potbellied old stockman who hankered to cut in tapped Charlie Moon on the shoulder. The Ute rancher graciously gave up a piqued Miss Spencer and tapped the Kyd, who released Sarah with just enough reluctance to please the young lady.

Ah, the resilience of youth! In an instant, all was forgiven. Dancing on air with the love of her life, the brand-new sixteen-year-old was lost in a dream. This was Sarah's day—and Sarah's night.

As the final twangy strain of "Pike County Breakdown" faded, there was enthusiastic applause, whistles, shouts of "More!"

Which was when Charlie Moon made his strategic retreat to the stage, got his banjo back in hand. Now firmly in the groove, the

Columbine Grass settled down to do their thing, which was to pick, pluck, and sing and create quite a big commotion that would compel even shy, uncoordinated folks into high-gear locomotion. All over the ballroom, chairs were shoved away from tables as the happy crowd got up to kick heels and stomp and shout.

Oh, and did they dance!

In the entire history of Granite Creek, Colorado—even back in the days of hardworking miners with little pouches of precious metal, coldhearted madams with rouged faces, shifty-eyed cardsharps with cuffed aces, and hardcase drifters with umpteen notches carved on ivory-handled six-guns—there had never been such a rip-tootin' celebration. Not even that time when they hanged Big Sam Carp from a cottonwood limb for shooting the mayor's brother in the . . . But that's another story, and one best forgotten.

Now it just so happens that the leader of the band is a natural-born traveling man and Charlie Moon likes to ride the rails, which is why they took the Orange Blossom Special over to Big Rock Candy Mountain, where they stopped to sit a spell with Cotton Eyed Joe and Old Joe Clark and boiled some cabbage down before they flagged down that New River Train, which got 'em to Cumberland Gap just in time to watch the Blue Moon of Kentucky rise and shine on the Little Cabin on the Hill, which was where they caught that *sixteen coaches long* Night Train to Georgia, which made an unscheduled stop In the Pines so's they could pick pretty Miss Patsy Poynter a bouquet of Wildwood Flowers. It was a mighty busy trip, but somewhere or another along the way, they found time to Walk the Dog.

In spite of the fact that the girl singer was absolutely first-rate, one or two Nashville music critics might've been of the opinion that the Columbine Grass was not right up there with such classy outfits as those put together by Bill Monroe or Flatt and Scruggs or Doc Watson or Ricky Scaggs, and that Mr. Moon's singers and string pluckers weren't quite ready for the Grand Ole Opry, but none by-gosh said so out loud—not that night in Granite Creek—because they dang well knew what was good for them! Besides, what the CG lacked in raw talent, they more than made up for with red-blooded, cowboy enthusiasm.

But no matter how much zest and zeal a musician has, he must be fed.

And so, after about a half-dozen more high-octane pieces, the Columbine fivesome put aside their instruments, rested their voice boxes, and joined the crowd for dinner—which was being brought on in sizable helpings. There was a huge iron pot of barbecued pork, a side of roasted prime Columbine beef, eight mouthwatering Virginia hams, and don't even talk about the gallons of pinto beans, trays of buttered corn on the cob, bowls of mashed potatoes (with enough thick brown gravy to float a twelve-foot bass boat), home-baked breads, and desserts— well, we could go on all night about fresh California strawberries and hand-cranked ice cream in six different flavors, and— But that is enough. Except for mentioning the towering birthday cake delivered on a six-wheeled cart by two nervous waiters. The cake's five layers weighed eighty-four pounds; it was topped by hand-made beeswax candles (sixteen, of course). The weighty centerpiece was ever-so-gently hoisted onto the table by Charlie Moon and Chief of Police Scott Parris.

It shall be mentioned that Sarah received a light kiss on the cheek from Charlie Moon (this almost resulted in a genuine swoon), a suffocating hug from Dolly Bushman, and a lighter embrace from Lila Mae McTeague, who—ever since Sarah had come to Colorado from Tonapah Flats, Utah—had realized that this little slip of a girl represented The Competition, and was taking what had initially seemed to be merely a frivolous teenage crush as something that might have to be reckoned with.

The sudden realization that Charlie Moon's sweetheart was present at her party was quite a shock to the birthday girl. But Sarah hugged her rival right back.

After the dessert, the tables were cleared. Great urns of coffee were brought into the ballroom, and a few flasks were stealthily removed from men's pockets and one woman's purse.

After whistles were duly wetted, the time had come for the giving of gifts.

It was one of those completely disorganized, totally delightful times that beggars description. Suffice it to say that as well-wishers passed by, a great multitude of prettily wrapped and ribboned parcels were piled onto the table in front of Sarah Frank. And though she would not examine the bounty until the following day, the loot including a thick red woolen shawl Daisy had knitted while Sarah was away at school, a lovely wristwatch Special Agent McTeague had purchased that afternoon, another lovely wristwatch from Scott Parris, and so on. When the thing was (almost) done, Charlie Moon made the observation that this was quite a pile of stuff. Why, it would take a pickup truck to haul all these gifts to the Columbine. Which just happened to remind him. . . . He reached into his jacket pocket, produced a small, white box that was just about big enough to hold a diamond bracelet or a state-of-the-art cell phone or . . .

Sarah stared at the enticing box, looked up at Charlie Moon.

He smiled back at the girl, who was happier, prettier than she had ever been. His eyes urged her on. *Go ahead. Open it.*

She did. And inside was a ring! No, not that kind—a silver key ring. On a smaller circle attached to it was a lump of turquoise. Also, there was a pair of keys. Ford keys. Sarah sighed a long, blissful "oooooohhh."

Moon laughed. "I hope you liked that rebuilt pickup Mr. Kydmann brought you here in. It's still parked out front by the curb, and it's all yours now."

She let out a shriek that would have startled the biggest, baddest banshee you can imagine, gave Moon a running hug that would have felled a lesser man, all the while yelping a long series of thank-yous, which eventually terminated with, "I'll drive it to the Columbine tonight!"

Scott Parris, who represented the law in these here parts, had something to say about that. What he said (loudly) was, "Ahem," which got most everyone's attention. He added, "You'll need a driver's permit before you can drive that pickup away from the curb." Taking note of Sarah's pitiful expression, he inquired, "You don't have one?"

The thin little girl shook her head.

Parris looked almost as sad as the sixteen-year-old. "I'm sorry, kid—

but you can't operate it on a public highway until you have a duly issued driver's permit." He brightened. "But that shouldn't be any trouble. I just happen to know that you took driver's ed at Ignacio High School and made the second-highest score in your class."

Moon scowled at his best friend. "She'll need that permit right away."

Parris scowled back. "I hope you're not suggesting—just because you're my buddy—that I use my influence as chief of police to pull some strings."

The Ute shot back, "I sure as shootin' am."

"Well, okay—if you put it that way." Granite Creek's top cop fumbled inside his jacket, produced a small envelope, and gave it to Sarah. As the girl opened it and stared at the document in her hand, Parris grinned so hard that it hurt his face. "That's your learner's permit. It's okay for you to drive as long as any of the people who've signed it are in the truck with you." He patted Sarah's shoulder. "Which includes me and Charlie and the Wyomin' Kyd and Pete and Dolly Bushman and a half-dozen Columbine ranch hands."

It was Scott Parris's turn to get hugged. There was no shriek this time, only tears on his shirt.

A few softhearted women started to sob again. Their men began to haw-haw.

Everyone was having a grand old time.

# CHAPTER EIGHTEEN

## AN UNSETTLING DEVELOPMENT

AFTER ENTERING INTO A CONSPIRACY WITH NANCY YAZZI THAT MIGHT turn out to be the most ill-advised enterprise she had ever undertaken, Millicent Muntz (who rarely ventured out at night) had returned home with no appetite. The elderly lady could not imagine even a light snack of crackers and cheese, much less an Italian sausage calzone—such a heavy meal as that would have to wait until her nerves and digestive system had settled down. She picked up her cat and withdrew to the upstairs corner room where she did her sewing, crocheting, knitting and kept a watchful eye on the neighborhood.

Leaving the sewing room lights off (the soft glow of a hallway lamp was sufficient to see by), she placed Mr. Moriarty in his favorite spot under the potted palm and seated herself in a comfortable armchair. As was her habit, the spinster lady began this period of relaxation by reviewing her day. She smiled at the memory of each modest accomplishment, pausing to reprove herself for a task that could have been done better. By this process, she passed quickly through the morning and afternoon hours, up to the point when she had crossed the street to initiate the intrigue with Nancy Yazzi. That was when things had begun to get—what was the saying? Ah, yes—things had gotten *dicey.* She shook her head and sighed. *When I was younger, this evening's exertions would not have been such a challenge, but the frenetic activities of the past hour have been almost too much.* She knew that despite an intelligent woman's most meticulously prepared plans, there were so many things that could go amiss as a result of small miscalculations, ill-advised assumptions, and general imponderables. And most vexing of all—unexpected developments.

Such as: *What if Hermann Wetzel came up from the basement while I was away and happened to be looking through a front window when I drove my car into the garage?* This worry begot a daughter fret: *If he did, he might wonder about my early return.* The fertile offspring promptly produced another: *What if Hermann calls me on the phone and asks to speak to Nancy?* The very thought of such a calamity made her spine tingle. *What would I say to that?* Miss M came up with a simple ploy: *If the telephone rings, I shall not pick it up.* She frowned. *But if I did not answer, he might assume that something was wrong over here and cross the street to pound on my door.* The worrier clasped her hands on the varnished maple chair arms. *It is enough to give a person a case of the flibberty-jibbers!* She smiled at her ludicrous thoughts. *Oh, I am a silly old goose to worry so much—I simply must relax.*

To that end, she leaned back in her chair and considered life's many blessings. *I have excellent health. Worthwhile things to do. A very nice home. And it is so peaceful here.* Not for the first time, the frugal woman congratulated herself on investing her inheritance in the two properties on Beechwood Road, and at a time when real estate was an excellent investment. The homes, built by the same contractor, were virtually identical, but . . . *I'm so glad I rented 750 Beechwood to Mr. Wetzel. When I lived over there, I could hardly see a thing for that veritable forest of trees in the front yard. But here at 751, and particularly from this upper window, I have a wonderful view. Especially of the mountains and sky.*

The landlady also had an exceptional view of her rental property across the street, though not for long at this hour. Already misty wisps of darkness—those sinister night-soldiers—were coalescing into menacing platoons that would creep in to occupy territory abandoned by sunlight. It happened every night: The ghostly brigades would convert cool shady glades into eerie black enclaves, and charming clusters of junipers into miniature jungles where all manner of red-eyed vermin rustled about with evil intent.

Determined to put her mind at ease, Miss Muntz assured herself that Hermann Wetzel—a creature of ingrained habits—had undoubtedly remained in the basement "rec room" to peruse his collection of fishing, hunting, and gun magazines. *Well, at least he doesn't spend all his time watching TV.* Aside from this observation, it was difficult for Miss M to think of anything positive about her tenant, but not because he was a vulgar, stupid fellow—he couldn't help that. Such conditions were, as Daddy used to say (prior to the discovery of DNA), "in the blood." What bothered her was how Hermann abused his pretty step-daughter. And not only verbally. Nancy Yazzi had never actually come right out and told her about it, but there were signs that Miss Muntz recognized, such as bruises on the girl's face and neck. Also on her wrists . . . and legs. Miss M shook her head. Men like that should be put in jail. Better still, eliminated from the face of the earth. But most of the women (and young girls!) they molested would not admit to having been victimized, much less testify in a public trial. The humilia-tion was too much to bear, the probability of a conviction too small. She rapped her knuckles on the chair arm. *But one way or another, Hermann will get what's coming to him.*

If someone had suggested that Miss Millicent Muntz had "second sight," she would have disagreed. She did not think of herself as special.

Her eyes having adjusted to the low light level, the lady picked up her knitting, got to work on a yellow cat-sweater that was not quite half finished. She made a valiant effort to concentrate on her work. Clickety-click. Clickety-click. *I just can't do this and look out the win-dow too.* On most evenings she had a magnificent view of soaring gran-ite peaks, great sprays of stars sparkling like tiny diamonds. But not tonight. It had been cloudy all day, with intermittent rain. At this very moment, a few plump little drops began to pelt the windowpanes.

So peaceful.

After another clickety-click or two, the neighborhood's self-appointed guardian set her knitting aside. She would spend this "quiet time" listen-ing to the light rain.

Several minutes passed. Also a motor vehicle or two.

Then, something quite interesting attracted her attention.

Miss M leaned closer to the window, frowned. *Well, now.*

## ACROSS BEECHWOOD ROAD

HERMANN WETZEL was thumbing through a dog-eared copy of *Rod & Gun* when the cell phone in his shirt pocket vibrated. He scowled at the caller ID. *What's Muntzy got ants in her pants about this time?* He pressed the Talk button. "Hey."

The voice in his ear said, "Mr. Wetzel?"

"Nope, it's the butler." A snicker. "What's up?"

"I thought that I should advise you that—"

"Hey—what was that?"

"I beg your pardon?"

"I just heard somebody upstairs." *And it ain't Nancy come home early—that little slut slinks around like a damn alley cat—never makes a sound.*

"That is what I was calling you about, Mr. Wetzel—" There was a sharp click in her ear. *Well—the man has the manners of a goat!* Leaving Mr. Moriarty behind, Miss Muntz hurried down the stairs.

◆ ◆ ◆

HERMANN WETZEL switched off the rec-room lights, listened intently as the footsteps passed rapidly over his head and continued for a few paces before falling silent.

*It's a burglar. All the lights are off upstairs—the thieving bastard must figure there's nobody home.*

More creaking of boards overhead.

Automatic pistol firmly in hand, Wetzel looked up at the darkened ceiling. *Where's he going now?* Miss Muntz's tenant thumbed the Safety button on his weapon and began a silent ascent of the basement stairs in his soft-soled house slippers. A thin fan of light flashed under the stairwell door. *The bozo's turned on the lights!* Unnerved by the brazenness of the intruder—who was either armed or stupid or both— Wetzel momentarily considered a strategic retreat to the cellar, a discreet telephone call to the police. *But only a brass-plated sissy would do that and I got a gun and this guy don't know I'm here.*

Which settled the matter.

Drawing a deep breath, Wetzel reached out to slowly twist the porcelain knob a quarter turn. The barely audible click of the latch set his teeth on edge. *I hope he didn't hear that.* But there was no turning back. He pushed the door open just a crack. Immediately saw the intruder. *What the hell—*

◆ ◆ ◆

MISS MUNTZ had barely gotten downstairs when she heard the crisp cracks of pistol shots. *Oh my!* She slipped on her black raincoat, snatched up a cordless telephone, and opened her front door just in time to see a shadowy figure burst from the rental house and make a dash for it. She did not see the intruder toss a pistol into the bushes, and perhaps it was just as well. For one who already had a serious case of the flibbertyjibbers, Miss M had heard and seen quite enough. Still, the cool-headed landlady dialed 911 and reported the unnerving incident.

As soon as Clara Tavishuts had the caller's name and address, she assured Miss Muntz that officers would be on the scene very shortly. The dispatcher also instructed the elderly lady (whom she assumed was safely in her home) to remain inside with the doors locked—and to stay away from windows.

Ignoring this sensible advice, the landlady dropped the telephone into her coat pocket and headed (at a trot!) directly across the street to 750 Beechwood. As she did so, an automobile turned a corner about a block away. The headlights illuminated a man who was crossing Beechwood in the opposite direction. There was a screech of brakes. Miss Muntz could not see the fleeing man's face, but it was apparent that he was a burly fellow, wearing a cowboy hat. At such stressful moments, it is odd which impressions pop into our minds. The thought struck her that for such a big fellow, he was certainly making tracks.

The driver of the automobile saw the elderly lady by the curb and stopped to ask what was going on. Breathless from the excitement, Miss Muntz paused long enough to explain to the neighbor (a young mother, with a toddler secured in a car seat) that there had apparently been a shooting in the Wetzel residence and that she had already called the police. The neighbor, now quite alarmed, said that she had gotten a pretty good look at the man who'd crossed the street, and thought she might recognize him if she ever saw him again.

The women heard a roar, turned to see a Jeep lurch out of a vacant lot near the GC Propane Company storage yard. It bounced over the curb and almost flipped over as the driver made a hard left turn. The sturdy vehicle righted itself with a thud and sped away straddling the white center line.

"Well," said Miss Muntz. "This used to be such a peaceful neighborhood."

The neighbor (who had forgotten where she was going) executed a quick U-turn and drove back home.

After watching the young woman depart, the landlady hurried up to Wetzel's front door, which was open. She went through the parlor, down the hallway, and into the kitchen, where she paused to inspect these familiar surroundings. Her Felix the Cat clock tick-tocked on the wall over the refrigerator. Even more arresting were familiar scents, some quite pleasant to the senses: the potted African violets in the south windows. Pine-Sol. The lingering aroma of an uneaten supper. But there was another, quite unpleasant odor. Fresh blood.

◆ ◆ ◆

AS THE neighbor pulled into her driveway and braked her minivan to a stop, she yanked a cell phone from her purse, punched in 911. "Hello, this is Hazel Burch, 220 Aspen Loop. I believe I've just been a witness to a crime and I want to tell you what I saw while it's still fresh in my mind. . . ."

◆ ◆ ◆

MISS MUNTZ found Hermann Wetzel crumpled at the top of the basement stairs, his shirt soaked with blood. The man had a 9-mm automatic pistol in his hand, an astonished expression on his homely face.

She knelt to make a quick examination. His pupils, which were completely dilated, reminded the elderly lady of Little Orphan Annie. *He's not breathing.* She pressed a finger under his jawbone. *And there's no pulse.*

Diagnosis: The spirit had departed.

The sensible landlady, who had been so reckless in entering a house where shots had been fired, was beginning to feel rather uneasy. Also distinctly queasy. *Oh, I mustn't throw up on the carpet . . . it was cleaned just last month!* She hurried back into the kitchen, steadied herself on the sink. It would be indelicate, also inappropriate, to describe what occurred during the next half minute. Suffice it to say that after completing her business, Miss Muntz was eager to be elsewhere.

Out the Wetzel front door she went, down the driveway, across Beechwood Road, and into the safety of her cozy home. Perspiration beading on her forehead, she paused to lean against the inside of her front door and gasp for breath, only to be assaulted by a wave of nauseating dizziness. *Oh, dear—I hope I don't faint.* It became apparent that *hope* would not get the job done; consciousness began to slip away. The determined old soul clenched her teeth. *I shall not faint.* Miss M called upon resources from deep within. *I simply refuse to!*

And she did not.

## WHERE IS A COP WHEN YOU NEED ONE?

OR TWO. COPS, THAT IS. IN THIS INSTANCE, BOTH OF THEM WERE AT a birthday party in Granite Creek's classiest hotel, having a grand old time. The Southern Ute Buffalo Drummers, the White River Gourd Dancers, a barrel-chested Taos Pueblo singer with a baritone that an Arkansas auctioneer would have envied—all were going at it with great gusto. Picture four serious men seated around a rawhide drum large enough to float Huck Finn and his friend Tom Sawyer down the old Mississippi with sufficient luggage for a three-week stay. One is tempted to add that ol' Jim could have come along for the ride, but that would be an unwarranted exaggeration, and besides, Jim had had quite enough of going "down de ribber," thank you very much. But it sure was a dandy drum, and when one of the foursome hit it a good lick with his big knobby drumstick, the *BOOM!* reverberated not only in the listener's head but in his rib cage as well. Add to this the rattling of piñon nuts in long-neck gourds and the voice of the stony-faced crooner who wailed a tale (about a girl who married a badger) in a Tewa dialect that no one present but himself could understand, and you get some notion of the general commotion. What a great party!

Not that officer Eddie Knox, who was an old grump, couldn't find something or other to grouse about. Like his beverage. Our man in blue was sipping at something insipid, wishing it were a cold brew, but what could you do when the birthday celebration was for a sixteen-year-old girl? Drink iced tea, that's what.

E. C. "Piggy" Slocum, Knox's five-foot-five, 210-pound partner, was sloshing down one cup of coffee after another, munching Dolly Bushman's homemade oatmeal-raisin-chocolate-chip-macadamia-nut cookies by the handful, all the while eyeing the huge birthday cake with gluttonous intensity.

The radio on Knox's belt made a bleeping sound, which was barely audible above the drum beats, gourd rattles, and the song about how Mr. Badger ate his bride's mother. No. Hold on. Tewa is a difficult language and there is some dispute about the translation—it may be that the toothy groom devoured his new wife's beaded moccasins. Whichever it was, this culinary indiscretion got the marriage off in a bad direction.

The senior partner put the radio to his ear, barked, "Knox here."

Clara Tavishuts advised the irritable cop that she was sorry to spoil the party for him and Slocum, but— "Officers Martin and Lopez are dealing with a family dispute and I have two callers who report suspicious activity at 750 Beechwood Road, residence of a Mr. Hermann Wetzel. A Miss Muntz at 751 Beechwood reports possible gunshots."

Knox groaned. *It'll be some old rattletrap that backfired.* He elbowed Slocum, causing his partner to spill half a cup of coffee onto his lap, which made Piggy let out a shrill yelp, which went unheard by the other guests seated at Sarah's table. Knox shouted into the chubby man's ear, "We got a call, Pig."

Slocum made a two-handed grab at the cookie plate, got a half dozen of Dolly Bushman's finest in his mitts.

And off they went, lickety-split, no one taking any interest in their departure except Chief of Police Scott Parris and Charlie Moon, who gave his best friend a questioning look. Parris shrugged, shook his head at what he considered to be a pair of latter-day Keystone Kops. Knox treated every response, whether to rescue a treed cat or soothe a marital spat, as if he'd been called upon to protect the town from a horde of crazed, armed-to-the-teeth terrorists. Slocum, a placid, dim-bulb sort, was mainly along for the ride.

Parris's judgment was unduly harsh. True, Eddie Knox was more than a wee bit eccentric, and also had a tendency toward drama. But Knox was also an officer with uncommonly reliable instincts and he was absolutely fearless. E. C. Slocum was not the brightest policeman on the force, but "Piggy" rarely missed a day's work, never complained about an unpleasant assignment, and was blessed with a bright outlook on life and perpetual good humor. And though he was always afraid of getting hurt, when push did come to shove, Slocum would not back down from a knock-down, drag-out fight—and he would never let his partner down *no matter what.*

What about tonight?

Officers Knox and Slocum arrived at the scene with emergency lights flashing, dual sirens wailing, tires squealing as their unit skidded to a stop. Miss Muntz hurried out to the curb to provide a breathless report about finding her tenant's dead body inside her rental property. Piggy immediately called for an ambulance. They entered the residence at 750 Beechwood Road with sidearms drawn, found Hermann Wetzel's bloody corpse, and called dispatch to request all available officers on the spot ASAP and assistance from the state police in setting up roadblocks along all major exits from Granite Creek. All this in *two minutes flat.* And that was that.

Not bad for a couple of "Keystone Kops."

◆ ◆ ◆

WHEN SCOTT Parris got the call from dispatch, gourds were still rattling, the big drum was still booming, the Taos Pueblo singer was still singing—now a humorous birthday song, in flawless English. The chief of police left the ballroom for the lobby, where the sound was merely a deafening roar such as would be caused by two speeding freight trains colliding head-on. Upon hearing the grim news, he silently mouthed the obligatory two-word expletive, then advised Clara Tavishuts that he'd be on the spot in six minutes. Made it in five and twenty seconds.

Like Knox and Slocum before him, Parris's departure had gone almost unnoticed. Those who did notice were Charlie Moon and FBI Special Agent Lila Mae McTeague.

An inveterate gambler, the tribal investigator figured the odds were thirty to one that blood had been spilled. Four to one it was an auto accident, most likely on one of the steep, winding mountain roads that spiraled out of town. Then there was the long shot—it might be a homicide. Every so often, some crazed drunk would put a knife between a drinking buddy's ribs or a disgruntled wife would club her cheating husband with whatever happened to be close at hand, such as a cast-iron skillet, baseball bat, or unabridged dictionary. *But whatever it is that's got Scott all red-faced, it's none of my business.* Moon caught Sarah's eye and smiled at the little girl who, it seemed, had grown up all at once and become a little woman. A *pretty* little woman.

Lila Mae, who had been cajoled into accepting a seat at the birthday girl's table, was sitting as close beside Mr. Moon as possible. She put her hand in his.

The Ute turned the bright light of his smile upon the good-looking lady.

At that moment, another guest approached the guest of honor's table. Nancy Yazzi.

She gave Sarah a big hug and a box of chocolates.

"Oh," Sarah shrieked, "I didn't know you were here!"

"I told you I was going to a dance tonight." Nancy explained that she had been sitting in a far corner, practically behind a potted rubber plant. She pouted her pretty lips. "I had to lean sideways to see the bandstand."

The birthday girl insisted that her friend take a seat beside her.

Which Nancy did.

Shall this day's wonders never cease?

Not for at least an hour or two. Or midnight, at the latest.

# CHAPTER TWENTY

## THE FUGITIVE

AS HE LISTENED TO THE ALARMING POLICE REPORTS ON HIS PORT-able scanner, Jake Harper realized that he was in a serious fix—he'd been seen hoofing it from the scene of a murder. *And the cops know what kind of car I'm driving!*

Nancy Yazzi's desperate boyfriend was fueled by a volatile mix of animal instinct and brutish determination. *I gotta hole up somewhere till this thing blows over. The cops pick me up, I'm toast.* As he turned onto Forest Road 1040 (known by the locals as IRS Road) and the Jeep leaped and lurched over the bumps and ruts, the wild-eyed man began to experience something akin to Miss Muntz's recent affliction. Nausea. Mrs. Harper's son came as near to praying as he ever had during his thirty-seven years: *Please . . . please . . . don't let me puke all over myself.* The desperate sinner had no idea to Whom he was addressing this urgent plea. Even so, the nausea gradually diminished. Probably because he had slowed down. Or perhaps his prayer had been heard and answered.

*At any moment, somewhere a sparrow falleth.*

The spunky little Jeep bumpity-bumped its way along IRS Road, passing a few year-round residences whose windows glowed with friendly illumination, a barn or two nestled in pastures that were half shrouded in darkness. Over the mountains, thunder rumbled—a cold rain began to pelt the dirty windshield. The unnerved driver could not remember where the wiper control was, fumbled and cursed until he found it, and watched with relief as the blades swiped away blotchy splotches of wetness. During the next mile or so, there was no sign of a dwelling. Finally, at almost two thousand feet above the valley where the lights of Granite Creek were spread out like a scattering of rhinestones on a party skirt, a sprightly display of lightning tap-danced along the mountainside—illuminating the dark landscape just long enough for Harper to see a hand-painted wooden sign (ROGER'S ROOST) and a two-level log home about fifty yards off the road. Following the heavenly fireworks, there was a thunderous applause as the dark curtain fell. Even as the stage was swallowed up in night, the essential impressions registered in his mind. *I didn't seen no car in the driveway. And there's no lights in the house.* Conclusion: *There's nobody home.* He gave the steering wheel a quick twist, sped along a graveled driveway, braking to a skidding stop just in time to avoid ramming the garage. He cut the ignition, switched off the headlights, found a small flashlight in the glove compartment, and got out to tug at the garage-door handle.

Locked, of course.

He abandoned the garage, found another door on the lower level, tried the knob. Also locked. Not a problem. The resourceful fellow picked up one of several ornamental cement blocks that had been arranged around a small, shriveled-up flower garden, smashed the door glass, reached inside to find the knob, gave it a turn, and let himself in.

When Harper switched on the lights he found himself in what is commonly known as a walk-in basement. This one had walnut wall paneling, acoustic ceiling panels with track lighting, and vinyl flooring that appeared to have been waxed recently. The furnishings included a sagging gray couch, a pair of bunk beds with colorful quilts (prancing pinto ponies rampant on a field of lime-green grass), and a massive 1970s-era RCA color television. Mounted on the walls were hockey sticks, tennis racquets, miscellaneous fishing equipment, and a striped bass that (if you included the spikes on its tail) was almost a yard long. He entered the attached garage, switched on the lights, and blinked at an almost-new Ford Escape. *Now ain't that a nice piece of luck.* He unlatched the garage door, drove his Jeep into the vacant space, and slammed the door down again.

This essential task accomplished, he returned to the kids' room, turned off the lights, and ascended the stairs to a spacious kitchen that was provided with stainless steel appliances and polished granite countertops. But, like Miss Muntz, the bearish fellow was not in the mood for food. What he required was liquid refreshment, and he found what he longed for in the tastefully appointed parlor, which was equipped with a well-stocked bar. Within half an hour, Jake Harper had drunk himself into a stupor. He stumbled over to a downy-soft couch, flopped onto it, and drifted off to a deep, dreamless sleep.

If he'd had the least inkling of how the local authorities were attempting to close the net around him, Mr. Harper might not have slept at all.

For just one example:

A steely-eyed forest official was motoring along the mountain road, looking for Hermann Wetzel's murderer. His spiffy green pickup was fitted with an umpteen-candlepower searchlight, which he was using to good effect. But when he slowed to illuminate Rogers' Roost, the man under the Smokey Bear hat did not notice the broken glass on the lower level.

Jake's good luck was almost uncanny.

# CHAPTER TWENTY-ONE

## THE WITNESS

AS HE ENTERED THE ELDERLY LADY'S IMMACULATE PARLOR, SCOTT Parris was glad that he had remembered to wipe his boots on the doormat. He removed his venerable felt hat. "Mrs. Muntz, I realize you've—"

"*Miss* Muntz, if you please." She took the hat, placed it on a maple end table.

"Uh . . . right." The chief of police grinned, restarted his speech. "I realize you've had a very stressful experience and I imagine you'd rather not be bothered right now. But after just an hour or two, witnesses tend to forget a lot of what they've seen and heard, so I'd like to ask you a few questions about what happened across the street this evening." He produced a small notebook and ballpoint pen. "First of all, did Mr. Wetzel live alone?"

"No. His stepdaughter shared the house with him. Which reminds me—" Miss Muntz glanced at a brass clock on the mantelpiece. "Oh my goodness!" She raised both palms, as if to push him away. "I'm sorry, but your inquiry will have to wait."

Parris cocked his head. "Wait for what?"

"I have an urgent errand to run." She smiled at the policeman's bemused expression. "You see, I promised to pick up Mr. Wetzel's stepdaughter at nine forty-five P.M., and"—she consulted her archaic Lady Elgin wristwatch—"it is now nine twenty-eight. I shall barely have time to get there." Her expression was suddenly very sober. "Which means that I must prepare myself to tell her what has happened." *And it will be extremely difficult.*

The cop shook his head. "No you won't. I'll see that the young lady is notified." But this was a new wrinkle. "How old is this stepdaughter?"

"Seventeen. Very close to eighteen, I believe."

He wrote this down. "Her name?"

"Nancy. Nancy *Yazzi.*" She spelled the surname.

After he jotted this information in his notebook, Parris looked through the front window at a gay display of flashing red-and-blue lights. "Just Mr. Wetzel and his stepdaughter occupied your rental property?"

"That is correct. I understand that the girl's mother left some time ago." Miss Muntz had heard rumors about Chiquita Yazzi running off with *another man,* but she would not repeat such distasteful gossip.

"Where are you supposed to pick up Miss Yazzi?"

"The Silver Mountain Hotel." The landlady glanced at her watch. "She's attending a dance."

*Holy smoke.* "Is she at Sarah Frank's birthday party?"

"Why, yes." *However did he know that?* "Nancy was invited about a week ago, by the gentleman who was organizing the event."

"Charlie Moon?"

"I believe that was the name Nancy mentioned." An amused smile. "You are certainly well-informed."

"Yes ma'am." Basking in the compliment, Parris returned the smile. "Hold on while I make a quick call." He fumbled for the phone in his jacket pocket, selected the programmed number for his Ute friend.

Charlie Moon answered after two rings, his deep voice almost drowned out by the happy pandemonium. "What's up, pard?"

"Uh, you know a guest of Sarah's—" Parris squinted at the scrawl in his notebook. *I got to learn to write so I can read what I wrote.* "Nancy . . . uh . . . Yoxxi?"

"You mean Nancy Yazzi?"

"Right. I understand you invited the young lady to the birthday party."

"Sure. She's a friend of Sarah's." *And the kid don't have many friends.* "What's up?"

Parris turned his back on Miss Muntz, lowered his voice. "Her stepfather's been shot and killed."

The Southern Ute tribal investigator digested this unpalatable piece of information. "Sorry to hear it."

"The dead guy's Hermann Wetzel. The two of 'em lived alone." The chief of police cleared his throat. "This is going to be a big shock for Miss Yazzi, and she's going to need someplace to stay for a few days. Maybe with a friend. Somewhere out of town would be nice. But not too far away." He let the heavy hint hang in the air.

Charlie Moon understood what was expected of him. "You want me to put Nancy up at the Hotel Columbine?"

Parris chuckled. "Now that you mention it, that sounds like a great notion."

Moon's close call with the ladies who were expecting an invitation to dance was still fresh in his mind. *If I take that pretty young girl out to the Columbine with me—and leave Lila Mae here at the hotel—that might not go down too well.* Which dilemma, it seemed, contained the seeds of a solution. "I'll see what I can work out."

"Great."

"But for tonight, I'll book Miss Yazzi a room at the Silver Mountain. Lila Mae's staying here, so she can help look after her."

"I really appreciate it. Otherwise, I'd have to refer the kid to social services."

"Consider it done."

"Thanks, buddy. Catch you later." Parris folded and pocketed the instrument. "Charlie Moon'll look after the stepdaughter," he told Miss Muntz.

"I am pleased to hear it." She seated herself in a rocking chair, closed her eyes and sighed. "To be perfectly frank, after all the excitement, I was not looking forward to driving into town—much less breaking the tragic news to poor Nancy."

"Don't worry your head about that, ma'am." Parris squared his big, brawny shoulders, set his prominent jaw. "When stuff like this happens, breaking bad news is my job." *But this time, good ol' Charlie will end up doing it for me.*

News of the shooting had already spread from the Granite Creek Police Department to the Silver Mountain Hotel, dashed in a flash from the front desk into the main ballroom. Within a few minutes of Parris's call to Moon, most of the attendees of the birthday party were privy to the information. One of the notable exceptions was FBI Special Agent Lila Mae McTeague. The aloof woman was not the sort of stranger to whom one sauntered up and passed on local gossip.

## HIS GOOD INTENTIONS

WHEN CHARLIE Moon jingled the bell on the registration desk, a helpful clerk appeared instantly. Over the party hullabaloo, he managed to reserve a room for Nancy Yazzi. As soon as this was accomplished, he found the dead man's stepdaughter in the ballroom, caught her eye, and gave her a barely discernible "come with me" nod.

Feeling oddly numb, Nancy followed the tribal investigator into the hotel lobby.

Only two persons at the birthday party noticed the subtle signal that had passed between Charlie Moon and Miss Yazzi and watched the pretty girl depart.

Sarah Frank was wide-eyed with curiosity. *Charlie looked awfully worried; something must be wrong.*

The other keen-eyed observer was FBI Special Agent Lila Mae McTeague, who arched a finely penciled brow. *What is this all about?* Her fertile imagination conjured up several possibilities. Including one that embarrassed her. *Oh, but that's so silly—I know Charlie better than that.* Her mouth, which apparently disagreed, went thin. *Or do I?* It took a distinct effort to suppress this uncharitable thought and substitute a generous impulse: *If there is some kind of trouble, perhaps I can be of assistance.*

As Moon and Nancy Yazzi withdrew to a far corner of the hotel lobby, the drums and gourd rattles in the ballroom suddenly stopped.

This unexpected silence was ominous to Hermann Wetzel's stepdaughter. She clutched a cheap plastic purse to her chest. "What is it?"

"Some bad news, I'm afraid."

She stared at him.

Moon was alarmed by the glazed look in her eyes. *She's gonna faint.* "Why don't you sit down."

"No. Just tell me." The girl felt her hands go ice-cold, her knees buckle. She also felt Moon's arms catch her.

◆ ◆ ◆

LILA MAE McTeague arrived at the ballroom door just in time to see the *embrace*. Stunned, she turned away, returned to her place at the table.

◆ ◆ ◆

MOON EASED the girl onto a leather couch.

"I'm okay." Nancy sat up straight as a steel fence post and looked him straight in the eye. "Please—just tell me."

"There's been a shooting at your home." He hesitated. "I'm sorry. It's your stepfather."

"Oh," she murmured. "Hermann . . . is he *dead*?"

"Yes." Charlie Moon was about to tell the young woman that he had made arrangements for her to stay at the hotel for the night, when Sarah, who had picked up the news that something terrible had happened to Nancy's stepfather, showed up. The brand-new sixteen-year-old grabbed Nancy in a hug and invited her to stay at Charlie Moon's ranch for a few days.

Nancy Yazzi accepted the invitation.

So much for a prudent man's plans.

# CHAPTER TWENTY-TWO

## THE INTERVIEW

NOW THAT THE POLICE HAD ASSUMED RESPONSIBILITY FOR NANCY Yazzi's welfare, Miss Muntz was sufficiently composed to submit to the official interrogation. "Please sit down, Mr. Parris." Being particular about such matters, she showed him where.

The chief of police eased himself into the spindly-looking armchair, hoped it would not collapse under his weight. It did not. Like the woman who owned it, the piece was more sturdy than appearances would suggest.

She seated herself opposite him, on a couch. "I've already told those two policemen what happened."

"I know, and I appreciate it. But I haven't had much time to talk to Officers Knox or Slocum, and anyway I thought it'd be better to hear it right from the horse's mouth." He blushed. "Uh—so to speak."

"Very well." *He is rather an amusing young man.* To better recall the unnerving events of the evening, Miss Muntz closed her eyes. "I was upstairs in my sewing room, attempting to knit a sweater. There is an excellent view of my rental property from the east window. I saw a shadowy form approach the Wetzel residence and enter the front door."

"What did this person look like?"

"I would prefer not to attempt a description—there wasn't all that much light."

The former Chicago cop pressed: "Tall or short? Fat or thin?"

"Oh . . . I'm not entirely sure."

He suppressed a grin. "Was it a man or a woman?"

"I'm sorry that I can't be of more help." Miss Muntz clasped her pale hands as if concealing something precious and averted her bright blue eyes from his steady gaze. "The sun had gone down and it was very hard to see."

*She must've only seen a shadow.* Then, there was the other possibility: *Or she's holding out on me.* He scribbled a question mark on the pad, circled it. "So what happened next?"

"I telephoned Mr. Wetzel to alert him, but I had barely gotten a few words out of my mouth when he said that he heard someone upstairs, and hung up. I assumed that he intended to find out who had entered his home. I went downstairs. When I heard the gunshots, I immediately dialed 911 and reported the incident."

Scott Parris smiled at the witness, who reminded him of his mother. "What happened after that?"

She hesitated, almost blushed. "I know it will seem extraordinarily silly of me, but I slipped on my raincoat and hurried across the street to find out what had happened."

The policeman assumed a stern scowl and shook his head. "That was very dangerous, Miss Muntz. The killer might've taken a shot at you."

She raised her chin defiantly. "I had a perfect right to check on my tenant."

*Silly old woman.* "I understand you saw the guy who crossed the road in front of the lady's car."

"Oh my yes—he was illuminated by Mrs. Burch's headlights. He was a big, husky fellow. And he wore a hat."

Parris nodded at his fedora on the end table. "Like mine?"

She gave the sixty-year-old hat an appraising look. "No. The man crossing the road wore a broad-brimmed hat. Like the ones cowboys wear."

"Anything else that might help us ID him?"

She took a deep breath. Held it for a few heartbeats. "I cannot be absolutely certain on this point, but he appeared to have a beard."

"Uh-huh." *That description matches what we got from Mrs. Burch.*

The lady also had a question to ask: "Do you believe that the big man who crossed the street is the same person who entered Mr. Wetzel's home—and shot him?"

"We'll have to wait and see how things play out, but it's pretty likely." Parris doodled a cartoon of a fat, bearded man in a cowboy hat onto his notebook. "Ten to one, he was a burglar who got caught in the act." *A burglar who was packing.*

"This is beginning to sound like what the police detectives on the TV shows call an 'open and shut' case."

"Most of 'em are, Miss Muntz. We've already got a bulletin out for a bearded guy who's about six-four, two hundred and fifty pounds. Chances are pretty good that we'll pick him up before daylight." *But if we don't, he'll likely be long gone.* Scott Parris snapped his notebook shut and got up from the armchair with a grunt. "I appreciate your help, ma'am." The chief of police gave the witness a business card that included his GCPD direct telephone line. "If you think of anything else I oughta know, give me call." He returned the hat to its customary, comfortable spot atop his balding head.

As she escorted the big, brawny cop to her front door, he stopped. "Oh, there's one more thing."

She blinked. "Yes?"

"Do you know whether your tenant owned a gun?"

"He certainly did—and more than one!" Miss Muntz clasped her hands and sighed. "I would not be surprised if you found a dozen firearms on the premises." After a thoughtful frown, she whispered, "Mr. Wetzel always had a pistol close at hand."

*Now that's interesting.* "What about the outside doors—did Wetzel keep 'em locked?"

"Oh my yes." She shook her head at the irony. "I believe he had a concern about intruders."

Parris thanked the helpful lady, tipped his hat, and departed.

As she watched the lawman take heavy, purposeful strides down the driveway to his sleek black-and-white Chevrolet, Miss Muntz drifted off into a reflective mood. *It would be so nice if life could be simple and straightforward. Why does everything have to be so complicated—so terribly messy!*

# MARTIN MAKES A BIG SCORE

ACROSS THE street from Miss Muntz's residence, a certain Lady in Blue had done her work extremely well.

Scott Parris was absolutely *beaming* upon Officer Alicia Martin. Had he not been restrained by (a) being somewhat shy and (b) the Official Copper's Rule Book of Professional Conduct, the happy fellow would have hugged her breathless. Kissed her on both cheeks.

What, one might ask, has engendered such passion in the heart of the grumpy, middle-aged chief of police? Here is the straight scoop. It was not only because Ms. Martin was one of his most competent officers. And not simply because she was a cute little blonde with eyes as blue as a summer sky, though that did help. His beam was particularly bright tonight because Officer Martin, while searching the grounds of the Wetzel residence with the aid of her five-cell thug-thumper flashlight, had discovered something of interest in a prickly huckleberry bush.

A Smith & Wesson .38 Special revolver, model 10.

This pistol was, almost without a doubt, the murder weapon—and if Fortune was displaying a toothy smile upon Officer Martin with half the candlepower emitted by her delighted supervisor, there would be fingerprints on the pistol. Nice clean prints that would identify someone of ill repute whose grubby fingertips had, at some previous date, been inked and rolled on the white cardboard, and were now among those millions of records residing in the FBI files.

# CHAPTER TWENTY-THREE

## WHAT IS IT ABOUT GIRLS AND THEIR PICKUP TRUCKS?

SARAH FRANK (BLESS HER INNOCENT HEART!) WAS DETERMINED TO step in and help her friend. After hugging a dry-eyed Nancy Yazzi and assuring her that things would be all right, the Ute-Papago orphan commenced to do everything in her power to distract the late Hermann Wetzel's stepdaughter from the evening's grim events. In her enthusiasm, the guest of honor had quite forgotten about the roomful of guests who had come to celebrate her birthday, and the huge pile of presents that must be loaded up and carted away to the Columbine— except for one. The spiffy red pickup truck.

Clutching Mr. Zig-Zag under her arm, Sarah used her free hand to grasp Nancy Yazzi's wrist and practically dragged her out of the hotel, where the F-150 waited by the curb.

A bemused Moon remained in the lobby, arms crossed, watching them go. The gratified gift giver presumed that Sarah's intent was to show off the best present of all.

Which was what she did.

The girls got into the cab with Sarah yammering at about three hundred syllables a minute, which was faster than Nancy could listen. She repeated practically every word the Wyoming Kyd had said about the recently rejuvenated truck, from the overhauled engine to the new brakes and rebuilt transmission, several coats of paint, brand-new AM-FM radio, oversized chrome bumpers, halogen headlights, even the cute little mirror on the driver's sun visor that lit up when you slid the cover off it.

As Nancy Yazzi offered the occasional mumble and nod, she stared unblinkingly through the windshield. She was attempting to penetrate the darkness that enveloped her, conjure up answers to the questions that bedeviled her. *I wonder where Jake is right now. Probably someplace as far away as he can get from Granite Creek.* She felt her lower lip tremble. *When he can, Jake will come back for me.* Tears glistened in her eyes. *And no matter how long it takes, I'll be waiting.*

But in the meantime, which might be a long time, Nancy realized that she must not utter the least hint about her connection with Jake Harper, or how her stepfather had abused her. *With a little bit of luck, the cops won't ever know who killed that filthy rotten bastard.* This hopeful thought was disturbed by a query from Sarah Frank, who had pushed a key into the ignition switch. Nancy turned to the driver. "Uh, what did you say?"

Sarah repeated the question: "Do you want to go right now?"

"Go where?"

"To the Columbine."

Nancy shrugged. "Why not?"

There was a very good reason why not. Sarah Frank was not allowed to drive without a licensed driver in the motor vehicle whose name was on her learner's permit. But it would be unreasonable, particularly at the end of such an exciting day, to expect her to remember such niggling little details as this. And she did not. With all the expertise one would expect of a student who had come in next to first in her driver's-ed class, she put her foot on the brake pedal, made sure the gear shift was in Park, cranked the engine to life, glanced at the rearview mirror, consulted similar reflectors mounted on each door, pulled the small lever down to signal a left turn, shifted to Drive, gave the steering wheel a twist, and let 'er rip. *Vrrrooom!*

At the instant he saw the turn signal, Mr. Moon made a dash for the street. As Sarah was pulling away, he had one boot on the sidewalk.

Good try, Charlie.

Jerome Kydmann had seen the boss sprint out of the lobby and, as they say in this neck of the woods, *took out after him.*

As Moon headed for his Expedition, he yelled at his employee, "I'm gonna follow those kids, Jerome. You take care of things here—look after Aunt Daisy!"

◆ ◆ ◆

ASIDE FROM a couple of amateurish slips (running a pesky red light that she thought should have stayed yellow *just a teensy-weensy bit longer,* doing thirty-nine in a twenty-five miles per hour zone, missing a right turn at the main intersection, driving over the curb when she made a wide U-turn, and turning right on red back at the intersection when the green arrow was permitting only left turns (which was why she came *this close* to colliding with a VW bug), Sarah Frank figured she was not doing all that bad. For a beginner. By the time she got back on track, Charlie Moon was *ahead* of the birthday pickup and already at the edge of town. He slowed down when he couldn't see a single tail-light on the straight-as-an-arrow highway that stretched off yonder toward the Columbine. *They've probably stopped at some ice cream or burger joint.* Knowing the location of every such establishment, the cowboy gourmand did a nice, tight U-turn and headed back into town. Immediately, he saw the red pickup coming right at him. Moon flashed his lights, which got Sarah's attention. As the they passed in the night he saw her flash a smile and wave.

"That was Charlie," Sarah told her passenger. "He's probably out looking for us." *He is such a sweetie.*

As he made another nice, tight U-turn, Mr. Sweetie was muttering something about teenage drivers that was just a tad on the critical side. As he pulled within sight of Sarah's pickup, he remembered something that he should not have forgotten in the first place. Make that some*one* he should not have forgotten in the first place.

Lila Mae.

*I guess I should've said something to her before I took off.* But, he reasoned, there had not been time. *She probably don't even know I'm gone.* Perhaps. But in an instance such as this, the volatile combination of guessing and reasoning and wishful thinking might just explode in his face.

On the other hand, he had left the Kyd in charge, and Mr. Jerome Kydmann was not only Moon's right-hand man; it was the general con-sensus of the Columbine employees (and everyone knows what keen judgment cowboys have) that the Wyoming Kyd was the smartest hand on the ranch. Now it's true that the Kyd was sharp as a tack when it came to things like dosing a horse suffering from the dreaded yellow-eye colic or mowing hay that was just a mite too wet, and he could set a line of fence posts so straight you could shoot your Winchester rifle from one end post to the other and the slug would pass dead center over every post in between. But, as we already know, he was a bit slow when it came to communicating with women. Which is no doubt why, when Miss McTeague (accompanied by Daisy Perika) entered the hotel lobby, spotted Moon's brightest employee, and inquired, "Where is Charlie?" he responded much as he had when Sarah Frank had posed the same question: "Some important business came up the boss had to attend to."

Now anyone who knows her will tell you that Miss McTeague has an imperious way of arching her left eyebrow that beggars description. But one must have a go at it. That dainty little line of hairs over her big, beautiful eyeball absolutely bristled, and as much as said, in rapid succession, *You're lying through your teeth, Buckwheat!* and *What kind of important business?* Now any woman you might come across would have understood that straightaway, but the Kyd (aka Buckwheat) didn't get it, so Lila Mae was obliged to repeat the second remark out loud. "What kind of important business?"

He flashed the disarming smile. "Oh, with ol' Charlie you never know—but whatever it is, I expect he'll be back before first light." By way of punctuation, he added a "ha-ha!" Mr. Kydmann, bless his happy soul, figured that any girlfriend of Charlie Moon's would be bound to have a sense of humor.

Which assumption was somewhat presumptuous. To quote the FBI agent's father, a quite jolly fellow, "Lila Mae's just like her mother. When senses of humor was being doled out, the both of 'em was elsewhere, probably tossing rotten tomatoes at Jack Benny or Red Skelton."

A little harsh. But McTeague's eyes went flat, like a well-fed rattlesnake about to fang a mouse just for the hell of it. "Indeed." That was all she said. It was sufficient.

Having just about shot his wad, the Kyd took to licking his lips. A sure sign he was bumfuzzled.

Daisy took this opportunity to insert herself into the conversation. "So what am I supposed to do, stand around here all night waiting for my nephew to drive me to his ranch?"

Hoping for better results with the tribal elder, Kydmann shook his head. "Oh no, ma'am." He tipped the white John B. Stetson hat. "I'll take you to the Columbine."

Always ready to start a fire, the Ute woman struck flint to steel. Nodding to indicate Charlie Moon's sweetheart, she said, as sweetly as honey dripping from the comb, "What about her?"

Now the Kyd was unaware that Moon had reserved a hotel room for Lila Mae, but, always ready to assist a lady, he found a faint remnant of the grin. "Oh, I'm sure Charlie would want me to take you wherever you want to go, ma'am."

Now, though they were, for the most part, worlds apart, Lila Mae McTeague did share one characteristic with Daisy Perika—she did not appreciate being "ma'amed." Especially by a man of more or less her own age. She raised her perfect chin to a haughty altitude. "You needn't bother yourself, Mr. Kydmann." With this, she turned on a high heel, clicked across the lobby to a chair, and used her cell phone to check on the red-eye flight from Colorado Springs to Los Angeles. Was about to book a seat when, realizing the finality of such a decision, she hesitated. *I'll wait awhile. Charlie should have an opportunity to explain his absence.*

As bad luck (Charlie Moon's) would have it, Columbine cowboy Oscar "Bud" Yirty had overheard Miss McTeague's conversation with Jerome Kydmann. While very few of Moon's employees were noted for having well-above-average intellectual capacity (Kydmann and Cassidy being the notable exceptions), Yirty would, in Foreman Pete Bushman's very words, "Have to take a five-year correspondence course to work his way up to half-wit." Surely an exaggeration. And being a bit slow would not have made Mr. Yirty particularly dangerous. The man was a walking calamity because he was completely unaware of having any cerebral shortcomings. Indeed, he considered himself not only danged clever but a top-rate humorist as well; he was famous on the Columbine for such knee slappers as pulling chairs from under fellows who were about to sit in them, or putting salt in the sugar bowl and live snakes (and other inappropriate creatures) into his comrades' bunks.

Yirty elbowed the one friend he had on the ranch, whispered a proposition in Six-Toes's ear.

"Awright," Six said. "But it'll cost you a case a beer."

A high price, but Yirty could not miss this opportunity of a lifetime.

After shaking hands on the deal, the comic and his straight man sidled up close enough for the FBI agent to overhear their conversation.

Yirty: "Even for a young man, that Charlie Moon sure beats anything I ever seen."

Six: "Uh-huh."

Yirty: "After a party that wore me plum out, that Injun's still frisky as a colt."

Six: "Uh-huh."

Yirty: "Just imagine, takin' off after two young wimmen." An idiotic leer. "I wonder what he'll do when he catches up with 'em."

Six: "Uh-huh."

If Charlie Moon's sweetheart was not quite to the point of grinding her teeth, neither was she taking this well. She reassured herself, *These are just a couple of stupid cow-pie kickers. Why should I listen to a word they say?* She closed her eyes, took a deep breath. *I'll go up to my room and wait for Charlie to call me.* But first things first. Like taking a look at the face, perhaps touching up the lipstick. She opened her purse and was about to remove the compact when . . . she spotted the piece of paper. That's right—the sales slip from Pippin's Fine Jewelry. She gave it a close inspection. *Well, Charlie certainly spent a pile of money on my engagement ring.* But wait. What was this? *This receipt is dated more than five years ago. Which is well before we first met.* The lady's face blanched. *Charlie bought this ring for someone else.* Searching her excellent memory for data about whom Charlie Moon was interested in at that particular time, the FBI agent came up with a name.

For Mr. Moon, this had been a day of missteps and misfortunes. One of these mistakes he could have survived. Probably even two. Maybe, and it's a long shot—the whole series.

McTeague stuffed the sales slip back into the purse, snapped it shut, and marched over to the desk. The drums in the ballroom were going full force again. "Excuse me." She was addressing the young man in the dark blue suit and red tie. "I am Miss McTeague. Mr. Moon reserved a room for me and—"

"Moon, oh sure." The clerk had not heard the "McTeague," which had been coincident with a rafter-rattling drumbeat. "Yes ma'am, we have it right here. You're in room 302, Miss Yazzi."

She raised the expressive eyebrow, and her voice. "I beg your pardon?"

"When Mr. Moon booked the room for you, he said put you in one at the end of the hall, so you'd only have one neighbor. And 302's the only end-of-hall we had left. But if you don't mind being next to the elevator, I could put you in 433."

She reached over to the old-fashioned registration book, turned it around. Sure enough.

MISS NANCY YAZZI

ROOM 302

*That could be either the attractive blonde Charlie danced with or the brunette teenager he hugged in the lobby when he didn't know I was watching.* She glanced at the clerk's name tag. "Herbert, are you absolutely sure that it was Mr. Charles Moon who made this reservation?"

Herbert Norbert nodded. "Oh yes, ma'am—it was Charlie all right. I took care of it myself, not twenty minutes ago."

◆ ◆ ◆

THE KYD had been keeping a close eye on Lila Mae McTeague, and though he was too far away to hear what Bud Yirty was saying to Six-Toes, the very presence of these two lowlifes so close to Moon's lady friend generated a queasy feeling under his belt buckle. Having almost forgotten the elderly Ute woman at his elbow, he mumbled to himself, "It looks like Miss McTeague is booking a room."

Daisy had her own pair of eyebrows. The one she raised said, *It don't look that way to me.*

◆  ◆  ◆

SPECIAL AGENT McTeague asked the helpful clerk to have her stored luggage brought around.

Most certainly. He pressed an intercom button, issued the order. Did the lady require transportation?

Yes indeed. The lady wished to rent a car that she could leave at the airport in Colorado Springs.

That could be arranged. But there was another option: The Silver Mountain provided limousine service to the airport.

"How soon could I leave?

"Immediately."

Lila Mae informed him that *immediately* would be quite satisfactory.

◆  ◆  ◆

AS THE Kyd entered the ballroom to manage the transfer of Sarah's birthday presents to another Columbine pickup, Daisy Perika watched the business being conducted at the hotel registration desk. She could not hear a word that was being said, but hearing was not necessary. Daisy could read eyebrows, and much more. *Well, this is turning out all right.*

An uncharitable thought?

Let us give Daisy the benefit of such doubt as there may be.

After all, in the Lila Mae/Moon/Sarah triangle, the Ute elder is rooting for the Ute-Papago orphan.

◆  ◆  ◆

AS CHARLIE Moon followed Sarah Frank's red pickup out of town, he found his cell phone and punched the button for J Kydmann. He barely heard the young man's hello over the thundering drumbeat. "Hey, Jerome—what's happening?"

"Everything's going pretty well here. The presents are all being loaded up to go, and soon as your aunt's out of the ladies' room, I'll take her out to the ranch. You catch up with them girls yet?"

"I'm right behind 'em." Sarah was staying just within the speed limit. "First chance you get, tell Lila Mae I'll head back to town soon as these kids are at the ranch."

"Will do, boss. Last time I saw your lady she was over at the front desk—getting her room key I guess."

*That's good. Lila Mae's had a long day since she woke up in D.C. and she needs some rest.* "Never mind then, Jerome—I'll call her in the morning. Oh, one more thing—I reserved a room at the Silver Mountain for Miss Yazzi. Please see that it's canceled."

"Consider it done."

Moon borrowed a thought from his aunt: *This is turning out all right.*

# CHAPTER TWENTY-FOUR

## BAD NEWS FOR BREAKFAST

WHILE HE WAS ENJOYING HIS FIRST CUP OF COFFEE, CHARLIE MOON placed the call.

A young woman's voice machine-gunned the words into his ear. "Good morning Silver Mountain Hotel front desk this is Hilda how may I help you today."

"Good morning to you, Hilda. This is Charlie Moon."

*Oh my.* Conjuring up a memory of the tall Indian cowboy who owned the finest ranch in the county, the clerk shifted to her human voice: "What can I do for you, Mr. Moon?" *You name it.*

He did. "You can connect me to Miss McTeague's room."

"Certainly. Just a moment." A good half-dozen moments passed while she consulted the computer terminal. "I'm sorry. The lady checked out last night."

"She's gone?" *That don't sound right.* "Are you sure about that?"

"Oh yes, sir. The record indicates that L. M. McTeague canceled her reservation at ten sixteen P.M."

Moon glared at his coffee cup. "Did she leave a message for me?"

"No."

He mumbled to himself. "Well where'd she go?"

"I'm sorry, sir, but I am not authorized to tell you." She added, in a whisper, "Assuming that I was privy to such personal information."

"Forget the 'sir,' Hilda. Call me Charlie."

"Yes sir. I mean . . . Charlie." A sigh.

"Now that we've got that straightened out, I want you to know that I'd never even *hint* that you should break a hotel rule. Not even if you were privy to some ordinary little fact that might be a great big help to me." An interlude of silence that practically shouted in her ear. "You understand what I mean?"

"Oh, I most certainly do . . . Charlie." Another sigh, this one with closed eyes. "Even if I knew something that might be of interest—such as how the lady had availed herself of our convenient twenty-four/seven on-call limousine service to the Colorado Springs airport—I would not be able to breathe a word of it. Not a *word*."

"Thanks, Hilda."

"Don't mention it, Charlie."

"Don't worry. I won't." *But I'll send you an armful of flowers.* After saying goodbye, Moon began to consider the most likely reasons for the sudden departure: *Lila Mae probably got a call about an emergency. Something work related. Or a family problem. Her dad's in poor health—already had two heart attacks.* He dialed his sweetheart's number.

## THOUSAND OAKS, CALIFORNIA

LILA MAE McTeague had just pulled into her driveway. She yanked the cell phone from her purse, saw C Moon on the caller ID, hesitated. *Charlie will try to sweet-talk me into believing there's nothing wrong. He'll come up with a plausible reason for making a hotel reservation for another woman and for leaving me standing in the lobby while he went chasing two more, and I'll believe him because I want to. And I can't even* ask *him why he was planning to offer me a ring he bought years ago for another woman—not without telling him that I had the jeweler's sales slip in my purse because I picked his jacket pocket and found the ring.* Deep breath. *So I suppose the best thing to do is not speak to him. Not right now.* There was another edge to this blade that pierced her heart: *But if I don't answer the phone, he might never call me again. So perhaps I ought to—*

Too late, Lila Mae. The telephone has stopped ringing.

Charlie Moon listened to a computerized voice that invited him to leave a brief message after the tone. He cleared his throat. "It's me." Two heartbeats. "I just called the Silver Mountain and found out that you checked out last night." As if it had a mind of its own, his hand found the black velvet box in his jacket pocket. "I hope everything's all right." Two more heartbeats. "Call me soon as you get a chance."

# CHAPTER TWENTY-FIVE

## A BUSY MORNING

DESPITE THE FACT THAT A WEEK HAD PASSED AND LILA MAE McTeague had not returned his telephone call, Charlie Moon was feeling about as good as might be expected, considering that a new-hire twenty-two-year-old cowboy had (on a ten-dollar bet from a savvy old-timer that he wouldn't stay in the saddle ten seconds) attempted to ride Sweet Alice. The unfortunate fellow had ended up with three busted ribs in his left side that hurt almost as much as his injured pride.

As the taped-up bronc buster was being hauled away to the hospital, Moon was assaulted by a dire prediction from Pete Bushman, a be-whiskered old stockman who had an uncanny knack for finding something new to worry about. The ranch foreman snapped off a chaw of Red Man tobacco and (between enthusiastic chews) reported the latest bad news: "Them damn range worms are swarmin' in Delta County and they'll prob'ly be here by next week and eat ever' damn blade a grass on the Columbine and then they'll chomp all the leaves off'n the cottonwood trees."

The owner of the outfit assured his second in command that if a caterpillar invasion threatened, he would hire a crop duster to spray the threatened pastures with Permethrin.

Bushman had no confidence in expensive pesticides or noisy little biplanes or—for that matter—any solution Moon might suggest to the vexing problems he delighted in tormenting the boss about. After spitting tobacco juice onto the porch step, he grinned under his scraggly beard. "If the spray plane don't stop 'em, whadda we do next—call all the cowhands together for a prayer meetin'?"

Pushing back the brim of his black Stetson, Moon looked to the heavens for a measure of peace. *What I need is some time off. A little bit of relaxation.*

◆ ◆ ◆

TOWARD THAT end, not too far into the afternoon Charlie Moon was in a rocking chair by the fireplace, a cup of sweet coffee beside him, a much-read copy of Zane Grey's *The Last Trail* in his hand. From what could be gleaned from this tale, it seemed a good bet that Jonathan Zane had never encountered a horde of famished caterpillars. The reader was enjoying the part about how Mr. Zane loved the lonely wilderness like other men lusted after— But wait.

What was that distant tapping? Someone rapping on Moon's chamber door? Something or other about a lady called Lenore? A raven who saith over and over: *Nevermore?*

No.

The Columbine ravens are a sensible clan, who limit their remarks to simple caw-caws and the occasional strident squawk. What the Ute's keen ears had picked up when the automobile was about a quarter mile away was an aged Volvo's valves tapping. Well, talk about your perfect day! He put the book aside, went outside with his coffee cup, and watched his best friend park in the shade of the Daddy of all Cottonwoods, slam the car door, and approach in that heavy, shoulder-swinging gait that always reminded the Ute of John Wayne about to take on a dozen armed bad guys. Ten paces away, Scott Parris waved. "Hey, Charlie."

"Hey yourself, pardner."

The Granite Creek chief of police mounted the porch steps with the heavy grunts of a man who is not as young as he used to be and feels it in his hip and knee joints. He was also beginning to present a belly. Not so much as to justify calling him fat. Not to his face. "That coffee smells good."

Charlie Moon raised his cup. "You like to have some?"

"Later, maybe."

"Want to go inside, sit by the fireplace?"

A fresh breeze caressed Parris's face. "Let's stay out here."

Moon seated himself on a redwood bench.

After considering a couple of wooden chairs, the edge of the porch, and the steps, Parris settled on the chain-suspended swing, which creaked under his 220 pounds. He kick-started the pendulum seat into motion, treated his lungs to a breath of the crisp-as-a-new-dollar-bill high-country air, and soaked in a healthy dose of a silence that was, by some deep magic, enhanced by the mystical whisper of the river that rolled a little slower now that most of the snowmelt was somewhere a long way downstream. "How're you getting along, Charlie?"

"Tolerable." This man who hung his wide-brimmed black hat smack in the middle of a piece of paradise that he held clear title to, knew it wouldn't do to push his luck by bragging.

"How's your aunt?"

"Oh, same as ever. Daisy's taking her after-lunch siesta."

"How're the girls getting along?"

"Okay."

The chief of police shot a glance at the front door. "They in the house?"

"An hour or so ago, Sarah and Nancy rode off on a pair of pinto ponies." Moon pointed his chin in a northerly direction. "By now, they'll be on the far side of Pine Knob. Probably won't be back until suppertime." *So you can talk all you want to about the Wetzel killing.*

The town's top cop didn't let on that he was pleased to hear this.

*Scott's as easy to read as a comic book.* But which one? *With that hat, Dick Tracy.* "I hope you'll be staying for supper."

"Thanks, Charlie. Maybe I will."

"Glad to hear it." It would be fun to tweak him a little bit. "So, besides shouldering your way up to the feed trough, what brings you way out here?"

Parris hesitated. The seasoned lawman had an overpowering sensation that someone besides Charlie Moon was listening to every word he said. And someone was, but that person was not Sweet Alice, the homely little mare who had a crush on the boss and was never far from Moon when he was on the Columbine. Nor do we refer to Sidewinder, the hound who was sleeping on the warm porch planks, dreaming of a meal where the main course was warm, furry cottontail. And of course, we would never suggest that Sarah's spotted cat (who was curled up by the dog) would eavesdrop. In the entire course of recorded history, no one of the feline persuasion has ever paid the least attention to a single word uttered by a human being—though, on occasion, the sly creatures have been known to pretend.

The guilty party is a third human being, recently arrived. Daisy Perika. By means of a mysterious episode of women's intuition, the crafty old shaman had awakened suddenly from her nap, realized that something was up, toddled out to the parlor to find out what it was, and had at this very moment concealed herself by an open window just behind the porch swing where Parris was back-and-forthing. Daisy's right ear was pressed close to the screen. She had not made a sound, but (ladies should take note of this) *men have intuition too.* Cops who are not well endowed with that essential gift do not stay healthy for very long, and Scott Parris's sixth sense was operating at full throttle. Which was why he responded to Moon's question ("So, besides shouldering your way up to the feed trough, what brings you way out here?") by suggesting an immediate change of venue.

Moon cocked his head. "Lake Jesse?"

"You heard me right."

The old woman, who had also heard him loud and clear, whispered a rude word.

The Ute, who was aware of his aunt's eavesdropping, greeted his friend's request with a wry twinkle in his eye. "A man of your mental caliber hankers to match wits with a fish that has a brain about the size of a piñon nut?"

The hopeful angler nodded his classic fedora. "I'm feeling lucky today."

◆ ◆ ◆

ON THE crest of Pine Knob, the young women eased their spotted ponies along at a slow walk. Their full-speed chatter was frequently punctuated by girlish laughs. As if she'd spotted a rattlesnake in her path, Nancy Yazzi suddenly reined her mount to a dead stop. Squinting in the sunlight, she pointed across the river at the Columbine headquarters. "Look. Charlie Moon and some guy are getting into a pickup."

Shading her eyes, Sarah Frank verified the truth of this statement.

Nancy leaned forward in the saddle. "Who's that man with him?"

"It's too far away to be sure." The sixteen-year-old frowned. "But that old car looks like the one Mr. Parris drives."

The name sounded familiar. "That policeman who was at your table last night?"

Sarah nodded, patted her spotted pony's neck. "Mr. Parris is the chief of police."

Nancy's eyes narrowed. "It looks like they're leaving."

Sarah watched the Columbine pickup kick up a puff of dust along the dirt lane that wound around the big horse barn before crossing a rocky ridge studded with spruce and pine. "They're headed toward the little log cabin." A grim memory of what had happened there a couple of years ago gave the Ute-Papago girl a sudden chill. "Or maybe they're going to the lake." Something terrible had happened there as well. In an attempt to chase the memories away, Sarah said, "There are lots of pretty wildflowers near the lake." She turned to gaze at her companion. "Want to head back to the house?"

Nancy shook her head.

Eager to get going, Sarah's mount stamped at the hard earth, whinnied. "What do you want to do, then?"

Hermann Wetzel's stepdaughter assumed a mischievous smile. "Let's follow Charlie and that cop—without them knowing it."

Sarah frowned. "You mean . . . *spy* on them?"

"Why not?" Nancy laughed. "It'd be fun, wouldn't it?"

"I don't know." But she did. "It doesn't seem right."

"Oh, okay—if you're going to be a wet blanket." The older girl rolled her big eyes. "I guess we can go sit on the corral fence and count horseflies."

Unable to abide the wet-blanket charge, Sarah came up with a compromise: "I guess we could flip a coin."

Nancy fished a quarter out of her pocket. "Call it in the air." She thumbed the silver-plated copper disk.

"Tails!"

Up, up it soared, sketching a perfect parabolic arc.

There was an infinitesimal pause at the apex, then— down, down to the ground.

So what was it—heads or tails?

As it happened, the quarter was difficult to see from their vantage point. Impossible, actually—the contrary coin landed behind a plump clump of prickly pears. The riders had to dismount to determine whether they would (a) go spying on the men or (b) count horseflies.

# CHAPTER TWENTY-SIX

## A FISHING EXPEDITION

DECKED OUT IN A SKIRT OF RED WILLOWS TRIMMED WITH CATTAILS and a blue and white blouse of reflected sky, Lake Jesse was dressed in her Sunday best. From the west, a sage-scented breeze barely rippled her glassy surface. From time to time, an iridescent, almost luminescent trout would break the water to snatch a tasty insect, then vanish into the blue-green depths.

On the shore, the alleged anglers sat about two yards apart, Scott Parris on a cottonwood log, Charlie Moon on the ground. The spinning outfits provided by the host were propped on a scarified basalt boulder left behind by the most recent glacier. Close at hand was a lard can filled with black river-bottom soil, coffee grounds, and about two dozen earthworms who might have just about concluded that they need not fear the dreadful fate of becoming fish bait that afternoon. As an afterthought, Moon had also brought along a minnow bucket, which stood beside the lard can.

The fishermen friends had not bothered to wet a line.

And why should they? Reeling in a sizable, scrappy fish requires intense concentration, which tends to distract a man from what he profits most from—which is a quiet hour away from work, worries, and needless conversation. Which was the reason why barely four dozen words had passed between them. Three and a half dozen of these had traveled from the white man's mouth to the Indian's ear. Not a word about local crime, county politics, or devastating bovine diseases.

About thirty feet offshore, a big rainbow rolled over the surface, slurped up an unwary six-legged creature. Moon watched the concentric ripples spread and vanish. *About a five-pounder.* He picked up his spinning outfit, fumbled in the bucket for a lively minnow, found the unlucky candidate, deftly slipped the hook through mouth and gill without injuring the scaly creature. Moon executed a skillful flick of the wrist to place the live bait on the spot where the trout had surfaced. *Bull's-eye!*

Parris admired the expert cast.

The happy angler released sufficient translucent six-pound test filament to let his line go slack, watched it run this way and that as the minnow began to dart about. *Come to dinner, Mr. Trout.* Moon waited. Not for long. A big tug as a relative from higher up the food chain hit the minnow. He let the predator take the bait down the shoreline for a few yards, then gave the line a jerk. The empty hook sailed out of the water, over his head, snagged on a willow branch. "Dang!"

A true-blue friend would merely have chuckled. Parris *sniggered.* And compounded the offense by offering unsolicited advice in a high-hatted, know-it-all tone: "You got overeager. Should've given that trout time to swallow the bait."

As the frustrated fisherman was extracting the barbed hook from a spindly branch, he loosed a sharp little dart: "You had any luck identifying the fellow who shot Hermann Wetzel—like finding some clean prints on the murder weapon?"

"FBI's still got the .38. It'll still be a while before we hear anything about prints." Parris flipped a pebble into the water. "But it won't be long before we know who he is."

"You sound pretty sure of yourself."

"Hey, you can take it to the bank—the shooter's as good as behind bars."

"Well, I'm glad to hear it." Moon put a fresh minnow on the hook, cast the line back to the sweet spot. *Next time, I'll let Mr. Trout swallow the tiny fish down past his tonsils before I set the hook.* "You must have a pretty good clue or two."

"Sure I do." Parris tugged his hat brim down to shade his eyes from sunshine reflecting off the water. "And I expect you'd like to hear all about it."

"Not particularly. But since you're just bustin' to make a big brag about what a great detective you are, go right ahead—let it all out." Moon flashed a toothy grin at his friend. "And I'll pretend like I'm hanging on every word."

"Thanks, Charlie—but I don't like to mix police business with fishing."

"That's a sensible policy." *He doesn't have anything to hang his hat on.*

But Parris did. Quite a lot. Which, for the moment, he was keeping to himself. The cleverest chief of police in Granite Creek inhaled, blew some smoke at his friend. "The perp entered the Wetzel home without breaking a window. Which means either a door was left open or he had a key. And Miss Muntz—she's the landlady, who lives across the street—tells me that Hermann Wetzel generally kept his doors locked."

Moon watched the line drifting slowly to his left. *This ain't a very lively minnow.* Another possibility occurred to him: *Or maybe he's just playing it smart.* "Maybe the burglar picked the lock."

"Can't be ruled out, but it's a long shot." The social critic commenced to explain. "It's a sad commentary on our society that not one housebreaker in fifty has the know-how to pick the sorriest fifty-cent padlock you ever saw. It's this younger generation, Charlie—they're too bone-lazy to learn a useful skill. Most of 'em toss a big rock through a window, or they break through a door with a crowbar or sledgehammer. So when the thief doesn't bust up something, it's almost a sure thing that he had a key."

"So where'd our lazy burglar get a key?"

"Now that's the question." *And wouldn't you like to know the answer.* Parris straightened his spine, pushed his hat back. "Hey, pay attention— you've got a bite!"

*A good one, too.* "That's just the minnow making a run for it." With exaggerated casualness, Moon leaned the rod into the crotch of a sturdy willow. Only a sure-enough ham would have faked a yawn. But that's what he did.

"Charlie, that's a bite for sure!"

He sat down on the log beside his buddy. "So how'd the burglar get a key to the Wetzel house?"

Parris put on a smug expression. "I've got an idea I'm working on."

## THE YOUNG LADIES

DID THEY ride over to the corral to count horseflies or trot off on a delightfully despicable little spy mission?

Sarah Frank and Nancy Yazzi were—at this very moment—sitting very quietly. Watching one of the most humongous horseflies that had ever been seen within the confines of the Columbine.

Sarah cringed as the massive insect landed on her knee. "You better not bite me!"

"If he does, you're good as dead." Nancy Yazzi's observation was offered with a smirk. "See his red eyes? That's a *vampire* horsefly and he's after blood. He'll sink his fangs into you, suck your dry."

The potential victim raised her hand, gave the hideous creature a healthy smack.

## THE ANGLING LAWMEN

AS HE counted his catch, which ranged from fourteen to twenty-two inches, Charlie Moon addressed Parris in a soothing tone that was fine-tuned to irritate his friend to the bone. "Don't feel so bad about hooking just one little fish. I doubt that cutthroat was much more than ten inches long." Well-timed pause. "Definitely not worth worrying about."

Parris's growl was low and throaty. Like a hungry old cougar who wanted to get some fresh, bloody meat between his teeth.

"Anyway, that pygmy trout is long gone." Moon managed not to grin. "Like the guy who shot Wetzel."

This did not help Parris's temper.

The Ute didn't let up. "I'll lay you even money—say twenty bucks—that this time next year, that'll still be an open case. It'll turn out to be one of those killings where you'll never have the least idea who did it. But someday when you're in the nursing home, some fresh-faced cop right out of the academy will take a glance at an old, yellowed file and spot something you missed—like a silver shirt stud found under Wetzel's coffee table that has the shooter's name and address etched on it. And it'll turn out the bad guy was an evil locksmith, who'd just broke out of Folsom Prison and—"

"Make it a hundred clams and you're on."

"What?"

"You heard me, Charlie. Let's shake on it."

"What exactly are we shaking on?"

"Just what you said. That this time next year, I won't know the shooter's name."

*Maybe he does know something.* Then again . . . *He might be bluffing.*

Whatever the case, your proud Rocky Mountain gambling man does not back down. Code of the West. Look it up.

Moon reached for the outstretched paw, shook it.

Parris's grin went Cheshire. No—better than that. No cat could split his face so wide, display all that enamel. This was in-your-face, grade-A *gloating.*

*Uh-oh.* Moon set his jaw, prepared himself for a big dose of bad news. "So what d'you know that you haven't told me?"

Parris looked away, to the center of the lake, where a handsome pair of ring-necked ducks were skimming to a landing. "Oh, not enough to impress a big-shot tribal investigator who figures us town cops for a bunch of doughnut-munching yokels." He watched one of the ducks go bottom-up. "But when we get back to the ranch headquarters, I intend to ask a certain somebody some questions."

Moon lowered his voice. "Nancy Yazzi?"

"Mmm-hmm."

"You figure she might know something that could help you ID the shooter?"

"Let's just say I intend to ask her a question or two."

"Sorry, pardner." Moon shook his head. "Not in my house."

"What?"

"If you want to interrogate the young lady, that's your business. But you'll have to ask your questions at the police station." Moon's tone was very firm. "Here on the Columbine—she's under the protection of my hospitality."

"I appreciate that." Parris didn't. "But if I take Wetzel's stepdaughter into town, she'll know something's up and it'll give her plenty of time to come up with a story."

"I appreciate the spot you're in, pardner. But it don't make any difference. Long as Miss Yazzi is a guest in my house, she can expect the usual courtesy offered by the Columbine."

Parris's face was getting red, veins were bulging on his forehead, and his voice was increasing in volume. "Now listen here, Charlie. That girl knows—"

"Shhhh!"

"What?"

"For quite some time now, we've had an audience. Sarah and Nancy tied their horses over at the cabin, tried to sneak up on us."

"Damn!" Parris peered through the willows, saw nothing amiss. "Why didn't you tell me?"

"Well, I didn't want to let on that I knew they were there—that'd spoil all their fun."

"Where are they?"

"About fifty yards behind us, in a shallow little arroyo, peeking from behind a juniper."

*I can't see a thing.* "You absolutely sure?"

"Hey, I'm one hundred percent Indian. Anybody who ever watched a grade-B Western picture show knows we can track a Mormon cricket over ten miles of solid sandstone, and spot a kangaroo mouse snacking on a grasshopper in the next county." The Ute grinned at his *matukach* buddy. "They couldn't have heard a word we've said so far—but just in case the wind shifts, you'd better speak softly."

It was an unnecessary caution.

# CHAPTER TWENTY-SEVEN

## SEATING ARRANGEMENTS ARE IMPORTANT

AS ANY ONE OF THOSE FORTUNATE SOULS WHO HAS CHOWED DOWN at the Columbine would attest to, the menu was invariably first-rate. The food was never fancy, but Charlie Moon was a pretty good cook, and whatever culinary skills he lacked were more than compensated for by the foreman's wife. When guests were expected for supper, Dolly Bushman was likely to show up right on time with her famous peach cobbler, a gallon of hand-cranked strawberry ice cream, and a side dish such as chived and buttered new potatoes or crispy fried green tomatoes. Though it was early in the season for those particular delicacies, the grub on this night was not bad.

The man of the house was seated at the north end of the dining-room table, gazing down its considerable length at his spunky relative.

Aunt Daisy had taken her rightful place at the southern extremity.

The chief of police had seated himself at Moon's left, where, from time to time, he smiled across the table at the young ladies.

Sarah Frank (sitting as close to Charlie Moon as she could) was still on a high from an afternoon of skulking around and spying that had proved to be lots more fun than she had expected. The shy teenager smiled back at the thoughtful gentleman who had provided her with the learner's permit.

Nancy Yazzi, whose expression suggested acute disinterest, had not so much as glanced at the visiting lawman.

From time to time, Moon shot his best friend a look that could not be misread. It plainly said, *You ask my guest what time it is, you've crossed the line.*

The chief of police made no inquires, and had very little to say, all the way from the appetizers (Dutch-chocolate mints, macadamia nuts, and prime buffalo jerky) through the main course: butter-grilled catch-of-the-day trout, potatoes fried in Sicilian olive oil, San Luis Valley pinto beans boiled in lightly salted well water, and home-baked sourdough bread.

Having progressed from lip smacking to hearty burping, Parris was helping himself to a second helping of Dolly's peach cobbler.

Moon was enjoying black coffee, sweetened with Tule Creek honey.

Ditto for Sarah, whose pleasure it was to match Mr. Right move for move.

Nancy Yazzi—probably just to be contrary—had opted for iced tea. Which the young lady sipped with a raised pinky. *La-di-da.*

Daisy was drinking unsweetened black coffee, thinking blacker thoughts. *This all seems so nice, but something don't smell quite right.*

Mr. Zig-Zag? Sarah's spotted cat was under the table, nibbling daintily at a finger-size morsel of grilled trout. Not a dog's life.

Which brings Sidewinder to mind. The Columbine hound was outside, under the porch, gnawing a meaty beef bone.

## A SLIP OF THE TONGUE

THE CONFIDENT expression on Scott Parris's mug was counterfeit; the lawman was feeling distinctly uneasy. Here he was, sitting across the table from a young woman who might be able to help him get his hands on the man who had murdered her stepfather. But he was strictly forbidden to ask her a single question. *And if I take her back to the station, she won't say a word. Except: "I never heard of anybody by that name." Or: "I want to talk to a lawyer." Somehow or other, I need to bring up the subject of the killing.* But it would have to be done with considerable delicacy or Charlie Moon would take umbrage. Tons of umbrage. And get all hot under the collar.

How to broach the subject of homicide? It was a knotty problem.

Solutions sometimes come from the most unexpected sources.

"So, have you figured out who killed this girl's stepfather?" Yes, Daisy Perika. Parris could've hugged the tribal elder.

All present gazed at the one who had offered the cop this splendid opening.

Parris put on a doubtful look, and replied with shameless hypocrisy, "I don't know as I should talk about that particular subject." He glanced at Nancy Yazzi, who quickly concentrated her attention on the tea glass. "I mean with the young ladies present and all."

Moon, who was eyeing Parris, had turned on The Look. Full intensity.

The old woman snorted. "These girls won't mind. Tell us what you've found out."

Ignoring his friend's steely gaze, the chief of police addressed the female members of his rapt audience. "Well, I guess it wouldn't hurt to tell you a thing or two. Most of it'll be in the newspaper tomorrow." He paused to spear a slice of fried potato, lift it to his mouth. Between chews, he said, "The shooter—who evidently ain't too bright—left us some prints on a doorknob."

Moon saw his one hundred dollars fly away. *So that's what he's been holding back.* "You got a match yet?"

A nod as Parris swallowed the starchy mouthful. "The fella's had a few run-ins with the law. His prints were on file in Texas, Nebraska, Florida—and with the FBI." He added, "This bad guy drives a black 2006 Jeep Wrangler—with Colorado plates."

Nancy Yazzi was staring at a slivery remnant of the last ice cube in her tea.

Daisy did not like the waiting game. "So what's the yahoo's name?"

Parris had fixed his gaze on the girlfriend. "Jacob Harper." *She didn't bat an eyelash.* "His friends call him Jake." Under Moon's Rules of Engagement, the chief of police could not ask a direct question, but this ex-Chicago cop was a cagey fellow. "I don't suppose that's a name anybody here has heard around town."

Nancy looked over her glass at Parris. "Did you say Harper?"

He nodded. *This is one cool cookie.*

"That does sound kinda familiar." As if attempting to recall a bit of trivia that was right at the edge of her memory, she cocked her head. "Maybe Daddy mentioned him."

Sarah could hardly believe her ears. *I've never heard Nancy call Mr. Wetzel "Daddy."*

The chief of police nodded. "We're already checking to find out whether Mr. Harper was someone your stepfather knew." Three heart-beats. "There's the question of how he got into the house without breaking a lock or window." Two more thumpity-thumps of the blood pump. "I'm guessing this burglar had some help."

Nancy stirred her tea.

Parris continued in the easy manner of one talking shop. "If Harper had a collaborator, that person could—from a legal point of view—be considered an accomplice to murder."

Hermann Wetzel's stepdaughter felt a sudden rush of nausea.

As if he'd just thought of something funny, Parris shook his head and chuckled. "Yesterday, a couple of Texas Rangers interviewed a tough little lady down in Waco that said Harper had better not show his face at *her* house—not after the way he'd behaved. And if he did, she'd by-gosh knock his block off!"

Again, it was Daisy who played straight man. "What woman was this?"

Parris glanced at Nancy Yazzi, who was about to take a sip of tepid tea. "Harper's wife."

*Slip! Slosh! Roll! Crash! Tinkle-tinkle!*

Those were the sounds of the slippery tea glass slipping from Nancy's hand, sloshing onto the table, rolling over the edge, crashing onto the floor, and tinkle-tinkling into a scattering of sharp-edged fragments.

Moon and Sarah came out of their chairs at the same time, both mouthing more or less the same line: "Don't worry about it, Nancy— we'll have that cleaned up in a jiffy." Which they did.

The late Hermann Wetzel's stepdaughter seemed virtually unaware of the broken glass, or the effort to soak up the tea with a napkin (Sarah) or pick up the larger pieces of glass (Moon).

Scott Parris, who might have been glued to his chair, was staring hard at Nancy Yazzi. Waiting for something else to pop.

Daisy Perika was shifting her shifty gaze from Parris to Nancy and back.

Though wearing a brittle, expressionless mask, Nancy was fuming inside. *So Jake has a wife, does he? The dirty bastard!*

Despite the dropped tea glass, the chief of police was impressed. *I'd never want to play a hand of poker with this little lady.*

## THE END OF PARRIS'S PERFECT DAY

AFTER SCOTT Parris had tipped his fedora and said his goodbyes to the womenfolk, Moon and the spotted cat followed him out onto the west porch. The Ute was not one to withhold a well-deserved compliment. "You put on quite a nice little show."

The leading man of the piece was appreciative, and he was not done yet. "Thanks."

They stepped off the porch, headed for the Volvo.

Moon brought up the subject of their wager at Lake Jesse. "And it looks like I might have to come up with a hundred bucks."

"Might?"

"Finding a man's prints on a doorknob don't prove he did a shooting."

Parris conceded the point. "All the same, you'd better start putting nickels and dimes into your piggy bank."

"You think so?"

" 'Deed I do." Parris opened the car door, slipped his belly under the steering wheel, inserted the key into the ignition switch, listened to the sweet old engine sputter to life, and cleared his throat for the finale. "Morning after the shooting, Judge Boudreau issued a warrant that enabled me to check on some phone calls."

Moon could see it coming. "Nancy Yazzi has a cell phone. I'm betting Jake Harper does too."

"Charlie, there's no hiding anything from you."

"So—has she called him?"

"Since the shooting, six times. So far, Harper's not answering. But last night, Miss Yazzi left him a message, which was more or less along the line of 'I sure miss you, Sugar Baby, and I hope you're okay,' and all the usual blah-blah-blah." The white cop grinned up at his tall Indian friend. "Best part was, 'I don't know how long I'll be staying at this ranch, but soon as you can, please call me.' "

Moon patted the Volvo's roof. "It's mighty nice of you to let me know what's going on."

"Hey, what're friends for?"

The Ute had a flinty-edged answer for that, but held his tongue on the subject. But another issue deserved comment: "That bomb you dropped about Harper having a wife in Waco—it's a wonder Nancy Yazzi didn't have a heart attack."

The finest amateur actor present on the Columbine assumed a puzzled expression that his one-man audience could not fully appreciate in the moonlight. "You're kidding—did I actually say Nancy's boyfriend had himself a *wife*?"

"Now don't you sit there and tell me right to my face you don't remember—"

"What I meant to say was that Mr. Harper's *mother* was all ticked off at him." Parris shook his head and sighed. "Well, don't that just beat all—a fella gets one little word mixed up, and just imagine how much trouble it might cause." A thoughtful pause. "If Jake Harper knew right now that Nancy Yazzi figures him for a married man, he'd damn sure steer clear of *her*. He's got troubles enough."

"Then he's not married?"

Parris switched on the Volvo's headlights. "He was a few years ago, but his mother told the Texas cops his wife died someplace down in Mexico. They're checking it out with the federales."

"Pardner, you are some piece of work."

"I'll take that as a compliment."

"If you do, you've either got skin an inch thick—or you're mighty easy to please."

"Now stop sweet-talkin' me or I'll get a swelled head." Parris admired a thin sliver of silver moon hanging over the Misery peaks. As he watched, a gluttonous cloud swallowed the celestial jewel. "It won't be long before Miss Yazzi moves back to town."

Moon drummed his fingers on the top of the car. "You got a particular spot in mind?"

"In the jailhouse. But I'd like to let things simmer for a few days, just on the chance that Jake Harper picks up one of her phone calls."

The tribal investigator listened to a chilly breeze rattling cottonwood leaves. "If you decide to arrest her, that's none of my business. But until you do, she's my guest."

Parris considered the long, dark road back to Granite Creek, a darker one into the future. "I'd better be getting on home."

Charlie Moon watched the taillights bounce as the Volvo rumbled over Too Late Creek bridge. *I wonder if those hungry caterpillars are any closer.* The worried rancher hardly noticed as a crackling fork of lightning did a few high-kicking steps across the back of Porcupine Mountain. *Last I heard, it cost a dollar seventy-five an acre to spray for range worms.* The white-hot dancer took a six-mile leap, landed atop Elk Tooth Peak to perform a sizzling little number that split an old-growth spruce down the middle. *Sometime tomorrow, I'll phone that crop-dusting outfit.*

As the indifferent spectator turned his back and headed to the log house, a long roll of thunder grumbled behind him.

Daisy Perika was watching her nephew from the parlor window. *Fire-Legs Woman is a big show-off, and she hates to be ignored.* The shaman shook her head. *One way or another, she'll get even with Charlie.*

◆ ◆ ◆

NOT THAT there is any connection. Not *necessarily.* Be it understood right up front that one does not wish to encourage anything that smells of superstition. But in the interest of what real estate attorneys refer to as "full disclosure," it shall be mentioned that Charlie Moon would awaken at dawn to learn that last night's lightning had struck the biggest haystack on the Columbine. This precious supply of bovine victuals had burned down to the last straw.

Pete Bushman, who was the bearer of the bad news, cheerfully allowed as how a man with a glass eye could've spotted the needle from thirty paces away.

Daisy Perika merely nodded in her knowing way.

As if the loss of a valuable supply of hay was not enough to ruin Moon's day, there was also that business about the cougar and the calf, and far worse than that—

But we get ahead of ourselves.

# CHAPTER TWENTY-EIGHT

## TENSION

NANCY YAZZI'S LIFE HAD BEEN TURNED UPSIDE DOWN WHEN SCOTT Parris had uttered that synonym for *spouse* that rhymes with *knife*—which cruel blade had pierced the girl to the heart. But, believing that her romantic liaison with Jake Harper was a secret, she carried on the charade as unfortunate stepdaughter of the lately deceased Hermann Wetzel with admirable composure.

The only soul on the Columbine who knew Nancy's secret continued to treat the young woman as if she were a young lady. Charlie Moon was a gentleman.

Even though they were not *in the know,* Daisy Perika and Sarah Frank sensed that something was not quite right, and breakfast on the morning after Parris's visit was tense, the conversation awkwardly cheerful with observations about how tasty the bacon was and how scrambling eggs was the safest way to go because any cook worth her spatula could hardly mess up a scrambled egg—but getting an egg *fried* just to someone's taste, well that was a yolk of a different color. And made-from-scratch biscuits—why, those doughy things that come in a can don't compare with the real McCoy. And homemade preserves—just try to find a jar on the supermarket shelf that tastes half as good.

After the morning meal was over, the diners scattered.

Nancy complained of a headache and withdrew to her room "for a nap."

Charlie Moon cranked up one of the Columbine pickups and headed off to an eastern pasture where a cougar had pulled down a purebred Hereford calf.

Daisy and Sarah went for a walk along the river, where the tribal elder lectured her youthful companion on the preparation of a bitter tea brewed from a concoction of yucca roots, picklefern leaves, and the tender bark of April bloodberry vines. The procedure, which required the practitioner to dry the roots and leaves in the sun for precisely seven days and soak the bark in brine overnight (during the Dark of the Moon), was complex and time-consuming. The end product, the self-taught pharmacist asserted, was well worth the effort.

Daisy stopped to lean on her sturdy oak walking staff and catch her breath. Her thought slipped away like driftwood on the river.

The sixteen-year old asked, "What's it good for?"

The shaman snapped at her apprentice. "What's *what* good for?"

"The tea. Is it for a stomachache or is it a sleeping potion or what?"

Daisy's old eyes blinked at the snow-capped Buckhorn peaks. *What is that medicine used for? The lumbago?* No, she didn't think so. *Maybe it's for menstrual cramps.* The teacher cast a stern glance at Little Miss Smarty-Pants. "That part will be in tomorrow's lesson."

◆ ◆ ◆

WHAT WAS that—a low rumble of thunder left over from last night's performance?

No, the sky is clear of clouds. Presumably, Fire-Legs Woman has departed to perform her thunderous tango upon another craggy stage.

The noise that Daisy Perika and Sarah Frank *did not hear* was the throaty stutter of an internal combustion engine. Their ears were filled with the uproariously happy laughter of the rolling river splishity-splashing over a multitude of slippery stones. Such soothing water music tends to drown out less pleasant sounds.

Which is not always a good thing.

## THE DISCOVERY

WHEN HE pulled up to the headquarters in the pickup, Charlie Moon noticed that Sarah's spiffy little red F-150 was not in its usual spot under the cottonwood. The birthday girl kept her favorite gift parked beside his Expedition. So near that the two Ford Motor Company products—had they had a mind and fingers to—could have reached out and *touched* each other.

Moon thought he knew what had happened. *Nancy's been pretty upset ever since Scott conned her with that "wife" business last night. I bet she asked Sarah to drive her into town so she could tell the police everything she knows about Jake Harper.* Whether or not the girl was connected to her stepfather's murder, that was the smart move to make. And whatever else she might be, Miss Yazzi was no dope.

Moon strode onto the redwood porch and into the headquarters parlor. He was about halfway across that spacious room when something in a shaft of sunlight caught his eye—something that sparkled like diamonds but was not. The fractured glass on the floor was from the shattered pane on his locked gun-case door, where he kept several sidearms, five rifles, two carbines, a double-barrel (over-and-under) 12-gauge shotgun. Not anymore. The shotgun and a .44-caliber revolver were missing, along with a box of 12-gauge buckshot and two boxes of ammo for the pistol. Moon held his breath. *Whoever did this is intending to conduct some serious business. And he might still be in the house.*

Which reminded him of what had happened to Hermann Wetzel.

The Ute removed his boots, slipped his .357 magnum revolver from its holster. Stepping softly, Moon searched every room in the headquarters, every closet, even the pantry. No one at home. That fact was worrisome enough. What made his skin prickle was what he found in Sarah Frank's bedroom. Her little black leather purse had been turned upside down, the contents spilled all over her neatly made bed. A pink plastic compact. Sunrise Surprise lipstick. A tiny bottle of perfume. A lace-edged hankie. Two cheap ballpoint pens. A wallet stuffed with snapshots. The critical issue was the item that was missing.

The keys to Sarah's F-150 pickup.

The tribal investigator imagined what had happened: *Jake Harper came here to get his girlfriend, broke into the gun cabinet, and stole the keys for Sarah's truck. Nancy's probably behind the F-150 wheel right now. Down the road someplace, they plan to ditch his hot Jeep—*

But wait a minute.

*Where are Daisy and Sarah?* Moon's hands were cold as marble. *Maybe he took some hostages.*

Grim-faced as he had ever been, the tribal investigator holstered the heavy pistol and headed for the west porch. *It's my fault. I should have seen this coming. Oh, God—if Sarah and Daisy are still alive, please keep 'em that way till I can get there and—*

This prayer was interrupted by the sweetest sounds he had ever heard.

Sarah's outraged scream: "Hey—where's my truck!"

Daisy's response: "One of them knot-head cowboys probably drove it into town to pick up a sportin' woman at some smelly saloon with brass spittoons and sawdust on the floor."

Sidewinder: Two and a half barks, presumably to affirm his agreement with the Ute elder.

The astonished females gawked at the tall, lean man in his stocking feet who burst through the door, leaped off the porch, and approached in a dead run to grab one of them in each arm.

Tears streamed down Charlie Moon's face.

When Daisy—who had not been hugged that hard in her entire life—was finally able to extricate herself, she flailed her arms and squawked, "What the hell is going on?"

Moon looked to the heavens and laughed. "Somebody stole Sarah's pickup."

The old woman glowered at her nephew. "Well, why didn't you say so right off—if we'd have known, me and the girl would've had us a good belly laugh too!"

# CHAPTER TWENTY-NINE

## ONE MINUTE LATER

WHEN THE TELEPHONE JINGLED ON THE DESK IN HIS SECOND-FLOOR office, Scott Parris was enjoying a brand-new CD. It was an off-label is-sue and there were no instruments—the performers were a local female-male duo, and though neither one could hold a tune in a five-gallon bucket, their a cappella performance was gripping. The chief of police had expressly told the day dispatcher (a rookie), "No calls unless it's my girlfriend or there's a national emergency." He pressed the Pause button on the CD player, snatched up the telephone, heard Moon's deep voice booming at him.

The abbreviated story that the rancher told might have been head-lined CRIME ON THE COLUMBINE. Bottom line: firearms stolen, also a motor vehicle.

Parris jotted notes on a yellow pad. "Got it, Charlie. Hold on a sec." He punched the Intercom button, instructed dispatch to set up a GCPD roadblock twenty-five miles this side of the Columbine Ranch gate and to ask the state police to plug the jug on the other end. While the dispatcher was saying "yes sir" he shut off the intercom and jammed the telephone hard against his ear. "Please tell me that Sarah and Daisy are okay." A pause while he did not breathe. "That's great news, Charlie—and don't you worry, we'll arrest the Yazzi girl in a few minutes." He chuckled. "Hey, how far can she get in that shiny red pickup?"

Two issues are of interest.

Number one: As it happened, the birthday pickup was farther along than Scott Parris had assumed. The roadblocks would be of no use.

Number two: Note that the chief of police said, "Hey, how far can *she* get. . . ." Did Scott Parris assume that Nancy Yazzi was alone in the stolen vehicle? Yes indeed.

As the chief of police would now inform Charlie Moon, the CD he had been listening to when the Ute called featured two "persons of interest" in the Hermann Wetzel homicide—i.e., Jake Harper and Nancy Yazzi. Shortly after Moon had departed to examine the carcass of the calf that had served as the cougar's midnight snack, and at about the time that Daisy and Sarah had left for their educational outing along the river, Miss Yazzi had placed her seventh call to Mr. Harper. Six-plus-one was evidently her lucky number. On this occasion, after peering suspiciously at the caller ID, Mr. Harper had answered his cell phone. The following transcript (from official GCPD files) is a verbatim account of the brief exchange:

"H'lo, Nance."

"Jakey—are you okay?"

"Uh, yeah." (Grunt.) "Where you callin' from, Peachy Pie?"

"I'm still at the Columbine Ranch. D'you know where that is?"

"Sure."

"Look—I've got to get away from here."

"Uh—right." (Burp.) "You want me to come get you tonight?"

"No. I'll have my own wheels. Now listen close, Jakey—I don't want to say the name of the place on the phone, but let's meet at that restaurant where you took me last Valentine's Day."

Three-second pause.

"Uh . . ."

"Jakey!"

"The McDonald's down at Durango?"

"No! Remember where we shared that great barbecue plate?"

"Uh . . ."

"I bet you haven't forgot that redhead waitress who was old enough to be your momma. The slut was wearing a see-through blouse about the size of a dinner napkin. she called you 'Honey Bunch.' "

"Oh—right."

"You sure you know which place I'm talking about?"

"Yeah. That damn barbecue kept me up half the night."

"I'll meet you there. This afternoon."

*"Okay, Peachy Pie."*

*"See you."*

*(Click.)*

*(Click.)*

# CHAPTER THIRTY

## WHERE HAS NANCY GONE IN SARAH'S PICKUP?

BEFORE ADDRESSING THAT PRESSING QUESTION, WHICH IS ON THE minds of Sarah Frank, Daisy Perika, Charlie Moon, Chief of Police Scott Parris, and a dozen GCPD coppers plus enough Colorado State Police to fill every Dunkin' Donuts in Denver, Colorado Springs, Pueblo—and Crested Butte to boot—let us back up a few minutes.

At the instant when Scott Parris and Charlie Moon terminated their telephone conversation, Miss Yazzi, having already passed through Granite Creek, was precisely 12.3 miles south of that fair city.

But that had been twenty-two minutes ago. At present, she was 36.1 miles south of Granite Creek, turning off the main highway onto a "scenic byway" that would take her into an unpleasant little depression between the mountains that hopeful locals call Pleasant Valley. After winding along the north bank of a meager little stream, the red pickup crossed into the adjacent county, which was named after one Zebulon Montgomery Pike, who also had a sizable mountain peak named after his fine self.

In this new jurisdiction, the road abruptly changed from "blacktop with potholes" to "gravel with bigger potholes." By and by, Nancy Y found herself a straight place in the road that extended to yon cloud-shrouded ridge. Her destination was a forlorn little hamlet known by folks thereabouts as Hamlet's Crossroads. At this intersection of gravel lanes, there were four cinder-block buildings, each occupying its as-signed quadrant. Hamlet's Service Station. Hamlet's Stop-n-Shop. Hamlet's Barber Shop. Hamlet's Cowboy Saloon. The proud owner of this prosperous quartet was one Hamlet Anderson, aka "Ham." Of par-ticular interest to Nancy was the latter enterprise, which served fair-to-middling barbecue.

She braked the F-150, eyed the motley assembly of motor vehicles scattered higgledy-piggledy about the Cowboy Saloon. There was the predicable selection of pickups, ranging from a 1957 Chevy that had been brush-painted a dreadful shade of green to a brand-new Dodge with dual rear wheels and chrome exhausts. Also a big GMC stake-bed, a 1964 red-and-white VW bus, a white Qwest Communications van, a matched pair of black Harley-Davidson hogs, and . . . a nifty little Ford SUV that seemed oddly out of place. Nancy did not notice the Escape. The intended object of her intense concentration was Jake Harper's Jeep—which was not present and accounted for.

Quick intake of breath as she turned into the dirt driveway, parked beside the Harleys. *Maybe Jake changed his mind and isn't coming after all. Or maybe he's just late, like he usually is.* She cut the ignition. *I'll just have to wait for him.*

Her wait would not be a lengthy one.

The engine had barely shut down when Mr. Harper opened the driver-side door and slipped in beside her. "Hi ya, Peachy Pie!"

Nancy let out a squeaky little shriek. "Jakey—where'd you come from?"

Being somewhat of a wit, he was sorely tempted to reply, *Fort Worth,* which was the city of his birth. Instead, he said, "I been here for almost an hour."

She looked around the parking lot. "Where's your Jeep?"

"That Wrangler's hot as two-dollar pistol. I got it stashed where I've been holed up."

"What're you driving?"

"Something I found in a garage." He patted the seat. "Where'd you get this nice truck?"

"I borrowed it."

"From who?"

Suddenly confronted by the image of an outraged Sarah Frank, Nancy felt a pang of guilt. "From a friend."

"Wish I had a friend like that." Harper scratched his beard. "Why're you wearing that great big raincoat?" This was not an idle query. It was not raining, and the man had not seen his main squeeze for some days now and just as many nights, and it irked him that the shapely form was concealed in the bulky covering.

Ignoring this reasonable question, Main Squeeze posed one of her own: "Did you find Hermann's money under the heat thingy?"

"Uh . . . afraid not." Harper felt his face blush. "Way things turned out, there wasn't time to look. I'd just got into the house when the shooting started and—"

"Shut up, Jake!"

Unless your companion is deaf, and Nancy's was definitely not, it is unnecessary to produce a 160-decibel remark inside the smallish cab of a standard F-150 pickup. The lady's screech caused Jake's left ear to ring, his diastolic pressure to rise, and blood to pool in his eyes. He turned a bushy-browed scowl on his sweetheart.

She lowered the volume. "I'm sorry, Jakey. I didn't mean to yell at you."

They both knew that this was not 100 percent true.

Even so, Mr. Harper was mollified by the gesture. "That's all right, Nance." To demonstrate his sincerity, he leaned over to give her a little kiss on the cheek.

She turned, planted a big one square on his mouth. After their lips were disengaged, Nancy used hers to speak as softly as that proverbial warm twilight breeze which barely rustles willow leaves. "Jakey, I'm *glad* you killed Hermann, but I don't want to hear a *single word* about it." The sly woman-child cunningly twisted a lock of his scruffy beard into a stringy little strand. "Do you understand what I mean?"

"Yeah, but—"

"Don't 'but' me, Jake!" She yanked the beard, pointed a sharp fingernail at his left eyeball. "Just try to wrap your brain around this *one simple fact*." Hermann Wetzel's stepdaughter spoke slowly, enunciating each syllable. "I don't want to know *anything* about the shooting."

"Well, all right—" Jake Harper caught himself barely in time to avoid committing another *but*. But he was no dunce and he understood well enough. *Nancy's afraid I might tell her something she don't want to know and then she might became a . . .* What was that fancy legal lingo the TV lawyers used? *An excessory after the fax? No, that don't sound right.*

She shifted quickly to another subject: "So where've you been hiding out?"

"Some rich guy's house up on Muleshoe Mountain."

She blinked. *Even Jake can't be that dumb.* "So close to Granite Creek?"

"It's a great place to hole up—loaded with fancy food and top-rate booze." He pointed at the Escape. "And the nice rich dude lent me his car." To this small piece of wit, Jake appended a small chuckle.

Nancy Yazzi drew in a deep breath. "Since *that night*—have you talked to anyone besides me?"

He grinned at this unfathomable female "Like who, Peachy Pie?"

"Oh, one of your buddies. Spike, maybe. Or Spider."

"Nah, I don't trust them bozos." Harper snorted. "If there was a ten-dollar reward out on me, they'd give me up faster'n you could say 'Peter Pepper picked a pint of pickled pipers.'"

"Then you didn't telephone anyone?"

"Nah."

"Not even your mother?"

"Nope." *Momma ever sees me again, she'll probably throw a brick at me.*

"Or your sister?"

"Huh-uh." *I owe Sis nine hundred bucks.*

"How about your wife in Waco?"

"Lulabelle don't live in Waco. Her and the kids have a double-wide down at Kerr—" Oops.

CHAPTER THIRTY-ONE

## MR. HARPER FINDS HIMSELF IN A SPOT OF DIFFICULTY

WHATEVER HIS SHORTCOMINGS, AND THE LIST WAS A LENGTHY ONE, Jake Harper was not a coward. Far from it. He had been in a dozen hard-knuckle bar brawls, and he generally came out on top. But the tough guy had a strong instinct for survival, which at this instant was shouting inside his head, *Make a false move, you're dead!*

His girlfriend had a six-gun in her hands. And not of a small caliber. This was what is known in the trade as a Great Big Number. He rightly deduced that she had produced the heavy-duty shooting iron from somewhere in the bulky raincoat.

"Uh, Nance—"

"Don't 'Nance' me, you two-bit . . ." Searching for just the right word, she furrowed her brow. It came to her. "You two-bit gigolo!"

"What?"

It was not that he required clarification. What Mr. Harper wanted more than all the gold in Fort Knox was to get out of the pickup without a perforation in his hide, and extending the conversation seemed to be the best means of accomplishing that objective.

It was not.

*Click!* This was Mr. Six-Shooter's way of saying howdy.

Nancy Yazzi had just cocked the thing, which, because it was a double-action machine, was not absolutely necessary. But it was absolutely terrifying.

Jake did not wish to be present to hear the next (very loud) word uttered by the .44, which would be the Big Goodbye. He made a desperate grab for the door, heard the thunder roar, and hit the ground to scuttle away on all fours. In the cover of the phone-company van, the fleeing man got onto his hind legs and made a remarkable sprint for a heavyset fellow.

Going now for the one-handed shot, Nancy stuck her left arm out the driver-side door and pointed the barrel more or less in Jake's direction. She pulled the trigger five more times to empty the cylinder. The first shot went into the sky; the second punctured a rear tire in the VW bus; the third went into Hamlet's rooftop sign (neatly drilling a bull's-eye in the second O of COWBOY); the fourth went through a window screen, across the saloon and over the bar, passed close to Ham's right ear, and smashed a full bottle of Jack Daniel's, which exploded just as the object of the shooter's fury banged through the swinging front doors to flail his way across the barroom floor, knocking chairs, tables, filthy spittoons, and startled patrons aside as if he were the Father of All Bowling Balls and they were balsa-wood tenpins.

The fifth slug? Where that one ended up is anyone's guess.

Nancy had additional armament behind the seat in the pickup. When the young woman toting a double-barrel shotgun came dashing in after her terrified boyfriend, things began to get downright *interesting*.

Big-hatted cowboys, sooty coal miners, sweaty oil-field roughnecks, a painted lady of questionable character, and a nice young couple from Hot Springs, Arkansas, who had stopped to soak up some "local color" scattered for the nearest exits and hiding places. Some of those who were already bellied up to the bar scrambled over the top to join Ham, who was facedown on the floor. Others dived out of windows and a few followed Jake, who had made a beeline for the kitchen. Six fellows who were about to lose their water managed to get inside the men's room, which was about twice the size of an old-fashioned telephone booth. Four panic-stricken gents pushed their way into the ladies' facility only to meet an outraged, middle-aged señorita who punched one in the nose and took to swinging her purse at the others—

◆ ◆ ◆

BUT THIS is altogether too much. The skin is flushed, the mind boggles, the pulse races, the blood pressure surges, the breath comes in short gasps. One needs a respite from these frenetic activities—a brief interlude of peace. What is called for is a visit to a park with serene paths that meander among stately maples in whose leafy boughs perky little bluebirds are all atwitter. But there is no such place in Pike County, Colorado. We shall go for second best, which is a visit with an elderly lady who is entirely sane, faultlessly honest, and is not known in the community for pursuing violent activities, such as shooting sprees with a passionate intent toward homicide. No, Daisy Perika does not qualify.

We refer to Miss Millicent Muntz.

◆ ◆ ◆

BACK IN Granite Creek, quite comfy inside her cozy abode at 751 Beechwood Road, the respectable bespectacled lady sits (primly, as you would expect) in an overstuffed mauve armchair, a small volume in her hand. *The Collected Poems of Emily Dickinson.*

Miss Muntz reads aloud to Mr. Moriarty from a favorite piece. Something about the *bleakness of her lot.*

The cat, sprawled in his usual habitat (the basket-bed), does not respond with any noticeable enthusiasm. It is possible that, being of the male persuasion, the feline would have preferred the manly verse of Robert Service.

◆ ◆ ◆

THERE. WAS that not a pleasant diversion? With the mind now at rest the pulse rate and blood pressure once again within the proper brackets, and breath coming easily, let us return to the fray.

◆ ◆ ◆

FOUR OTHERS pushed their way into the ladies' facility, only to meet an outraged, middle-aged señorita who punched one in the nose and took to swinging her purse at the others—

But let us dispense with these not-so-innocent bystanders and concentrate on the principal characters.

Watch Jake Harper come a-running out the back door of Hamlet's

Cowboy Saloon, make a hard left around the corner of the cinder-block building, and hotfoot it to the Escape, whose name had never seemed so appropriate.

Three racing heartbeats later, watch Nancy Yazzi emerge from the same door, fire in her eye, the over-and-under 12-gauge tucked under her arm, primed and ready for action. Watch her stop, stare, wonder, *Where'd that $%&#* so-and-so go?* What the frustrated young woman needs is a clue. *Aha!* She hears any number of engines being cranked to life, just as many vehicles departing as fast as they can go—destination: anyplace but *here!*

She rounds the corner, points the shotgun in the direction of Jake's recently pilfered Ford Escape. The top barrel says *ka-Booom!* The bottom repeats the earsplitting statement.

More or less shielded amid the fleeing pack, the diminutive SUV was not struck by a single pellet. The aforesaid pair of *ka-Booms* did pepper three pickup trucks, and the lumbering stake-bed loaded with hay, which (as a consequence of the fellow behind the wheel being un-nerved by the assault) rammed the VW bus, flipping that vehicle onto its side. Seven of the ka-zinging lead spheres also struck a passing FedEx van, whose stalwart driver (without so much as batting an eyelash) took note of that little cluster of stars that made a brand-new constel-lation on his sandblasted windshield, jutted his clefted chin, kept right on going. No matter what, come heck or high water—*the parcels must go through.* The fellow definitely had the right stuff.

Nancy Yazzi's stuff might not have been entirely *right*, but she was not short on grit. Undaunted by the knowledge that the hateful man was picking up speed, she leaned the spent shotgun against the over-turned VW bus, got the pistol and a handful of .44 cartridges from her raincoat pocket, and reloaded Charlie Moon's revolver. Realizing that this might be her last opportunity to severely injure the former lover, she held the pistol in both hands, closed her left eye, sighted down the barrel with the other one, pursed her pretty lips, held her hot breath, got a steady bead . . . pulled the trigger.

When operating a firearm, the importance of applying proper technique cannot be exaggerated.

Just as Jake Harper was pulling onto the gravel road, the slug passed through the rear window, buzzed like a bumblebee between the front seats, and smacked into the dash-mounted AM/FM radio. The next one—and this is not an exaggeration—*parted his hair* before it smacked into the windshield. Two of the next four lumps of lead came close enough to the terrified driver to clip an earlobe and penetrate a loose undergarment. This caused his teeth to clench, his mind to generate what is aptly called an HNDE (Harrowing Near-Death Experience). But, as scary as the HNDE is, Near is not the same thing as Dead Center, and by the time the stolen pistol was empty, Jake was roaring past other fleeing vehicles as if they were backing up, running one off the road into an irrigation ditch, another through a *bob-war* fence and into a slime-encrusted pond.

Long before the state police arrived to investigate this most recent hullabaloo at Hamlet's rowdy roadhouse, all the witnesses had fled the scene. Ham, who had spent the exciting interlude with his nose pressed against the filthy floor behind the bar, informed the officer that the joint had been shot up by a gang of *at least* six guys. Great big guys, with automatic weapons. And hand grenades.

Which was why the incident was never connected with Nancy Yazzi and her errant boyfriend. Not that either one of them gave it a thought. Both had other, more urgent business to tend to. Nancy, a persistent soul, had not given up the chase. Moreover, she was not all that far behind Jake Harper. The outcome hinged on whether that distance would stretch or shrink.

The Escape's top speed on a conventional highway exceeded what the rebuilt F-150 could muster by about fifteen miles per hour, which is a considerable advantage. The problem was (for Mr. Harper) that the potholed gravel road was several notches below *conventional,* and he was a long way from a paved highway. This being the case, the outcome of the race was—*problematic.*

Even though not a single drop of Jake Harper's blood had been spilled, the day was not yet over and neither was the saga of these star-crossed lovers. While the outcome remains in doubt, one feels justified to offer the following observations:

With practice, Nancy Yazzi's aim was improving.

If the romance had not ended, it had definitely experienced a set-back.

# CHAPTER THIRTY-TWO

## SHE HAS A NOTION

REFRESHED BY A LONG, SOAPY SOAK IN THE MOTEL TUB, NANCY
Yazzi (wrapped in a bedspread) sits in front of the TV, munching buttery popcorn hot from the microwave. Has the passionate young woman cooled off, given up on getting even with Jake Harper? Not for a minute. While the entertainment-craving portion of her brain absorbs a dose of *America's Funniest Home Videos,* her dark, sinister lobe mulls over serious business.

*I've got to get rid of Sarah's pickup before the cops spot it and pick me up.* Another handful of popcorn masticated by her perfect molars. Crunch-crunch. *First thing tomorrow morning, I'll dump it someplace.* The enthusiastic man-hunter would require an alternate means of transportation, and was considering her options. Then, there was the overriding issue.

*How do I find him? Even Jake won't be dumb enough to go back to his hideout on Muleshoe Mountain.* Which would make things difficult. A man who would cheat on his faithful girlfriend by having a wife on the side—the rascal was devious in the extreme. *What I need is a really good idea—*

Bang!

No, that was not a gunshot. Not even a fifty-cent firecracker.

Nancy had experienced one of those explosive *eureka!* moments.

Indeed, the answer appeared as if it were a gift—though definitely not from heaven. And the notion was what a thoughtful gambler would call a long shot. Never mind. Elated, the pistol-packin' momma tossed the popcorn bag aside, raised clenched fists over her head, and yelled, "Jake—you are as good as dead!"

At the very instant that Nancy shouted, the object of her threat—who was huddled in the backseat of the stolen Escape, shivering under a wool blanket—awakened from a troubled sleep, banged his head on something or other, and yelped, "No, Nance—please don't shoot me! I got a wife and two kids. . . ." Or was it three kids? As he floated up from the semigroggy state, Jacob Harper was relieved to realize that his vengeful sweetie was not about to administer lead poisoning to his person. It also occurred to him that if Nancy had been ready to pull the trigger, mentioning the wife and young'uns would probably not have gained the sought-for sympathy from his judge/jury/prosecutor/executioner. Girlfriends, he had learned at that recent rendezvous at Hamlet's Cowboy Saloon, tended to be sensitive on such subjects.

Jake groaned, laid his head back on a makeshift pillow, which was a rolled-up copy of last Sunday's *Rocky Mountain News.* Though he tried ever so hard, the bone-weary fugitive could not drift away to Dreamland. Too many thorny issues pricked at his mind. *Nance's out there somewhere. She finds me again, she'll shoot me dead.*

# CHAPTER THIRTY-THREE

## A HUNTED, HAUNTED MAN

IT HAS BEEN ESTABLISHED THAT JAKE HARPER IS NO SISSY. BUT EVEN the most stalwart soul has its limits, and as he drove southward his fevered thoughts festered with a corrosive fear: *Nance won't ever give up.* For the hundredth time in the past hour, he glanced at the rearview mirror. The fact that he saw nothing on the strip of Texas asphalt that stretched off to the horizon provided little comfort. *She's still back there somewhere, sniffin' at my trail.* As it happened, this fear was totally groundless. But Mr. Harper would not have been greatly surprised if his sweetheart had popped up in the backseat, jammed the cold pistol muzzle against his head, and shot him dead.

With every minute, his anxiety increased.

And though he had put hundreds of miles between himself and Hamlet's Cowboy Saloon . . . *It feels like the farther I go, the closer she gets.* Odd that the normally sensible fellow should entertain such a counterintuitive conclusion. Put it down to stress.

*That little gal won't stop till she puts enough bullets through my hide to let all my blood leak out.* The contemplation of such an undesirable outcome is what has kept him going in the Escape, which stolen vehicle the police in several states are *not* looking for because the owners of the summer home where Jake left his Jeep Wrangler as a trade-in for this spiffy little Ford SUV have not yet shown up to discover the exchange.

It is too bad that worry about his angry girlfriend has prevented the nervous tourist from enjoying his travels. He has recently paid calls on such exotic tourist meccas as Pueblo, Lamar, Dodge City, Amarillo, Tulia (the home of Charlie Moon's favorite honey), Plainview, Lubbock (he lunched there on Texas-style red chili with a half inch of grease floating over the fiery ingredients), Abilene (where he purchased a bottle of

Granny Hodad's Old-Fashioned Stomach Remedy and Nerve Tonic), and, last, Comanche (a quick stop for ice cream). Despite all this excellent recreation, his trip cannot be said to be a true vacation. And though our desperado is in desperate need of some R & R, Harper must stay on the road until he reaches a particular destination. Waco, of course. As Scott Parris and the Texas Rangers know, Jake's momma lives there, and everyone knows that no matter how badly a boy treats his mother or how many times she warns him that if he ever shows his hairy hide at her door again she will fill it so full of buckshot he won't be able to walk faster than a duck-waddle, the one who gave birth to him *doesn't really mean it.* Really, now—how many mothers can you count on all your fingers and toes who are sufficiently mean-spirited to carry out such a violent threat?

That many? You must come from a sure-enough tough neighborhood.

Waco, on the other hand, is the heartland of Texas, which is the friendly Lone Star State and home of the Dallas Cowboy Cheerleaders, for goodness' sake. Mommas in these parts want their boys to grow up to be good-looking cowboys who drive old pickup trucks and such, and the little tyke under that big-brimmed hat cannot very well do that if Momma employs deadly weapons to enforce parental discipline.

Which was why Jake Harper had no doubt that his dear old mom would welcome him with open arms, big hugs, and kisses. His judgment may also have been affected by the fact that he had an overpowering hankering for home-cooked victuals. After all that had occurred recently, it would be mighty gratifying to belly up to the old family trough and chow down on big helpings of Momma's pinto beans and pork enchiladas. And, best of all—*sleep in his own little bed again.* But when Harper motored up to the venerable homestead, Momma was conspicuously absent from the premises. The outraged felon banged on the front door, kicked on the back one so hard that he injured his big toe, and shouted foul obscenities that scandalized the drug-pushing pimp who plied his trade next door.

Mrs. Harper's son broke in a window (a nasty habit he must learn to overcome), found nothing in the refrigerator but a quart of skim milk, a moldy onion, and two shriveled lemons. The cupboard was empty except for a fifteen-ounce can of a cornlike vegetable with the notice: BEST IF USED BY 6/22/96. As he sat at the table, eating cold hominy from a can with a plastic spoon, Jake Harper could not help being miffed. When a man can't even count on his own dear old momma to be there when he needs her, on who can he count? Even though this was merely a rhetorical question, an answer came to Jake. His wife, that's who. But Lulabelle was also on the outs with Jake on account of how he had run off about two years ago with a waitress about half his age and left his missus flat broke, with a pile of unpaid bills and children to look after.

But wives, as all husbands know, are almost as forgiving as mothers.

Which is why Harper, now in desperate straits, took I-35 south through Austin, hung a right just before entering good ol' San Antonio, rolled along I-10 in a northwesterly direction, and before he knew it he was practically to Kerrville. By the time he pulled into the familiar dirt lane (which was getting muddy on account of a thunderstorm that had drifted down from Kimble County), and pulled to a stop at the wife's double-wide, the poor boy was all tuckered out. And no wonder: He'd been hard at it since dawn, and it was now close to midnight. It was hard to see anything through the downpour—such as a stray elephant that might have wandered into the front yard, or for that matter Lulabelle's 1993 F-250 pickup. But in a window, a dim light flickered. *She's still up watching TV.* Feeling a sudden unease (a woman would have called this *intuition*), Jake chewed on his lower lip. *I hope Lulabelle lets me in.*

After several knocks, she turned on the outside floodlight, which illuminated the small porch and caused the weary pilgrim to squint. After getting a good look-see at the late-night visitor through the window, Lulabelle shouted, "Jake—is that you?"

He yelled, "Sure is, Peachy Pie." Yes—this was also the pet name by which he called the missus. Particularly when he wanted something, such as hot food and a safe place to sleep. "Lemme in. It's raining up a reg'lar Noah's flood out here!"

No response from Lulabelle. For the longest time he stood there, water dripping off his hat and running down his collar, waiting for Wifey to open the door. This, he knew, was not the best possible sign. *Maybe she don't like me anymore.* His vanity begged to disagree—it couldn't be *that.* A more likely explanation occurred to him: *She just needs a little while to fix up her hair, slap on some makeup.* Women wanted to look their A-number-one best when their man showed up unexpected. He was relieved when the doorknob finally turned and the portal to the warm, cozy parlor opened just enough that he could see her face, and the half-smoked cigarette hanging limply from her lips. True, she did not exactly reach out and grab an armful of the errant husband, smother him with passionate kisses and urgent caresses. But neither did she spit in his eye. Indeed, when she removed the cigarette, her lips smiled. And what did she say, in that honeyed Texas drawl?

"C'mon in, Jake."

"Thanks, Peachy Pie." Half blinded by the floodlight that had flashed in his face, he tripped on the threshold.

Lulabelle pointed to a chair he could barely see in the twilight gloom of the living room. "Siddown."

It may have been the abrupt way she'd said, "Siddown." Or the fact that the smile had vanished. For whatever reason, he did not feel entirely welcome. "Uh, I been doin' a lotta sittin' today—maybe I'll just stand here for a little while."

"Suit yourself." His wife also remained standing, and, backlit by the television screen, her profile from head to knee was clearly visible. Lulabelle was looking good and she knew it. "So what've you been up to, Jake?"

"Oh, this and that."

"You might ask how I've been doing."

The mouth under the unkempt beard curled into a silly grin. "How've you been getting along, Lulabelle?"

"Things have been tough." She took a puff. Blew smoke in his face. "But I've been able to manage."

"That's good."

"You haven't asked about the kids."

"Well, that was right on the tip of my tongue. How're little . . . uh . . . Sally and—" No. *It's not Sally.* This was embarrassing. *Acutely* embarrassing.

"You don't even remember their names." Lulabelle laughed.

He was relieved to know that the missus still had a sense of humor.

"They're Lilly and Bobby and Annie."

He nodded. "Oh, right."

"No, that's not right. I just made those names up. And before you ask, the kids ain't here. There up in Lubbock, staying with my momma."

"Oh. I hope your old lady's doing okay."

Lulabelle flicked the cigarette butt, which bounced off his knee. "You are a sorry piece of work, Jake." She lit up another smoke. "And you've got a lot of explaining to do."

Jake Harper knew this was true. He was also aware that an idle mind was a something or other. Had to do with a workshop. He couldn't remember whose workshop, or what the saying meant, but work was definitely a negative subject, which made him pretty sure what the bottom line was: When a fella was in deep trouble, he shouldn't while away his time thinking about bass fishing or watching football or other stuff of that sort. He needed to apply his brain to finding a solution to his difficulties. This was why, all the way from Waco, Jake had considered a long string of more or less plausible lies. Several he had rejected out of hand, as no-sells. Two were definite keepers, but he hadn't been able to decide between them. Not until right this minute. The business about the kids' names settled it. He drew in a deep breath and got right to it. "Lulabelle, I'm awfully sorry about not being able to call the kids' names to mind, and I feel really bad about not being in touch for a while, but—"

"A while?" Her tone was distinctly brusque. Almost to the point of being curt. "Jake, two-years-plus, ain't *a while,* it's a huge chunk of a woman's lifetime!"

Such interruptions tend to unsettle a liar who has a dandy excuse right on the tip of his tongue, even make him entirely forget what he was going to say, which had something to do with having been kidnapped by a bunch of Arabs who'd found out he was a secret agent working for the FDA or BIA—one of those top-secret government intelligence agencies. But Harper had dropped the thread and could not just stand there all night trying to come up with a good story. The staunch fellow fell back on one that was almost as good: "It was on account of magnesia."

"On account of *what*?"

Harper clarified, separating the syllables best as he could: "Mag-nee-zee-uh."

Her expression remained blank.

Recalling that Lulabelle hadn't made it past the ninth grade, the high-school graduate explained with admirable patience for a hunted man who has had a very tense time getting all the way from Hamlet's Cowboy Saloon to a double-wide way down yonder by Kerrville: "Magnesia is a brain sickness a man can get. Like if he gets hit on the head too hard. It makes him not able to remember nothing that's happened to him." He assumed a sad-eyed expression calculated to elicit pity. "Like what his name is, or where he's from, or—"

"Or whether or not he has a wife?"

"That's right, Peachy Pie." *She's buying it!*

"So you got bopped on the noggin—and forgot who you was—and who I was?"

He nodded. "That's pretty much the long and short of it."

"Then you must not remember that teeny-bopper waitress you run off with."

"No, I don't remember a single thing about her." He shook his head at the wonder of what a bad bout of magnesia could do to a man. "But a couple of days ago, my name just come to me, *bang!* Jake Parker."

As wives are wont to do, she corrected him.

"Oh, right." Sheepish expression. "Harper."

Oh, Jake was *good*! And he was just warming up.

"And soon as I knowed who I was, it wasn't long before I figured out that I had me a sweet, lovin' wife by the name of Lulabelle and I hoped she was still living in our fine home down by Kerrville, and waiting for me. And you was!" He raised his arms in a triumphant gesture. "So here I am." There was a slight crack in his manly voice, the hint of a salty tear in his eye. "Home again."

She touched a flame to another Lucky Strike. "I'm glad you're back, Jake."

"Me too, Peachy Pie."

Well. All's well that ends nicely. Now, let us leave Mr. and Mrs. Harper to themselves. Lovers so long separated require privacy. Even if they are married. To each other. And so we bid a fond farewell to Jake and Lulabelle— Wait a minute.

What was that?

Was there a slight movement, barely discernible in Lulabelle's dimly illuminated living room?

And did someone (in a muffled tone) utter the sort of remark that can fairly be described as "of a caustic nature"?

It wasn't Jake. His store of conversation was quite spent.

Neither was it Lulabelle. No part of her, including her lips, moved by as much as a millimeter.

Moreover, the person who moved was *not* the one who had made the remark.

Well. This is beginning to get interesting.

# CHAPTER THIRTY-FOUR

## THERE REALLY IS NO REST FOR THE WICKED

THAT DESCRIPTOR MAY BE A BIT OVER THE TOP; AS MEMBERS OF HIS hormone-driven gender go, Jake Harper was not particularly *wicked*. But neither was he to be counted among the righteous, nor in the company of that great centrist multitude who are "neither hot nor cold." But in spite of his shortcomings, we may be allowed just a smidgen of sympathy for the aggravated felon who has recently been shot at by the Queen of His Heart, chased by Her Majesty across a parking lot, in and out of Hamlet's Cowboy Saloon, shot at again, and pursued with extreme malice and ill intent until he finally eluded the vengeful girlfriend. Exhausted from these trials, Jake retreated to the Texas family homestead in Waco in search of the kind of love only a mother can give—only to find dear old Momma absent without leave. You might think this last disappointment would be the icing on the nasty-cake. But no.

Now, in his legally wedded wife's living room, Lulabelle switched on a floor lamp and—

Jake could hardly believe his eyes. *I must be seeing things.* What Jake beheld in the living room were two additional characters.

His mother, Mrs. Petunia Harper. The hook-nosed old lady, whose hard visage glinted with congenital bitterness, was leaning on a walker that someone with a perverse sense of humor had painted *purple*. She did not look at all pleased to see the bearded, dripping-wet offspring.

The second character?

The *other* Peachy Pie. The young lady was just as Jake Harper remembered her from the prior encounter—the shapely form concealed under a bulky raincoat, the .44-caliber revolver gripped in both hands. Nancy Yazzi's trigger finger was white-knuckle taut.

The terrifying apparition spoke. "Hello, Jake."

*She's real!* Which raised a couple of perplexing questions: *How did Nance find out about my wife? And how did she find Lulabelle's house?*

Women, bless them all, have mysterious powers of which the hairy-legged gender know nothing. His teenage girlfriend appeared to be a mind-reader. "After you told me your mother lived in Waco, I got on a bus headed for Texas, and found her." Nancy nodded to indicate the grimacing crone. "When I told Petunia why I was looking for you, she agreed to introduce me to Lulabelle."

The intensely curious lobe of his brain was tempted to inquire, *So now that you've found me, what are you going to do?* The much smaller, sensible section of the gray matter was fairly shouting, *Don't ask!* And so he did not.

Didn't matter. In her disarmingly direct manner, the mind-reader announced, "I'm going to shoot you, Jake."

"Uh—listen, Nance—"

"Shut your mouth!" She pointed the stolen revolver at his belly button, which was showing under his dirty T-shirt. "First one goes in the gut. That'll hurt *real* bad." A sugary-sweet smile. "And while you're writhing on the floor and hollering for mercy, I'll put another one in your kneecap. Then I'll shoot you right in the [expletive deleted]."

Harper tried to swallow past a crab-apple-size lump in his throat.

"Now hold on a minute!" Lulabelle's voice was firm, her expression resolute. "Jake's my husband."

*Yes!* Relief flooded over the threatened man. Picture Mr. Harper standing in a cool mountain pool, under a crystalline waterfall.

"And he's my youngest son!" This, of course, was Petunia piping up.

As far as Jake knew, he was his mother's *only* son, but what mattered in this crisis was Blood Will Tell, and in the Lone Star State a wife will Stand by Her Man. The exultant fellow wanted to shout, but because of the crab apple in his throat, he could not come up with a joyful "hallelujah!" or a lusty "wa-hoo!"

Without taking her eye off her boyfriend, Nancy Yazzi raised the pertinent issue: "So what do we do?"

As the women thought about it, the silence in the living room was thick enough to roll up and chink between logs.

The wife suggested a solution: "I say we cut cards."

Jake was puzzled. *Cut cards for* what?

Nancy Yazzi was not the only woman present who had the gift of responding instantly to his innermost questions.

"I like it." Petunia giggled. "High card gets to shoot the dirty rascal!"

The dirty rascal, who had swallowed the pesky crab apple, was opening his mouth to protest, when Lulabelle snapped, "You don't get no vote, Jake!"

He watched his legal spouse produce a new deck from a voluminous purse, strip off the cellophane seal, remove the cards from the box, perform a dexterous shuffle, slap the stack of fifty-two plus a joker facedown onto the coffee table, and spread them into a perfect fan. "Who wants to go first?"

Nancy: "It's your house and your cards."

"Okay." Lulabelle pursed her lips, pulled a card from the center of the array, turned it over. Five of diamonds. A shadow of distress settled over her finely chiseled features. Ever since she had tied the knot with Jake Harper, the lady's life had been just one disappointment after another.

Jake watched the grim proceedings with the mesmerized fascination of a field mouse cornered by a trio of famished alley cats. A plump field mouse. Smeared with catnip jelly.

Both hands filled with Charlie Moon's six-shooter, Nancy Y asked her host to select a pasteboard. Mrs. Lulabelle Harper complied, flipped the queen of spades onto the coffee table for all to see. Nancy's brilliant smile could have adorned a Madison Avenue toothpaste advertisement. She cocked the hammer. Took careful aim at the boyfriend's navel—

"Hey!" Momma again. "I didn't get to pick me a card."

Miss Yazzi murmured an apology, urged the senior citizen to get on with it, and reminded all present that time was a-wasting. After the fun part was over, it would be necessary to dispose of the corpse.

The potential corpse watched in numb disbelief as his aged mother clumpity-clumped the purple walker over to the coffee table, grunted and wheezed as she leaned to take the nearest candidate, which was on the end of the fan. "Hah!" She held the ace of clubs over her head, gloating as she flicked the card at her son. "Gimme that big pistol!"

After a slight hesitation, and with some reluctance, Nancy yielded the revolver to the elderly lady.

Knowing Jake's natural limitations, also the state of his physical and emotional exhaustion, one might not have expected much from him. But a man whose girlfriend, wife, and mother are drawing cards for the high privilege of executing him is obliged to come up with a plan, and quickly. All the while the ladies were fussing with the cards, the intended victim had been easing himself closer to the floor lamp. Just as Momma took aim with the .44, the offspring gave the lamp a healthy yank, pulling the cord from the wall, which put the room into near darkness. All three women let out outraged howls, and the revolver boomed. A shot drilled a big hole in the wall just behind where he had been standing, while another shattered the television screen—which made the darkness total. Jake had crawled across the floor toward the door, only to arrive there and find it latched. Amid all the confusion while Lulabelle was attempting to wrestle the pistol away from Petunia, the intended victim redirected his crawl to the nearest exit, where he kicked off like a bullfrog to launch his bulky self through the window as Lulabelle fired three .44 slugs. Two missed his behind by inches.

The third hit him where it hurt. No; in the wallet. And though his skin was not broken, the concussion impact on his butt might have been a ninth-inning whack by a Major League pinch hitter wielding a Louisville Slugger. This parting blow enhanced his ambition to become the first human being to break the sound barrier solely by muscle power. Mr. Harper was a blur on the landscape!

And do not underestimate the performance of American automotive products.

Before the pistol could be reloaded, the women heard the valiant little

Escape go *vrrrooom!* as it lurched away like a jackrabbit with three she-wolves about three lopes behind. Mother, wife, and girlfriend—all responded with outraged shouts, rude curses, and, finally—streams of salty tears.

It was all for naught.

◆ ◆ ◆

JAKE HARPER was about sixty miles from Kerrville when he realized that his left buttock was beginning to ache like all get-out.

Bad news has a habit of arriving hand in hand with like companions.

Mr. Harper also noticed that the little SUV was running on fumes. *Damn. All I need now is to get stranded out here in the middle of nowhere.* But not a quarter mile down the road from nowhere was an all-night gas station. He pulled in, put his hand on his hip pocket, and discovered that his wallet had been badly chewed up by the .44-caliber slug, as had most of the currency therein. Only three twenty-dollar bills remained unscathed. He limped inside and gave the sleepy-eyed young woman at the cash register forty dollars.

As he pumped eighty-eight-octane into the tank, Harper mulled over his desperate financial situation and what might be done to remedy it. *I could bop that cashier on the noggin and take what's in the till.* But this was Texas. *She probably has a pistol under the counter.* He had no desire to face another armed female. Another option was more to his liking. *That cash Hermann Wetzel stashed under his office heating vent sure would come in handy. If the cops don't know I'm driving this rich guy's car, I could drive back to his big home on Muleshoe Mountain without much chance of being spotted. And if things have cooled off some at Hermann's house, I could slip in there at night and snatch his bag of money.*

It would be easy enough to drop by a public library somewhere up the road and check out the Granite Creek newspaper on the Internet to find out whether the local cops were still looking for his Jeep, or had discovered the break-in and knew he'd stolen the Escape. Despite the ache under his hip pocket, Jake Harper smiled as the pump shut off at

$40. No, make that $40.02. He saw this as a good omen. No doubt about it, Lady Luck was beginning to smile upon him.

Such a possibility cannot be discounted. She might have been laughing out loud.

# CHAPTER THIRTY-FIVE

## LOST AND FOUND

WHEN HE RECEIVED THE NEWS AT SIX MINUTES BEFORE MIDNIGHT, Scott Parris was enjoying a bedtime snack of Oreo cookies and chocolate milk. He thanked the Pueblo chief of police and immediately placed a call to Charlie Moon, who picked up on the second ring. "What is it, pard?"

"You'd never guess in a month of Mondays."

Maybe not. But Moon was willing to give it a shot. Perhaps it was because Sarah Frank had been deeply despondent since her friend swiped the cherished birthday present. Or because Aunt Daisy was nagging him every chance she got about when he was going to get off his butt and go find that truck and what had he been a tribal cop for all those years not to mention a big-shot tribal investigator nowadays if he couldn't even find a shiny red pickup. No wonder Daisy's nephew was grasping at straws. "Sarah's pickup has turned up."

"Dang it all, Charlie, I wanted to enjoy surprising you. Nancy Yazzi left the F-150 in a strip mall parking lot." The dieter popped an Oreo into his mouth, chewed, gulped it down.

"Surprise me by telling me that the guns Nancy took were in the truck."

"You'll have to settle for a half surprise. The shotgun was stashed behind the seat, but it looks like she took the pistol with her."

Moon groaned. "I hope she don't shoot somebody with that big .44."

"I hope so too." Parris took a sip of chocolate milk.

"Is Sarah's pickup messed up?"

"Don't know for sure. Battery was flat because the parking lights had been left on. But when the Pueblo cops jumpered it, it started up and ran—so it's probably drivable. Oh, I almost forgot—there was a note to Sarah in the glove compartment, which is where Miss Yazzi left the keys. Some stuff about how sorry she was, had to 'borrow the truck without asking.'"

"That was mighty thoughtful."

Parris reached for another Oreo. "You gonna tell the kid the great news?"

"I'll check her truck out first. How soon'll Pueblo PD be willing to turn it loose?"

"I fixed things so you can pick it up by noon tomorrow. The chief over there is a buddy of mine." To close the deal, Scott Parris had mentioned that the stolen vehicle was Charlie Moon's birthday gift to a sweet little orphaned Indian girl, and that Sarah was a straight-A student who was taking care of a feeble old Ute woman.

"I appreciate that."

"I told 'em you'd probably show up tomorrow to sign for it."

"I'll get Jerome to drive me. We'll head east at first light."

"No need to pry the Kyd away from his work. I'll show up at sunup and take you to Pueblo myself."

And that was that.

Except for one small matter.

We refer to what was about to occur in Daisy Perika's bedroom.

## WHAT IS PERCHED ON THE FOOT OF HER BED?

NOT THAT *Daisy has the least doubt. But it is a reasonable question, and one that is difficult to answer. Perhaps it is merely the persistent remnant of a bad dream. However the experience should be classified, when the shaman opened her eyes—there it was. Looking back at her.*

◆ ◆ ◆

DAISY WAS mightily displeased and she had every right to be. It was one thing to encounter the odd disembodied soul in the environs of her remote home on the Southern Ute reservation, where such invasions of her privacy were almost commonplace. Her isolated dwelling was barely outside the wide mouth of Cañón del Espíritu, which had that name for a good reason. And do not assume that locals called it Spirit Canyon because a mere two or three disembodied souls drifted about in the shelter of a few soot-blackened Anasazi overhangs. The spirits absolutely *swarmed* there. No recent census had been taken, but Daisy believed there were hundreds of the departed in the canyon, waiting for the earthshaking blast of that final trumpet. With this sort of eccentric population so close at hand, it was not surprising that from time to time one would accost the shaman as she strolled in the canyon. Less often, one of these lonely souls would enter her bedroom while she was trying to get some rest, and wake her up. This might be accomplished by giving her big toe a painful twist or yanking the quilt right off her, and a wild-eyed Apache spirit would shout his unintelligible gibberish in her ear! (Daisy referred to the Apache tongue, and all others excepting Ute, English, and Spanish, as gibberish.)

The point was that here on the Columbine, such disturbances were not supposed to occur. Especially when she was in her cozy downstairs bedroom, snuggled up under the covers. It just wasn't *right.* But it did happen tonight.

Which was why, when she awoke around about midnight to see the dead woman sitting on the foot of the bed, Daisy was greatly annoyed. With the darkest scowl she could muster in the middle of the night, she addressed the uninvited guest in this manner: "Chiquita—you are beginning to get on my nerves."

Because only the shaman could see and hear the presence, we have only her word for it that the apparition apologized for being such a nuisance—and gave every appearance of being truly remorseful. Which softened the Ute elder somewhat.

"Well, that's all right." *I guess she's lonesome and don't have nobody to talk to except the monkey.*

Daisy referred to the agitated squirrel monkey with the red collar fastened around its neck. The homely little fellow, restrained on a leash gripped firmly in Chiquita's right hand, sat on Daisy's bed, tail curled over its head. The creature gawked at the Ute elder, waved its skinny arms—jabbered at her in silly monkey gibberish.

Ignoring her noisy pet, Chiquita explained that she had come to thank Daisy.

The Ute woman arched her left brow. "Thank me for what?"

Why, for doing what she could to help Nancy. The apparition also stated that she was grateful to Sarah Frank and Charlie Moon for their kindness to her naughty daughter, and Chiquita was mortified that the silly girl had stolen Sarah's red pickup truck.

Daisy shrugged. *Now get out of here and take your ugly monkey with you.*

The visitor was not quite ready to depart. She allowed as how, if she ever had the opportunity, she would like to do something to return the favor.

Daisy was about to repeat the instruction about hitting the road with the monkey *aloud* when she recalled a tantalizing tidbit of gossip about the late Hermann Wetzel. "Back when you folks lived in Ignacio, folks said that Hermann wouldn't keep any of his money in the bank. Word was, your husband put his life savings in a coffee can and buried it someplace in the backyard."

The ghost begged to disagree. Chiquita knew for a fact that her husband had kept his liquid assets in a zippered canvas bag, which he'd kept hidden someplace in the garage. Or the workshop. Or maybe the tool shed. Sadly, she had never been able to find it.

This was not encouraging, but Daisy persisted. "After Hermann moved to Granite Creek, where d'you suppose he kept it then?"

The confounded monkey, who had been remarkably still for these past few moments, bared a fine set of pointy teeth at the shaman.

Chiquita gave the leash a cruel yank that almost pulled the creature's tiny head off.

The startled primate flailed its skinny arms and legs and, as soon as it got its breath, let out one of those raucous shrieks that scatter flocks of multicolored birds in tropical rain forests and startle sweaty scientists who are busy netting exotic insects.

Having gotten her pet's attention, the leash holder ordered the agitated beast to answer Daisy's questions.

The creature shook its head and rattled off what sounded (to Daisy) like a string of monkey curses.

Puzzled by this peculiar interplay between the dead woman and her pet, the Ute woman posed a pertinent question: "How would this little booger know where Hermann hid his—" Daisy had gotten a close look at the animal. *Oh my goodness—the ugly face on that monkey is Hermann Wetzel's!*

After more harsh jerks of the leash applied by his mistress, the Hermann Wetzel look-alike revealed (in monkey gibberish, which Chiquita evidently understood) that the bankroll was in a small bag concealed under the floor of his final earthly home.

Daisy craved more-specific information: *Where under the floor?*

But Hermann W was a spunky little monkey, and no matter how many neck jerks and dire threats Chiquita applied, he would say no more. Moreover, he gave his former mate an enthusiastic bite on her thumb. Which was when Daisy noticed that the leash was fastened to Chiquita's wrist with an iron band. The unhappy couple were mutual prisoners, fastened together for . . . how long?

Thankfully, Daisy was not privy to such information.

As the tribal elder contemplated their terrible entanglement, Chiquita and her monkey-husband vanished. Not in a puff of vaporous smoke or a flash of blinding light, but they were definitely gone.

The weary old woman fell back onto her pillow, lay there with eyes wide open. Stretched out beyond her were those gray, lonely hours that linger ever so long before touching dawn. But, by and by, when a rising sun bathed her bedspread in liquid gold, Daisy Perika knew what she was going to do. More or less.

# CHAPTER THIRTY-SIX

## DAISY'S OPPORTUNITY

WHEN THE SUN WAS BARELY OVER THE BUCKHORN RANGE, DAISY Perika and Sarah Frank got out of bed to find themselves alone in the house. No Charlie Moon. This was not remarkable; the busy stockman often departed before daylight to attend to the latest emergency, which might be anything from a busted pump in an irrigation well to a drunken employee in the GCPD jail who expected the boss to go his bail.

They found a note on the dining-room table:

I expect to be back a little while after sundown.
Charlie

Daisy had little to say during breakfast with Sarah. The sly old woman was too busy *thinking*. Always a risky occupation, though not so much for the tribal elder as for Western civilization, which seems always to be teetering on the brink of the abyss. In this particular instance there was no telling what the outcome might be.

After breaking her fast, the cranky old soul stood at one of the parlor's large west windows, gazing in the direction of Too Late Creek bridge. It was unnaturally quiet. The Ute elder put her nose close to the glass; her gaze darted this way and that. No sign of the usual hireling lurking about. The reference is to the unfortunate employee whom Daisy's nephew assigned to "keep an eye on the old lady." *Maybe he forgot.* Charlie had a lot on his mind lately, what with that silly Yazzi girl making off with Sarah's pickup and some guns. *That one's just as bad as her mother and I'd bet a shiny silver dollar to a wooden nickel that Nancy'll end up just like her. Dead and pulling an ugly little monkey around on a leash.* Daisy breathed a melancholy sigh. *It'd be just like Chiquita Yazzi to bring her wacky daughter along when she comes to pester me.* The shaman nodded to agree with herself. *Some night, I'll wake up and there they'll be—the both of 'em sitting on the foot of my bedstead, yapping their heads off about how all their troubles are my fault and why don't I go and do this and that to get things straightened out.* She ground her teeth. *Why can't dead people just let me alone?*

The old woman felt two pairs of eyes staring at the back of her head. Daisy turned to discover Sarah Frank and the spotted cat gazing at her. The Ute-Papago orphan was clutching Mr. Zig-Zag to her neck. "I wonder when Charlie will be back." She rubbed her chin on cat fur. "I wish he'd asked us if we wanted to go with him."

Daisy snorted at such a silly notion. "Men don't think about things like that—not a one of them." She banged her oak staff on the floor. "When they get ready to take off somewhere and have a good time, they just get up and go—and leave the women behind to cook and clean and wash their dirty clothes!" Neither Daisy nor Sarah was expected to do any chore at the Columbine, but never mind. This impromptu lecture on the war between the sexes had nothing to do with facts. Daisy leaned on her staff and pointed a crooked finger at the girl. "And I know what I'm talking about—I've had me three husbands and not one of 'em who'd take me to town to get a hamburger or see a picture show unless I threw a fit!"

The sixteen-year-old's eyes filled with tears. "Charlie's not like that."

"Oh he's not, ain't he?" Daisy jerked a thumb over her shoulder. "Then why's he gone and left you and me behind to mope around this big house?"

Sarah had no answer to that. A salty tear dripped off her face, onto the cat's ear, which flicked.

Daisy muttered under her breath, "One thing you have to say for Nancy, when she decided it was time to go, she didn't wait around for some man to take her—she stole some guns and a truck and hit the road." Seen from this perspective, the Yazzi girl's action seemed pardonable. Almost admirable. Daisy's wrinkled brow managed to furrow even deeper. *Which gives me an idea.* An impish smile curled her lips. "Sarah, something just come to me."

"What?"

Daisy told her.

Sarah could hardly believe her ears. "You want me to steal one of Charlie's pickups?"

This girl had too many principles, scruples—bothersome stuff like that. Daisy assumed a doubtful expression. "Did I say 'steal'?"

"Yes!"

"Well, imagine that. I guess it's because I'm getting old as Moses, but sometimes when I try for one word—out pops another one." Her hunched little frame shook with a chuckle. "What I meant to say was we could *borrow* one of Charlie's trucks and go for a ride into town."

Sarah thought it over.

Daisy patted her on the arm. "We'd be back long before Charlie gets home."

The girl shrugged. "I guess that'd be okay."

Daisy pointed toward the kitchen. "The spare truck keys are on a pegboard by the back door."

Sarah placed her cat on a leather couch, departed to select an ignition key.

The Ute elder smiled at the pliable child's skinny backside. *She could grow up to be just like me.*

◆　◆　◆

THE TRUCK started right up and they pulled away from the Columbine headquarters without incident. Things seemed to be going their way, which is to say that no startled cowboy assigned to guard duty came running after them yelling, *Hey—where do you two think you're goin'!* As they proceeded along the miles of dirt lane toward the paved highway, there was not the slightest indication that the same irate cowboy had cranked up his assigned motor vehicle and was following them.

But he had. And was.

After they passed through the ranch gate and Sarah made a left to aim the vehicle toward Granite Creek, the road in front of them was clear of traffic as far as the eye could see. Both driver and passenger believed that they were in for clear sailing.

What Sarah had in mind was a quick trip into town, then back to the Columbine hours before sundown. Charlie Moon would be none the wiser.

Escapades of almost any sort are considerable morale boosters for teenagers with the blues, and *getting away with something* that feels just a little bit dangerous is great fun, so Sarah was feeling pretty good for the first time since that other teenager had heisted her pickup truck. Sad to say, the innocent lass did not realize that she had fallen under a Dark Influence.

Ever so pleased with herself, Daisy Perika began to flesh out her plot for finding Hermann Wetzel's money.

# CHAPTER THIRTY-SEVEN

## ON THE ROAD AGAIN

AFTER STOPPING AT A BAKERY IN SALIDA TO PURCHASE A BROWN paper bag of breakfast, Charlie Moon and Scott Parris were rolling east on Route 50 toward Cañon City.

Accustomed to doing the driving himself, Moon was enjoying this rare time in the passenger seat. He held a steaming cup of sugary black coffee in his left hand, a warm-from-the-oven thickly glazed apple fritter in the other. The satisfied diner paused between a slurp and a chomp to cast a glance at the driver. "So what's the latest on Nancy and her boyfriend?"

"Telephone tap hasn't picked up anything since their conversation about meeting in some restaurant. Pueblo PD are making all the usual checks, but it's not likely Nancy's still in town." Parris slowed as a lame old dog limped across the road. "There've been reports of one or the other of 'em all over Colorado. And there've been sightings in Arizona, Wyoming, Kansas, Utah, New Mexico, and Michigan."

"Michigan?"

"Why not?" Parris shrugged. "Those two could be in Alaska by now."

Moon emptied the Styrofoam cup.

A magpie who had been dining on feathered roadkill took flight. It may have been this small incident that reminded the driver of something unpleasant.

Except for the hum of new tires, a mile passed in silence. Then another.

Finally, Parris steeled himself and said, "Charlie, I need to talk to you about something that's, well—personal."

"Pardner, if you don't mind—I'd rather not hear about stuff like that."

"Like what?"

"Intimate stuff you should only discuss with your family physician."

Parris set the formidable jaw that his girlfriend (an anthropologist) considered "quasi-Neanderthal." It took some time for the caveman to get up sufficient courage to make the admission. "I'm worried that my mind is going soft."

Moon choked on a chunk of pastry.

Parris gripped the steering wheel. "Last night, I dreamed that I was a chicken farmer in Florida." For specificity, he added, "Key West."

"Sounds like a fine way to while away your declining years."

Parris shook his head. "It was extremely weird—I was raising genetically modified Rhode Island Reds." Reliving the nightmare, Parris shuddered. "Those Reds all had two heads. And four legs."

Moon mulled this over. "I don't know that there's much of a market for chicken heads in Florida—unless it'd be in the Haitian voodoo trade. But you'd have the drumstick market cornered in no time flat."

Parris was not amused. "When I woke up in the middle of that dream, for a few seconds I laid there flat on my back, trying to remember—do chickens have four legs; or only two?"

"Well don't leave me in suspense—which was it?"

"This ain't funny, Charlie."

"Sorry, pard." *Now he'll come up with some way to get even.*

A mile down the road, the town cop said, "Oh, by the way—have you managed to patch things up with your lady friend?"

Caught off guard, Moon took this one square on the chin. "Patch what things up?"

"How would I know?" Parris was feeling much better. "But word is, she's pretty ticked off at you over something or other."

"Is that a fact?"

The rumormonger nodded. "From what I hear—not long after you left her standing in the Silver Mountain lobby, Special Agent McTeague checked out of the hotel. Headed straight for the airport."

Charlie Moon forced a smile. "That's what Lila Mae did all right. And she had a good reason to leave town that night." *I wish I knew what it was.*

The driver nodded. "Bureau business, I expect." The cop glanced at his passenger. "Then you two ain't on the outs—you're still talking to each other?"

"I called her last night." *Twice. Got her answering machine both times.* He had not left a message.

This exchange was interrupted by the buzz of Moon's cell phone. He checked the caller ID. "What's up, Butch?"

Little Butch Cassidy's voice boomed in his ear: "Thought you ought to know, boss—your aunt and the girl left the Columbine a while ago. The kid drove off in one of your pickups."

"Where are they now?"

"Headed toward Granite Creek. I'm about a half mile back, so they don't know they've got a tail." Cassidy was not your typical Columbine employee—the former museum curator had several university degrees and an intellect to match. But he had given up everything to fulfill his childhood ambition, which was to become a sure-enough cowboy. During his several semesters at the Columbine Cowboy School, Butch had cleaned horse stables, ridden a sullen little mare to check and mend fences, cleared brush with the Farmall tractor and Bush Hog, assisted pregnant Herefords during troublesome deliveries, injected frisky calves with antibiotics, and generally surprised his skeptical comrades by passing with a B-plus average. Now he was playing at private eye. What a life.

"Thanks for the heads-up." Moon had lost interest in his sugary breakfast. "Keep a close eye on 'em."

As the Ute pocketed the telephone, Parris inquired, "Problem?"

"It's Butch's turn to look after Aunt Daisy."

"So what's she up to this time?"

"That's what I'd like to know."

"Hey, how much trouble could a tired old woman cause?" After letting that hang in the air, the chief of police added with a smirk, "Things get really nasty, the governor could declare martial law."

❖ ❖ ❖

AS THE borrowed Columbine pickup chugged along toward Granite Creek, Daisy Perika had developed a distinctly uneasy sensation that something was wrong. She could not see anything worrisome in the door-mounted mirror—just the big Mayflower van that had followed them for the past few miles. But this seasoned veteran of countless conflicts had developed a habit of acting on her instincts. If Daisy had been trudging along a deer path in Cañón del Espíritu, she would have stepped into a cluster of the willows by the stream and waited to see if another creature was soft-footing it along behind her. Perhaps an old cougar who figured that the elderly Ute was easier pickings than a swift-footed mule deer. She reached over to touch the youthful driver's elbow. "Turn in at that big truck stop down there on the right."

Sarah slowed to make the turn. *I bet she needs to go to the bathroom.*

Daisy pointed. "Go around back, where all those big trucks are."

As they bumped across the graveled parking lot, Sarah noticed that the fuel gauge was reading a tad below the quarter-tank mark. Which provided the brand-new driver with an opportunity for another first. "I'd better put some gas in the tank."

"Not right now." Daisy pointed at an eighteen-wheeler loaded with irrigation pipe. "Pull up behind that big red truck."

Sarah shot a worried look at the tribal elder. Aunt Daisy had no qualms about relieving herself wherever it was convenient. *Oh my—I hope she doesn't intend to go* outside. "Uh—are you feeling okay?"

"I'm fine as frog hair—now shut the engine off."

Sarah watched the enigmatic woman—purse hanging from the crook of her left arm, oak staff in her right hand—grunt and groan her way out of the pickup. Her worst fears seemed justified when Daisy went to peer around the cab of the huge semi, as if to confirm that no one was likely to invade her privacy. The mortified girl prayed, *Oh please, God. Please don't let her pee right here in the parking lot where somebody might see her. Please please please!*

Teenagers are a sensitive lot.

Sarah's apprehension was transformed to relief when Daisy toddled off toward Hoke's Truck Stop. The grateful youth tagged along, hands clasped under her chin. *Thank you thank you thank you!*

The successful roadside business was housed in a one-acre-square, steel-paneled building with a multitude of large windows and double doors on all sides. In addition to twenty-one fuel-pump stations (a dozen out front, nine behind), Hoke's various departments provided almost everything a tourist might need or desire, including jackalope picture postcards, road maps for all fifty states plus Mexico and Canada, a line of high-quality automotive supplies, sundry over-the-counter medications, a two-chair barbershop where Mrs. Hoke and her brother-in-law wielded old-fashioned shears and electric clippers with frightful enthusiasm, a convenience store stocked with essential groceries and a thirty-foot magazine rack, and, best of all—the old-time café that dished out Hoke's Famous Oklahoma Barbecue. The mouthwatering chopped-brisket sandwiches attracted gourmands from neighboring states. Not only that, the spacious restrooms were clean and functional.

As they entered the rear door, Sarah Frank caught a delicious scent from the restaurant kitchen.

Daisy Perika headed across the convenience store to a fly-specked window that faced the highway. The wary old woman peered through the glass, looking for she knew not what. She observed traffic going this way and that, lots of people pumping gas and wiping at dusty windshields with squares of blue paper, but she saw nothing that looked the least bit suspicious. *Well, if there was somebody following us, he ain't there now.* If she had gotten to the window a mere six seconds earlier, Daisy would have seen Butch's Columbine pickup pass by on the highway, and the sight would have caused her to gnash the aged bicuspids and feel the bile rising in her throat. As it was, she felt a tug on her sleeve, and turned to see Sarah's hopeful expression.

"Could we please go into the restaurant and get something to eat?"

"We just finished breakfast a while ago." Daisy lifted her nose, took a sniff. *But that barbecue does smell good.*

◆  ◆  ◆

ABOUT A mile beyond Hoke's, Butch passed the Mayflower van and was puzzled by what he saw in front of him. Aside from miles of empty straight-as-an-arrow two-lane—not a thing. *That little Indian girl drives slow as sap running down a cedar stump* [this was dandy cowboy talk he had picked up], *so I don't see how she could have got out of sight so fast.* Which raised the question: *What is going on here?* The answer came in a flash. He braked, did a neck-jerking U-turn, and headed for that truck stop where he frequently enjoyed the famous barbecue sandwiches.

By the time Butch had backtracked his way back to Hoke's and parked his pickup by one of the out-front gas pumps, Daisy and Sarah were seated in a booth, chowing down on today's lunch special. He spotted them as soon as he was inside the front door, and spied on the pair from behind a postcard carousel until a suspicious clerk inquired whether there was something she could do for him. Butch blushed, mumbled something unintelligible, and retreated to his pickup, where he could keep an eye on Daisy and the girl through the café window. To help while away the time, he filled the gas tank, checked the oil level on the dipstick, and measured the air pressure in the tires, adding or subtracting a couple of pounds per square inch as required. Butch also used up considerable time wiping at the pickup windows. All except the rear window, which was difficult to reach and hard to see through because of a thick layer of Columbine dust. Are any of these details significant? We shall see.

◆  ◆  ◆

BY THE time Daisy and Sarah were finishing their tasty lunch, they were feeling pretty good. And why not? The food was delicious, they had a comfortable booth with a vase of plastic flowers on the table, and they were blessed with neighboring diners who did not talk loudly, belch, or remove earwax with toothpicks. The nice young couple behind Sarah were holding hands and whispering. The heavyset man

seated back-to-back with Daisy was alone. He was also bald as a bil-
liard ball, clean shaven, and wore pink-tinted sunglasses.

Having had enough escapade for one day, Miss Frank was becoming
concerned that Charlie Moon might get back to the ranch headquarters
early and find out that she had borrowed a pickup. "Maybe we ought
to go back to the Columbine now."

The frugal diner wrapped the remainder of her brisket sandwich in
a paper napkin, shook her gray head. "Not yet."

Sarah slurped the last of her Coke thorough a straw, then: "You still
want to go into town?"

"Sure." Daisy put the half sandwich into her purse, snapped it shut.

"To the supermarket?"

"Nope." Before the chatterbox could ask, *Where, then?* Daisy
told her.

Sarah stared wide-eyed at her peculiar companion. "Why would we
want to go to see Mr. Wetzel's landlady?"

Daisy did not respond immediately. *I still feel like someone's watching me.* After glancing this way and that, she said, "I'd like to take a
look inside the house where Hermann Wetzel got shot."

"What for?"

The aged woman presented a smug expression. "That's for me to
know and you to find out."

◆ ◆ ◆

FROM THE very moment when Sarah Frank had mentioned the
Columbine, their conversation had attracted the attention of the lone
diner seated back-to-back with Daisy Perika—the heavyset, bald-as-
a-billiard-ball, clean-shaven fellow who was wearing pink-tinted sunglasses. Once upon a time and not so long ago (about six hours or so),
he'd had a goodly supply of hair on his head, a manly beard on his
chin. That's right. Jake Harper, ever since his return to the rich man's
summer home above Granite Creek, had been hankering for someone
else's cooking, which had tempted him out of hiding for a Hoke's

Famous Barbecue brisket sandwich and a Daddy-Bear Bowl of Hoke's (infamous) Firehouse Chili, which is reputed to burn holes through Hoke's Tennessee Forge iron cook-pots, but that's a crock—or at the very least a slight exaggeration.

Whatever the case may be, a hungry man sometimes does foolish things, and on top of exposing his digestive tract to a helping of gastric dynamite, our daring diner was close enough to Charlie Moon's volatile aunt to lean back and nibble on her ear, which would have annoyed the old woman quite a lot and then some.

The fugitive was startled by the snatches of conversation he had picked up, which raised such issues as: *Who 'n hell are these people? What connection do they have with the Columbine Ranch? Why does the old lady want to get into Hermann's house?* Provocative questions without satisfying answers tend to ruin even the most healthy appetite.

Harper wolfed his food down, paid the bill, and withdrew to the magazine rack, where, peering from behind a copy of *Motorcycle Mommas*, he eyeballed Daisy and Sarah. *The old woman looks like a real weirdo. She probably read about the shooting in the newspaper and wants to go snooping around where somebody got killed.* Which was no big problem. *Not unless she knows more than she's letting on. I'd rather wait till after dark, but maybe I'd better get over to Hermann's house right now and grab his money while the grabbing's good.* But, though he was eager to hit the road, there was something about the elderly woman that made him feel uneasy. *I'll hang around for a minute or two and see what they do.*

Daisy, who felt a sudden (and urgent!) demand from her bladder, pushed a few dollars across the table to Sarah. "Go pay for the food."

The girl stared at the greenbacks. "Can I have some money for gas?"

*Kids these days must think a person is made of money.* Daisy, who still lived in that era when gasoline cost twenty-seven cents a gallon, slapped a five in Sarah's hand.

"Uh—that won't pay for very much—"

"Well that's all you're going to get from me." Daisy hobbled off to the ladies' facility, shouting over her shoulder, "I'll meet you out back by the gas pump."

As it happened, the heavyset, bald, beardless man in the pink shades who lingered at the magazine rack was directly between Daisy and the restroom, and though he had intended to keep an eye on the elderly woman and the girl, Jake Harper's attention had been distracted by the centerfold, which featured a motorcycle momma from Memphis who was of no mean proportions. Which was why he did not see Daisy coming. He did feel the prod of her oak staff on his shin, and hear her bark, "Hey, Onion Head—get outta my way!"

He did, and in a big hurry.

As she passed, in a voice loud enough for Harper and a dozen other customers to hear, Daisy offered this observation: "You ought to be ashamed of yourself, looking at that trash!"

Enough was enough. His freshly shaved head now as pink as his shades, Jake Harper put the current copy of *Motorcycle Mommas* back on the rack, turned his back on the belligerent senior citizen, and headed for the parking lot.

As Harper stomped out the front door, he almost collided with Butch Cassidy, who was coming in. Daisy Perika's appointed guardian had been temporarily distracted for a minute or so by a nice-looking lady in a classic red 1967 Mustang who had engaged him in a conversation about pressing issues such as the high price of gasoline, the nice weather they were having, and whether or not he was married. When he'd happened to glance at the restaurant window, Butch had been startled to see the empty space in the booth where Daisy and Sarah had been only a minute earlier. Or had it been ten minutes? Time passes so quickly during conversations with attractive ladies. Thinking it likely that Daisy and her young companion were already on the road, he had cranked up his pickup. But just on the off chance that they might still be inside Hoke's cavernous building, he hurried in for a quick look-see. But just in case his quarry attempted a quick getaway, Butch had *left his engine running.* It was the wrong thing to do. There were signs on every gas pump warning motorists against this dangerous practice.

As Butch strode into the restaurant, Daisy was in the ladies' room and Sarah was outside, headed for the far end of the rear parking area, where her borrowed Columbine pickup was concealed behind the eighteen-wheeler.

Which was why Butch found neither hide nor hair of either female, and headed out the back door.

Sarah eased her truck up to a vacant gas pump, checked out the prices. *I wonder what "octane" means.* She opted for the least expensive option.

Butch's progress was impeded by the clutter of every sort of motor vehicle imaginable. In addition to the usual assortment of big, brawny diesel rigs and glistening hundred-thousand-dollar RV motor homes, the lot was beginning to fill with dozens of old, rusty, battered pickups. Remembering what day it was, Butch understood. On Tuesdays, Hoke's take-out lunch special was a brisket sandwich with two sides of your choice and a fizzy fountain soft drink—all for the amazing low price of $5.98. It took him a little while to spot Sarah putting gas into the other Columbine pickup. When he did, the situation raised a thorny issue: What should a rookie gumshoe do when he found what he'd been looking for? March right up to the kid who was like a daughter to Charlie Moon and say something like, *Well, what are you two doing here with a Columbine vehicle?* Butch decided to call the boss and ask for instructions.

◆ ◆ ◆

A FEW miles east of Cañon City, Moon's cell phone buzzed. "Tell me some good news, Butch."

"I located your aunt and the kid, boss—they're at Hoke's. The girl's gassing up the pickup."

"Good work. Keep an eye on 'em."

"Will do." *And they won't get out of my sight again.*

◆ ◆ ◆

SCOTT PARRIS grinned at his stern-faced Indian friend. "Daisy and the kid creating havoc in Granite Creek?"

"Not yet. They made a stop at Hoke's."

"Today's when they have the special on that brisket-sandwich lunch."

Moon nodded. "Daisy must've got a yen for some barbecue." *I was worried over nothing.*

# CHAPTER THIRTY-EIGHT

## AN UNDERSTANDABLE ERROR

AFTER USING THE FACILITIES, DAISY PERIKA EMERGED AND AIMED her nose at the exit, where a thoughtful Mormon gentleman from Provo, Utah tipped his wide-brimmed hat, smiled, and held the door open for her. Isn't that nice? Not entirely.

The elderly woman, who tended to get confused in places she was not intimately familiar with, had not aimed her nose at the *rear* door. No. Daisy exited on the highway side of Hoke's commercial establishment. She might have noticed her mistake if she could have seen the passing traffic, but her view of the road was blocked by a big truck hauling enough baled alfalfa to feed all the Columbine stock for a full day, and that is a lot of hay. The error was compounded when Daisy spotted Butch's Columbine pickup (they all had the blue-and-white official state flower on both doors), which was where she expected it to be—i.e., parked at one of the gas pumps. The misdirected woman naturally assumed that this was the vehicle that she and Sarah had arrived in.

As Daisy got into the cab with the aid of her trusty walking stick, she wondered where the girl had gone to. *Probably off looking for me. Well, I'll just sit here till she comes back.* Had she been the observant type, Daisy might have noticed a few things that were different in this pickup, such as the copy of Kenoyer's *Ancient Cities of the Indus Valley Civilization* on the dashboard, Butch's sunglasses hanging from the sun visor, and the fact that the key in the ignition was mounted on a sterling silver ring from which dangled an eighteenth-dynasty Egyptian glazed steatite scarab.

It was not as if Daisy were sleepwalking. She did notice that the engine was throbbing. *Isn't that just like a teenager, going off leaving the motor running?* Precious fuel was being wasted. *I'd better shut it off.* She could have reached over from the passenger side and twisted the ignition key, but Daisy decided to perform the operation from behind the wheel. Scooting across the bench seat, she got her hands on the steering wheel and was thrilled by a sudden joy of recollection as her feet touched the pedals.

What did she remember? A prior escapade.

About three or four years ago—but it seemed like only last month—Daisy had piloted Louise-Marie LaForte's 1950s-era Oldsmobile along this same road from the Columbine to Granite Creek, and quite a distance beyond. That had been quite a fine adventure, despite the fact that she had come *this close* to getting into really serious trouble. *If I could, I'd do it all over again.* As the sweet memories flooded over her, the tribal elder tapped the accelerator, was delighted to hear the engine pick up rpm's. She also jigged the steering wheel back and forth, all the while smiling like a happy child. Tiring of accelerator tapping and steering-wheel jiggling, she put her right hand on the gear shift and gazed at the letters and numbers: P R N D 2 1 She tried to remember what these indicators meant. Fragments of what she had learned from driving Louise-Marie's venerable Oldsmobile began to come back to her. *P is for park. D is for drive.* R and N remained unfathomable mysteries, and the numbers made no sense at all. But after all, how to park and drive was all a person really needed to know. *Making a car go isn't hard, not unless it has a clutch.* Her confidence surged. *If I was of a mind to, I bet I could drive this old truck all the way from here to . . .* She tried to think of a suitable destination. And did.

No. We must not leap to conclusions.

Daisy had no intention of driving the pickup anywhere. Why should she, when Sarah Frank would do the driving for her? What happened next, as Daisy would tell you herself, was not her fault. It was that "loudmouthed yahoo" who was to blame.

At about this time, the designated scapegoat was approaching the pickup. From behind. Which was why Daisy, lost in her pleasant remembrance of past acts of madcap violence and general mayhem, did not see Charlie Moon's employee coming.

Which was also why Butch Cassidy saw only the indistinct outline of someone's head through the dirty rear window of the cab. *Who the hell is in my pickup?* This was a reasonable question to pose, and he might have marched up to the driver's door and made a polite inquiry, but this namesake of that famous member of the Hole-in-the-Wall Gang was all hot under the collar and wanted to know *right now,* which was why, when he was within about a yard of the tailgate, Butch yelled, "Hey, you—what d'you think you're doing!"

For a man of his modest proportions, he had a loud voice. A more apt nickname for the cowboy might have been Foghorn Cassidy.

Which was why Daisy was severely startled. Startled folks do unpredictable things, like gasp and grasp on tightly to whatever they happen to have in their hand, such as an F-150 gear shift—and in this instance *tug on it.* As it happened, she only pulled the shift one notch down from P. Ask any guru you happen to run into and that authority will tell you that *illumination* can come oh so slowly, or it can be an incandescent experience conferred in an instant, which is precisely how long it took our elderly student driver to learn what R meant.

How long did it take for Butch to become aware of his precarious predicament? Less than a heartbeat. As the instrument of his destruction lurched toward him, the cowboy made a grab for the ground and yelled loudly enough to attract the attention of several bystanders.

Realizing her error, Daisy pulled the gearshift all the way down. She did this while putting her foot on the accelerator instead of the brake, which caused the rear wheels to spin and toss an impressive arc of gravel. The pickup lurched away in the forward direction, at which point (we know not why—angry men do inexplicable things) Butch reached up and grabbed hold of the bumper. This was an ill-advised decision.

Daisy had temporarily forgotten the concept of what brakes are for or where to find the right pedal to push, which was the one just to the left of the accelerator. Off she went like a shot, not realizing that the "loud-mouthed yahoo" was attached to the pickup by eight fingers and an iron will that boggles the mind and excites considerable admiration.

As she swerved to avoid a large woman carrying away eight of today's lunch specials, Daisy barely missed clipping the fender of a shiny

Mercedes, ditto of a brand-new Toyota pickup. She did demolish the last working telephone booth in the county (empty because the tourist who was talking to his stockbroker had seen the truck coming and made a mad dash for safety). The pickup romped its merry way across the prairie, making hash of sage and mesquite alike, and leaped over a shallow ditch and onto the paved road, at which point Daisy—steering along the center line—was a woman with but a single thought: *I'm not stoppin' for nothing.*

And she didn't. Not even the big Mac truck hauling a load of feathery livestock. Daisy was not fazed by the truck's lights flashing, its horn blaring, the wild-eyed driver cursing up a storm and shaking his fist. A heartbeat before a head-on collision, the professional truck driver went for the ditch, spilling several crates of excited turkeys. Those fowls who were able to escape went dashing helter-skelter over the landscape.

About a mile down the road, very near the spot where Butch had made his U-turn, Daisy let out the breath she had been holding. By the time another half mile had passed, her abdominal organs had stopped churning out pints of bile and acid, and the aged heart had slowed to a mere ninety-eight beats per minute. She consulted the rearview mirror. *Nobody's chasing after me.* She inhaled deeply. *That didn't turn out so bad.*

Butch? Despite his best intentions, the gutsy fellow was no longer attached to the rear bumper by his digits. Our cowboy hero had been tossed aside when Daisy took out the antique telephone booth. And speaking of Daisy . . .

It occurred to her that Sarah was still at the truck stop. *Tough cookies. I ain't going back there.* The Ute-Papago orphan was sixteen years old now and could take care of herself. When Daisy was younger than that she had gotten married to a fellow twice her age, and just four months later she'd ridden a big bay mare to Cortez and back, killed a man, and— No. Don't ask. Daisy hardly ever talks about that. But when she does, she insists that the Apache rascal *had it coming.*

In all the excitement, Daisy had forgotten about her important mission. But, like P and D, it began to come back to her.

*Let me see. Beechwood Road is the third stoplight, which is by the Walgreens. And I'll have to make a right turn.*

Which she did, but by then the road was four lanes and Daisy turned right from the left lane, directly in front of a FedEx van. Yes, driven by the very man whose windshield had been pitted by shotgun pellets fired by Nancy Yazzi as he'd passed by Hamlet's Cowboy Saloon.

As the stalwart fellow jammed on the brakes, his heart did not miss a beat. Neither did he bat an eye. All in a day's work.

How cool is *that*?

# CHAPTER THIRTY-NINE

## STUPEFIED

THAT IS WHAT SARAH FRANK WAS. ALSO SPEECHLESS. BUT LET US back up a minute.

The girl, who had put a gallon and a half of gas into the borrowed pickup, went looking for Aunt Daisy in the ladies' room and emerged from that facility to hear a big commotion out front. She got to the door just in time to see the tribal elder back the pickup over the cowboy who was bellowing like an angry bull, and watched in stunned disbelief as the crusty old woman—apparently believing she'd done him in—roared away with her victim clinging to the rear bumper. Sarah watched in gaped-mouth horror as Butch was tossed aside like a used-up rag doll, screamed and wrung her hands when Daisy totaled the telephone booth and went bumpity-bumping across the prairie in a cloud of yellow dust. Sarah watched in awe as Butch got to his feet. "Oh-oh!" she yelped, and clapped her hands.

Having no idea that the Indian girl he'd been tailing had witnessed his humiliating ordeal (or that Daisy Perika was responsible for it!), the tough little fellow ignored the inquiries of sympathetic onlookers. In the best tradition of tough-as-boot-leather rodeo cowboys, he brushed himself off and walked away. All without uttering a word. Despite the fact that his body was screaming with pain. What a man.

◆ ◆ ◆

WHAT ABOUT Sarah? Realizing that someone was going to have a heap of explaining to do, and having no plausible explanation for this bizarre event—even for Aunt Daisy, attempted vehicular homicide was somewhat over the top—the sensible girl opted for a tactical withdrawal, which took her through a throng of spectators to Hoke's rear exit, outside, and into the borrowed pickup. With a cunning stealth that her Ute and Papago ancestors would have been proud of, the girl wove a circuitous route among the multitude of vehicles. As soon as she managed to get onto the highway without being seen by the ill-treated cowboy, Sarah's single-minded objective was to catch up with Daisy Perika. She was, in a word, focused. What could have distracted the young lady from her duty—a sudden deluge of rain, wind-driven sleet? No. A blinding blizzard of snow, a low-flying UFO? Certainly not. How about the marvelous spectacle of a bewildered flock of escaped turkeys rushing about in search of who knows what? Not a chance. Our hardy pursuer of the runaway auntie glanced neither left nor right; neither did she slow. The silly birds strutting around on the highway were forced to flee and fly for their lives. What a girl.

◆ ◆ ◆

BUTCH SUMMED up the day's misfortunes: *First, I lose Daisy Perika and that little Indian girl. Then, some thieving bastard steals my pickup in broad daylight. But not before he tries to run me down! Well, it wasn't exactly* my *pickup. It belongs to Charlie Moon.* Recalling how the Yazzi girl had absconded with Sarah's shiny red birthday pickup, it occurred to him that truck stealing was getting to be a regular epidemic on the Columbine. *This keeps up for another couple of weeks, we'll be all out of motorized transportation.* Which raised a prickly issue: *How am I going to break the news to the boss?* The brow furrowed. Behind the formidable forehead, billions and billions of neurons and synapses generated astonishingly complex patterns of electrochemical impulses. Quite a lot of activity for the meager result: *I guess I could call Charlie up and say guess what, boss—while I was at Hoke's keeping an eye on your aunt and the girl, well—you won't believe this—but damned if some jackass didn't steal my Columbine pickup and try to run over me with it.* No, that wouldn't quite do it. Charlie Moon was known for his sense of humor, but the loss of prime stock or motor vehicles was not likely to get a chuckle. Butch's neurons and synapses had another go at it: *Somehow, I've got to get that truck back without the boss ever knowing it was gone.* Considering the fact that he was without transport and the murderous car thief had a good head start, this was a pretty tall assignment. But when there's a job that needs doing your sure-enough American cowboy *gets right at it.* Butch pulled his hat brim down, hitched up his britches, limped over to the highway, and stuck his thumb out.

A hopeless gesture?

The first automobile to pull out of Hoke's parking lot was an immaculately restored red 1967 Mustang convertible with the top down. It eased to a stop. The attractive lady behind the wheel, who had not witnessed the dazzling demonstration of Daisy Perika's ability to use a motor vehicle as a deadly weapon, gazed over her sunglasses at the sorry spectacle. "Look's like you've gotten bucked from the saddle and landed on a pile of rocks." She looked around. "Where's your pickup?"

Butch was not in the mood for small talk or explanations. The Columbine cowboy uttered something between a growl and a grumble.

The only phrase she managed to catch was "some trouble." Men of few words appealed to the lady. *He's cute as a spotted puppy.* "You need a lift into Granite Creek?"

The injured party nodded.

◆  ◆  ◆

ONE MIGHT reasonably assume that Sarah would have a small chance of catching up with Daisy. Such assumption would be a mistake, but a natural one considering the fact that we have failed to mention that the old woman, who still had not figured out the significance of the 2 and 1 on the gearshift indicator, drove all the way into town in "1." Even with the accelerator on the floorboard, running in low gear tends to severely limit a vehicle's forward velocity. Which is why that, by the time Daisy made her alarming turn in front of the FedEx van, Sarah was barely a block behind Charlie Moon's aunt. Cutting across the Walgreens parking lot, Sarah caught up with the aggressive motorist, and being too polite to honk the horn, she flashed the headlights.

Which was a good thing, because there's no telling what Daisy might have done had she heard another loud noise behind her. When she noticed the headlights in the rearview mirror going on and off, and the fact that the truck behind her looked a lot like the one she was driving, and . . . *That looks like Sarah behind the wheel!* By this time, Daisy had recalled the concept of braking, and was able to pull over to the curb in front of Jerry's Pawn Shop.

The excited girl ejected from the pickup like a jacqueline-in-the-box, and while running, waving her arms, and hyperventilating (Sarah was a multitasker), she shouted at Daisy, "What are you *doing*?"

The tribal elder considered this a peculiar query and the girl to be hysterical. She responded in a calm, reassuring tone, "I'm sitting here in this pickup truck."

"No, I mean"—hand-wringing—"there are turkeys all over the road—"

"I know. One of 'em tooted his horn at me."

"And back there at the barbecue place—" Sarah gasped, pointed, "You ran over that man—"

"Now that's silly talk." Daisy jutted her chin. "I didn't run over *nobody*."

Sarah banged her fist on the pickup door. "Yes you did!"

*Oh.* "Is he dead?"

"No. But he's—"

"If he's not dead, what's all the fuss about?"

More hand-wringing, plus some jumping up and down. "You drove away in his truck!"

*Oh, so that's what happened. I got into the wrong pickup. Well, I guess the joke's on me.* "Who'd I run over?"

"I don't know his name, but he's that cowboy with the icky tattoo on his head."

*Oh, him.* Daisy rolled her eyes. "That's Butch Cassidy." *I bet Charlie Moon told him to look after me.*

"Well he's *really* mad about you taking his truck!"

She was determined to pacify this silly girl. "Now calm down and listen to me. This old, beat-up old pickup—which is probably worth about thirty-five dollars—ain't that sawed-off cowboy's property. It belongs to my nephew." The very thought of Butch annoyed her. "The little sneak must've followed us all the way from the ranch." *He's a real pest.*

Sarah had ceased jumping and her hand-wringing was gradually diminishing in amplitude. She raised a pressing question: "What should we do now?"

*Kids nowadays don't know how to think for themselves—you have to tell them everything.* "We'll head on down this road till we find the house where Hermann Wetzel lived before he was dead. But we don't need both pickups, so I'll leave this one here and ride the rest of the way with you."

## OSCAR "BUD" YIRTY

BY WAY of a reminder, Mr. Yirty is that Columbine employee who enjoys harmless little pranks. Such as pulling chairs from under fellow employees who are about to sit in them, putting salt in the sugar bowl, and stashing wriggly serpents in his comrades' bunks—*and* convincing Lila Mae McTeague that Charlie Moon was such a cad as to go chasing other women the moment the lady he is practically engaged to looks the other way. Generally, this is not the sort of character who deserves much attention, but he should get what he does deserve, and at this very moment Mr. Yirty happens to be right on the well-known spot, which is to say that he is exiting Jerry's Pawn Shop, where he has just purchased an absolutely spiffy Morgan silver-dollar bolo tie. By a most fortuitous coincidence, this is also where Charlie Moon's aunt has abandoned Butch Cassidy's Columbine pickup at the curb.

Unlike Daisy, Yirty did not mistake this vehicle for the truck he drove to town in, a big flat-bed that is parked a block away in the Miner's Ball Park parking lot. But he did notice it. *That looks like the pickup Butch drives when he runs errands for the boss. Wonder what Half-Pint Cassidy's doin' in this part of town.*

Not the sort of man to approach anything directly, he sidled up to the old pickup, shot a sideways glance into the cab to make sure it was empty. Yirty, who had twenty-twenty vision, saw the key Daisy had left in the ignition and grinned like a Tennessee possum eating a ripe paw-paw. The reason why this particular opossum look-alike grinned was that he saw this apparent oversight on Butch's part as an opportunity to have some good, innocent fun. Slipping into the pickup and behind the steering wheel, he removed the key from the ignition, stared hard at the brassy implement as he considered how a clever fellow such as himself might gain maximum satisfaction from the prank.

*When Butch don't find the key in the ignition, he'll figger it must be in his pockets. When he don't find it there, he'll figger he must've lost it.* So far, so good. But what to do with the key? *I could put it in the ashtray—Butch don't smoke, so he'd never think of lookin' there. Or I could just take the key with me back to the ranch. Or I could toss it into a trash can.* Yirty sighed. *If I didn't have me so danged much imagination, this kinda stuff would sure be lots easier.* With so many excellent ideas, picking the best of the bunch certainly did strain a fellow's brain. Which tended to make the same fellow less aware of what was going on in the immediate vicinity. Such as the fact that a red, 1967 Mustang convertible with the top down had stopped about a block away, at the intersection, and a very angry Butch Cassidy had gotten out of the classic car and was approaching at a pretty good pace for a man who ached all over.

◆ ◆ ◆

THE COWBOY who had recently been the victim of a blatant hit-and-run was prepared to deal severely with the villain of the piece, whom he assumed to be a total stranger. *Probably some dumb, vacant-eyed punk with a cigarette dangling from his lips.* But when Butch got close enough to recognize Bud Yirty (whose dangerous pranks he had suffered on several occasions, including the time he woke up to find a viper wriggling in his undershirt), it is fair to say that that his temperature spiked. Mr. Cassidy, as the saying goes, had *blood in his eye.*

Which was why, though Yirty was twice Butch's size and a fair-to-middling barroom brawler, he was caught completely by surprise when the angry man jerked the truck door open and snatched the keys from his hand. Yirty had just enough time to grin and say, "Hello, half-pint— *urk!*"

No, Yirty had not invented a new word right on the spot. The *urk* was due to the fact that Butch had grabbed the hated prankster by his brand-new bolo tie, yanked him clean out of the pickup, kneed him hard in the crotch, applied a crisp uppercut to the hairy chin, punched the bulbous nose flat, and, when Yirty fell onto his face, proceeded to jump up and down on his back. Which, when the fellow doing the jumping is wearing cowboy boots with pointy heels, is no Sunday picnic for his victim.

The lady in the Mustang, a marriage counselor with a master's degree in sociology, had parked not far away. She observed the unprovoked attack in wide-eyed horror. Shocked is what she was. No, more than shocked: Her mental state might be fairly described as one of utter horror. *Oh—I have never seen such mindless violence—that seemingly gentle little cowboy is a beast, a veritable mad dog!* She felt strangely febrile (warm), giddy, and numb. All at the same time. *Oh— I think I'm falling in love.*

Now we understand more about the root cause of such events as schoolyard fistfights and world wars.

After Butch wore himself out, he dragged Yirty behind the rear wheels of the stolen pickup. His firm intention was to back over the offender. Four or five times, if necessary. *That'll teach him a lesson he won't forget.*

He was prevented from these homicidal plans by the sensible lady, who trotted up on her high heels to advise him that he had accomplished enough for one day. Would he care to accompany her to her motel, where there was a fine restaurant and bar?

Butch stared at the pretty woman for long enough to catch his breath and remember who she was. After a glare at what was left of Oscar "Bud" Yirty, he said, "Yes ma'am, I could use a bite to eat. And something to drink." *A tall glass of cold lemonade sure would hit the spot.*

Just as the battered prankster was regaining the first stirrings of consciousness, the lady pulled away in the Mustang, and the spunky little cowboy followed in his recovered Columbine pickup.

◆ ◆ ◆

YIRTY, WHO was certain that every bone in his body was broken, every joint dislocated, wondered what had happened. *Oooooh . . . I must've got run over by a freight train. Or maybe it was a stampede.* After he rolled over onto his back, and saw several faces looking down at him, it took the disoriented fellow quite some time to string a few thoughts together and recall the gist of what had happened. Like many of life's painful experiences, this one had been educational. As a result of today's lesson, he arrived at this conclusion: *I guess it ain't such a good idea to mess with Butch's truck keys.*

◆ ◆ ◆

BARELY THREE miles away, Daisy Perika was sitting placidly in the Columbine pickup that Sarah Frank was driving along Beechwood Road. The old woman was pleased that the nervous girl had finally settled down. *The trouble with young people these days is they get all excited over nothing.*

# CHAPTER FORTY

## HE RETURNS TO THE SCENE OF THE CRIME

AFTER DRIVING PAST THE LATE HERMANN WETZEL'S FORMER RESI-
dence three times and seeing no sign of the local police, Jake Harper
had deposited the stolen Escape two blocks away, in a church parking
lot. Now, crouched on a forested ridge behind the rental home, the burglar behind the pink shades grinned. *The place looks dead as Nancy's
nasty stepdaddy.*

After a stealthy approach, he used a pocketknife to slice through the
POLICE tape on the back door, which he then opened with the key that
Nancy had provided. Once inside the open doorway, Harper spliced
the severed tape with a transparent Scotch product he had purchased
for that very purpose. His intention, upon departing with a bag of cash,
was to crawl under the tape. If Confucius did not say this, it was an
oversight: In any enterprise, a successful outcome depends upon attention to details.

## HOUSE HUNTING

WHILE HARPER was making his unlawful entry, Sarah Frank was driving the borrowed Columbine pickup along Beechwood Road practically at a crawl, so that Daisy Perika could read the house numbers
painted on mailboxes.

"Seven thirty-seven." She muttered a few additional addresses. "It
must be coming' up pretty quick." Daisy uttered an expletive in her native language, which is untranslatable. "We must've passed it—there's
seven fifty-one."

"Seven fifty is right across the street." Sarah pulled to the curb and
turned off the engine. It was a serenely quiet neighborhood. She eyed

the house. *It's a pretty place. I wonder if Mr. Wetzel's ghost is haunting it.* She enjoyed a delicious little shiver. *If he is, I bet Aunt Daisy could see him. Maybe he's in one of those upstairs windows.* The shaman's apprentice knew very well that haunts prefer upper floors. *He could be looking down at us right now, wondering who we are and what we're doing here.* Sarah suddenly thought she saw the dead man's face between the curtains in a *downstairs* window. A blink of her eyes and the face was gone.

Sarah's follow-up shiver was anything but delicious.

A youthful fantasy? No.

◆ ◆ ◆

BEFORE HE got down to the serious business of plundering the murdered man's earthly treasure, Jake Harper, aka Onion Head, had gone from window to window, surveying the landscape for any sign of curious constables or nosy neighbors. The count in each instance was zero, but one item had piqued his interest—the pickup parked across the street, which was distinguished from other such vehicles by the blue-and-white Colorado state flower painted on the door. And just below the logo COLUMBINE RANCH. The skinny little girl from the restaurant was behind the wheel, which made it a cinch that the mean-mouthed old woman was with her. Harper was torn. *Should I grab the money and get out of here? Or should I keep an eye on these two until I know what they're up to?* Unable to make up his mind, the burglar would withdraw to Hermann's office for a moment, then—anxious about the prospect of unexpected visitors—he would hurry back to the front window.

## A FORTUITOUS ENCOUNTER

MILLICENT MUNTZ, who had seen the Columbine pickup from her parlor window, approached the passenger-side door. "Hello there."

Because the window adjacent to Daisy was closed, the occupants did not hear the greeting.

The resident of 751 Beechwood Road tapped on the glass.

The Ute elder lowered the window, growled at the paleface, "Who're you and whatta you want?"

Miss Muntz lifted her chin, the better to stare down her perfectly straight nose at this impertinent tourist. "I might well ask you the same."

"You might, but I asked you first—so who are you and what's on your mind, toots?"

Being addressed in this manner called for a stiff reply: "I am Millicent Muntz." She pointed over her shoulder at the dwelling partially concealed by dwarfish juniper and piñon. "I live here." The local resident sniffed. "Now perhaps you will identify yourselves and explain your presence in the neighborhood."

Daisy's scowl was transformed into a semisweet smile. "You must be Hermann Wetzel's landlady." *Just who I wanted to see.*

"Indeed I am." Miss M raised her chin another notch. "But if you do not identify yourselves, I shall be compelled to—"

The girl intervened. "Uh, ma'am—I'm Sarah Frank and this is Aunt Daisy. We just wanted to stop for a minute or two and look at Nancy's house."

The youngster's name seemed familiar. The landlady leaned to get a better look at the young person behind the steering wheel. "Are you one of Nancy Yazzi's young friends?"

Sarah hesitated, nibbled at her lip. "We *were* good friends—until she ran off with my pickup truck."

"My goodness—what a dreadful thing to do!" *And it doesn't sound a bit like Nancy.* "Perhaps she only borrowed it, dear—and intends to return it."

"Sure she does." Without losing the smile, Daisy snorted. "And I bet she'll probably bring it back loaded with groceries." She rubbed her hands together. "I hope she don't forget to pitch in a case of canned peaches."

Among Miss Muntz's few deficiencies was an occasional difficulty in recognizing sarcasm. "Well . . . though I suppose that cannot be entirely discounted, I rather imagine that a simple apology is more likely."

Daisy barely suppressed the urge to roll her eyes. *This white woman don't have enough sense to pour cider out of a boot. But among her people, she was probably the smartest of the lot.* "When you was younger and could hold down a job, I bet you was a schoolteacher."

Wide-eyed with astonishment, Miss Muntz reflected Daisy's counterfeit smile with what is commonly known as the real McCoy. "Well, that is quite a remarkable insight. I taught in the Denver public school system for almost forty years."

Daisy: *I knew it!*

Oblivious to the Indian woman's amusement, Miss Muntz continued. "My specialties were mathematics and music. After my retirement, I have continued to teach piano to a few gifted students." Unhappy memories pulled the smile off her face. *One should not dwell too much on days gone by.* Suddenly feeling lonely, Miss Muntz made a proposal: "Would you ladies like to come inside and visit? I could brew us a pot of tea. And I have some absolutely scrumptious oatmeal-raisin cookies that I made this morning."

"Cookies would be very nice." Sarah gave Charlie Moon's crotchety aunt a pleading look. Big eyes and all.

Though eager to conduct some shady business with Hermann Wetzel's landlady, Daisy grimaced. "I don't like tea. It gives me cramps."

Miss Muntz reached inside the cab to pat the crabby woman's shoulder. "What do you like to drink, dear?"

Flinching under the white woman's feather-light touch, Daisy shot back, "Rotgut whiskey laced with lye!"

"I shall call the local saloon and order up a quart."

Daisy looked up at the twinkling blue eyes. *Maybe she's not so bad as I thought.* "Could you boil a pot of coffee?"

"Blindfolded. With one hand firmly tied behind my back."

"At home, I don't make nothing but Folgers." Daisy's small black eyes twinkled wickedly back at the landlady. "But none of that sissy decaf stuff—I use the hundred-proof kind in the red can."

◆ ◆ ◆

ACROSS THE street, in the former Wetzel residence, Jake Harper's right eye peered between a pair of heavy drapes. *They're going into the land-lady's house. Now's my chance to get the job done.* He backed away from the curtain. Paused. *But maybe I better stay at the window for a few more minutes . . . just to make sure they don't come over here.*

Regarding the formerly decisive fellow, it is hard to say what the matter was. Being shot at with malice aforethought had no doubt taken its toll on Harper's psyche. Shaving off his curly hair and manly beard may also have been a factor in this crippling attack of uncertainty.

Unable to come to a decision, the burglar *dithered.*

A pitiful case.

# CHAPTER FORTY-ONE

## A PLEASANT LITTLE INTERLUDE

THE COFFEE WAS BLACK AND BITTER, WHICH SUITED DAISY PERIKA.

Sarah Frank had a ginger ale. Because she was "watching her figure," the skinny girl limited herself to two cookies. Then, two more.

After taking a dainty sip of green tea, Miss Muntz directed her guests' attention to an array of framed photos on the parlor wall. "Every one of my piano students is represented in this group. Most have children of their own by now." She yielded to a wistful sigh. "Two that I know of have . . . passed on." After a moment's melancholy reflection, she dismissed the distressing recollection, turned from the display of youthful faces to regard the Ute elder's wrinkled visage. "Would you like more coffee, dear?"

Daisy shook her head.

"A cookie, perhaps?"

"No, thanks." It was time to get down to business. The Ute woman fixed her gaze on the kindly old lady. "I don't expect Hermann's stepdaughter's likely to come back anytime soon." *If she does, she'll be slapped in jail for stealing Sarah's truck.* "And even if she did, it's not likely she could pay the rent on that big house across the street."

"No, I suppose not." Miss Muntz, whose mind had been occupied with so many pressing issues, had hardly given a thought to the future of her vacant rental property. "Once the police investigation is completed and they take down the yellow tape, I suppose I shall have to advertise it."

"So what'll you be asking?"

Miss Muntz blinked at the tribal elder. "Are you interested in the house?"

"Oh, I suppose I might be. If it suits me." The wily old bargainer gulped the last swallow of coffee. "And if the price was right."

"Well." *I don't know whether you are quite the sort of tenant I would be looking for.* "Do you live by yourself?"

Daisy nodded.

Sarah cleared her throat.

Daisy jerked her head to indicate her companion. "Except for her."

*The girl seems very sweet.* "Any pets?"

Sarah nodded. "I have a cat."

"Oh, that would not be a problem." *Cats create very little fuss.* Mr. Moriarty was a particularly easy pet to live with. "But you would have to keep your kitty inside at night. I would not want to hear it yowling about the neighborhood."

Daisy put her china cup on a marble-topped coffee table. "How about you show us the place."

"Oh, I don't think I could." The landlady pointed in an across-the-street direction. "The police have put up yards and yards of official tape, and there are stern signs on all the doors that warn—"

"That's just to keep nosy people from snooping around." Daisy grinned at the innocent. "They wouldn't mind if you was to show the place to somebody that might want to rent it."

Miss M put her teacup down, frowned. "I don't know. . . ."

The sly old Ute shot a poisoned arrow: "Who owns that house—the cops or you?"

The barbed projectile hit one of Miss Muntz's sore spots. Though brought up to be respectful of both civil law and civilized traditions, the prim little spinster resented being pushed around by the authorities. She also had a way of coming to snap decisions. "Very well." She got up from her armchair. "Shall we go have a look?"

◆ ◆ ◆

FINALLY DONE with his dithering, Jake Harper also made a snap decision. He abandoned the front window, hurried into Hermann Wetzel's office, got down on his knees, shone a penlight through the heating vent, and—*Wow!*

There it was, just like Nancy had said—a black leather pouch. The alluring object was hanging on a small nail, just inches away. As Harper commenced to lift the register, he was practically counting the green-backs—

But wait.

What is this—is the confounded thing stuck?

Not exactly.

*Damn! Hermann has fastened the register down with a dozen screws.* But that was not the worst news. These were not ordinary fasteners. *Oh, great. The jerk used tamper-proof screws.* The frustrated burglar put his face close to the problem, focused on one of the offending screw heads, and concluded that it was a Torx.

Useful information, to be sure. But what size?

*Looks like either a twenty-five or a twenty-seven. Either way, ol' Hermann must have the matching Torx bit somewhere in the house. But it won't likely be in a toolbox—the sneaky bastard probably hid it somewhere.* Harper considered his options. *I could come back later with the tools I need.* That would be the sensible course of action. *Or I might be able to find a crowbar or something to pry the register up, screws and all. But that would make a lot of noise and—*

The burglar heard the distinct *click* of the front door latch.

The squeaky *creak* of hinges.

The soft *thud* of the door closing

Faint voices in the hallway. Getting louder by the second.

In a flash, Jake Harper slipped into the office closet and closed the door.

# CHAPTER FORTY-TWO

## THE BURGLAR IS CORNERED

AND THEREFORE, EXTREMELY DANGEROUS. JAKE HARPER STOOD MOtionless among Hermann Wetzel's coats and sweaters, listened to the voices and footsteps come down the hallway, into the kitchen, and then—into the dead man's office. He held his breath.

## THE LANDLADY MAKES HER PITCH

BELIEVING IT better to deal with the lurid issue of murder right up front, Miss Muntz pointed at the open cellar door and the masking-tape outline the medical examiner had placed on the floor. "That is where I found the body." With a barely discernible hint of self-importance, she added, "I was on the scene only moments after the killer fled." She frowned at the dark-brown stains on the top steps and door sill. "I was too late to be of any help. Mr. Wetzel was quite dead."

Sarah Frank was barely able to suppress a fit of the cold shudders. *It must hurt awful to get shot with real bullets. I wonder what it's like to die . . . all by yourself.* Nancy's brutish stepfather must have experienced terrible pain and loneliness as he slipped away from this bright world of warm sunshine and sweet birdsongs to . . . to *what?* Aunt Daisy could have told her, but would the sensible sixteen-year-old have believed such a tale of ghostly monkeyshines?

During her long, difficult life, the Ute elder had encountered more corpses than she could count on both hands—including three husbands. This being the case, Daisy had little interest in the dwelling's recent history of violent death. What galvanized her mind was the dead man's alleged treasure trove of hard cash. But even though she was posing as a prospective tenant to conceal her money-hunting motives, the tribal elder was beginning to take her assumed role more seriously. *I wouldn't mind living in a nice place like this that was so close to town. If I was to get bad sick or fall down and break my hip, I'd be close to a hospital. And this place isn't all that far from the Columbine—Charlie Moon could stop by every day or two.* Her mouth curled into an avaricious grin. *And if I lived here I'd have all the time I needed to look for Hermann's money.* "Does this house have city water and sewer?"

Miss M nodded. "Oh yes."

"How about natural gas?"

"Indeed it does, which is quite a rare blessing in such a semirural setting. Only about a half mile farther out of town, everyone burns either wood or propane."

The comfort and peace of mind that such conveniences would provide made the Ute elder fairly prickle with envy. *When this old* matukach *woman has a problem, all she has to do is pick up the phone and call the county and they send somebody out to take care of it.* Which was not so at the yawning mouth of Cañon del Espíritu. *Just imagine, never having to worry about well pumps breaking or septic tanks backing up or the propane deliveryman not showing up because the snow's knee deep or the summer rains turned the road into muck that'd bog his truck up to the axles.* The calculating old soul did some adding and subtracting. *If I was to rent my place for a fair price, maybe I could afford to move into this one.* "Let's go have a look at the kitchen."

◆　◆　◆

BEING AN ordinary mortal with run-of-the-mill lung capacity, Jake Harper had not been holding his breath for this entire interlude. *What the hell—it's just two women and a girl.* But the burglar concealed in the closet was just beginning to be dimly aware of a more potent threat. Something evil was brewing here . . . he could feel it. Practically *taste it.*

◆　◆　◆

BARELY AWARE of the departure of Daisy and the landlady for the kitchen, Sarah Frank stood in the office, gawking at the bloodstains and the tape outline of the body. There was also a bullet hole in the wall, marked by a blue tape-on arrow and a yellow sticky note upon which someone had hand-printed:

#2. 9 mm (?)

*I wonder what that little sign means.* There was so much to wonder about in this mysterious life. *I wonder if Mr. Wetzel's ghost is still here and that's what I saw at the front window. I wonder if he can see me right now—*

An unseen Something passed by her face. A cold and *clammy* Something. And it smelled funny. Like an animal. Probably an effect of the girl's active imagination.

Sarah's blood ran cold; her teeth began to chatter. She wanted *more than anything* to run, but her shoes might have been nailed to the floor.

◆ ◆ ◆

JAKE HARPER could not see the girl from his dark concealment in the office closet. Nor could he hear Sarah Frank's rapid breaths. But he knew she was there. And the boxed-in burglar was beginning to experience what those spin doctors in the medical profession refer to as *discomfort.* Considerable discomfort. Compared to this, the dull throb in his left buttock was downright comfortable.

◆ ◆ ◆

DAISY WENT from one kitchen appliance to another, touching this, tapping on that, taking every opportunity to look doubtful. But, whatever she pretended to examine, *what was beneath her feet* continually occupied the old woman's attention.

Miss Muntz commenced to point out features that commended her property. "The refrigerator is less than a year old, and it has a wonderful ice maker."

"There's one of them things on my refrigerator," Daisy said. "It's been nothing but trouble."

"Really—what sort of trouble?"

"For one thing, it leaks." Daisy rubbed the small of her aching back. "My nephew's had to fix the water hookup two or three times. And it's noisy as a pig eating corncobs. Sometimes it wakes me up in the middle of the night."

Miss M's tone was firm. "This ice maker has never leaked a drop. And your sleep would certainly not be disturbed by the slight noise it makes—the bedrooms are located well away from the kitchen."

Daisy cast a suspicious gaze at the cooking stove. As if it might explode and incinerate them all.

Sensing an imminent complaint, the landlady launched a preemptive defense. "This gas range was installed just last month. Neither Mr. Wetzel nor his stepdaughter ever used the oven." Shaking her head to express disapproval, Miss Muntz confided, "I doubt that Nancy could bake a pan of biscuits if her life depended on it. Aside from warming up canned soups and such on the range, those two managed with just the microwave. Nancy and her stepfather preferred . . ." she could barely get the horrid phrase past her lips, "frozen dinners."

Daisy grunted as she bent to open the oven door. There was not the least blemish on the enamel. Not a stray crumb to be seen.

Considerably more flexible than her guest, Miss Muntz squatted beside Daisy. "Isn't that oven just as spotless as one you'd expect to see in a Sears and Roebuck showroom?"

The Ute elder, who had not heard anyone tack "Roebuck" onto "Sears" for at least thirty years, was pleased that someone besides herself remembered such significant historical lore. She might have agreed with the landlady, who had every right to talk up the place. But, being who she was, Daisy sniffed at the oven. Cocked her head just so. Frowned. "Oh, I expect they must've used it once or twice."

From Miss Muntz's slightly elevated eyebrow, one might have concluded that this response did not please her.

Daisy noticed this, and more. *This old white woman is awfully edgy about something or other. Something must be wrong with this kitchen. But what? One way or another, I'm going to find out.* The Ute elder's mind, which had a talent for conjuring up trouble, was beginning to froth and bubble. She played a hunch. "I think you know a lot more than you're telling me."

Miss Muntz's rosy little face blanched. "Why, what do you mean by that—I've been quite forthcoming about my rental property and I must say that I resent—"

The tribal elder raised a hand to silence the protest, assumed a stern "I already know" expression, which invites confession. "You'll feel a lot better if you get it off your chest."

The white woman stared at the inscrutable Indian for the longest time, then finally hung her head and said, "Yes. You are quite right."

*Hah! I knew it.* Daisy guessed that the dark secret would have something to do with bad plumbing.

The landlady held her a breath for a moment. Pursed her lips. Tapped her fingers on a granite-topped counter. "I suppose I should go to the police."

*Police?* Daisy blinked. *What is she babbling about?*

"Ever since the shooting, I have existed in a state of confusion." Miss Muntz raised her palms, stared at the ceiling. "I awaken in the morning, certain that I understand exactly what happened here. But by the time I go to bed, I wonder whether I really know anything at all. This whole business really has me quite beside myself!" She gazed at the shifty old Indian. "I'm just *bursting* to tell someone—a person I can trust."

Daisy assumed a brand-new expression, this one absolutely reeking of saintliness and wisdom. Imagine a combination of Mother Theresa and Abe Lincoln. "You can trust me."

Well.

"Yes, I believe I can." Miss M, bless her soul, had no idea whom she was talking to. In that manner that is so often described as *meaningful,* she glanced toward the adjacent room, where Sarah Frank tarries near the scene of the crime and Jake Harper fumes and fidgets in the closet. Mr. H fumes because he is annoyed at those three females who have interrupted his attempted burglary without so much as a by-your-leave. But why does the felon fidget? One would rather not say.

"Don't worry about the girl." Daisy took a firm grip on her walking stick. "I know how to get rid of her."

## IN HERMANN WETZEL'S OFFICE

JUST AS the woman with the sturdy oak staff advised Miss Muntz not to worry about the girl, Sarah's heels clicked. No, not together, as if she were attempting to transport herself from Oz back to Kansas. The heels made the clicking sounds as she walked across the hardwood floor.

◆　◆　◆

CLICKING SOUNDS on the floor that are getting closer and closer to his place of concealment are just the sort of noises that make a burglar concealed in a dark closet get a case of the clenched-teeth cringes. Which, when added to fumes and fidgets, tend to create considerable agitation. And this was not the best possible time to agitate Mr. Harper. As so often occurs with lowlife malefactors, a recent discretion had come back to haunt him. Or perhaps it would be more to the point to say that it had come *up* to *torment* him. What was the nature of this dreadful visitation? In a word, *gastronomic.*

The imprudent diner could feel the red-hot fire of Hoke's Firehouse Chili rising in his throat.

◆　◆　◆

AS IF drawn forward by some perverse magnetism, the half-frightened girl slowly approached the closet. As if by its own accord, her right hand reached out, the fingertips touched the white porcelain knob on the door, gave it just the slightest turn . . .

"Hey!"

Startled by this exclamation, Sarah turned to see Aunt Daisy, who was not alone. The prim little landlady was looking over the Ute elder's stooped shoulder.

◆ ◆ ◆

JAKE HARPER was also startled by the "Hey!" So much so that he al-most . . . But it is a delicate matter. And there are legal issues to be considered. Yes, burglars who are ill have a right to privacy. But here is a hint: Harper's distress is related to the potential projectile ejection of partially digested Firehouse Chili.

◆ ◆ ◆

DAISY SHOOK her walking stick at the embarrassed girl. "What're you doing?"

In response, the sixteen-year-old uttered one of those childish replies that sounds like a pack of bald-faced lies: "Um—I don't know—I mean . . . I'm not sure . . . um . . ." In this instance, it was the perfect truth right down to the final "um," but Sarah had no doubt that she was about to get a tongue-lashing for snooping around in the dead man's office.

Imagine the girl's surprise when Daisy gave her a twenty-dollar bill.

Sarah stared at what appeared to be a rather generous reward for unseemly behavior.

Like a kindly old granny, Daisy patted the girl's head. "Drive that old pickup over to the supermarket and buy us some ice cream."

"Oh, your needn't bother." Miss Muntz, who had already forgotten Daisy's promise to "get rid of the girl," beamed at Sarah. "I have some strawberry ice cream in my freezer."

"She don't like strawberry," Daisy snapped.

Sarah Frank responded with a bright-eyed, "Yes I do!"

"Well I don't." The Ute woman glared at the girl. "Strawberries give me the hives." Having made her point, Daisy switched on a wicked little grin. "Go buy us some butter pecan. Or peach. Or plain vanilla. But don't bring it here—we'll be across the street by the time you get back. Now scat!"

And that was that.

◆ ◆ ◆

EXCEPT THAT Jake Harper was hanging on every word. And praying that he would not vomit all over himself. Do not doubt it for a moment—when they're in a tough spot, burglars pray up a storm.

◆ ◆ ◆

A MOMENT after the girl had departed, Daisy addressed her host: "What's got you so worried?"

Millicent Muntz blinked owlishly at her guest. Licked her lips. Blinked again. "I hardly know where to begin." She braced herself. "I can tell you this—if I were to go to the police with what I know, it would—what do they say on those TV cops-and-robbers shows?" She tried to recall. "Oh, yes—it would blow this case wide open!"

Daisy cocked her head. "This fella who did the shooting—could you help the police put the cuffs on him?"

Miss Muntz cocked her head. "Yes. I believe I could."

◆ ◆ ◆

JAKE HARPER'S gut rumbled. The desperate man chewed on his lip, clenched his hands. *Oh, please. Not here. Not now.*

◆ ◆ ◆

HOPING TO be the exclusive co-owner of whatever juicy secret her new friend was about to share, Daisy wondered how closemouthed this white woman really was. "You haven't said a word about what you know to Scott Parris?"

"I suppose I should have. And perhaps I shall decide to do just that." Miss Muntz's arid sigh was like a dry breeze in the pines. "But the situation is rather complex."

The Ute woman suppressed a groan. With whites, everything was complicated. *Most of these* matukach *can't fry an egg without making plans the day before.* She opened her mouth to offer some helpful advice, when—

Sarah's face appeared in the doorway. "Is it okay if I get chocolate ripple?"

Daisy raised her sturdy oak walking stick in a menacing gesture. "If you don't get outta here right this minute and go to the store I'm gonna ripple *you*!"

The face vanished.

"Oh dear," Miss Muntz said, clasping a hand over her mouth. "I wonder how much she overheard."

"Kids are born sneaks," the Ute moral philosopher asserted. "You can't trust a one of 'em." *Especially when they're half Papago.*

The landlady waited until she heard the front door close, then addressed her confidante. "I suggest we retire across the street to my parlor."

Daisy agreed.

◆ ◆ ◆

JAKE HARPER clenched his fists. *Yes! Go across the street or to Oklahoma City or Doo wah diddy—just vamoose, so I can get outta this damn closet!* Of all the worldly treasures sought after by men, what he wanted most was a stiff dose of baking soda stirred (not shaken) in cold water.

◆ ◆ ◆

IT APPEARS that Hermann Wetzel's money bag will have to wait until another day, when his former earthly residence is not crawling with landladies, prospective tenants, and curious teenagers. On his next visit, Mr. Harper will undoubtedly come prepared with the proper tool kit, and one might expect that his preburglary meal on that occasion will consist of plain low-fat yogurt and a slice of white bread.

# CHAPTER FORTY-THREE

## THE PURLOINED PICKUP GOES HOME AGAIN

WAS CHARLIE MOON HAPPY? INDEED HE WAS. IT WAS A PLEASURE TO be behind the wheel of the recovered birthday truck, imagining how happy Sarah Frank would be. As Moon rolled serenely homeward, he conjured up images of the sixteen-year-old squealing, jumping up and down, squealing again, then turning cartwheels across the Columbine driveway. There were also several backflips. Such an imagination.

Scott Parris was locomoting gloomily along behind the Ute, trying not to think about malformed chickens. This impossible task was interrupted when the chief of police received a radio call from Officer Eddie "Rocks" Knox. He pressed the microphone against his chin. "What's up, Eddie?"

"Hemlines and hog bellies. Heh-heh!"

His teeth on edge, Parris tried again: "Why're you calling?"

Like other die-hard comedians, Eddie Knox was unfazed by those members of the audience who did not appreciate his art. "You'll never guess."

"So tell me!"

Knox was determined to drag this out. "You remember that ol' Muntz woman—Hermann Wetzel's landlady?"

Parris's stomach churned. *I hope this ain't bad news.* "Is she okay?"

"I'd say so. When Me 'n' Piggy spotted her a few minutes ago, she was moving along at a pretty lively clip."

"Then what's the problem?"

"Well, it had to do with her crossing the road." Knox loved to create little mysteries. "And *where* she was crossing it."

*What is he babbling about?* "So what's the charge—jaywalking?"

"Now, I'd a never thought of that." The jolly cop whistled. "I s'pose that's why you're the grand high mucky-muck and I'm just a flatfoot grunt."

The chief of police set the formidable jaw; his ominous silence roared at the insubordinate subordinate.

Knox was not intimidated, but he got the point. "The landlady was walking across Beechwood toward her house." Pause. "She was coming from the residence where Hermann Wetzel got shot to death, where we used about two hundred yards of pretty yellow tape to seal the premises off from curious civilians."

Parris groaned. "I hope she hadn't been inside."

"While you're at it, you might as well hope for thirty-cent-a-gallon gasoline." The wit chuckled at this snappy comeback, cleared his throat, and got back on track. "Me 'n' Piggy checked out the Wetzel residence, took a close look at all the doors and windows. Turns out that somebody—and we all know who *that* was—has messed with the tape on the front door."

Parris's roared "What?" boomed inside the black-and-white, and without waiting for a response to this vague query, he shouted into the microphone again, "Why didn't you and Slocum stop her?"

Knox, who knew how to set his boss up, assumed an injured tone. "Because when we spotted Miss Muntz, we'd just showed up."

"Oh."

The constable on patrol was enjoying every word of this conversation. "You'd never guess who was with the landlady when she crossed the street."

"Right again." Parris's tone was deadly cold. "But you're going to tell me in two seconds flat."

"It was that wacky old Indian woman—Charlie Moon's aunt."

Parris murmured to himself, "Daisy Perika?"

"Far as I know, Daisy's the only wacky old aunt Charlie's got. And her and the landlady was real chummy with one another. Matter a fact, Daisy's in Miss Muntz's house right now, and I bet that them two old hens are cacklin' up a storm and hatching a batch of trouble."

Parris cringed at the feathery reference. It occurred to his troubled mind that between them, Daisy and Miss Muntz had four legs and two heads. Had the chicken-farmer dream been a dark omen?

Knox assumed a blatantly phony apologetic tone. "Normally, I wouldn't bother a busy man such as yourself with a piddlin' little matter like this—me and Piggy would take care of it ourselves. But seeing as how you and Charlie are good buddies and Daisy is a favorite dancin' partner of mine, there's all kind of nasty opportunities for conflicts of interest to pop up. So I thought maybe you'd like to advise me on how to proceed."

*Silly nitwit.* "You and Slocum go knock on Miss Muntz's front door and—and . . ."

"Yes sir?" *And what?*

Which was precisely Parris's thought. He furrowed the highly expressive brow. *This could get dicey. Miss Muntz owns the house we taped off and she probably believes she has a right to go inside. She don't, of course, but she could cause me a lot of heartburn if she phones the mayor and kicks up a fuss about private-property rights and whatnot. And if Knox goes barging in, it'd be just like Daisy to get excited and whack him over the head with her big walking stick. And Knox don't have any more sense than Daisy, so he might arrest her for real this time, and it'd take him and Slocum both to haul her away to jail.* He could imagine the headlines.

**LOCAL COPS BRAWL WITH AGED NATIVE AMERICAN WOMAN**

"Uh, you and Slocum go back to your regular patrol. Soon as I get back to town, I'll take care of this business with Miss Muntz."

"Thanks, Chief. I told Piggy that you'd know the right thing to do." The insolent cop appended a final "heh-heh."

Parris ground his teeth. *Someday, Knox—you're gonna push me too far.* But this wasn't someday and he had a more immediate problem to deal with. The thought of facing the Daisy-Muntz combination alone was unsettling. Then, he remembered what best friends were for. He switched on the emergency lights to get Charlie Moon's attention, also toggled the siren switch twice.

As the Ute pulled the pickup into a wide spot on the shoulder, Parris parked beside him, lowered the passenger-side window, and passed on the troubling news.

Moon was not surprised. "Sounds like Daisy sweet-talked the landlady into giving her a guided tour of the murder house." *I bet she wanted to see the bloodstains where Hermann Wetzel got shot to death.* Another thought occurred to him: *I wonder why Knox didn't mention Sarah. Maybe she was smart enough to stay clear of the Wetzel house.* Also: *I wonder where Butch is.* He grinned. *I bet Daisy gave him the slip.*

Parris switched off the flashing lights. "Charlie, seeing as how Daisy's your aunt—"

"I don't appreciate the reminder."

"—You've got to help me with this."

The Indian raised an eyebrow. "How?"

"You can go with me to Miss Muntz's house and give Daisy a good talking-to." The chief of police glanced at the rearview mirror, watched a yellow Corvette approaching at a good clip, and switched the emergency lights back on. "Explain to your aunt how she don't have any business mucking around a crime scene."

"I don't think that'd help." Moon adjusted his black workaday John B. Stetson hat to a jaunty angle. "The elderly relative don't pay me much attention." *It'll be like talking to a fence post. Only less fun.*

"Well you gotta try." Parris watched the spiffy sports car slow and pass by. A pretty redhead waved. The distracted cop returned a half-hearted salute. "This could turn into a real mess."

The tribal investigator's smile went off like a dozen flashbulbs. "Hey, how much trouble could a couple of little old ladies get themselves into?"

# CHAPTER FORTY-FOUR

## A COUPLE OF LITTLE OLD LADIES

OFFICER KNOX'S IMAGE OF DAISY PERIKA AND HER NEW FRIEND AS two old hens "cacklin' up a storm" was somewhat off the mark, but "hatching a batch of trouble" was an apt metaphor. As might be expected, it was the Ute woman who had settled onto the nest, which was the most comfortable chair in a cozy sanctum chock-full of comfy places to sit.

Daisy got right to the point. "That silly girl's liable to show up again and ask me if it's all right to buy ten dollars' worth of bubble gum, so tell me what's on your mind."

"I shall." Her back poker-straight, Miss Muntz was seated across from the Indian woman. "But there is a condition—this is *for your ears only.*"

Oh, this was sounding good. "I won't breathe a word of what you say. Not unless you give me the okay."

"You solemnly promise?"

A nod.

With this assurance, Millicent Muntz commenced to tell her hair-raising narrative. When she had finished, the tribal elder was struck dumb. But only for a few rapid heartbeats. "You're in a real fix."

"Indeed I am." The landlady clasped her hands in her lap. "But now that I've shared my secret, I feel much better."

The tribal elder offered up an off-the-cuff proverb: "Feeling better won't get the job done." As she thought things over, Daisy studied the carpeted floor. Also the landlady's feet, and Miss M's tasteful footwear. "If I was in your shoes, I'd figure out a way to fix things."

Convinced that her guest was already figuring, she leaned forward. Expectantly.

The Ute problem-solver took quite some time to mull it over. By and by, after discarding a few so-so notions, Daisy came up with what she *knew* was a surefire solution.

When Miss Muntz heard the result of Daisy's brainstorm, she clapped her hands. "That is just splendid—you are absolutely brilliant!"

The recipient of this generous compliment shrugged with a modesty that was as genuine as a politician's election-day promise. "It oughta work."

True. It oughta. And cottonwood trees oughta grow crispy twenty-dollar bills instead of shiny green leaves. But Daisy's track record for schemes that actually worked was not one to brag about. Perhaps one in twenty.

Miss Muntz, of course, was unaware of these dismal statistics.

◆　◆　◆

CHARLIE MOON and Scott Parris were about three blocks away, approaching the address on Beechwood Road, when Sarah Frank pulled up at the curb at Miss Muntz's home with a half gallon of chocolate-ripple ice cream.

◆　◆　◆

THE GRANITE Creek chief of police turned into the Wetzel driveway, braked to a stop near the front porch, and got out to watch Charlie Moon arrive in Sarah's red pickup. Without exchanging a word, the good friends took a hard look at the official yellow tape, labeled in large, bold letters: POLICE–DO NOT CROSS. Knox's description "messed with" was a euphemism bordering on rash understatement. The tape had been ripped from across the front door and tossed onto the porch to curl up and rattle in the breeze. The Miss Muntzes of this world are ever so tidy. This messy, in-your-face infraction had "Daisy Perika" written all over it.

Charlie Moon shook his head. It was not as if Aunt Daisy set out with the intention of creating havoc. Her penchant for causing trouble was more like . . . a gift.

A half-dozen molars in Scott Parris's massive jawbone were

clenched hard enough to produce hairline cracks in the enamel. The already elevated blood pressure was edging up toward that bright red section of the dial marked DANGER. What made him so doggoned angry was not so much the *fact* of the unauthorized entry into the house where the homicide had occurred, or even the brazenness of the act. If the intruders were ordinary malefactors, there would be a ready remedy. What made Parris's blood boil and his teeth ache was that Daisy Perika was undoubtedly responsible for egging the mild-mannered little Miss Muntz into collaborating in the misdemeanor. That and the fact that Charlie Moon's irascible aunt was simply impossible to deal with. So now that he was here . . . *What should I do?* Or to put it another way: *What* can *I do?* Or still another way: *How can I just walk away from this without looking like an idiot?*

As if he had posed the questions aloud, the answer was provided verbally.

"Pardner, if I was you—I'd forget about this."

Though enormously grateful for this face-saving suggestion, Parris turned to scowl at his buddy. "Oh, you would, would you?"

Moon nodded.

Parris kicked at a chunk of white gravel. "Tell me why."

"First of all, whatever damage is done can't be fixed."

"Okay. What's second of all?"

"Well, there's a slim chance that Daisy might've learned something important from the landlady about Wetzel or his stepdaughter. But if you go read the riot act to her, she won't tell you a thing."

The cop pretended to think it over. "Okay, Charlie. For the time being, I'll play it your way."

"You won't regret it."

"I hope not." The overworked chin jutted again. "But Daisy can't keep on messing in police business and getting away with it."

"That's the spirit!" Moon patted him on the back. "Next time she spits on the sidewalk, throw the whole doggone book at her."

"Right." *That'll be the day.* But his jaw was relaxed and the blood pressure was drifting down toward that orange section labeled CAUTION.

What the burned-out lawman figured he needed was a nice quiet vacation in a pleasant retreat that came equipped with warm ocean breezes, stately palm trees, soothing sounds of softly strummed guitars, the heady scent of exotic tropical flowers . . . *tropical flowers. Flowers. Daisies.* He scowled. No, this would be a Daisy-free zone. Which reminded Parris that it was high time he put some distance between the tribal elder and himself, which he did. But not before reminding Charlie Moon that he must have a stern face-to-face with the aged auntie, explain how breaking yellow tape labeled POLICE—DO NOT CROSS was frowned upon in their fair city.

Now anyone who knows Charlie Moon will tell you the Ute is a man that a friend can count on. Like those resolute Roman soldiers who stood their posts even as Mount Vesuvius exploded in a pyroclastic eruption over doomed Pompeii, the stalwart tribal investigator would remain behind to do his duty.

For about thirty seconds.

Which, after Parris's official vehicle slipped out of sight, was how long it took Mr. Moon to conclude that there was no point in informing Aunt Daisy that she had broken the law. She already knew that, and had undoubtedly ripped away the official yellow tape with considerable gusto. *She'd just laugh in my face. Which would give her considerable satisfaction and me a bad case of aggravation.* Moon could imagine any number of experiences that would be more fun than exchanging words with the elderly relative. Such as . . . *gouging out my eyeball with a rusty tablespoon.*

The alternative to a confrontation with the cantankerous auntie was a strategic withdrawal. There was no shame in it. After all, hadn't the Dunkirk option worked just fine for Winston Churchill and the beleaguered troops? Certainly. And the British Expeditionary Force had survived to fight when the conditions were more favorable. It helped that Moon's withdrawal would accomplish another, more noble goal. *I'll drive the ranch truck they came in away with my spare key, and leave Sarah's pickup here for her to find—with the copy of Nancy Yazzi's apology on the driver's seat.* Which was what he did.

◆  ◆  ◆

WHEN SARAH emerged a few minutes later to find her recovered birthday gift waiting by the curb, the teenager was ecstatic. There were no cartwheels or backflips, but her happy shriek could be heard a quarter mile away, where Charlie Moon had parked the less attractive member of the F-150 family.

Why was the tribal investigator hanging around? Because he intended to follow the red pickup to ensure that Sarah and Daisy returned safely to the Columbine.

Also, to hear the earsplitting shriek. This was the main reason.

# CHAPTER FORTY-FIVE

## KNOX AND SLOCUM'S EXCELLENT ADVENTURE

APPROXIMATELY TWENTY MINUTES AFTER SARAH FRANK'S SUPEREC-static shriek, E. C. "Piggy" Slocum was piloting the GCPD black-and-white and Eddie Knox was in charge of communications. When the dispatcher put in a routine call to unit 240, Slocum's partner snatched the microphone. "What've you got for us, Clara?"

"Neighbor reports vandalism at the Roger Grilly residence. It's one of those summer homes on Muleshoe Mountain. Address is 980 Forest Road 1040; sign by the driveway says Roger's Roost. Caller was walking his dog when he noticed a broken window in a door on the lower level."

"Was the caller a neighbor?"

"Probably, but I don't have an ID. Just as I asked his name, his cell-phone connection starting breaking up and I lost connection. The new computer's acting up and didn't record his cell number— Hold on Eddie. I've got another 911."

After listening to Clara Tavishuts attempt to calm a hysterical woman whose aged Chihuahua (Mousie, aka Pookie) had just swallowed a cigar butt and was having a coughing fit, Knox hung up. "Well, you heard what she said, Pig—let's motivate over to IRS Road."

Slocum stepped on the gas, stuffed the last bite of doughnut into his mouth, brushed the powdered sugar off on his dark blue trousers, and said, "Obby fum bum kib fewwa wok."

Knox nodded. *Piggy's right—some halfwit juvenile delinquent probably tossed a rock through the window.* At the beginning of every shift, the gung-ho cop prayed for a crime he could really get his teeth into. A hostage situation or bank robbery topped off his wish list.

As he swallowed a mouthful of doughnut, Officer Slocum turned onto Forest Road 1040.

As was his standard practice on any call where there was the slightest prospect of encountering a felon who might put up a fight, Eddie Knox checked his revolver. All six cylinders were loaded for bear.

As GCPD unit 240 was nearing the high-altitude, multiple-level, thirty-eight-hundred-square-foot log mansion (eight bedrooms, seven baths) that Mr. and Mrs. Grilly humbly referred to as "the cabin," Knox began to feel a tickling abdominal sensation, as if energetic spiders were playing volleyball in the pit of his stomach. Almost immediately, he received Alert Number Two, as the short hairs on the back of his neck bristled. As if these subliminal signals might be insufficient to get his attention, all five of his missing toes began to tingle. (The business about the absent appendages will be fleshed out later; the point at the moment is that the cop had an overwhelming premonition that there was something *dinky* about this call.) "Stop the car, Pig—block the driveway!"

Slocum skidded to a halt, glanced at his partner. *Uh-oh. Eddie's got that "we're about to have hell for breakfast" look in his eye.* Having no food in his mouth, he was able to enunciate clearly, "Whassup, Rocks?"

"I got a feeling this call ain't about some run-of-the-mill vandalism." Knox rested his meaty hand on the grip of his holstered pistol. "This is gonna turn out to be a break-in by a sure-enough bad guy."

The driver frowned at the Grilly residence. "You figger he might still be in the house?"

*I sure hope so.* Knox's face split in that crooked grin that reminded his partner of a criminally insane chainsaw murderer in an old horror flick. Despite his reputation for being a dim bulb, Slocum was not eager to shoot it out with a desperate felon. Moreover, the chubby cop knew the GCPD rule book by heart. "If the suspect is still on the premises, we're supposed to put in a call for backup and sit tight till some of our guys show up."

"Pig, we don't know for sure anybody's in the house—it's just a little hunch I got." *But he's in there all right, and I'm gonna take him down without any sissy call for help.* "If it turns out he's still inside, we'll put in the call." *But by then he'll either be dead or wishin' he was.* As the senior officer was getting out of the unit, Knox instructed his subordinate thusly: "You go around back, Pig—and make sure he don't get away."

Slocum used all the cover available to slip around to the rear of the house.

It shall be stipulated that Eddie "Rocks" Knox had not earned his nickname for carrying gravel in his pockets. There would be no slipping around for Knox. His practice in such situations was to march right up to the front door and kick it in. The point was to force the bad guy into a violent confrontation, during which Knox would put slugs one and two through the thug's pump, the third right one between the eyes. He would reserve four through six in case there was a Thug Number Two. This straightforward tactic was what Knox had in mind when he approached the log house and paused to peer through a small window in one of the garage doors. Twilight was rapidly fading into night, so it was fortuitous that the day's final reddish ray of sunlight passed helpfully over Knox's shoulder and through the glazing to illuminate the backside of a muddy Jeep. It was also fortunate that there was not enough mud to conceal the letters and numbers on the license plate, which Eddie Knox and every other GCPD officer had committed to memory.

To assert that the bloodthirsty cop was pleased would be a flagrant act of understatement. Knox was transported into a state of pure, unadulterated bliss. Which is why he may be excused for garnishing his happy thoughts with a fragment from Jerry Lee Lewis. *Great balls of fire—that's Jake Harper's Jeep!* He could hardly believe his luck. *Ten to one, Harper's inside right now.* He unclipped a PSRCD (portable short-range communications device) from the assortment of nine essential items fastened to his equipment belt, pressed the button that would make Slocum's matching PSRCD unit vibrate. Knox held his breath until he heard his partner's hoarsely whispered, "Whassup, Eddie?"

Eddie K told him whassup: "Jake Harper's Jeep's in the garage."

A low whistle, then: "You one-hundred-percent sure?"

Knox repeated the license number.

Slocum whistled again. This was a dangerous situation. "Harper shot Wetzel dead, so he's probably packin' right now."

"I expect so." Knox licked his lips.

Slocum was determined to go by the book. "We got to put a call in for some backup."

"Not till we make sure he's inside." *But he's there. I can feel it.*

◆ ◆ ◆

AND HE was.

Jake Harper was a persistent fellow. Now *obsessed* with the notion of getting his hands on Hermann Wetzel's hoard of cash money, the burglar had concluded that the Grilly residence was a good spot to lie low for another day or two, until he made one last attempt to retrieve the little black pouch from the dead man's heat register. Which is why, when Knox and Slocum arrived to investigate the broken window, the felon was in the Grilly kitchen, enjoying scrambled eggs, marbled-rye toast, imported English marmalade, and a fresh pot of Kona coffee.

◆ ◆ ◆

PISTOL DRAWN, Officer Knox approached the ground-level door, inhaled a deep breath that swelled his barrel chest, and bellowed loudly enough to unnerve the diner in the Grilly kitchen, "We know you're in there, Harper!"

Harper, who was in the process of swallowing his third forkful of eggs, choked. But this did not deter him from trotting from the kitchen to the parlor and looking out the window.

Knox spotted the indistinct figure behind the glass, grinned, and shouted again. "We've got you surrounded, dipstick—come out with your hands in the air or we come in shooting!"

In spite of his many shortcomings, Harper was a congenial fellow. And being, in a manner of speaking, the host, he felt an obligation to be hospitable. So, though partially blinded by the setting sun, he raised his right hand high and waved at the unseen visitor. With one finger.

Eddie Knox, who was beginning to take a liking to this plucky fugitive, took time out for a "heh-heh" before bellowing, "Come out before I lose my temper and maybe I'll go easy on you." He'd not had so much fun since that day about fourteen years ago when he had faced down the Mexican toting a shotgun loaded with slugs. (The murder suspect had shot him in the leg, which is why Knox limps about on a prosthetic limb and occasionally feels eerie tingles from the phantom toes.)

When Harper's blurry form disappeared from the window, Knox assumed the worst: *He's gonna start popping lead at me and Piggy.* He used the PSRCD to alert his partner to the prickly situation, stated the obvious remedy, and was annoyed when Slocum quoted another one of those pesky rules.

"You can't rush the guy. Eddie, you ain't yet announced that we was the police."

"Dammit, Pig—I'm in uniform and he saw me from the window!"

"Don't matter. You got to *tell* him."

*Half-wit nitpicker.* "Okay. First chance I get, I'll show him my official picture ID, read him his rights, and introduce you as my partner and official legal adviser."

"Okay, Rocks. Hey—guess what I found back here?"

"How should I know?"

Slocum's voice betrayed the hurt he felt. "It wouldn't cost you nothin' to make a guess."

Knox sighed. *Big cabbage head.* "You found a pink rhinestone big enough to choke a rhinoceros."

"Huh-uh." But, satisfied with his partner's effort, Slocum told him what.

"So you found the electric power meter. How's that gonna help us?"

Slocum, whose daddy used to work for the Granite Creek Utilities, told him.

Knox was, well . . . *electrified* by this information. "You can do that?"

Dang right. Slocum assured his partner that it was as easy as eating apple pie for breakfast.

Eddie Knox was impressed. *Just imagine, ol' Piggy coming up with something like that.*

It was quite simple, really. E. C. Slocum was prepared to remove the power meter, which, on his partner's signal he did.

As the lights in the big log house went out, Knox yelled, "Police!" and shouldered the downstairs door off its hinges. The brawny cop landed flat on the floor, rolled aside to take cover behind a couch, aimed his revolver at nothing in particular, and heard a loud report as Jake Harper (now stumbling around in the darkness) knocked over an excellent bronze reproduction of a Remington sculpture depicting a charging cavalry officer (six-shooter in one hand, raised saber in the other), which landed *bang!* in an antique copper pot. Not having the benefit of X-ray vision, Knox interpreted the *bang!* as a gunshot, and yelled, "Look out, Pig—he's shootin' at us!" He returned fire through the ceiling. There was little chance of hitting the suspect, but Knox fired two shots just to make a point.

Which it did.

Jake Harper stomped across the darkened parlor, dived through a second-level window, landed like a bushel of bricks on the redwood deck, and was over the railing and onto the ground quicker than Greta Garbo could have said, "I want to be let alone."

Before either policeman was aware of his hasty departure, the heavyset fellow had sprinted up the mountain and across several acres of adjacent property and broken through the back door of a modest bungalow, where he took a minute or two to hyperventilate and consider his precarious situation. *I'll have to make a run for it before those crazy cowboy cops find me here and start shooting again. I'll need some transportation.* Full of hope, he entered the garage. It was empty. Bummer. *I'll have to hoof it.* Which he did, but not before hurriedly filling a stolen knapsack with victuals from a well-stocked pantry and snatching an armful of blankets off the beds.

As soon as he was safely concealed in a thickish glade of quaking aspens, Harper paused to catch his breath. As he gazed into the valley, where the night lights of Granite Creek flickered mockingly, the fugitive was faced with the eternal question. *Where can I hide for a few days?* Dusty caves, smelly barns, and muddy culverts under roadways were not appealing, but . . . *If I have to, I'll sleep in a hollow log. I'm not leaving the county without Hermann's money bag.*

◆ ◆ ◆

FACED WITH the fact that Jake Harper had given them the old slip, Eddie Knox was obliged to endure some of Slocum's lip.

"I told you we oughta called for some backup." Which the smug partner now proceeded to do.

By the time a half-dozen GCPD officers, Chief of Police Scott Parris, and a lone state-police officer had arrived on the scene, Jake Harper was miles away.

Officer Knox was a stand-up guy. He confessed that his partner had urged him to call for backup when they arrived on the scene, and took all the flak, which amounted to nothing more than a dark scowl from Chief of Police Parris. Despite the fact that the suspect in the Wetzel homicide had escaped capture, Officers Knox and Slocum had discovered Harper's hideout, which was the first big break in the murder case.

# CHAPTER FORTY-SIX

## THE TIP

"JUST *LOOKING* FOR SOMEBODY TO HAMMER." THIS WAS HOW ONE of Scott Parris's subordinates at the GCPD described the chief of police to a fellow officer, with this warning: "Stay out of the boss's way."

If Parris was in an intemperate mood, it was understandable. The prime suspect in the murder of a local citizen had evaded arrest for the second time. Parris's statement days ago to the local media that the shooter would be apprehended "within a few hours" had turned out to be—as one of his more generous critics had observed in today's newspaper editorial—"somewhat optimistic." More polite than "really a dumb thing to say, which makes both of us look damned silly," which was how District Attorney Bill "Pug" Bullett had put it. Desperate for anything that even smelled like a lead, the harried cop was pleased to receive a telephone call from the elderly spinster.

"Mr. Parris, this is Millicent Muntz. You asked me to contact you if I happened to think of anything that might prove useful in your investigation of Mr. Wetzel's untimely death."

"Yes ma'am, I remember that all right." The edgy man drummed the fingers of his free hand on the desk. "What've you got for me?"

"Probably nothing of any importance, but I thought it was my civic duty to call and let you know."

His phone-gripping hand was beginning to show white knuckles. "Just take your time, and tell me what's on your mind." The finger-drumming hand snatched a ballpoint pen, made ready to take notes.

"I don't think I should tell you over the telephone."

He scratched a big *X* on a yellow notepad. "You don't, huh?"

"Under the circumstances, it might prove to be indiscreet. Also, I'm in my car now, headed into town." A nervous little titter of a laugh.

"But I'm not driving while using my cell phone—I want to make that quite clear. I pulled over to the curb before placing the call."

Parris closed his eyes, took a deep breath, and recalled how his mother had warned him that a career in law enforcement would be stressful. "If you want to drop by the police station, I'll be in my office—"

"I am on my way to Sunburst Pizza. I suggest that you meet me at that location."

"Why there?"

"For one thing, I have some business to conduct at that establishment." She whispered, "And Sunburst is where I am virtually *certain* that I saw the suspect."

"If you've spotted Jake Harper, the first thing I need to know is—"

"I do not wish to appear rude, Mr. Parris, but I really must be going."

"But—"

"As it happens, I am parked in front of the fire station and a big red truck has just pulled out and the young man driving it is gesturing and suggesting—quite vehemently, I might add—that I should move my automobile out of the way." She waved at the distraught fireman. "If you wish to meet me at Sunburst Pizza, that will be fine. Otherwise, we must continue this conversation at another time. Good day." *Click*.

Parris slammed the phone into the cradle, grabbed his battered felt hat off the coat rack, exited his office at a dead run, went down the stairway considerably faster than was sensible for a man of his bulk and coordination, made it to the bottom unscathed, and figured he could make it to the pizza joint in six minutes flat. Which he will. With twenty-odd seconds to spare.

But before the chief constable arrives at his destination, an interesting coincidence deserves mention.

◆ ◆ ◆

AS PARRIS was speeding down Beechwood toward the Sunburst Pizza Restaurant, passing motorists left and right, one such citizen was behind the wheel of a dusty old Chevrolet Camearo he had stolen that very morning from a trail head where a hiker had left it.

Imagine Jake Harper's panic when, on his way to take a gander at the Wetzel house in preparation for still another try at grabbing Hermann's money bag, he glanced at the rearview mirror and saw the GCPD black-and-white coming up fast behind him, emergency lights flashing. Presuming that he was about to be either arrested or shot dead, the felon uttered a coarse expletive, and appended this addendum: "How'd they get on to me so damn fast?"

The burglar was numb with relief when the chief of police roared around him and *kept on going.* As the wanted man recovered from this unsettling experience, he took note of the fact that the police car had pulled into the Sunburst Pizza parking lot. As he passed by, Harper also noticed that the cop was chatting with an elderly woman standing by a Buick. Both the woman and the automobile looked awfully familiar. Not a half block away, he remembered. *It's that ditzy old landlady I thought was going to flush me out of Wetzel's closet when she was there with that ditzy old Indian woman.* Which raised a troubling possibility: *Maybe the landlady found the place where I cut and mended that yellow police tape across the back door. She knows someone's been inside Hermann's house and that's what she's yakking to that big cop about.* His brow wrinkled. *But why are her and the cop at the pizza joint?* A sudden flash of insight. *I bet the old lady saw me talking to Nance that night and she's telling the cop all about it.* One worry begets another. *And maybe Nance told the landlady some other stuff about me. Something that would help the cops pin the shooting on me.*

Jake Harper hung a hard right at the next corner, circled the block, and parked as close as he dared to Sunburst Pizza.

◆ ◆ ◆

SCOTT PARRIS gave Miss Muntz his semi-stern look. "So what's all this about you seeing Harper?"

"Young man, I hope you will not think me unreasonable, but I do not wish to be interviewed in a parking lot." The prim little lady glanced at the restaurant. "I suggest that we go inside."

*Well, I haven't had my lunch yet.* "Tell you what—how about I buy us both a bite to eat?"

"How sweet of you." She took the offered arm, which felt like a cedar post. "I generally stop here about once a week."

As they crossed the threshold, Parris took a hard look at the grimy interior and began to have doubts. "The eats here okay?"

"I can recommend the calzone." She turned her face to smile at the brawny policeman. *He looks rather dapper in that old-fashioned hat.* "But I generally get a take-out order. I prefer not to dine here—the ambience does not appeal to me."

"Yeah. I see what you mean." *It'd have to get better to qualify as a dump.* He led her to a moderately clean booth, scooted onto the seat opposite her, and withdrew a menu that was wedged between a napkin holder and a plastic sugar dispenser. *I wonder if I could handle a pepperoni and green chili.* His small intestine, which was a fractious organ, answered the question with a sharp pain.

An attractive, gum-chewing waitress arrived. The elderly lady might have been invisible, but the girl exchanged big smiles with the big cop, asked what looked good to him.

Parris resisted the temptation to tell her. "Coffee and a meatball sandwich." He restored the menu to its rightful place. "Don't be stingy with the marinara sauce."

Pretty Face giggled and wriggled. "I'll tell the chef to slop on an extra glop."

After getting the waitress's attention with a barely audible cough, the elderly lady ordered a tossed salad. House dressing. Cup of tea. "And please ask Alvin Burkowitz to come to our table."

The gum chewer ceased masticating long enough to say, "You mean Al?"

"Yes."

"Awright." She cast a parting smile at the broad-shouldered cop. "I'll go get 'im."

"Thank you." Eyeing grease spots on the table with no little dismay, Miss Muntz held her purse in her lap.

After enjoying the shapely young lady's departure, Parris returned his attention to his elderly companion. "So tell me when and where you think you saw Harper."

Miss Muntz was about to reply when a man in a red-and-yellow Sunburst Pizza vest appear in the kitchen doorway. She waved. "Yoo-hoo—over here!"

Like a wary coyote being offered a scrap of meat at a cowboy's campfire, he approached in a wary, shuffling gait.

Miss M lifted a gloved hand to indicate her luncheon date. "Alvin—allow me to introduce my friend Mr. Parris. He is the chief of police."

The cop nodded at the rat-faced fellow, who averted his gaze.

She spoke crisply to the Sunburst employee. "There is some unfinished business between us, young man—involving a calzone delivery."

Burkowitz gawked at the elderly woman.

"You needn't be concerned that I have a complaint about the food. As it happens, I have not taken a bite of it—it is in my freezer."

The pizza deliveryman took a step backward, stumbled, grabbed a plastic chair for support.

The policeman's face prickled with suspicion. *This punk's pupils are big as dimes—he's high on something.*

Did Miss Muntz show the least sign of discomfort? Certainly not. Breeding will tell. The polite little lady continued as if nothing awkward had occurred. Smiling at the Sunburst employee, she said, "But I can assure you that the calzone shall not remain amongst the frozen foods much longer. I intend to share it with a friend." She shot a meaningful glance at Parris.

Still grasping the chair, Burkowitz might have been miles away. As he stared over Miss M's gray head, his eyes rolled upward, and his lower lip begin to jerk in spasmodic little tics.

Parris saw it coming. *This yahoo's gonna pass out.* He tensed for action. *I'll try to grab him before he hits the floor.*

Apparently oblivious to the possibility that the deliveryman might fall flat on his face, Miss Muntz continued her monologue. "The issue has to do with your gratuity, which was not where I told you to look for it." She removed a letter-size envelope from her purse, held it out to him. "Please accept my apology—and this."

The wild-eyed man steadied himself, stared at the offering like it was a snake about to fang him.

Parris snatched the envelope from the lady's fingers and jammed it into Burkowitz's vest pocket. "That'll be all, Alvin." *But I'll be checking on you later.* There had been street talk about someone dealing drugs from Sunburst Pizza.

The deliveryman hurried away, bumping into tables and chairs.

Parris addressed his elderly companion. "Okay, the wacko's got his tip. Now tell me about seeing Jake Harper."

Miss Muntz snapped her purse shut. "As you already know, on the night when Mr. Wetzel was shot to death, I drove his stepdaughter into town. I had agreed to drop Nancy off at the Silver Mountain Hotel so she could attend that sweet little Indian girl's birthday party. On the way, I stopped here." She paused, pursed her lips. "Aren't you going to write this down?"

"Sure." Parris found the necessary equipment in his shirt pocket.

"My, what a fancy little leather-bound notebook."

"Thank you." A silly grin. "It's a present from my girlfriend." He resumed the official expression. "So what happened when you made your stop at Sunburst?"

She tapped a gloved finger on the table. "I was inside placing my order when I noticed a vehicle that pulled up very close to my Buick, where Nancy was waiting for me. When I came outside, it was apparent that she was having a conversation with the driver. And the moment I appeared, off he went." She waved her hand to demonstrate the rapid departure.

Parris's arched eyebrows said, *So?*

In preparation for the punch line, Miss M inhaled. "The driver had a beard, and the car was one of those boxy little Jeeps—just like the newspaper account said the suspect in the Wetzel homicide was driving." She clamped her mouth shut.

Disappointment fairly dripped from Parris's face. "You think you might've seen Harper here in his Jeep on the night Hermann Wetzel was shot?" *I was hoping she'd spotted him today.*

A pert nod. "That is correct." She cocked her head as if expecting some expression of thanks.

"Well . . . that's very interesting, ma'am." He pocketed the notebook.

At about this time, the salad and meatball sandwich were delivered.

Aside from a few remarks about the food and the nice weather, they dined in silence.

After Parris had signed the credit-card receipt and halfheartedly flirted with the saucy waitress, he escorted his elderly date to her automobile.

Clutching at Scott Parris's arm, Miss Muntz inquired whether her possible sighting of Harper's Jeep—tardy as the report was—might be of any help in his ongoing investigation of the Wetzel homicide.

The gallant lawman did the best he could. "You can never tell what'll turn out to be the critical piece of information." He smiled at the senior citizen, tipped the venerable hat. "I sure do appreciate your help."

She appreciated these encouraging words, and as Miss Millicent Muntz watched the chief of police's automobile roar away at twice the posted speed limit, she shook her little gray head. *Such a nice young man. If I had a son I would be quite satisfied if he turned out to be just like Mr. Parris.* She was reminded of an exception. *Except for that little potbelly. He really should cut back on his calories.*

◆ ◆ ◆

A HALF block away, crouched behind the wheel of the classic Camaro, the bald, beardless version of Jake Harper watched the little old lady get into her Buick. *I wonder how much she knows. And what she's told that cop.*

# CHAPTER FORTY-SEVEN

## COPS GET HEARTBURN TOO

JAKE HARPER WAS NOT THE ONLY FELLOW IN GRANITE CREEK COUNTY who needed a place to hide out and lick his wounds.

The third time the district attorney had called to demand an "up-to-the-minute progress report," Scott Parris had (through clenched teeth) advised that assertive public servant to pack a bag and go straight to— But that unseemly travel suggestion does not bear repeating. And getting the DA off his back did not measurably ease the stress on the harried chief of police. The phone line fairly hummed with impertinent inquiries from journalists who posed smart aleck questions like: "How'd this desperado manage to slip away from you guys twice—he been dipped in grease or what?" Then, there were alarmed citizens who figured that they were next on Harper's hit list. Typical of these was a nervous widow lady whose home was within two blocks of the Wetzel "murder house." Without stopping to catch her breath, she demanded to know, "Why is this bloodthirsty killer still on the loose right here in my neighborhood and what do we pay these outrageous property taxes for—to buy fancy uniforms and expensive cars for dumb cops who couldn't find their [vulgarity deleted] with both hands? Next election I intend to vote for a whole new slate—we'll throw all of you bums out and start over!"

By midafternoon, Scott Parris was desperate for someplace to escape the ongoing persecution. He jammed the felt hat down to his ears, stalked out of the station without a word to anyone about his destination, which was the one place on earth where he could count on a warm welcome, a free meal, and—best of all—a few hours of peace and quiet. Charlie Moon's Columbine Ranch.

## PARRIS PUTS IT ALL TOGETHER

AS DAISY Perika was saving her appetite for an evening out, and Sarah Frank was absent from the ranch headquarters, Scott Parris and Charlie Moon dined alone.

Following a hearty supper of melt-in-your-mouth beefsteaks, baked and buttered Idaho potatoes, and hot apple pie, the best friends took their coffee onto the west porch, seated themselves on sturdy redwood chairs, and settled down to view the evening's prime-time performance—a pink-and-violet sunset so stunningly gorgeous that it took their breaths away. But, as is the way of temporal blessings, the soul-warming glow over the snow-capped peaks soon faded, and as the rainbow-hued display was relegated to that secret place where cherished memories are kept, a chill breeze passed by to rattle cottonwood leaves and sweep dust off the porch. Then came twilight, that bittersweet foretaste of true night. Crisp shadows tugged impotently on solidly built horse barns and sturdy tree trunks. Even though the rainbow presentation had gradually faded to black-and-white, this was the Ute's favorite portion of eventide, when day fled and took all its worries with it.

By and by, the highlands were abandoned to dusk's cool hand.

Was it quiet? The Ute could hear his heartbeat. Perfection.

The white man shattered the silence. "Where's Sarah?"

"Spending the night over at the cabin."

Parris's brow furrowed. "The one by the lake?"

Moon nodded. "She took some things to eat and a couple of books." *Sarah's a good kid.*

"Is that little girl all by herself?"

The Ute grinned. "She thinks she is."

"You posted a guard."

"Two keen-eyed men with Winchesters." Charlie Moon clasped his hands behind his head.

Inspired by the breeze in the eaves, Parris sighed. "There've been some breaks in the Wetzel homicide."

The rancher closed his eyes.

The town cop sipped some brew from his coffee mug. "If you're interested, you don't have to go to all the trouble of saying so—just grunt."

*I've hurt his feelings.* "Has Jake Harper been picked up?"

"Not yet." Parris blushed. "But it won't be long before we'll nab the bastard."

"Then you must've arrested Nancy Yazzi."

The blush was promoted to a tingling burn. "Afraid not."

Count a dozen ticktocks of the clock.

*Ol' Charlie's drifted off again. This is like trying to have a conversation with one of them knotty-pine cigar-store Indians.* Parris leaned back in the redwood chair, stretched his legs. "I got a fax today from FBI forensics. They've traced that .38 Smith & Wesson that Officer Martin found in Wetzel's front yard. The ballistics report verifies that it's the firearm used to shoot Wetzel, which is what we expected all along. But you'll be surprised to know that—"

"The .38 was part of Hermann Wetzel's gun collection—which the burglar probably found while he was burgling and used it to shoot Mr. Wetzel dead."

"Dammit, Charlie—you sure know how to steal a man's thunder."

"Sorry, pardner." Through his boot heels, the Ute felt the Columbine hound move under the porch. "So—that's it?"

"Pretty much." After counting off six heartbeats, Parris murmured, "Oh, there was one other little thing. You want to hear about it?"

"Mmm-hmm."

"The Bureau geeks found two clean prints on the pistol."

The Ute's ears pricked at this news, but he kept his eyes shut. "Since you need all the thunder you can lay your hands on, I won't speculate about whose fingerprints were on the murder weapon."

"Thanks, Charlie—that's very thoughtful of you." *Now I'll let him stew.* The chief of police counted again. At ten: *Okay, if you won't ask, I won't tell you.* At sixteen, he blurted out, "The prints on the gun—"

"Weren't Harper's. And the FBI hasn't made a match yet."

Parris ground his molars. Felt his pulse thumpity-thumping in his temple.

It hurt Moon's mouth not to grin. "Sorry, pardner. Just couldn't help myself."

"So how'd you know?"

The tribal investigator shrugged. "Wild guess."

Parris counted to ten again. Slowly this time. Somewhat relaxed, he said, "So we know Harper didn't do the burglary by himself." He rested his left Roper boot on top of the right one. "And that it was his partner who pulled the trigger on Wetzel."

Moon opened his eyes to get a gander at the lawman's face, which glowed with self-satisfaction. "And you've got a pretty good notion of who the partner was."

"Maybe I do." Mimicking his buddy, Parris clasped his fingers behind his head. Closed his eyes. "But I don't want to spoil your fun. So go ahead—tell me."

The Ute was listening to a sinister sound his friend had not heard. "Wetzel's stepdaughter?"

Scott Parris did a fine imitation of the tribal investigator's "mmm-hmm." He opened one eye long enough to let it twinkle at his buddy. "All Nancy Yazzi had to do was get away from the festivities for a few minutes."

Moon recalled how much confusion there had been at Sarah's birthday party. "I guess that can't be ruled out." He could not pass up an opportunity to tweak his best friend. "But I can think of another possibility."

Parris was haunted by the certainty that this had all happened before. But it was not déjà vu—the clever Ute had scooped him time and again. "So tell me."

"No. You wouldn't appreciate it."

"Don't let that stop you—I'll pretend like I do."

"Okay, then. Way I figure it, the shooter's that little landlady who lives right across the street."

Parris's eyes popped wide open to goggle at his host. "Miss Muntz?"

"Oh, I expect she's the sort that wouldn't swat a fat greenfly even if it was squatted on a fresh blueberry pie. But my momma always used to say to me, 'Eat your green beans, Charles,' and, 'Still waters run deep.'"

The Ute fixed his gaze on a silvery-gray glow over the Shining Mountains. "You ought to run a background check on that one. I bet she's got a rap sheet long as your—"

"Charlie, get *serious*!"

Moon assumed a defensive tone. "With what little I know, the landlady's the best suspect I could come up with."

"This ain't nothing to joke about." Once again, Parris calmed himself. "What we need to do is question everybody that was at Sarah's birthday party, find out if anyone saw Nancy slip away from the shindig—or sneak back in."

"What's this 'we' stuff?"

"About a third of the men in the ballroom were from the Columbine, so it's only natural I'd expect you to help in the investigation."

"Why's it only natural?"

Parris did not mind telling him. "During that nasty business over at the Yellow Pines Ranch last year, I deputized you. And before you say, 'That was a heck of a long time ago,' I'll remind you that you ain't never been undeputized."

"And I'll remind you that this particular deputy is still waiting for his first paycheck."

"That's not my fault." Parris waved the coffee mug. "I turned your time in to the county."

"Well, that puts things in a whole different light."

"Don't be sarcastic, Charlie. You know I've done my level best."

A small, raspy voice said, "He's always been a big gourd head."

Parris felt a sudden chill. *First, four-legged chickens. Now I'm hearing voices.* "Uh, Charlie . . ." This was downright embarrassing. "Did you just hear something?"

Moon was wearing his high-stakes-poker face. "Like what?"

The cop blushed. "Oh, nothing."

"That was Aunt Daisy. She's been sitting in the parlor, listening to every word we've said."

This assertion was verified by a witchy cackle at the screened window.

The chief of police turned to glare at the invisible eavesdropper.

The disembodied voice spoke again. "I can't sit here much longer. The van'll be showing up any minute now."

Parris blinked at the window screen. "What van?"

"The one from St. Anthony's in Granite Creek."

Moon laughed. "She's hoping to clean up at tonight's bingo game."

The chief of police, who was all for religious activities, forgave the old sinner. "I hope you hit the jackpot, Daisy."

"So do I." She snorted. "But from what I'm told, all they have in the prize box is little bags of sugar-free candy and dime-store handkerchiefs and bottles of hand lotion. I don't see why they can't give away some hard cash."

Parris grinned. "You seem to worry a lot about money."

"You would too if you was a little ol' lady who lived hand-to-mouth on Social Security and that piddlin' little check I get from the tribe." She might have mentioned the generous monthly allowance from her nephew.

The hairy-chested man, who could not imagine himself as any sort of ol' lady, had no snappy comeback.

There was a grunt as Daisy Perika got up from her seat by the window. "Well, I'd better go to the bathroom before some old duffer shows up in the van. Don't you two say a word till I get back."

They didn't and she would not.

Clarification is required. The men did not say a word until she returned and Daisy would *not* go to the bathroom. Why would she practice this deception? Partly because it was in her nature to deceive, also because Daisy had a more urgent job to attend to (which had almost slipped her mind). In her view, this particular task was none of their business. Though in fact, it was—very much so.

*Just look at her go! The old woman hurries across the parlor, hobbles down the hallway past the dining room and across the kitchen, and opens the door to the headquarters tool room, where Charlie Moon keeps everything a handyman might need, from an antique muscle-powered auger a stout fellow can use to bore holes through oak logs—to a brand-new 120-volt Makita HM1211B demolition hammer capable of breaking concrete. Daisy has no interest in drilling holes or pulverizing cement. Without pulling the string to switch on a hundred-watt bulb hanging from the beamed ceiling, she heads straight for the pine shelf where her nephew keeps his fishing gear, opens a blue metal tackle box, fumbles around until she finds what she needs, and stuffs it into her sweater pocket.*

*What did Daisy take?*

*Sorry—there was so little light, and she moved so quickly.*

*But never mind. It is probably of no importance.*

*What is this? Now she is heading to the bathroom—undoubtedly to confound our prediction that she would not. Such a contrary old soul. But perhaps we are too hard on the cantankerous character. It is possible that the excitement of committing a minor theft has activated the aged bladder.*

◆ ◆ ◆

AS WE are obliged to leave Daisy to her personal business, and faced with a break in the lawmen's conversation, let us check in on Sarah Frank.

◆ ◆ ◆

THE GIRL is not in the priest's cabin. Ah—she is over there, where the breeze caresses her long black tresses. Bathed in the luminous moonshine, Sarah stands on Lake Jesse's pebbled shoreline.

The armed Columbine bodyguards who keep watch from a discreet distance are puzzled. It appears that the frail little body they guard is having a conversation with someone who (as far as the sharp-eyed cowboys can tell) is *not there*.

Oh—we have barged in on a sacramental situation. She is making a confession.

Our apologies, young lady. We shall leave you to converse with your unseen companion.

◆ ◆ ◆

SO WHO *shall* we visit? How about that notorious felon who is at the top of the Granite Creek Police Department's most-wanted list. Please be patient. It may take a moment to locate the slippery fellow. . . .

Aha—there the rascal is, skulking around in the darkness. Up to his old tricks, no doubt.

Since his dramatic eviction from the Grilly family mountain chalet by Officers Slocum and Knox, Jake Harper has been sleeping wherever he can find a place to lay his head and keep tolerably warm, such as in a tool shed or horse barn. Such a crafty fellow, and so full of felonious intent. But let us not judge him too harshly. Whatever his faults—and Mr. Harper is endowed with a multitude of them—he has his strong points, such as those sterling twin virtues Determination and Persistence. His resolution hardened by recent setbacks, Harper is more determined than ever to have what is *rightfully his* and will persist until he gets his grubby hands on Hermann Wetzel's legacy. Only a few hours earlier, he made several purchases at ABC Hardware, and the single-minded fellow is, once again, using the keys Nancy Yazzi provided to enter the rear door of the former Wetzel residence.

Watch the hopeful burglar scurry across the kitchen and into the office with his black canvas tool kit, which includes an orange plastic container labeled 100 BITS IN A BOX. Jake is betting on the Torx 25 to do the trick on the tamper-proof screws. He kneels on the floor to remove the heat register from the duct and—

But what is this?

The heat register is not firmly in place. Moreover, there are marks on the hardwood which suggest that someone has pried the thing from the floor.

Fearing the worst, Harper lifts the register from its rectangular well, uses his small flashlight to peer into the opening. Nothing is hanging from the nail.

The angry man growls. *Some rotten no-good stinking lowlife thief has come and swiped it.* The nerve of some people. *I'd like to get my hands on the guy and strangle him till his eyeballs pop out and roll down his cheeks.*

But let us pause and consider a pertinent question: Was his gender assumption politically correct? Must stinking lowlife thieves inevitably be of the *guy* persuasion?

Now, as petty criminals go, Jake Harper was a fair-minded fellow, and as he considered the possibilities he was forced to conclude that the pair of elderly ladies who had interrupted his previous attempt to retrieve the Wetzel loot were the most likely suspects. And of the two, Miss Muntz was the odds-on candidate. *I bet that nosy old landlady was dusting or something and noticed that the heat register had been screwed to the floor and she asked herself why, of all the registers in the house, would Hermann Wetzel fasten this one down? There was only one way to find out, so she pried it up and found his bag of money, which is rightfully mine.*

Which scenario presented Harper with a dilemma.

*The smart thing would be to write the whole thing off as a loss and leave town before the cops pick me up.*

On the other hand—

*I could sure use some hard cash. And the landlady's right across the street. And she knows she ain't got no legal right to Hermann's money, so she ain't told the cops about it. If I was to go over there and put a bad scare into her, she'd hand his money bag over so fast it'd scorch my hand.*

In addition to those virtues of Determination and Persistence, is Mr. Harper also endowed with even a meager helping of Wisdom—or the most minuscule portion of Common Sense? Presently, we shall find out.

## AT THE COLUMBINE

As DAISY returned to the front porch, and the men obligingly renewed their conversation, the St. Anthony's activities van came rumbling over the Too Late Creek bridge and pulled under the cottonwoods in the headquarters yard. Moon escorted his aunt to the roomy vehicle, where she insisted that she could get inside without any help. He spoke to the driver, a slender white man with a crown of snowy hair. "Like I told you on the phone, you don't have to come all the way out here. Anytime my aunt wants to go to church, I'll be happy to drive her into town."

"And like I told you, I don't mind a bit." Snowy Hair smiled at the rancher. "It's fun to make a run out into the countryside."

Moon watched Daisy settle into the seat behind the driver. "When should I expect her back?"

"Bingo generally goes until about ten P.M. and after that there's snacks and punch, so I won't get away from the church before eleven." The driver scratched his chin, which helped his thinking process along. "I'll have some other folks to drop off in town before I head out here, soooo . . . it'll prob'ly be a little while after midnight."

"That'll be fine." Before closing the van door, Moon smiled at his relative. "Have a good time."

She intended to do just that. Daisy Perika tapped the driver's shoulder with the knobby end of her walking stick. "Okay, bud—let's get this thing rolling."

As they watched the van pass over the bridge again, Parris recalled one of his worries: "I'm kinda concerned about Wetzel's landlady."

The Ute stretched out in the porch chair. "Why's that?"

"Oh, just a bad feeling." *I'd sure like to have another cup of coffee, but I'm too comfortable to go into the house for it.* "I had lunch with Miss Muntz today. On the night she drove Nancy Yazzi over to Sarah's birthday party, she stopped off at Sunburst Pizza for a few minutes."

"That's mostly a hangout for kids."

"And it's a regular dump. But the old lady don't eat there." *Except for today.* "She picks up to-go orders to take home." He grinned at the recollection of Miss M's determination to give the weirdo Sunburst employee his gratuity. "Point is, when she came out of the pizza joint that night, Miss Muntz saw Nancy talking to some guy in a Jeep. It was probably Jake Harper."

"Even if it was, that's old news."

"Yeah. But what nags at me is if it *was* Harper Miss Muntz spotted, then he probably saw her too and he might be worried that—one way or another—she knows a lot more about him than he'd like."

"Like if Nancy Yazzi talked to her landlady about her love life."

"Right."

"So what are you gonna do about it?"

"There's not much I can do, except have our regular patrols do a pass-by check of Miss Muntz's house every few hours. But most of the time, we're so short-handed I can't even manage that." Scott Parris waited for the hoped-for response.

Charlie Moon, who knew this man like they were blood twins, provided it. "I could ask Daisy to invite her new friend to spend a week or two at the Columbine."

The chief of police grinned. "I'd be much obliged."

*I thought you would.* The rancher gazed at the mountains, recalled what had happened the last time he'd opened the Columbine door to another woman Parris was worried about. *I hope this one won't run off with a pickup truck and what's left of my guns.*

# CHAPTER FORTY-EIGHT

## THE NIGHT STALKER

FOR THE SIXTH TIME IN AS MANY MINUTES, THE FELON'S RIGHT HAND found the knife holstered on his belt. The Buck Kalinga was a wicked-looking instrument, with a blade that curved sinuously upward as if eager to slide under someone's ribs. *There's no lights on in the house. The old biddy's probably gone to bed early.*

Like so many of his generation, the young man supposed that senior citizens consisted entirely of worn-out grandmas and grandpas who are obliged to spend eighteen of the day's hours in sleep. The fact that he had not caught a single Z for almost forty hours, had a pounding headache, and was running on a potent combination of alcohol and caffeine probably clouded his judgment. *This little job will be easy as spending somebody else's money.* The confident scoundrel counted off the reasons why.

One. The old lady lived all alone.

Two. Not a soul had witnessed his approach.

Three. No one could see him in his shadowy hideaway. (He was concealed beneath the drooping branches of Miss Muntz's Japanese cherry bush.)

But was he correct?

If we disregard the presence of Mr. Moriarty in her home, it is a fact that the elderly spinster lives alone.

Okay so far. But when the game is deadly serious, only a born loser would consider *one out of three* to be a satisfactory score.

So what about assumptions Two and Three?

As it happened, more than a dozen locals had witnessed the prowler's arrival and just as many knew where he was hiding. In the interest of brevity, we shall consider only two of these alert local citizens.

A mildly inquisitive chipmunk peeks from his cellar entrance, which is artfully concealed under the arch of a gnarled juniper root. As he is entertained by a drama far surpassing anything a rodent is likely to see on TV, the furry little fellow is fresh out of buttered popcorn, which is why he gnaws on one of last year's piñon nuts.

Eleven floors up (in the penthouse), a tiny wren is warming three pinto-bean-size eggs. No, not for the evening meal. This is an expectant mother, who has pressed herself into a nest so snug that her feathered tail sticks straight up behind her behind. She watches the prowler with unblinking black eyes set immediately above her beak, which rests on the finely wrought cup of twigs and grass. She has no piñon nut to gnaw, but Mr. Wren is out looking for something tasty for the common-law wife, whose taste runs toward victuals that scuttle about on six legs. Tiny beetles are her version of lobster thermidor.

◆ ◆ ◆

IN MOST (if not all) of the lower forty-eight states, *breaking and entering* is a legal term, and the first requirement under the law is that something must be broken. Such as a door latch or a pane of window glass. The latter is what the felon had in mind, which is why he had a roll of masking tape (to minimize the scattering of shards) and a heavy glove on his left hand (to avoid injury to his precious flesh). What else could he do—tap on the front door in the hope that Miss Muntz would invite him in for tea and crumpets? In light of the murder that had recently occurred just across the street, the woman would surely not be so careless as to leave her door unlocked. Even so, before breaking the glazing, he reached out with the gloved hand, gently twisted the doorknob.

It turned. The latch clicked. Well, shall wonders never cease?

The inside of the house was dark—though not quite as black as the depths of a coal mine in Anthracite County, Pennsylvania. He had brought along a small flashlight, but (hoping to surprise the elderly resident) was loathe to use it just yet.

◆ ◆ ◆

AS IT happened, Miss Muntz was not napping.

Like the piñon-nut-gnawing chipmunk, she was in her basement, which is where the contractor who built the house had installed the electrical panel. Fumbling around in the dark, she had not heard the front door open, but as the intruder walked across the floor over her head, Miss M heard the boards squeak. An interesting situation, and eerily similar to those events that had immediately preceded Hermann Wetzel's murder.

So what did she do?

The elderly spinster called out, "Yoo-hoo!"

The response from above was the ceasing of footsteps.

From below, another "Yoo-hoo," to which she appended, "I'm down here messing about with the circuit breakers, and cannot come upstairs until I get the lights turned on. Please stay right where you are—the basement stairway is rather steep and hazardous."

When an old lady yoo-hoos from the cellar and advises a dangerous felon to stay put, what is he to do? Wait until the lights go on? Possibly. Switch on his flashlight and find the basement stairway? Or should he withdraw, return on a more auspicious evening?

The fellow with the knife in his hand was obliged to make a choice, and whatever his shortcomings, he was not one to dilly-dally when faced with a critical issue that must be dealt with right on the well-known spot. After only a few ticktocks of Miss Muntz's grandfather clock, he came to a decision.

As she stood by the circuit-breaker panel, Miss Muntz heard the floorboards begin to squeak again. Having spent quite some time in the inky cellar darkness, which was *exactly* like a coal mine deep under Anthracite County, Pennsylvania, perhaps the old lady's sense of direction was a bit befuddled. Was her visitor returning to the front door, or moving toward the top of the cellar stairway? At first, she could not decide. But give the boards over her head time to make a few more squeaks.

Squeak. Creak. Squeak-creak. Creak-squeak.

Now she knows for sure.

Evidently, Miss Muntz has exhausted her supply of yoo-hoos.

◆ ◆ ◆

APPROXIMATELY THIRTY-FIVE minutes later, when Charlie Moon's wristwatch read half past ten o'clock, the tribal investigator and the chief of police were seated in the Columbine headquarters' kitchen, enjoying a penny-ante game of Texas Hold-'em Spit into the Wind—a highly complex contest that we shall not attempt to describe. Moon was a dollar and change ahead when the telephone rang. He took the call, grinned when he heard his aunt's voice. *I bet she's tired of the bingo game already and wants to come home before the van leaves.* "You want me to come get you?"

Yes, she did.

"Soon as this hand is played out, I'll be on my way."

That would be satisfactory. But there was one other thing. A minor detail.

"You're *where*?" The grin slipped off Moon's face.

A grin is a terrible thing to waste.

Parris picked it up, put it on. *Daisy's probably creating a big row over at the Catholic church.*

Daisy repeated what she had said to her nephew.

"Okay. I'll leave right away." Moon hung up the phone.

The chief of police eyed a pair of jacks and some trash. "So what's the old lady up to this time?" He imagined the aged Ute with a hammerlock on another elderly bingo player.

The rancher frowned at a framed print of a majestic bull buffalo standing in knee-high grass. "I guess we'll find out when we get there."

Scott Parris folded his hand. "We?"

"Aunt Daisy says I should bring you along." Moon, who had a modest portion of manly vanity, was putting the black hat on *just so* when something caught his eye. The tool-room door was not quite closed. *I know I shut it behind me about three hours ago when I put that sledgehammer back.* The rancher entered the small room, switched on the light. *Every-thing seems all right. No. Somebody's been messing with my fishing-tackle box.* The puzzled angler lifted the lid. *Looks like everything's there. No. Wait a minute . . .*

An item was missing.

*Who could have taken it?*

The name of a prime suspect immediately sprang to mind. And with that realization, a far more disturbing question:

*What would she want with something like that?*

# CHAPTER FORTY-NINE

## OLD-FASHIONED HOSPITALITY

AT THE FIRST RAP OF CHARLIE MOON'S KNUCKLE, MISS MUNTZ jerked the door open, gawked up at the tallest man she had ever seen in the flesh. "Oh, my—you must be Daisy's nephew."

The lean seven-footer tipped his black John B. Stetson lid and admitted to this singular misfortune.

The miniature Muntz lighthouse beamed a bright smile at the Ute, turned a lesser light on his companion. "How very nice to see you, Mr. Parris—and so soon after our luncheon today." The frail little lady drew in a deep breath. "Daisy advised me that this was your card-playing night, and assured me that I could expect two for the price of one—ha-ha!" She ushered them into her immaculate parlor, where Daisy Perika, hunched like an aged toad in an armchair, barely raised her chin at the men to acknowledge their formidable presence. The lawmen were directed to a spindly-looking pair of antique chairs.

The elderly spinster darted about with the nervous energy of a schoolgirl, her eyes sparkling like a pair of blue embers that might set the house afire, hurried words spilling out of her mouth. "I have prepared some refreshments." Miss Muntz clapped her hands to applaud this happy announcement. "Something very tasty!"

The dyspeptic chief of police shook his head. "Thank you, ma'am, I'll pass."

"Oh!" The disappointed lady turned her hopeful expression to the Indian. *He has a hungry look.* "Would you like something to nibble on, dear?"

"You betchum." Flashing a big smile, the Ute jerked his chin at Parris. "You can give me his share too."

*What a nice young man.* Off she went, with that blissful expression that adorns a child's face on Christmas morn.

Moon eyed the aged aunt. "I imagine you've had an interesting evening."

Avoiding his gaze, Daisy smoothed an imaginary wrinkle from her skirt. "Oh, it's been all right."

He eyed and pried a notch harder. "So how'd you end up here?"

"Milly was at the bingo game. She asked me to come over to her place for a while, so I did."

*"Milly," is it?* The Ute cocked his ear to enjoy the cacophony of snack-making sounds emanating from the kitchen. Refrigerator and microwave doors opening and shutting. Dishes rattling, pots and pans clanging. An old-fashioned coffee percolator cluggity-clugging, a teakettle shrieking a shrill whistle. His nose was delighted to detect the delectable aromas of various victuals.

Scott Parris also took notice of these sounds and smells, but after an evening of poker that had been interrupted when he was a dollar and sixteen cents down, the gloomy fellow was in no mood for having fun. The most he could look forward to at dawn was another hard day's work, and what he wanted in the dark meantime was some serious sack time. And no nightmares about hideously deformed chickens, thank you very much.

By and by, the occupants of the parlor heard the official Call to Snack, which summons was made by a vigorous clang-clanging of the retired schoolteacher's 1950s-era handbell. The treats would be served in her dining room, which was so squeaky-clean that the men *could have eaten off the floor,* but they sensibly chose to receive nourishment at the antique cherry dining table, whereupon a diner could—if so inclined—see reflections of tall yellow tallow candles in silver candelabras, as well as images of fellow chowhounds seated across the table.

Which is where Millicent Muntz was (across the table from her menfolk guests), but she preferred to observe the actual men rather than their foggy images on the polished wood. Though she would limit herself to tea, the prim little lady folded a lace-edged linen napkin in her lap. "I daresay, this is nothing at all like high tea at the Brown Palace Hotel, but I do hope you enjoy it."

Moon was adept at enjoying every blessing. "This looks great." Accustomed to more rowdy companions of the cowboy persuasion, the rancher barely caught himself before adding that time-honored compliment: *Good enough to eat.*

The very soul of modesty, their host made an admission: "Some of this is worked-over leftovers, but I have done my best to make it palatable."

The layout on the immaculate dining table included a matched pair of silver decanters whose spouts steamed forth tempting aromas of New Mexico Piñon coffee and Earl Grey tea, a miniature silver pitcher of Wisconsin whole cream, and two circular trays (also silver)—one heaped with homemade cookies (thin almond wafers and plump coconut macaroons), the second with a cunningly displayed array of miniature rectangular pastries that were filled with a delectable concoction of vegetables and meats, each topped with either aged cheddar, imported Swiss, or Wisconsin mozzarella.

Scott Parris observed that this was "some high-class treat, especially for a couple of ordinary galoots like me and ol' Charlie Moon." Despite his earlier tendency toward abstinence, the slightly paunchy chief of police had suddenly developed a healthy appetite. *Them cheesy little horse-doovers look good.* Tomorrow would provide plenty of time for dieting.

While Miss Muntz sipped tea and Daisy concentrated on a cup of coffee, Moon and Parris began to shovel it in. Food disappeared like an inch of May snow when the midday sun suddenly slips from behind the clouds to show its fiery face.

Miss Muntz touched her lips with the linen napkin. "I do enjoy seeing hungry men clean their plates."

Daisy rolled her eyes. "If that's all it takes to make you feel good, you ought to cook full-time for Charlie. I've never seen him leave a single bean on his platter."

Daisy's nephew smiled at the lady who had prepared the food. "That was a dandy snack."

Parris burped. "Sure was." And he was not finished.

Gratification sparkled in the eyes of the lady who had prepared the food, but her voice betrayed just the slightest hint of anxiety. "Now that you gentlemen are refreshed, there is a matter I am obliged to tell you about." She blinked once at Charlie Moon, twice at the chief of police. "Earlier this evening, Daisy and I experienced a bit of unpleasantness."

The town cop popped a macaroon into his mouth, proceeded to chew. "Umpesamess?"

Inwardly, Miss Muntz cringed. *I do wish he would not attempt to talk with his mouth full.* "The whole business was disagreeable. Indeed, it would not be going too far to characterize the occurrence as"—she pursed her lips—"*distasteful.*"

Parris choked the chewy cookie down. "What happened?"

"I hardly know where to begin." Miss Muntz shot a quick glance at the Ute woman, whose face had all the expression of a doorknob. "Shortly after Daisy and I arrived here from St. Anthony's, I was down in the cellar—messing about with the circuit breakers. At the time, all of the lights in the house were out."

"Well, the power's on now." Always ready to state the obvious or assist a citizen who didn't know an ampere from a volt, Scott Parris was on his feet, gung-ho to have a go at whatever needed fixing. "But I'll be happy to go check your breaker panel."

Miss Muntz opened her mouth, searched for appropriate words, gave up, and clamped it shut. Life's many vexations were so difficult to explain to men, who were always eager to *fix* any problem you might mention with a screwdriver, hammer, or, worst of all—sound advice. Without uttering another word, she led her male guests to the cellar door, opened it, and switched on the light over the stairway that descended into the damp, murky depths.

For an indefinable moment, that phenomenon that Professor Einstein referred to as "the persistent illusion of time" was suspended.

Clocks neither ticked nor tocked, neither did fleshly hearts beat.

The stunned men might have been made of stone. Or ice.

The lawmen had witnessed dozens of gory scenes, which tended from time to time to transform their dreams into nightmares. But what they saw at the bottom of Miss Muntz's cellar stairs was, in a word—*unique.*

Without taking his gaze off the mortal remains of the man whose face he could not see, the chief of police descended the steps.

Moon followed.

The unfortunate creature was stretched over a wooden barrel; his right hand had a death grip on a hunting knife.

No big deal.

What galvanized their attention was the sight of four bloody prongs protruding from the dead man's back. He was impaled on a digging fork—that common garden tool used for heaping compost and unearthing potatoes.

As he held his breath, Parris felt the sting of four distinct pains in his chest.

Miss Muntz, who had remained at the top of the cellar stairway with Daisy Perika, found her voice. "When this man entered the front door—which I had not yet locked for the night—all the lights were out. I was down in the cellar by the circuit-breaker panel, which is there—just to the right of my freezer. After I had specifically warned him not to, he came down the steps. . . ." A thoughtful pause, as she considered how rare it was for a man to accept sensible advice from a woman. "During the descent, he lost his footing and fell." She drew in a breath. "When I found the big circuit breaker and pulled the handle, the lights came on. And there he was, just as you see him now, on the barrel where I keep my gardening tools. With that horrible knife in his hand." She could not suppress a slight shudder. "I don't think anything has been disturbed, but as you might imagine, it was rather off-putting to have to squeeze past his corpse so that I could ascend the stairs." Blushing pink, she made a frank admission: "I very rarely drink strong spirits, but following this experience I felt compelled to pour myself a half ounce of cooking sherry."

Daisy smiled. "I had me a little glass too." *Or was it two little glasses . . . ?*

The tribal investigator was plagued by a worrisome thought. *If a man took a tumble on these steps, he'd be likely to injure himself, maybe even break a bone. But the odds against falling on that fork are at least twenty to one.* Charlie Moon took a long look at the stairway steps. Blinked. *So that's how they did it.* Confronted with a terrible dilemma, Daisy's longsuffering nephew made an instant decision. He turned, ushered the elderly women away from the cellar-stairway door, and closed it.

◆ ◆ ◆

"WELL," MISS Muntz sniffed. "That was rather abrupt."

Daisy scowled at her unseen relative. Charlie Moon, who was always so courteous, had shut the door in their faces without so much as an "excuse me."

◆ ◆ ◆

SCOTT PARRIS was grateful for the privacy. "Thanks, buddy."

"Don't mention it." Charlie Moon sat down on the steps, pulled a Meerkat from his pocket. No, not that excitable member of the mongoose family that comes equipped with a mouthful of pointy teeth—his jacket pocket was an unsuitable habitat for such ferocious contraband. This was a nifty little folding knife whose stubby blade could be flicked open with one hand, which is what he did. In a heartbeat, Mr. Moon and Mr. Meerkat got the job done.

Unaware of the felony that his unpaid deputy had committed, the chief of police squatted beside the barrel and shone a penlight onto the corpse's face.

Alvin Burkowitz's pale countenance looked back at him with bulging, startled eyes. The pizza deliveryman had encountered that ultimate surprise.

# CHAPTER FIFTY

## CORPSES WERE HIS LIFE

LIKE MOST PRACTITIONERS OF HIS ARCANE TRADE, THE GRANITE Creek County medical examiner was a deliberate, methodical worker. But if he would not be hurried, neither was Walter Simpson a dawdler. Being of the literalist persuasion, he would have snorted at the assertion that time is money—his hours were far more valuable than currency. After much probing, frowning, and clucking of the tongue, Doc Simpson instructed one of his assistants to make temperature measurements in the corpse's various orifices and (at Scott Parris's request) directed the other technician to take fingerprints from both hands.

The efficient ME completed his preliminary examination of Alvin Burkowitz's mortal remains in a mere forty-five minutes and officially declared the man dead, which declaration seemed somewhat superfluous considering the fact that four pointed steel spikes had penetrated the subject's thorax.

No small effort was required to maintain the garden implement *in place* as the assistants partially bagged the body, strapped it to a gurney, muscled the macabre assembly up the cellar stairs, and rolled it outside to the van.

It was a few minutes after one A.M. when the medical examiner's vehicle pulled out of Miss Muntz's driveway and sped away to the morgue, which was in the basement of Doc Simpson's 1870s-era Victorian home.


## PARRIS PUTS IT ALL TOGETHER (AGAIN)

CHARLIE MOON, Daisy Perika, and Scott Parris had joined Miss Muntz in her parlor, where she had turned on the fireplace's gas flames, whose yellow-tipped blue tongues licked lethargically at tasteless ceramic logs. Though lacking in pine-scented authenticity, the artificial hearth produced sufficient heat to dispel a chill that had descended upon the premises, which was not entirely related to temperature.

As stiff-backed little seconds marched away into the past, no one stirred, nor said a word.

If Mr. Moriarty purred, the mutter of that cat-motor passed unheard.

All waited for the Legally Constituted Authority to speak his piece.

The chief of police had used the respite during the coroner's visit to re-think the general scenario—all the way from Hermann Wetzel's death by gunshot to tonight's bizarre fatal accident. When the furrowed-brow re-thinker concluded that he had fitted enough pieces of the puzzle together to discern the major features of the emerging picture, he cleared his throat. "It's pretty clear what's happened here." He inhaled a breath that swelled the barrel chest. "This wacko guy from the pizza restaurant— who's probably been burgling homes to finance a drug habit—was in Hermann Wetzel's house that night with Jake Harper. Burkowitz and Harper were partners." He shot a glance at Moon, who shared his knowl-edge of the unidentified prints on the murder weapon. "The prints Doc Simpson's assistant took off Burkowitz's corpse will prove he shot Wet-zel." The lawman was correct in this assumption. "And Burkowitz showed up here tonight to . . ." *To carve up Miss Muntz with that hunt-ing knife.* Parris watched firelight flicker on translucent skin stretched tightly over the elderly woman's face. "Burkowitz was probably already worried that you knew something that'd tie him to the killing across the street. Then, when we showed up at Sunburst Pizza today and you gave him a tip for making you a take-out pizza that night—"

"I detest pizza." If her tone was a bit curt, the lady may be excused. This had been a very trying evening; what with encountering a knife-wielding murderer and entertaining guests, she was all tuckered out. "Alvin delivered a calzone."

"Okay. A calzone." *Fussy old nitpicker.* Parris bunched the bushy brows. *But wait a dang minute.* "Uh . . . run that by me again—did you say *delivered*?"

She gazed affectionately at her cat. "You heard me correctly."

"Let me make sure I got this straight—Burkowitz was Sunburst's pizza-delivery guy?"

"That is correct."

The cop glared at the elderly citizen. "And you asked him to make a delivery on the *same night* Wetzel got himself shot?"

"I did."

Parris felt the pulse throbbing in his neck. "You never bothered to mention that fact to me—or any of my officers?"

Miss M cocked her head. "Now that you mention it—I suppose I did not." A bright, tight little smile. "But I do see your point. Had you known about the calzone delivery, you would no doubt have interrogated Alvin and inquired whether he had noticed any suspicious characters in the vicinity of Mr. Wetzel's residence."

The chief of police bit his lower lip. Hard.

Aware that the policeman was somewhat chagrined, she attempted to soothe him. "I doubt very much that such an interview would have aided your investigation." The retired schoolmarm addressed Parris as she would a slow-witted pupil. "Though Alvin was admittedly not very bright, it seems highly unlikely that he would have admitted to being involved in a murder. He would undoubtedly have claimed that, while making his delivery, he had witnessed nothing out of the ordinary."

"Maybe so." Feeling his hands begin to tremble, Parris knotted them into fists. Big, hard-knuckled fists that craved to punch big, ugly holes in the paneled parlor wall. "But all the same, you should've told me."

The landlady's response was icy. "I have told you *now*."

A dull pain alerted Parris to the fact that he had bitten a hole in his lip. He closed his eyes. Imagined the Too Late Creek running under the rickety board bridge. Imagined himself leaning on the railing, watching gleaming rainbow trout break the blue-green water for mayflies. The hopeful angler's intent was to count ten cold-blooded, bug-gulping vertebrates of the superclass Pisces. He made it all the way to four before a sudden ache in his gut interrupted the reverie. "What's done is done," he said. "Water under the bridge."

Miss M's thin smile indicated that his clichéd apology was acceptable. But just barely.

Parris unclenched the meaty fists, flexed his fingers. "What matters now is we know that Al Burkowitz and Jake Harper were in on the Wetzel killing together." He made the necessary adjustments to his story: "After Burkowitz delivers your food, he drives up the street where Harper's waiting in his Jeep. They go over their plan one last time, then head for Hermann Wetzel's house." He licked at the swollen lip, tasted salty blood, and fixed his gaze on the old woman who vexed him so. "But you happen to see one of 'em across the street, snooping around your renter's residence. You call Wetzel, who's in the basement, and tell him about it. He goes upstairs with a pistol in his hand. There's a confrontation and he gets shot dead by Burkowitz, who's found one of Wetzel's loaded handguns." The violent encounter was playing across his imagination like an old black-and-white movie. "As the two of 'em was clearing out, you and that neighbor—Mrs. Burch—spotted Jake Harper making a run across the street for his Jeep." As if salty blood in his mouth were insufficient, Parris was treated to an acidic surge of heartburn. Having no bicarbonate of soda handy, he took a sip of tea. "But nobody saw Al Burkowitz coming or going. When we put out a bulletin on a guy matching Harper's description and didn't mention a second party, Burkowitz figures he's in the clear. But it's not long before Pizza Guy begins to fret. 'What if Jake Harper gets picked up and spills his guts about how it was his *partner* that shot Wetzel?'"

Apparently entranced by the narrative, Miss Muntz nodded.

Parris glared at the enigmatic lady. "Your name was in the newspaper along with Mrs. Burch, and Burkowitz must've been wondering whether either one of you might've seen anything that could tip us to a second suspect. And then you show up at the pizza restaurant today with the chief of police and give him a tip for delivering your order the evening that Wetzel got popped. That must've scared the daylights out of Burkowitz, so he came here tonight to make sure you'd never cause him a problem." *Yeah. That all hangs together.* Parris's tone was patronizing. "I hope you've learned your lesson, Miss Muntz. You've got to learn to be more careful."

She regarded him with a curious expression—as one might view an exotic beetle under a magnifying lens. "Yes . . . In retrospect, I suppose I should have been more circumspect."

*She just don't get it.* "Your first mistake was not telling me about Burkowitz delivering your calzone." Parris donned his *extremely stern* expression. "And tonight, when you're having trouble with the lights, what do you do when you hear someone come into your house? Call 911? Or at least keep quiet?" He shook his head. "No, you call out and tell him you're in the basement. And then, when he comes after you with the knife, that should've been the end of it. But the bozo—who's probably been popping pills all day—trips over his feet, tumbles down the cellar stairs, and lands on your barrel of garden tools." The recollection of that grisly image reproduced those nasty little pains that had prickled in Parris's chest. He waited until the discomfort subsided before issuing his reprimand to the senior citizen. "Don't you see, Miss Muntz, that if it wasn't for some lucky accidents, that corpse in the cellar would be *you*?"

She stared at her inquisitor without expression.

*I'm not getting through to the old biddy.* "Let me put it like this—if I was having a run of dumb luck like yours, I'd go out and buy me a fistful of lottery tickets."

Miss Muntz winced at this. *Dumb luck?*

The exasperated cop raised clenched hands. "*Two* fistfuls!"

The prim little lady gazed at the gas fireplace as if she could see something behind the flames waltzing so languidly in the sooty chamber. Something fascinating. "I appreciate your concern for my well-being. Really, I do." She turned to see the policeman's sunburned face gleaming redly in the firelight. "Please do not take offense, but I find your account to be, well . . . how shall I put it?" After a moment's reflection, she found a suitable phrase: "Not entirely satisfactory."

Having run out of words, Parris resorted to a snort.

"I hope this will not sound vain," Miss Muntz said. "But in your version of what has transpired, I play the role of a silly old woman. A mindless victim who, but for the vagaries of unpredictable circumstances, would have been murdered this evening." She shook her head. "No. I simply do not like it."

His grin was more annoying than the snort. "Sorry. I didn't mean to rattle your cage."

*My cage?* Another clumsy impertinence. But over her lengthy career, Miss Muntz had dealt with scores of adolescent personalities and understood that one must make allowances.

The whole business would probably have ended at that instant—had Scott Parris's grin not morphed into a superior little smirk, which irked the lady.

Sufficiently so that she felt compelled to strike back. "I do not deny that your explanation of the recent unpleasantness presents a certain inner consistency—not to mention a certain childlike simplicity which some minds would find appealing." She reached down to stroke Mr. Moriarty's fur. "But it strikes me as being rather arbitrary."

Parris's smirk had faded. "What does that mean?"

The well-bred lady was making a valiant attempt to remain civil. "Only that your narrative seems rather contrived to provide a string of events which suits you." Sensing the lawman's growing discomfort, she continued ruthlessly. "In most instances, a given set of facts can be accounted for in a variety of ways." Her cold blue eyes flashed hot sparks at the chief of police. "In the example under consideration, certain alternate explanations might prove more plausible than the theory you espouse—and certainly more interesting."

Scott Parris attempted a nonchalant shrug. "Okay, let's hear one."

"Very well." Millicent Muntz got up from her chair. "But I shall need a few minutes to construct a suitable narrative. While I do, I shall brew us a fresh pot of tea. Considering the lateness of the hour, chamomile seems most suitable." She turned a warm smile upon Charlie Moon. "As there are no more homemade cookies, I shall open a store-bought bag of gingersnaps."

# CHAPTER FIFTY-ONE

## MISS MUNTZ HAS HER SAY

CONSIDER ANY OF YOUR ROUTINE DAILY CHORES, WHETHER IT BE stocking a supermarket shelf with thirty cartons of canned goods, changing an old-fashioned diaper on a yowling tot without pricking her skin with a safety pin, or using a .50-caliber Thompson submachine gun to carve a smiling jack-o'-lantern face into a five-hundred-pound pumpkin whilst the oversized vegetable is bumpity-bumping its way down a steep hillside. None of these tasks is as easy as it looks to one who has not given it a try, and so it is with preparing a plausible story—as any practiced liar can attest to. Which was why, even after the tea was brewed and the gingersnaps distributed, Miss Muntz required a few additional moments and all her considerable faculties.

The very picture of concentration, the lady paced in her parlor.

Back and forth she went.

On occasion, she would pause to gaze thoughtfully at Mr. Moriarty, which feline did not return even a glance to his elderly mistress.

Back and forth again.

Finally, the lady's countenance brightened. "Aha!"

That said it all. There was no shortage of engaging characters, and she had the plot *nailed*.

### A NECESSARY PREAMBLE

CLASPING HER hands tightly, Miss Muntz eyed her expectant audience. "Before I begin, I wish to make it perfectly clear that—like Mr. Parris— I shall tell you a story that suits me. In contrast to being cast as a passive bystander who is *lucky to be alive*," she shot a barbed glance at the chief of police, "I prefer to be the central character in the piece." The prim little lady's mouth curled into an impish smile. "I ask you to allow me this harmless self-indulgence. Ever since I was a child, I have day-dreamed fantastic adventures, where I was invariably the heroine." The effect of her girlish blush was charming. And quite disarming.

"I can go with that." Parris took a noisy slurp of too-sweet chamomile. "I like to think of myself as the best dang chief of police west of the Mississippi—a latter-day Wyatt Earp."

"Good for you." Miss Muntz reached out to pat his hand. "We all have our limitations, and it does no harm to maintain these little illusions."

Daisy Perika cackled.

Charlie Moon almost choked on his gingersnap.

How did our Marshal Earp–wannabe react? With a thin smile. But the sugary tea was now bitter in Parris's mouth.

Miss Muntz raised her hand for silence. "I shall now commence."

### THE LANDLADY'S STORY

"LET US return to that evening when Mr. Wetzel was shot to death. While driving my tenant's stepdaughter to the sweet little Indian girl's birthday party, I made a stop at Sunburst Pizza. While Nancy Yazzi waited in the car, I went inside and asked Alvin Burkowitz to deliver my order *within the hour.* I instructed him to take the calzone into the kitchen and put it into the oven, and I told him that his gratuity would be in the office just off the kitchen. More specifically, in the desk." Seeing a quizzical look on the white cop's face, the narrator added a small detail. "The house was unlocked."

Parris grunted. *That I can believe.*

Your ardent storyteller does not appreciate being interrupted by any sort of critical comment, most especially a grunt. Miss M arched an eyebrow at the rude fellow. "Now pay very close attention—the following point is of some importance." She held her breath, then: "Alvin Burkowitz did *not* put a calzone in my oven that evening." Seeing Parris's mouth about to open, Miss Muntz asked the burning question: "But *why* did Alvin fail to make the delivery to my home?" Like a willowy fairy queen about to pluck the fabled golden apricot off the enchanted tree, the performer lifted her right hand in a theatrical gesture. "Because I gave him the wrong address. I directed him to Mr. Wetzel's residence!"

Daisy Perika chuckled.

Charlie Moon's expression was inscrutable.

Scott Parris offered a gaped-mouth stare.

Was the performer enjoying herself? Most certainly. Was her pale face luminous with delight as she continued her monologue? Of course. "But—and this is a critical point—the error did not occur because I am an old woman teetering on the brink of senility." She raised her chin in a defiant gesture. "For several years I lived across the street at 750 Beechwood, and moved here just a few months ago when I rented my former home to Mr. Wetzel. Therefore, it is hardly surprising that when someone—such as a deliveryman—asks for my address, I am in the habit of saying, '750 Beechwood Road.'"

There is nothing as thrilling for an entertainer as an entranced audience. Aware that she was on a roll, Miss Muntz did not pause for applause. "I may well have repeated the error when I called the police station that evening and the dispatcher asked for my address." Her eyes sparkled merrily at Scott Parris. "But of course, as all 911 calls are recorded, you would already know that."

But of course, he did not. And like so many who encounter a well-crafted piece of fiction, the chief of police had slipped into that well-known state of suspended disbelief. "But if you knew the pizza guy went to the wrong house, why didn't you tell me right off—"

"Please do not interrupt." Stern glance. "And do keep in mind that this is merely a made-up story."

The bearish fellow raised both paws. "Sorry."

"Very well. Now where was I?" Her smooth forehead came very near wrinkling. "Oh, yes." The elderly narrator picked up the string. "After dropping Nancy off downtown, I finished my other errands rather quickly and returned home earlier than I had planned. I went upstairs to sit by my sewing-room window, which is where I was when I witnessed the arrival of the pizza restaurant delivery van." She waved a fragile hand. "Imagine my surprise when I saw it turn into *Mr. Wetzel's* driveway and watched Alvin get out of the motor vehicle and approach the front door—which Mr. Wetzel often forgets to lock. I realized, of course, that my tenant might also have ordered an evening snack. But just in case Alvin had arrived at the wrong address, I immediately called Mr. Wetzel to advise him that someone had entered his residence. Before I could explain my concern about a possible delivery mix-up, my tenant hung up. Moments later, I heard gunshots—and as I stepped outside, I saw Alvin emerge from the house and flee in his van as if a dozen demons were pursuing him. As I was crossing the street, I witnessed the hasty departure of a second person—a rather beefy fellow, who I did not realize at the time was Mr. Harper—the young man Nancy had been chatting with in the Sunburst Pizza parking lot *not an hour earlier.*" She shook her old gray head. "After I found Mr. Wetzel shot to death, I realized that I was almost certainly responsible for Alvin's bungled delivery. But had this unfortunate error led to the shooting of my tenant?" She paused, apparently to consider this question. "That, of course, depended upon who had fired the fatal shot. Was it that big, burly, bearded fellow Mrs. Burch and I saw trotting across Beechwood Road? Or, unlikely as it might seem, did Alvin customarily go about his rounds with a pistol in his pocket? And if so, had he—perhaps in self-defense— fired at Mr. Wetzel? As you can imagine, the situation presented me with a terrible dilemma." She focused her gaze on the chief of police. "Under the circumstances, you can surely appreciate why I preferred not to mention the fact that I saw Alvin's van arrive and depart."

Scott Parris returned a squinty-eyed stare.

Miss M continued with her narrative. "When the authorities concluded that Mr. Harper was the murderer, and I realized that he was most probably the young man I had seen with Nancy at the Sunburst Pizza parking lot, I decided that I was quite justified in shielding Alvin— and myself—from undue public attention. But a day or two later, after I had time to think things over, I tended toward the conclusion that

Alvin—even if he had entered the dwelling unarmed—might well have shot Mr. Wetzel." She smiled expectantly at Scott Parris.

He was on the edge of his chair. "Why would you think that?"

Having practically invited this interruption, Miss Muntz was obliged to tolerate it. "It was because of one of those peculiarly unfortunate co-incidences. You see, I had instructed Alvin to look for his gratuity in my desk, which is in a small office just off my kitchen. As it happens, there is a similar room adjacent to the late Mr. Wetzel's kitchen, and there is also a desk in it—which is where my tenant kept a loaded pistol."

Parris murmured like a man in a daze, "How would you know that?"

She felt almost sorry for the clueless cop. "As Mr. Wetzel's landlady, I have a passkey to 750 Beechwood. I daresay there was precious little about either my tenant's possessions or habits that I was unaware of."

Scott Parris bowed his head, studied his scuffed Roper boots. "So, in your story, Jake Harper and Al Burkowitz aren't partners. Burkowitz was just making a botched food delivery and didn't know Harper was—"

"Please do not presume to sum up my account before I am finished." Having made her point, the tale teller continued. "To recap, it was quite possible that on account of a slip of the tongue on my part, a sim-ple calzone delivery had turned into a killing. If so, I was obligated to report what I knew to the authorities. On the other hand, Nancy's boyfriend might well have fired the fatal shot—in which case I bore no responsibility. Moreover, informing the police about Alvin's presence in the Wetzel residence at the critical moment might well implicate him in a crime which he had no part in." She sighed. "One way or another, I felt compelled to determine the truth of the matter. But I was stymied as to how to do that." She turned to the Ute elder. "Daisy, I find myself in need of an extra character. Would you mind terribly if I included you in my tale?"

The character, who had been back-and-forthing in a maple rocking chair, paused long enough to give her consent. "Not a bit, Milly—as long as I come out looking good."

"Thank you, dear—you certainly shall." Miss Muntz returned her attention to the male portion of her audience. "With my friend's permission, I shall assert that Daisy was extremely helpful—that this clever lady came up with the thrilling finale to my plot."

At this mention of his elderly relative in the context of *plotting,* Charlie Moon felt a sudden sense of dread.

Scott Parris's grim visage resembled chiseled stone. Visualize Wyatt Earp on Mount Rushmore.

Daisy Perika took no notice of the suspicious looks she was getting from the lawmen.

With admirable skill, the star of the drama drew attention back to herself. "Alvin Burkowitz did *not* arrive unexpectedly tonight." She pointed toward the front door. "I *lured* him here."

Scott Parris was gripped with the eerie sense that he was drifting into another nightmare. Any moment now, he might be attacked by an enraged flock of two-headed, four-legged Rhode Island Reds.

Miss M was having *so* much fun. "You are no doubt wondering how I managed that. I shall not keep you in suspense. When Mr. Parris was with me at Sunburst Pizza earlier today, I gave Alvin an envelope. No, wait—that is not entirely accurate." Her satisfied smirk easily trumped Parris's earlier effort. "*You* gave it to him for me." She was pleased to see the lawman's red face turn chalky white. "There was no check inside; merely a note printed in capital letters." Again, she patted Parris's hand. "Now, you may interrupt to ask what was in my message to Alvin."

"Okay," he grumped. *I'll play your silly game.* "You ginned up a blackmail note. 'Pay attention, Dirt Bag—here's the deal. I know you offed Wetzel and I can prove it. Show up at my place tonight with a satchel full of greenbacks or I spill my guts to the coppers and you're dead meat. And I'm talking roadkill!'"

Miss Muntz pressed her hands to her face. "My goodness—you are considerably more imaginative than I had given your credit for. Though my prose was not nearly so colorful, if you will give me a moment to recollect, I believe I can recite the message almost word for word."

The chief of police leaned back in his chair. "Take all the time you need."

Miss M gazed dreamily at a paneled wall that was covered by photographs of her former piano students. Two of whom had died of drug overdoses. "Ah . . . yes, I have it." She addressed the town cop: "You may feel free to write this down in your cute little leather policeman notepad."

"This is my day off," he shot back. "I left it in my cute Wyatt Earp shirt."

"How unfortunate." Shutting her eyes, she began the recitation:

"I WATCHED YOU ENTER MR. WETZEL'S RESIDENCE IMMEDIATELY BEFORE HE WAS SHOT TO DEATH. I ALSO SAW YOU FLEE FROM THE PREMISES IMMEDIATELY THEREAFTER. AFTER MUCH SOUL-SEARCHING, I HAVE DECIDED THAT I AM OBLIGATED TO INFORM THE POLICE. HOWEVER, BECAUSE I AM RESPONSIBLE FOR SENDING YOU TO MY TENANT'S ADDRESS WITH THE CALZONE, I SHALL WAIT UNTIL NOON TOMORROW TO REVEAL WHAT I KNOW TO THE CHIEF OF POLICE. THIS DELAY WILL PROVIDE YOU WITH APPROXIMATELY TWENTY-FOUR HOURS TO MAKE YOUR ESCAPE."

She opened her eyes so that they might sparkle at the most important member of her small audience. "What do you think of that?"

"Fair to middling," her critic said.

"Thank you. I was rather pleased with it myself." She made a scribbling gesture in the air. "Once I get pencil in hand and the creative juices begin to flow, I have a tendency to get quite carried away."

The middle-aged cop felt a sudden rumbling in his gut. "But Al Burkowitz didn't make a run for it." *I wonder if she's got any Alka-Seltzer.*

"No." Miss Muntz spoke very softly. "Alvin came here tonight, intending to murder me." She could not suppress a shudder. "With that terrible knife."

"But you were expecting him."

"Certainly." She cocked her head. "Men of that sort are so predictable." What the lady had almost said was an abbreviated version: *Men are so predictable.* "When Alvin entered my front door I was waiting in the cellar, where I had turned off the main circuit breaker more than an hour earlier. Hearing his footsteps, I called out a warning so that he would know precisely where to find me."

"A dandy plan." The chief of police recovered a feeble remnant of the smirk. "And you hoped he'd trip on the way down the stairs."

Miss M opened her mouth, then shut it.

"Aha!" Parris pointed at the somnolent Mr. Moriarty. "A hole in your story big enough to pitch that fat cat through!" He re-aimed the finger at the gray-haired lady. "I can practically see those conniving little wheels turning in your head—you're trying to think up some way to plug it."

"Let's see if I can help her." Waving off an imminent protest from Millicent Muntz, Daisy Perika glowered at her nephew's best friend. "I'm in this story too, y'know. What do you think I was doing when that murdering *matukach* pizza guy showed up—taking a nap?"

Parris, who knew the Ute elder well, was beginning to feel uneasy. And, because of something he had eaten, slightly queasy.

Charlie Moon's intense expression pleaded, *Keep your mouth shut.*

Daisy jutted her chin. "When that white man was about two steps down the cellar stairs, telling Milly what he was gonna do to her with his knife, I slipped up behind him, jammed the end of my walking stick right between his shoulder blades, and give him a good shove! Down he went—and landed on that big garden fork we'd put at the bottom of the steps."

How did Moon respond to this assertion? Oddly, with a measure of *relief.*

Chin-deep in denial, Parris slapped his thigh. "Way to go, Daisy— that's a big save for Miss Muntz's fantastic tale. I'm sure she's grateful."

"Indeed. I am quite appreciative." Miss M smiled at her presumed coconspirator. "Daisy is very resourceful. She has been more help to me than you might imagine." The enthusiastic storyteller smiled at Scott Parris. "Well, what do you think of my version of recent events?"

The weary chief of police got to his feet. "I've got to hand it to you, Miss Muntz. Not only have you got ten times the imagination of a dumb cop like me—you also spin a pretty good yarn." He waved the battered fedora. "But it's been a long day and it's time for me to go home and hit the hay." He aimed a weak grin at his host. "I imagine you'll be glad to get some sack time yourself."

"You imagine wrongly, Mr. Parris." Miss Muntz was standing with her spine ramrod straight. "I am not at all tired. On the contrary, I feel quite energized." *And very much alive.*

But after such a stunning performance, to what end could our innovative storyteller apply all this pent-up energy?

And what about Daisy Perika—was the tribal elder tired to the bone and ready to go home with her nephew?

Shortly, we shall see.

## A FLAW IN THE PLOT?

"EXCUSE ME, ma'am . . ." This was Charlie Moon.

Miss Muntz flashed a motherly smile at the Indian. "Yes, dear boy?"

Parris shook his head. *Why do all the women like Charlie so much?*

"I enjoyed your story." Dear Boy frowned at a plate of gingersnaps in his lap. "Would you mind very much if I asked you something?"

"Of course not." The gracious lady had forgiven her tallish guest for the door-shutting incident. *Daisy's nephew is such a sweetie.* "Ask away."

"It has to do with food."

*And he has such a healthy appetite.* "If you wish to take the surplus gingersnaps home, you certainly may."

"Well, thank you, ma'am." Moon set the cookie plate on the coffee table, then unfolded his long, angular frame as he got up from the chair. "But that wasn't what I was going to ask you about."

"What then, pray tell?"

"In your story, Mr. Burkowitz would have taken the food you ordered into Mr. Wetzel's rental house." Moon looked down his nose at the ninety-pound lady. "If he followed your instructions, the Sunburst Pizza deliveryman would have put the calzone in the oven—then went looking for his tip."

"Yes," she said. "That is exactly what Alvin would have done. How very clever of you to realize the critical importance of that point."

Daisy Perika was bursting to tell the lawmen that she had smelled the lingering scent of calzone in an oven that *"neither Mr. Wetzel nor his stepdaughter ever used."* But the Ute elder held it all inside. This was Milly's time in the limelight.

Moon shot a glance at Scott Parris. "Did any of your officers find a calzone in Wetzel's oven—or anywhere in his house?"

"No, they didn't." *Ol' Charlie's done it again.* The chief of police turned to Miss M. "But I bet you can explain that away with no trouble at all."

"Well, I shall give it my best effort. But please allow me a brief moment to gather my thoughts." She frowned. Pursed her lips. Blinked at Mr. Moriarty's still form in the wicker basket. And (this is always helpful) cocked her head. "Ah—I have it! When I entered my tenant's home after the shooting, I removed the calzone from Mr. Wetzel's oven and slipped it under my raincoat. Upon arriving home, I put it in my freezer."

Scott Parris frowned at the mention of that major appliance. *That's what she told the pizza-delivery guy today—that the calzone was in her freezer.* "Then let's have a look at it."

"I would be happy to oblige you, but it is no longer there."

The chief of police rolled his eyes. "Why am I not surprised?"

"Forgive me, Mr. Parris, for this candid observation—but you are a rather cynical young man." She regarded him with sad eyes. "I suppose that comes with being a policeman."

He laughed in her face. "You bet it does. And this cynical copper figures you're cornered—and stalling for time."

"Not in the least. In a modest little addendum to my story—which I'm sure you will admit is more interesting that your version—the calzone is concealed in a very secure location. Actually in *two* locations."

Parris laughed louder this time. "But you're not gonna tell us where."

## THE LADY ADMINISTERS THE COUP DE GRACE

"OH, BUT I am." Miss M observed the chief of police with an expression of enormous gratification. "Do you recall the snack I served upon your arrival? In particular, the hors d'oeuvres with the delicious bits of cheese on top?"

Parris felt himself nod. His stomach grumbled.

The teller of tales pointed a finger at his slightly bulging tummy, then at the slender Indian's flat-as-a-washboard abdomen. "This evening, you gentlemen consumed that critical evidence."

As the lawmen gawked at the elderly lady, Daisy Perika began to grin. What a fine evening this had been! The grin was joined by a jolly chuckle that caused her belly to shake and tears to well in her eyes.

# CHAPTER FIFTY-TWO

## ALL IS NOT WELL IN MUDVILLE

*SINCE VACATING MISS MUNTZ'S COZY ASYLUM FOR NIGHT'S INFINITE space, neither Charlie Moon nor Scott Parris has uttered a word. Standing elbow-to-elbow at the curb, the men gaze at heaven's black velvet curtain and wonder what marvels might lie beyond that dark veil the cosmic architect has studded with white-hot diamonds. Until the end of time and history the answer must remain a deep mystery, but to us mortals who cannot fully comprehend the violence of an exploding sun or see beyond a billion whirling galaxies to perceive the warp of space and time, the vast void appears to be so wonderfully quiet . . . so dreamily peaceful.*

◆  ◆  ◆

SCOTT PARRIS treated himself to a long, wistful sigh. *I wonder if there's aliens living way out yonder among all those sparkly little stars and whether they have as much aggravation to contend with as I do.* The policeman conjured up an image of a six-legged praying-mantis version of Miss Muntz, complete with huge bulbous eyes, a pair of knobbed antennae sprouting from her lime-green forehead. Miss Mantis was upbraiding a local constable who wore a nine-point kryptonite shield on his shirt pocket and a glum expression. She was addressing him thusly: *Sheriff Zorp, you could not solve a crime if the felon snuck up and bit you on the butt!*

◆  ◆  ◆

AS CHARLIE Moon gazed at the night sky, his thoughts also drifted to a woman. In contrast to his friend's dreadful vision, this one was young, lovely, and as bright as any star he could see. But, like others of her gender, Lila Mae was a mystery. *I wonder why she's mad at me.* The way to find out was right from the pretty lady's mouth. *But she hasn't returned my calls.* No matter. When a cowboy gets bucked out of the saddle, he gets up, dusts off his britches, and gets back onto the horse. *I'll phone her right now.* He remembered how late it was. *She's probably been in bed for a couple of hours.* Which might give him an edge. *If I wake Lila Mae up from a sound sleep, she might not realize it's me.* Mr. Moon flashed a crescent smile at his orbiting counterpart. *She'd probably think it was an FBI emergency and pick up before she looked at the caller ID.* The Ute found his cell phone, scrolled down to the programmed number in Thousand Oaks, pressed the button.

During the third ring, the familiar voice crackled in his ear. "Wha-what—who's calling?"

"We've got us a serious situation, Agent McTeague."

"What kind of sit—"

"Code Crimson."

She was wide awake now. "Code *what?*"

"Crimson. Burgundy. Red. As in Native American."

"Charlie?" A moaning groan. "Is that you?"

"Hey—who else would call you this time of night?" Three heartbeats. "I miss you."

A long, languorous sigh. "I miss you too." It was true.

"There's a ready remedy."

"Charlie . . ."

"Say the word and I'm on my way to California."

Eight heartbeats. (Three of Moon's, five of the lady's.)

"No."

"Ahh . . . that wasn't exactly the word I was hoping for."

"I'm sorry, Charlie."

He turned away from Parris, broached the fearful subject in a hoarse whisper. "Tell me what's wrong."

"Not now. Not on the phone."

"When, then?"

"I'm on flights between L.A. and D.C. at least once a month." She inhaled deeply, crossed her fingers. "Next chance I get, I'll arrange a stopover in Colorado Springs."

"I'll be waiting for you at the airport."

"Okay. Goodbye, Charlie."

"Good night, Lila—" Moon was talking to a dead line. He stuffed the cell phone into his pocket. *What's going on? Might be something I did at Sarah's birthday party. Like when I danced with Bea Spencer.* Other possibilities crossed his mind. Such as: *Lila Mae's a big-city girl. Maybe she doesn't want to spend the rest of her life on a cattle ranch.* The mystified man heard Scott Parris's voice croak behind him.

"So what'd your sweetheart have to say?"

"Goodbye."

"Oh." *Poor ol' Charlie.*

Long, heavy silence.

"D'you figure your aunt actually shoved that pizza guy down the cellar stairs?"

"No, I don't." *She didn't have to. Not with an ankle-high trip cord stretched across the seventh step down.* Moon's hand was in his jacket pocket with the trusty Meerkat and the remnant of evidence the elderly women had carelessly left on the basement stairway banister post— a loop of six-pound test fluorocarbon fishing line that Daisy had taken from his tackle box.

Parris removed his battered hat, rubbed an aching forehead. "What do you think about Miss Muntz's tale about how she got mixed up and gave the pizza-delivery guy Hermann Wetzel's address, and how tonight her and Daisy was waiting for Burkowitz to show up and—"

"Don't think I ever heard that one."

"What d'you mean you never—"

"But I do love a good story." Charlie Moon also loved a pretty lady who worked for the FBI, and he was thinking about Lila Mae as he watched the winking wingtip lights on a red-eye flight to L.A. "When I was about knee high to a cricket, my grandmomma told me one about how little Black Hair Girl got in a heap of trouble. Way it happens, she goes out to gather some wild plums but she can't find none and she gets lost in the forest. By and by, when she's hungry enough to eat a porcupine, hide-toenails-and-all, Black Hair Girl comes across this fine log house—we're talking three bedrooms, two baths, and a Jacuzzi. Seems like she's drawn four aces, but as it happens this is where these three black bears live. There's Papa Bear and Momma Bear and—"

"There ain't no Black Hair Girl in the Three Bears. That was Goldilocks."

"That's her name in the European version, which is what we Indians call a derivative."

"A *what?*"

"A more recent version—a shameless knock-off where a few minor details like names get changed to suit the audience. About a thousand years ago, when the Utes made up the original Three Bears tale, the hungry little girl who got caught eatin' Baby Bear's corn-and-squash mush was Black Hair Girl—you can take my word for it."

"I don't give a tinker's damn about any three bears you care to name—"

"Well, you should. It's a Native American classic."

"What I asked you was what you thought about Miss Muntz's story."

"Did that sweet little lady spin us a yarn?"

"Don't play games with me, Charlie—you know damn well she did!"

"Then I must've disremembered it." Moon patted his buddy on the back. "My daddy used to tell me that a man's head is like a clay bowl—it can only hold so much stuff before it starts running over. That being so, it's best to pour out those memories you never needed in the first place. Like recollections of gossip and rumors and . . . *bad news.*"

Somewhere on the wooded ridge behind the Wetzel house, a wise old owl got off a triple hoot.

Somewhere close-by, a chief of police got wiser. *Charlie's daddy was right. I guess I ought to disremember what Miss Muntz said too.* He watched the red-eye flight vanish over the mountains. "I ain't been serious drunk since my wife got killed by that lumber truck up in Canada." Scott Parris put the comfortable fedora back on his head, pushed it down to his ears. "But I'm thinking I'll drop by Soapy's Corner Bar and order up a quart of the cheapest rye whiskey he's got in stock. Soon as I'm feeling no pain, I'll trade a twenty-dollar bill for eighty quarters and play 'I Still Miss Someone' till I run out of change or the jukebox breaks. After I've said good night to Johnny Cash and emptied my bottle, I'll pick a fight with the two biggest guys in the joint." He elbowed the Indian. "You want to come along and watch?"

"Thanks anyway, I'll pass."

"Oh, right—you've got to take your aunt back to the ranch."

"Not for a while." *She's having too much fun.* "It's way past midnight, pardner—every bar in the county's closed up tight." Moon hung a pearly smile in the darkness. "But over at the Chicky's Daylight Bakery, it won't be long before they start lifting glazed doughnuts out of the hot grease."

The white man considered this option. "Chicky's coffee's the best in town."

"That's a fact. And what we both need right now is a big dose of caffeine and sugar, so I say let's you and me ooze on over in Chicky's direction and tie on a big one."

Which is what they did.

Which is a good place to leave the lawmen. And we shall also say good night to Millicent Muntz and Daisy Perika, who have had a long day.

But wait . . . what is this—do these aged ladies never tire?

They are in the kitchen. Cleaning up after the evening snack. And chatting.

About what? Oh, this and that. Mostly about *that.*

◆ ◆ ◆

WHILST DRYING a flowered teacup, Daily raised a delicate issue. "I thought you was gonna tell 'em the *good* story—about how you moved Hermann Wetzel's loaded pistol from his bedroom to that desk drawer and that you unlocked his front door that night when you went across the street to get Nancy—" She paused to place the cup on a shelf. "And that you gave that pizza guy Hermann's address *on purpose* because you hoped that either him or Hermann would get gut-shot and take a long, painful time dying a horrible death and the other one would go to prison for doing the shooting."

"I did consider presenting that version." Miss Muntz, who rarely used her noisy dishwasher, scrubbed a blue china platter with a soapy brush. "The drawback, as I saw it, was that I would have been expected to explain my motive. As a result, the narrative would have become rather too complex."

It seemed simple enough to Daisy. "The pizza guy was selling dope to kids who came into the restaurant, including some of those young people you used to give piano lessons to. And Hermann Wetzel was . . . well . . ." The old-fashioned Ute woman could not quite bring herself to say it *out loud.*

Prim little Miss M had no such compunctions. "It is possible that the police had heard rumors to the effect that Mr. Wetzel was sexually abusing his stepdaughter." *I wonder what has happened to poor Nancy.* "And I imagine that Mr. Parris would have eventually found out that Alvin was providing dangerous drugs to the local youth." She sprayed the platter with hot water. "But it is unlikely that anything would have been done to remedy either deplorable situation. Our system of justice rarely provides satisfactory solutions."

The Ute elder accepted the squeaky-clean platter from Miss Muntz, dried it. "But you and me—we take care of things right on the spot."

"Indeed we do." The *matukach* woman smiled at her Indian friend. But, as a glorious sunset must inevitably give way to a cold gray sky, the smile faded into a melancholy sigh.

"What is it, Millie?"

"I do not wish to burden you."

Daisy could not resist such delectable bait. "Oh, I don't mind."

After a thoughtful hesitation, Miss Muntz said, "In Granite Creek County, there are several vile criminals who—for a variety of reasons— the authorities *cannot touch.* Most of them conduct their nefarious business elsewhere."

"Sure-enough bad guys, huh?"

"Extremely so."

As often happens at such moments, a pregnant silence ensued.

The Ute woman turned Miss M's tentative proposal over in her mind. "I haven't had a bite to eat since I left Charlie's ranch. And you've got a hungry look about you." Daisy Perika's expression was at once enigmatic and terrifying. (Try not to imagine a short, dark, wrinkled reincarnation of Mona Lisa—whetting a bloody butcher knife.) "How about we make us an omelet?"

While Daisy's question hung in the air, an unborn cluster of potential futures waited in rapt anticipation.

"Yes." Miss M's lips went thin. "But we must be prepared to *break some eggs.*"

Their eyes met.

Bright blue fire sparked in one set.

Red flames danced in another.

Well.

# EPILOGUE

## DOWN THE ROAD A PIECE

HOW IS CHARLIE MOON GETTING ALONG? *SEÑOR LUNA* MISSES HIS former sweetheart, who did not place the hoped-for telephone call to arrange an airport meeting in Colorado Springs. Neither did Special Agent McTeague respond to a subsequent letter. Ditto for a dozen yellow roses he sent on her birthday. It appears that Lila Mae must be relegated to his past. But the owner of the Columbine Ranch has little time to dwell upon his troubles, as there is more than enough work to keep him busy. And if he should decide to take a day off once in a blue moon to go fishing with Scott Parris or enjoy an elegant dinner with Patsy Poynter, the pretty girl singer in the bluegrass band, or Beatrice Spencer, the wealthy widow who has had her eye on Charlie ever since her husband's untimely death—guess what happens. That's right. Something untoward will occur to divert Mr. Moon from the well-deserved recreation. Like putting out a fire started by *you know who.* Right again. The troublesome auntie.

How is Daisy Perika's life percolating along?

One day is much like another. We might find her dealing harshly with the occasional specter who wanders out of Cañón del Espíritu to disturb her night's sleep, or Daisy might be carrying on a conversation with a talkative raven who wings in bearing a dark rumor. From time to time, she will match wits with the diminutive *pitukupf* who resides in the abandoned badger hole in Spirit Canyon, or take a few hours to teach Sarah Frank how to cure warts with an obscure Ute phrase and an odorous poultice concocted from yucca root, oil of skullcap, and a thickish green tea brewed from leaves of the—

Sorry, that is a Top-Secret recipe.

What of the shaman's youthful apprentice?

Extremely happy to have her spiffy red F-150 back, Sarah Frank locomotes hither and yon every chance she gets, and she is definitely *going places.* The Ute-Papago orphan will have a mere seventeen candles on her birthday cake when she graduates from high school next spring. (While in the *Tohono O'otam* reservation school in southern Arizona, the bright little lass completed the fourth *and* fifth grades in a single year.) The teenager's major goal in life remains the same—to become Mrs. Moon.

Scott Parris? After considering a run for the Granite Creek mayor's seat, Charlie Moon's best friend decided he was best suited to be chief of police. His decision (after giving the matter considerable thought) was based upon his conclusion that being top cop was the righteous thing to do in a community that needed a seasoned hand at the helm. That and the fact that in a poll of likely voters, Parris came in fourth in a field of three. How could such a humiliation occur? Blame an organized write-in campaign for Alley Oop, whose candidacy was enthusiastically promoted by various local wits, including student members of the Rocky Mountain Polytechnic Anthropology Society.

Jake Harper's current whereabouts remain problematical, but the last sighting of the hapless burglar was in Punta de Alambre, which is in Mexico—where Harper was allegedly keeping body and soul together by peddling imported Cuban conch shells and Genuine Pirate Treasure Maps to the occasional tourist. It is reported that Mr. Harper sips his tequilas and eats his tortillas while standing up, and sleeps on his stomach. Evidently, the buttock remains rather tender. Poor fellow.

Which brings up the burning question—how is Nancy Yazzi getting along? There is no mystery about Jake Harper's former sweetheart. Immediately after the hot-tempered young lady fired the final shot at her errant boyfriend, Nancy got a yen to go home again, which is what she did, but for just long enough to rip up the heating vent and remove her late stepfather's leather bag of cash. Now in the chips, she turned over a new leaf, which including dying her hair platinum blond, assuming the moniker Sheila L'Amour, and moving into the three-bedroom double-wide with Lulabelle where they shared the rent. Bedroom number three, the one whose window catches the mellow rays of the rising sun, is occupied by the elder Mrs. Petunia Harper.

It is perhaps worth mentioning that the legacy from Nancy's dastardly stepfather was not wasted on pretentious frippery, whatever that may be. The enterprising L'Amour–Harper–Harper trio opened a coffee-and-pastry shop in a prosperous little Texas community not far from Kerrville. No, not another Starbucks look-alike. This business is the old-fashioned kind where a citizen can purchase a cuppa joe for fifty cents and a quarter-pound glazed doughnut for a greenback dollar. Word is, they're doing fine and dandy.

We must not forget Miss Millicent Muntz, who still resides at 751 Beechwood Road. The spinster lady rented the dwelling across the street to a nice young couple with five adorable children and a good-natured black Labrador to which the landlady feeds tidbits at her back door. Isn't that nice? Also, Miss M has acquired a new cat (a live one, this time) to provide some companionship for herself and Mr. Moriarty, whose sawdust was beginning to leak. What? Did we not mention that Mr. M had passed away nearly thirty years ago, and was represented in his basket by a fine example of the taxidermist's art? So sorry. An oversight.

With that, we shall bring the narrative to a close and—

What was the question?

"Have Millicent Muntz and Daisy Perika been up to any serious mischief?"

Not to the best of our knowledge. But it has come to our attention that from time to time they get together for tea, coffee, and discussions. About what? Nothing of great interest; just elderly-lady chitchat about one thing and another. Miss M and Miss D complain about their aches and pains (which get worse with every winter), the weather (which was much more agreeable when they were young), and the increasing cost of life's necessities. The charming old darlings also exchange recipes for such perennial favorites as green chili lamb stew, coconut-walnut fudge, buttermilk biscuits, and . . . *omelets.*

◆ ◆ ◆

THERE. IT is done.

Thank you. May God richly bless you.

Let us turn out the light, say good night, and *Now I lay me down to sleep* . . .